INFERNO

STAR TREK
DEEP SPACE NINE®

MILLENNIUM
BOOK III OF III

INFERNO

JUDITH & GARFIELD REEVES-STEVENS

POCKET BOOKS
New York   London   Toronto   Sydney   Singapore

An *Original* Publication of POCKET BOOKS

POCKET BOOKS, a division of Simon & Schuster Inc.
1230 Avenue of the Americas, New York, NY 10020

Copyright © 2000 by Paramount Pictures. All Rights Reserved.
Excerpt from The Chronicles of Galen Sword #3: *Dark Hunter* © 2000 by Softwind, Inc. All Rights Reserved. Reprinted with permission.

STAR TREK is a Registered Trademark of Paramount Pictures.

A VIACOM COMPANY

This book is published by Pocket Books, a division of Simon & Schuster Inc., under exclusive license from Paramount Pictures.

ISBN: 0-671-02403-5

First Pocket Books printing April 2000

10 9 8 7 6 5 4 3 2 1

POCKET and colophon are registered trademarks of Simon & Schuster Inc.

Printed in the U.S.A.

Since before our sun burned hot in space, every writer of a *Star Trek* novel or nonfiction book has had an unsung partner—a heroic captain whose mission it is to keep them true to the *Star Trek* universe, its history, its characters, and its ideals. In return, she's faced with *Star Trek* book writers (okay, like us) who push her unmercifully on deadlines, who grumble about her notes (*especially* when she's right), and who rarely share with her the bottom-line truth: she makes all of our books better. After sixteen of them, we thought it was about time to come clean.

So, with respect, appreciation, and many, many thanks, this one's for Paula Block.

batlh Daqawlu'taH!

As for the sand of that hourglass we sailed through, each speck an infinite echo of the Temple of All That Had Been and Was Still to Come, I walk through it still, today, among the stones of that city out of time that in these words is called V'halla, the one place and the true place where all paths lead. And even now, as I stand—a man far older than He Who Found This City ever was in this realm—my hand on the ancient blocks that bear his name, he is with me, and his hand guides mine, even as does his heart. ANSLEM, I whisper in that soft sweet tongue of this world we have adopted. FATHER, I say in the language of our first home. And on all of those paths that stretch out from this moment, I hear his answer, telling me that what we leave behind continues, and that our Journey, still, is without end . . .

—JAKE SISKO, *Anslem*

PROLOGUE

In the Hands of the Prophets

"THIS MUST END," Captain Jean-Luc Picard says.

The Sisko laughs as he pushes back his catcher's mask and strides toward the pitcher's mound. The scent of fresh-cut grass explodes within him, bringing with it every summer day he's ever known.

"But that's just the point," the Sisko says. "It didn't end!" He throws the baseball to Picard.

Admiral Ross angrily gets to his feet in the Wardroom of Deep Space 9 and catches the baseball. "Because it does not begin!"

Beside him, General Martok says, "Because it does not happen."

The Sisko points at the casualty board where the names of the Dominion War dead appear and disappear in endless nonlinearity. As an unseen crowd chants for a hit, the baseball leaps by itself from Ross's hand and the Sisko swings and the baseball drives through the casualty board which shatters into a sparkling, glittering comet's tail, *and again they are all on the field, under the stars, as the night game begins, the scent of fresh-cut summer grass mingling now with a crisp autumn chill that carries the delicate smoke of burning leaves.*

"No," the players protest. Vash and Rom and Kira and Lwaxana and Dulmer and Lucsly and Ezri and Arla—they are the Sisko's team, unhappy, staring at the images on their hats and shirts—the Station and a baseball? Juxtaposition is lost on them. "No!" they say. "No!"

But "Yes," the Sisko says as he holds up the baseball. "This is the essence. This is why you brought me here. This is what I am here to teach you." He tosses the ball straight up into the air. He swings the bat. A line drive to the right of second base. No one runs for it.

"You throw the ball," the Sisko says. "You hit the ball. You throw the ball. You hit the ball. And each time, everything is different."

Base swings his bat'leth and knocks the bat from the Sisko's right hand. "Adversarial," the tiny Ferengi squeaks.

Satr snatches a new baseball from the Sisko's left hand and gives it to her sister, Leen. "Confrontational," the Andorian sisters say together.

Interruption.

In the light space, Kai Winn stands before the Sisko. "He must be destroyed," she says.

"You've said that before," the Sisko reminds her.

"I always say that," the Kai replies.

"But why destroy your Emissary?"

The Kai spins around and the Sisko falls through the flames of the Fire Caves with Gul Dukat at his side.

"Pay attention," Dukat says as his gray flesh crisps away from his bones and then is restored in cycles without end. "Deep Space 9 is not destroyed. The Defiant is not in the future. There is only one Temple."

The Sisko thinks of a time, of a moment, makes it real, takes them all to the bridge of the Defiant *as Bajor is consumed by the supernova of that world's sun.*

"This does not happen," *Kai Weyoun says.*

"Then why do I remember it?" *the Sisko asks.*

"You are linear," *Kai Opaka says.*

"I realize now that so are you," *the Sisko says.* "In a different way than I am, but linear just the same."

Jake stands before the Sisko, twelve years old, the legs of his overalls rolled up, a fishing pole on his shoulder. "Explain," *he says.*

The Sisko smiles, reaches out to rub the boy's head, walks with him through the torchlit tunnels of B'hala, Ranjen Koral at their sides.

"Here," *the Sisko says. He points to the stone on which his name is carved.* "This is the past." *He turns around on the bridge of the* Defiant *to point to the main viewer on which the red and blue wormholes reach out tendrils of negative energy to entwine and combine and end the realm of linear time forever.* "This is the future." *He turns around on the dark and deserted Promenade and points toward Quark's bar where the Red Orbs of Jalbador float in alignment, the red wormhole beginning to open.* "And this is the* now *which followed from the past and from which the future* might *follow in turn."*

The Sisko's father stops in midstep on Bourbon Street, the sounds of a dozen jazz bands blending in the night, each from its own club on the rain-slicked streets around them. "Might?"

The Sisko understands the Prophets' confusion. "Might," *he says. He inhales deeply, drawing in the sweet, damp scent of New Orleans.* "You throw the ball. You hit the ball. And each time . . ."

"Everything is . . . different?" *his father says.*

"It* might *be a pop fly," the Sisko says. "It* might *be a*

3

line drive. It might *be fair. It* might *be foul. It* might *be caught.* Might *be fumbled.* Might *go over the fence or the batter* might *even miss and strike out."*

Worf walks up a narrow set of stairs, carrying a saxophone. "So the wormholes—the two wormholes—they are a 'might'?"

"A possibility," the Sisko says. "One result or another. One time or another."

They stand on the Promenade, on the first day the Sisko steps onto it, his path blocked by debris, by work crews cleaning and repairing.

At the door to the temple, the monk bows his head to the Sisko and says, "Another time."

"Another time," the Sisko agrees. "It might *be this time. It* might *be the next time."*

"Different times?" Kasidy asks.

"Different possibilities?" Odo asks.

"Always," Sisko says. "You throw the ball . . ."

Jake swings and the crack of the bat echoes and the ball soars and—

Jadzia swings and the crack of the bat echoes and the ball bounces foul over the third base line and—

Nog swings and misses and—

Vic swings and the crack of the bat echoes and the ball drives straight at Solok on the pitching mound who ducks and—

Keiko swings and the ball ticks and—

They all swing and each time—

Another thing happens. A different thing happens.

"A different time," Jennifer Sisko says.

Sisko nods, the lesson taught. "Another time."

An infinity of eternities in just two words. An infinity now within the understanding of the Prophets.

The Sisko rides the turbolift down with Worf and O'Brien and Jake and Nog. They are in the unmapped section, standing before the door that opens into the hidden room of Deep Space 9.

The Sisko looks around at the Prophets. He does not bring them here. He does not know who does.

The door to the hidden room remains closed.

The Prophets wait.

"Do you want me to open this door?" the Sisko asks. "Is that why you brought me here?"

"This is the Emissary's door," Quark says.

"My door?" the Sisko asks.

"Uh, no," Rom says. "Not yours. The Emissary's."

The Sisko smiles suddenly, another mystery revealed. "You still don't know, do you?" he asks. "When I first came to you, you didn't know who I was. You wanted to destroy me. You didn't recognize me as your Emissary."

Kira puts her hand on the Sisko's shoulder. "You are not our Emissary. You are the Emissary."

The Sisko stops smiling. "Is there another?" he asks.

"Open the door," Curzon Dax says.

The Sisko faces the door to the hidden room in the unmapped section of Deep Space 9. He thinks of it opening, makes it real.

The door remains closed.

As if he is in a linear realm, the Sisko puts his hand on the door control, inputs the 'open' command.

The door opens.

Inside, a wormhole tunnel of slowly pulsing light—full white, the perfect blending of blue and red and all the other colors of the spectrum.

The white tunnel is open, waiting.

The Sisko doesn't hesitate. He steps through the portal.

There are walls to either side of him, glittering with every color of light, sparkling, not like a comet's tail, but in a pattern of regular, repeating . . . shapes.

Hourglass shapes.

The Sisko is in a tunnel with walls made of Orbs.

Countless. Endless.

He turns to—

—a human in clothes that are centuries old, with transparent lenses held over his eyes by a frame of thin metal that—

The Sisko gasps, for even here, there can be surprise. "Benny?" he asks.

Benny Russell takes off his glasses. "Welcome, Messenger. The Gods of the Spacewarp Passage await you."

The Sisko thinks he understands. "I know what you're doing. You're showing me another possibility. Another time."

Benny shrugs. "It . . . might be."

The Sisko looks at the endless tunnel of Orbs. "But what about these? Are they real? So many of them?"

"Yes," Benny says.

"Why did you make so many of them?"

"We don't," Kai Winn says.

"They are here," Kai Opaka says.

"In another time . . . before us," Kai Bareil says.

The Sisko looks at Bareil and the robes he wears. "You were never Kai."

Bareil bows his head. "Another time."

The Sisko looks back at the Orbs. "You didn't make the Orbs? You didn't build the Temple? They were already here when you arrived?"

"Possibilities," Solok says.

"But leading where?" the Sisko asks.

Curzon points ahead, past the Orbs, to the end of the new Temple.

The Sisko peers in that direction, unable to picture himself traveling there, but able to see . . . to see . . .

Jake, older, in the excavations of B'hala, carefully brushing soil from a stone carved with ancient Bajoran glyphs which the Sisko can almost recognize.

Beside Jake, Kasidy waits. Unthinkingly, the Sisko reaches for her. She is watching Jake, cradling a young child, no more than three years old, but with wisdom far older reflected in attentive eyes—

"My child," the Sisko says, arm outstretched. "Kasidy—our child."

The dust of B'hala swirls around Jake and Kasidy and the Sisko's child. The three turn as if sensing his presence.

The walls of Orbs come together. The end of the Temple. The new wormhole an infinity away now.

"Why bring me here?" the Sisko demands.

"You brought us here, Lieutenant," Captain James T. Kirk says.

The Sisko is on the bridge of the first Enterprise. He feels the old-fashioned warp generators vibrating through the deck, smells the faint odor of tetralubisol from the air circulators.

"What is this?" the Sisko asks.

"A possibility?" Kirk asks.

"I don't understand," the Sisko says.

"Then finish your story," the Sisko's mother says from behind him.

The Sisko turns around at his desk in his office above Ops. His mother stands framed by the viewport, the white light from the opening Temple refracting through her lustrous hair.

"That is why you are here," his mother says. "And when you have finished your story . . ."

At last, the Sisko understands. "Then you will tell me why you are here."

Gul Dukat steps up to the plate, taps his bat on home. "Throw the ball," he says.

The Sisko laughs as he winds up on the mound, no longer merely describing the game to the Prophets, but at last playing the game with them.

"Hit the ball!" he calls out to Dukat.

The baseball speeds through the bright summer air of Ebbets Field.

Dukat swings his bat beneath the dome of the Pike City Stadium.

The crack of the bat echoes and—

—in a superposition of infinities, all *possibilities happen at once.*

And the Sisko's story continues . . .

CHAPTER 1

CAPTAIN BENJAMIN SISKO of space station Deep Space 9 fell backward as the flight deck of the *United Space Ship Defiant* burst into unholy flames around him. Then, huddled, panting, gasping, he saw bank after bank of calculating tubes and visi-screens detonate in response to the spectacular heat, saw Jean-Luc Picard rear up on mightily thewed reptilian legs, completing his incredible transformation into a six-limbed Venusian Firebeast!

Because what had at first appeared to be the legendary captain of Starfleet was in reality that hideous energy lifeform known in the whispered legends of a hundred fantastic alien worlds as an Antigod of the Spacewarp Passage.

Ben Sisko willed himself to his feet, his proud African features glistening in the hellish light of the awful surrounding flames of destruction. As a child growing up in New New Orleans on Venus, he had once been chased by a Firebeast and almost devoured alive—a singular experience which to this day brought him pulse-pounding nightmares.

I must assume the Antigod is able to read my mind through some advanced telepathic technique, Ben Sisko thought urgently. That might explain how it has been able to reach into my subconscious mind and extract a frightening memory from my childhood. It wants to disorient me--make me incapable of fighting back.

"You will never withstand me in this timeless void without dimension!" the Firebeast thundered, its cavernous voice still eerily echoing that of the genteel starship captain whose form it had assumed. "The Moibius Effect has destroyed the universe. Now you must do battle with me for all eternity!"

"If that is my fate, then I shall face it like the Starfleet officer I am!" Ben Sisko exclaimed proudly as he raised the only weapons he had against the loathsome creature that towered above him—his two bare fists!

"Bravely said, Earthman," the Firebeast hissed, each breath a sibilant sussuration of reptilian evil. Then, in a motion too quick to describe, it launched itself and flew swiftly by means of telekinetic atomic projection to land on Ben Sisko, and with hind claws the size of a strong man's forearm, rip open his chest and—

"Damn," Benny Russell muttered.

He stared at the typewriter on his rickety desk. The typing paper curled up in it stared back, the incomplete sentence describing Captain Sisko's fate taunting him. Through his open window rumbled the sounds of midnight traffic in Harlem, in the summer of 1953. An almost nonexistent breeze merely teased his open curtains, making his cramped apartment as hot as he imagined the flight deck of the *Defiant* to be.

"Okay," Benny sighed. "Firebeast is too powerful. Unless . . . Sisko's dagger collection!"

He snapped the crisp white paper from the typewriter, making the platen whirr. Along with it came a nearly exhausted sheet of carbon paper and a crinkly, semitransparent sheet of onion skin. Benny slipped the carbon out from between the other two sheets, then balled them up and—

Sisko screamed as all the dimensions of space collapsed upon him at once, twisting the bulkheads and deck and ceiling of the *Defiant*'s bridge, crushing the bodies of his fallen crew, leaving him compressed and forcing him into an inescapable, dimensionless point, a singularity in which his only thought and knowledge was that his life had been from its beginning an illusion, mere letters on a page, now discarded.

He screamed in despair and frustration and outrage until there was no more room to move or to fight or even to breathe.

He was nothing now. A figment of a dead man's imagination. A fleeting dream. Meaningless.

And then Starfleet met the Borg at Wolf 359 and the whole senseless story began again . . .

Bashir calmed himself. After the lights of the *Defiant*'s bridge had flickered into darkness, he had experienced a momentary flash of panic. As a Starfleet officer, he had had to contemplate the possibility of his own death on numerous occasions. In the abstract, he felt confident he could face the actual moment with composure.

But to experience the destruction of the *universe?* The obliteration of *everything?* Bashir was not sure that was something he was prepared to face with a stiff upper lip and the determination to do his duty.

Yet even now, after the light had fled, he was aware of sensation. The *Defiant*'s artificial gravity generators were still working. He could hear the compact vessel creak softly around him—the normal sounds of the ship as far as he could tell.

And then the emergency lights switched on, dim but steady.

"It didn't happen!" Bashir said to the empty corridor. He grinned. Rom's and O'Brien's calculations had been wrong. Existence continued. Everything was going to be—

"Julian!"

The urgency of that shout struck him like the crack of a whip in his ear, and Bashir wheeled to see Jadzia Dax motioning him into the *Defiant*'s engineering section. As he was, she was dressed in the standard-issue Starfleet uniform of the year 2400—ribbed black-fabric trousers and jacket, the shoulder of which was blue to designate Jadzia's science specialty, with her lieutenant commander pips vertically centered just below the jacket's collar.

Bashir raced down the corridor, through the open doors, and skidded to a halt as he saw who was waiting for him with Jadzia and Captain Sisko.

His parents.

They were holding on to each other, obviously upset, both wearing Federation penal uniforms. Bashir was startled to see that his father's once-black mustache was almost all white now.

"Mother? Father? How—"

Sisko didn't let him finish. "There's no time, Doctor. Show him, Dax."

At once, Jadzia pulled him over to what seemed to be a large power converter in the center of the deck, which Bashir couldn't remember having noticed before.

"But how did *they* get here?" Bashir glanced over his shoulder at his parents. Sisko had an arm around Richard and was holding Amsha's hand. All three looked extremely worried.

"Converging realities," Jadzia said crisply, annoyed.

"Twisted timelines. I don't know. We can work it out later. But right now, the only thing that's keeping the universe from ending the way Starfleet feared is this singularity-containment generator." She pointed at what Bashir had taken to be a power converter. "The *Defiant*'s been pulled into the red wormhole and the presence of the black hole fueling our warp engines is preventing the final collapse of normal space-time."

"But . . . singularity containment is a Romulan technology . . . and this is a Cardassian control interface."

"Exactly," Jadzia said. "Just like in the Infirmary on Deep Space 9. You know how to operate Cardassian controls in your sleep, Julian. All you have to do is adjust this interface to stabilize the singularity-containment field, and the universe will be saved."

She swung him around to face her, catching him off-guard as she pulled him tight and kissed him. "I know you can do it," she whispered, her breath warm in his ear. "We all know you can do it." Intensely blue, her eyes captured his. "And then we'll have the time we need to be together, the way we're supposed to be."

Jadzia stepped back then, leaving him shaken and stirred and at the controls.

"Save us, son," his mother cried out behind him.

"We're counting on you," Sisko added.

"Yes, yes," Bashir muttered as he studied the controls. Jadzia was right. They *were* simple, grouped in the same standard Cardassian logic patterns as the medical equipment in his Infirmary. All he had to do was to—

The deck pitched and the *Defiant* groaned.

"Hurry, Julian!" Jadzia urged him. "The field will hold for only fifty-two seconds!"

Bashir put his fingers over the master-sequencing control surfaces. He saw exactly what he had to do to stabilize the field—the equations were identical to those he used with medical isolation forcefields. He tapped the surface that would tell the power converter to stand by to receive a new command string.

But sirens wailed first.

"What did you do?!" Sisko shouted.

Bashir stared down at the controls in disbelief. They were different from what he had thought. Everything was shifted. He had hit the wrong control and—

"You dropped the field!" Jadzia said.

"Julian!" his father pleaded. "Save us!"

Jadzia yanked Bashir away from the controls. "You idiot! You've killed us all! The whole *universe,* Julian!" She slapped him hard across his face as tears streaked her own. "How stupid can you be?!"

"No! Jadzia! I know what I did wrong! I can fix it!" Bashir turned back to the controls.

But shafts of unbound energy were already beginning to puncture the control surfaces as the *Defiant*'s singularity began to unravel into useless cosmic string.

"No!" Bashir said.

"It's your fault!" Jadzia railed at him. "It's all your fault because you're so stupid!"

"Stupid!" his mother and father cried.

"Stupid!" Sisko echoed.

Now all the controls were melting, becoming unusable as the bulkheads of the engineering section began to fade into nonexistence. And in those last moments of awareness as all light vanished, Julian Bashir realized that the one thing worse than being present at the end of the universe was being present at the end and knowing it was all his fault . . .

Then, after darkness enveloped him, all around the compact vessel creaked softly—the normal sounds of the ship as far as he could tell. A moment later, the emergency lights switched on, dim but steady.

"It didn't happen!" he said to the empty corridor. He grinned again. Everything was going to be—

Then Jadzia called to him from engineering. And everything began again . . .

Elim Garak sneezed, and when he opened his eyes, his customer was laughing at him.

"Can't take the heat, hmm?"

"I'm sorry?" Garak said politely. He looked down at his body. The last thing he remembered was being clothed in the stultifyingly unfashionable robes of the Bajoran Ascendancy, monitoring the computers of the bridge of the *Boreth*, trying to understand exactly what was happening. Gul Dukat—at least, the crazed maniac who claimed to be the Dukat of the year 2400—had not been particularly forthcoming.

"Are you all right?" the customer asked. "I know we prefer the temperature to be higher than you do."

Garak looked up, nodded. "Quite fine, actually. I was merely—"

"Then get on with it."

Garak looked down at his body again, trying to recall what was wrong with what he saw. Instead of the loose-fitting robes, he was now garbed in a rather dull gray tunic. And he was kneeling on the floor of . . . he glanced around, then relaxed. He was in his tailor shop on DS9. Home ground. Safe.

But then he caught sight of the small piece of tailor's chalk he was holding in one hand and the measurement sensor in his other. He frowned, puzzled, as he tried to remember exactly how he had come to be here. Then a vicious backhand blow hit his temple and he rocked back with a gasp.

"Oww," Garak said as he placed his hand to the smooth side of his head. He looked up at the customer and—"Father?!"

He fell to the floor as Enabran Tain, chief of the Obsidian Order, Garak's father, and dead two years in Garak's own time, kicked his son in the shoulder.

"You insolent filth!" Tain exclaimed. "You think being a trustee is a gift that cannot be taken back?"

Garak pushed himself upright, overwhelmed by confusion. "Trustee?"

"Typical," Tain grunted. He tugged off the pinned-together, half-made jacket he'd been wearing, crumpled it into a ball, threw it to the floor. "Dukat finally finds one of you with a steady hand and an eye for detail, and you've got ore poisoning."

Garak leaned back against the purchasing counter for support. For an instant, he looked past his father to the Promenade. But it was wrong, somehow. Dark, its few lights too blue, the air clouded with the aromatics as the Cardassians preferred.

"Pay attention to me!" Tain commanded.

I've traveled through time again, Garak guessed, *to the time of the Occupation of Bajor.* Just as the *Defiant* had been thrown forward when the station had been destroyed, something must have happened when the *Boreth* reached the wormhole. But now, he decided quickly, instead of going forward in time, he'd gone back—far enough to warn everyone about the Red Orbs of Jalbador and the second wormhole in the Bajoran system. Far enough back to prevent the destruction of Cardassia Prime by the Ascendancy, and save the universe.

"Father," Garak said, "I apologize for my seeming confusion, but I have just had a most remarkable experience which—"

"You're mistaken," Tain said. He reached behind his back to get something from his belt. "What you mean to say is that you're *about* to have a remarkable experience."

"I beg your pardon?"

"Too late for that," Tain said as he aimed a small disruptor at his son.

Garak held up his hands. "No!" Then at once he realized what had seemed so wrong. His skin was pale pink, his nails clear.

He ran those alien hands over his neck, felt something distressingly scrawny, no sign whatever of a strong, doubled spinal cord. He touched his face—no eye ridges, no forehead umbilicus, that proud circle of flesh worn by every Cardassian since the creators had raised Ailam and Neeron from the swamps of Cardassia. Since a spark of divine lightning had imbued them with souls, leaving the sign of their elevation on their foreheads for all to see.

Instead, in the midst of unbearably smooth flesh, the only texture Garak could feel was on the bridge of his nose, and that was a small series of . . .

Garak wheeled to face a fitting mirror, then stared in horror as he saw himself. "I'm . . . a Bajoran."

"And a bad tailor to boot," Tain said in disgust. "Dukat must have chosen you to insult me on purpose."

Garak whirled to face his father. "No! Father, wait! I can explain!"

But all Tain did was to press the firing stud on his disruptor and Garak saw everything in his shop, in the station, and in the universe shrink back from him at warp speed as he fell into darkness.

Only to be prodded painfully awake by an overseer in the ore-processing chamber. "You can sleep when you're dead, Bajoran!"

Mind numb, body aching, Garak loaded ore all that shift, until Gul Dukat himself had him pulled aside to ask if he had ever considered being a tailor . . .

* * *

Miles O'Brien opened his eyes and for a moment thought he was back in the half-excavated city of B'hala. The sand he lay upon was searing hot. The air dry. The sun blinding.

But as he stood up, trying to recall what had happened in those last moments of consciousness on the *Boreth*, he realized there were no ancient stone-block buildings nearby. Nor any randomly scattered rocks, nor mountains in the distance.

Only an endless plain of flat sand stretching out boundless and bare in all directions.

"That doesn't make sense," O'Brien said. His voice sounded odd to him. The air was far too still, not even a hint of a breeze to stir the sand.

His engineer's mind sought the pattern and made the connection at once.

"No wind," he said. "That's why there're no sand dunes." He peered around again, trying to see how far the horizon was. But it melted into the soft distortion of rippling heat, unseen and unmeasurable.

"That's not right," O'Brien said. All that heat radiating from the sand should warm the air, form convection currents, drive winds. "What kind of planet is this, anyway?"

He squinted up at the pitiless sun, trying to judge its color. Too white for Earth or Bajor-B'hava'el. He held up his hand to cast a shadow over his eyes, tried to find evidence of clouds or any other type of atmospheric disturbance.

Then, despite the omnipresent heat he shivered. Because what he *was* able to see was so unexpected, so impossible, yet so obvious.

There was a structure in the sky.

He could just make out the vast geodesic pattern of its framework, some beams gleaming in the sunlight, the thickness and colors of others subtly changing as they neared the horizon and the angles of their shadows changed.

"No . . ." O'Brien said as his eyes, attuned to the structure, now traced it all through the sky, reaching down to every point on the surrounding horizon and stretching up to the sun—

—and *behind* it.

He was in a Dyson Sphere.

An artificial structure built *around* a star.

And if this was anything like the Dyson Sphere the *Enterprise* had discovered near the Norpin Colony, it had to be the greatest feat of engineering that could ever be attempted in . . .

"The universe," O'Brien whispered. He shook his head in confusion, felt sweat break out on his scalp. *The universe was supposed to end,* he thought. *We were heading into the wormhole . . .*

He looked around again in growing panic. There were too many unanswered questions.

How had he come to be here? Who had built the sphere? How was such a structure even possible?

He needed to make notes, to plan, to organize the thoughts cascading in his mind. Automatically, he patted the robes he wore, trying to find something, *anything* to write with.

But his flowing garments held nothing, no matter how many times he searched their folds.

O'Brien stared out for a long time at the unchanging vista, and when he ceased, there was nothing else he could do but begin again.

Because there was nothing to come to an end here. No action to take and then to repeat. He was alone and useless, an engineer without tools, trapped in a structure not even Miles O'Brien could comprehend, not even if he took forever . . .

* * *

Jake Sisko input faster, causing the words of his novel to appear on the padd at superhuman speed.

But the delete cursor was gaining on him, only eleven lines behind, devouring the words he wrote almost as fast as he could input them.

Jake's fingers ached, his eyes blurred, his mind swam with words as he struggled to lay down his thoughts and emotions in some intelligent order.

But the cursor was only seven lines away now, erasing all his thoughts and emotions before they were a minute old. Soon, he knew, each word would vanish as he wrote it.

Jake felt a cramp building in his wrists. Blood from his fingernails smeared the input controls, making his fingers slip, slowing him down.

He had almost run out of thoughts, out of words, of life . . .

He input faster yet.

But with a certainty that horrified him in its inevitability, he knew he could never input fast enough . . .

For his part, Quark was almost blinded by the shocking radiance of pure latinum as the doors to the Divine Treasury opened before him. Here at the celestial source of the Great Material River, there was no need for that oh-so-precious metal to be debased by being pressed with gold. The stairs he ascended, the coins he used to bribe his way to the head of the line, even the robes he wore, all were pure latinum, gleaming, somehow liquidly solid, and endlessly beguiling.

A choir of accountants burst into song as Relk, the Chief Auditor, opened both sets of books in which Quark's life was recorded.

Quark waited as he faced his final audit. He told himself he had nothing to fear. That the ledgers of his life would balance and the threat of spending eternity in the

Debtor's Dungeon was nothing to be concerned about.

And it wasn't.

Relk shut his books with a double thump as he congratulated Quark, informed him he had shown a most admirable return on investment and would be admitted to the Head Office to take his place at the Counting Board of the Divine Nagus himself.

Quark felt as if he were floating, every care of his past life lifting away from him. Dimly, he now remembered something about being beamed aboard the *Boreth* with Gul Dukat. Something about the . . . what was it now? Oh, yes, about the universe ending.

But why should he have to be concerned about the universe ending when he was this close to his final dividend?

The Junior Assistants in their latinum robes hovered around him as he stepped onto the executive floor.

He followed the latinum-paneled corridor until he came to the solid latinum door that awaited him.

Overwhelmed, Quark gazed at the shining door before him. Every childhood fantasy he had had about the Divine Treasury was turning out to be true.

It all worked out, Quark thought as he surrendered to bliss. *Life makes sense—or, at least, made sense after all.*

He had lived a good life of greed and self-absorption, and now he was to be rewarded for all time.

He lifted his hand and knocked on the Divinely Nagal door.

The booming voice that addressed him by name bade him enter.

If possible, it seemed to Quark that the light inside was even brighter, issuing forth from latinum even purer than he could imagine, surrounding . . . *Him.* The Divine Nagus. Sitting in his executive chair behind his executive desk, mounds of latinum coins waiting to be counted before him.

It was all too much. Quark dropped to his knees, hung

his head in supplication with only one quick glance around to see if anyone before him might have dropped a spare coin or two, or anything else of value. Then he abjectly thanked the Divine Nagus for granting him an eternal position here.

To which the Divine Nagus replied, "Uh . . . sorry, but there appears to have been . . . a mistake, brother."

Quark's head snapped up at once, and his appalled gaze fell on—

"ROM!?"

And no matter how loudly Quark squealed in that small dark cell that was forever his in Debtor's Dungeon, it was never loud enough to drown out the mocking laughter of his idiot brother—mocking laughter that echoed forever . . .

Arla Rees struggled through mud that stung the raw wounds on her arms and legs and mixed with her blood.

Phaser blasts crisscrossed the air around her, each shot coming closer, making it harder and harder to run.

She fell to her knees in the mud. Looked back.

The Cardassian soldiers were still advancing, implacable, sure of their victory.

Arla tried to stand, but the thick mud held her hands and feet prisoner. Fighting panic, she concentrated on reaching one hand forward to grab a rock and pull herself forward. Instead, the rock broke free of the mud and came away in her hand.

And it wasn't a rock.

It was a head.

Bajoran.

Unseeing eyes wide with terror.

She dropped the grisly object.

"Help me," Arla cried out, hopeless. "Please . . . in the name of the Prophets . . ."

And before her plea had ended, a shaft of warm protective blue light fell across her, and she looked up from the mud to see Kai Opaka, as she had been when she was but a simple prylar, young and slender, come to New Sydney to raise funds to aid the resistance on Occupied Bajor.

Arla sobbed with relief and happiness as she realized that the light was not shining *onto* the figure, but was shining *out* from her. Now she knew exactly what was happening. "You're not Opaka, you're a Prophet!"

Opaka nodded with a beatific smile, and Arla held out her hand to that light and to that comfort.

"Save me," she whispered, at last sure of the Prophets' love.

The shining figure shook her head. "If only you had believed in us while you were alive, my child. If only you had believed . . ."

And then the light vanished.

And with it, Opaka.

And Arla screamed as Cardassian hands grabbed her from behind and ripped at her clothes and . . .

Days later, when the soldiers were through with her, she was thrown into the mass grave and buried alive with the others from the camp, all the while fighting for breath as the dirt covered her, until she awoke to find herself struggling through the mud of the battlefield, pursued by Cardassians, forsaken by the Prophets, by her own choice, again . . .

Worf, son of Mogh, battled unceasingly upon the flat black rocks beneath the storm-filled sky and felt the thunder of the fire geysers as they shot upward transforming the landscape with flame.

He did not know what had happened to the *Defiant* or to his captain or to his wife or to his universe.

He was not sure where he was or how long he had been here.

But none of those questions concerned him now because in his hands he held the Sword of Kahless, and whatever had happened to him, that weapon's edge was true and sliced through the flesh and bone of his enemies as if the fire of Kri'stak still burned within it.

On this endless battlefield, Romulan warriors fell like wheat before his scythe, and the rocks were slick with steaming green blood.

Worf could taste the coppery tang of the mist it formed as he roared his battle cry, swinging, slicing, thrusting forward to twist and disembowel, wading through the Romulan invaders as did Kaylon at the battle of the Straker Dome, when the two Empires had ended their first war with the Romulans so deservedly crushed.

Worf savored the power of Kahless in his arms and back and legs as he endlessly pressed his attack. From time to time, he would have a moment's respite as the Romulans regrouped, their numbers never seeming to diminish. In those moments, Worf would wonder if this was *Gre'thor,* the land where the dishonored were consigned upon their deaths. But then he would lose himself again within the pure and absolute sensations of combat, and he would know that in some way, he had arrived at *Sto-Vo-Kor.*

All he had to do was to vanquish enough Romulans, and he would arrive at the doors of the Great Hall where Kahless himself would greet him and invite him to join the honored dead and the bloodwine would flow for all eternity.

Yet even if that bloodwine were never to flow again, even if Kahless were an infinity away, Worf suffered no remorse or frustration at his fate.

Endless battle.

What better use for eternity could there be for a Klingon?

He intensified his attack and swung his *bat'leth* so swiftly the edge of it glowed and sparks flew as it carved through his enemies' armor.

A Centurion flew apart in a spurt of bright green.

Two Proconsuls spun into each other, spilt blood and entrails mixing.

A female with Trill spots raised her hands as if to beg for mercy. But Worf cut her in two as well and charged on.

Now humans came before him, but since they wore the earliest uniforms of Starfleet, Worf knew they were from the time of the atrocities of their first contact with the Empire, and that they deserved death even more than did the Romulans.

Now the alien blood that flew was red, and his *bat'leth* blurred in frenzied action, its blade beginning to thrum.

Humans fell by the scores, by the hundreds. Another Trill female rose among them, and she also carried a *bat'leth*. Her mouth opened in a soundless cry, her face turned toward him, as if she wished him to hear her above the constant roar of battle.

But Worf could not be fooled by his enemies' tricks and he brought his weapon down across her shoulder to fling her head from her lifeless body.

Now his boots crushed chittering tribbles with every step. Wild *targ* nipped at his legs as Romulans and humans and Breen massed before him. Until every enemy of the Empire he fought here and now. Fought and vanquished.

And the Sword of Kahless no longer thrummed—it *sang*.

Now Worf added his voice to that of his weapon's, chanting the Warrior's Anthem, keeping time with each deadly stroke of his blade.

Now his boots splashed through an ankle-high basin of blood, and the flickering tongues of the fire geysers reached higher and the Trill female *blocked* his deathblow and made him stumble.

For a timeless instant, Worf knelt, braced for the inevitable impact of a dozen blades as his enemies took advantage of his fall. But death did not come.

Someone was keeping his enemies at bay.

He looked up to see the Trill female fighting in his place.

Worf leaped to his feet, raised his *bat'leth*, profoundly troubled. He had no doubt that a female could be a warrior bound for *Sto-Vo-Kor.* He knew the Trill species to be valorous and fully expected to find warriors of other worlds honored at Kahless's table. But though this female was fighting bravely and fiercely, it seemed wrong to him that she fought at all.

Somewhere, deep in the memories of whatever his existence had been before this time, it was as if he knew this one female should not be placed in danger, ever.

He responded instinctually.

With a roar of unbridled passion, Worf swept his *bat'leth* through a mass of Breen and from the thick mist of their venting coolant he jumped to the Trill's side, then brought his weapon into perfect synchronization with hers.

She took the upstroke, gutting a Romulan centurion, and as she withdrew her blade, Worf covered with a sidesweep that dropped two humans. As he brought his weapon back to strike again, the Trill's blade flashed up to deflect a Breen's cryodagger.

They were in perfect balance, she and he, Trill and Klingon. Aligned, finely tuned, two warriors fighting as one. What higher ideal could there be? What greater eternal reward could be bestowed?

Turning for an instant from the battle, Worf bared his teeth in a full-throated growl of victory at the blood-drenched face of the female. "I am Worf, son of Mogh, warrior of the House of Martok! Identify yourself!"

The female lifted her weapon high to brush her arm across her face, for a brief instant wiping away the blood of their enemies so that Worf glimpsed her pale skin, her dark spots, her pale blue eyes so familiar.

"I am Jadzia, symbiont of Dax, warrior of the House of Martok!"

The female's words echoed so loudly in Worf's mind he no longer heard the roar of battle. How was it possible that she—an alien—had been admitted to Martok's house?

Then Worf became aware that somehow time had slowed. His enemies still advanced on him, yet they no longer moved closer. Even the fountainhead of fire geysers hung motionless against the dark sky's unmoving storm clouds.

"Jadzia?" Worf repeated.

The Trill female's *bat'leth* melted from her hands as some bright light shone upon her from a source Worf couldn't see, the glare stunning him so he was no longer aware of the frozen battle around him.

"Worf!" the Trill cried out. "Look at me!"

But Worf shook his head, tried to step away. It had to be a trick, an illusion to break his fighting spirit. The only way a Trill could ever join a Klingon House would be through marriage to—

The female slapped Worf so hard his ears rang.

"Look at me!" she commanded.

The blow was proof enough for Worf. She was no illusion. She was another of his endless, infinite, eternal enemies, no different from the hundreds of other female Trills he had killed in this battle. Female Trills that looked exactly like—

"Jadzia," he breathed again as he raised his *bat'leth* to dispatch her.

But then, before his weapon could descend, in that one split-second in which she might have escaped, the Trill rushed forward and took his face in her hands and she kissed him so hard that his bottom lip split and he tasted his own blood as he remembered he had on his wedding night when his bride had—

A light of piercing intensity struck Worf as he felt himself lifted, then propelled through a tunnel of darkness until he was someplace else where he fell to his knees and there before him, her face slick with tears, not blood, was . . . Jadzia.

Jadzia of the House of Martok.

His bride.

"You're safe now," she whispered, reaching out for him.

And with that, Worf remembered.

Everything.

And was the second of them to be free.

CHAPTER 2

AFTER THE FIRST thousand years in the Dyson Sphere, O'Brien noticed that something was moving on the horizon. A dark shape, indistinct, shimmering, flickering in and out of existence in the turbulence of heat that rose from the level sand surrounding him.

Part of him wanted to cry out and run toward the illusion, to beg forgiveness for whatever he had done that had brought him here. But another part, the reasoning part, the engineering part bludgeoned into submission by the mere fact of this Dyson Sphere's existence, saw no reason for moving.

This part of him had remembered the old legends of Earth and that the point of this place, this hell, was that there was no point to anything. At first, O'Brien had been surprised that the old legends had turned out to be true. But after a century or two of simply standing in the sand, not even able to die, the surprise had left him, along with logic.

He had even given up his last hope that eventually he must go mad.

After another thousand years had passed, O'Brien noticed that the dark shape no longer shimmered as much as it had. It was more distinct. And larger.

Someone was walking toward him.

The engineering part of him tried to calculate the interior surface area of a sphere with a diameter approaching three hundred million kilometers. This part of him wanted to comprehend the incredible length of time it would take for someone walking on the interior of that sphere to randomly meet the only other being in the sphere. But his consciousness could no longer handle the numbers. Zeroes fell away from the pictures he built in his mind like infinite particles of sand.

He could no longer think or reason, except for whatever faculties were required to understand that he could no longer do so.

Within another century, at most, the person approaching was almost within earshot. O'Brien thought if he concentrated he might be able to hear the crunching of the sand under the person's feet. But after millennia of hearing only his own heartbeat, his own breathing, the sound of those footsteps proved almost painful. Even to focus on something other than an infinity of sand hurt his eyes.

A year went by. The person stood before him, dressed in robes that were . . . O'Brien couldn't even recall the names of their colors. The person, however, had gray skin and a wide neck, and O'Brien knew he was from another world, though he was unable to remember which one.

"Miles O'Brien," the visitor said.

O'Brien understood that that was his name. He wanted to say something in greeting but only got as far as opening his mouth. Whatever he was supposed to do after that—and he knew there was something—he had forgotten.

The visitor looked around at the desert, at the overwhelming ghostly lattice work that stretched through the sky and arched behind the blazing sun, as if he hadn't spent centuries walking through this same unchanging landscape, as if he were seeing it for the first time.

"I understand," he said. "And I can take it away. Would you like that?"

Only one thought formed in O'Brien's mind: *Yes* . . .

The gray-skinned figure smiled as if he had heard O'Brien's reply. "There is a price."

Pain ripped through O'Brien's throat as he forced himself to gasp out, ". . . yes . . ." The first word he had spoken in thousands, perhaps millions of years.

"Do you know who I am?"

O'Brien thought he should know. There were many things he thought he should know. But he didn't. He shook his head.

"You've just forgotten. Just from the look of this place, I'd guess you think you've been here for a long time, isn't that right?"

O'Brien couldn't answer. He had forgotten all the names he had once known for the units of time.

"But it's only been a few minutes. Remarkable, isn't it?"

O'Brien squinted, frowned, stretched his facial muscles, licked his lips as if waking up after a late night drinking Romulan ale with . . . "Julian," he said.

"I presume you mean Dr. Bashir." The visitor sounded amused. "He's not with us, but I am heartened to see that your memory might still function. I have need of an engineer."

O'Brien felt a shiver of recognition along his back, across his arms. "*Chief* Engineer," he corrected.

The visitor grinned. "You'll be fine." He held out a hand to O'Brien, a gray hand with black nails. "Now remember what I said. I will take you away from here, and in return, you will serve me."

O'Brien reached out to take that gray hand. He heard the sinews of his arm creak in protest after so many centuries of absolute immobility.

"That's right," the gray-skinned man said as he gave O'Brien's hand a hard squeeze. "Now, can you say that? Can you say, I will serve you . . . ?"

O'Brien's words were little more than escaping voiced breaths, but in his mind, he said what must be said. "I . . . will . . . serve . . . you . . ."

The gray hand squeezed O'Brien's harder. "Louder," the visitor said. "I *will* serve you, Kosst *Dukat*."

"Dukat," O'Brien croaked, as if that word had been about to be spoken for millennia. "Kosst Dukat, I will serve you . . ."

Dukat's face took on an expression of bliss, even as his dark eyes momentarily seemed to flash with the color of the armband he wore on his robes. "Then you are free," he said, and he pulled O'Brien forward, and with that single step—

—O'Brien was on the bridge of the Klingon battleship *Boreth*.

And he remembered.

Everything.

O'Brien took a step forward and swayed, dizzy, overcome by the instantaneous transition from millennia of damnation to reality. At least, some type of reality.

"Dukat?"

"No questions," the Cardassian ordered. "Get to work!" He pointed to the engineering consoles to the side of the bridge. On the deck by most of them, O'Brien registered the unconscious forms of his friends and coworkers, six in all, including Quark, Odo, and Garak.

"Doing what?"

Dukat hissed, "It's not going the way it should! The way *he* promised."

O'Brien stared at Dukat, completely baffled. He remembered being in a prison cell in a restored ancient building in B'hala, with Rom and Quark and Odo. In nearby cells were Garak and the ten others rescued from Deep Space 9's destruction by the *Defiant,* then transported twenty-five years into the future to become prisoners of the Bajoran Ascendancy. Only Captain Sisko, Commander Arla, and Major Kira were not among them, apparently held prisoner at another location on Bajor. O'Brien hadn't seen any of them since the terrible day they had all been forced to witness the public execution of Tom Riker.

Then O'Brien remembered working with Rom on what was supposed to have been the universe's last day of existence, to prove that when both Bajoran wormholes opened together, they would *not* be close enough to merge and unravel the hidden dimensions of space-time, instantaneously destroying the universe.

But then the wall of their cell had somehow melted, and Dukat had walked through some kind of dimensional portal from the Mirror Universe to join them. This version of Dukat, twenty-five years older, white-haired, and completely mad, had then told them that Weyoun and the Ascendancy were planning to induce a nova reaction in the Bajoran sun. Their goal: To distort the space-time metric so that the two wormholes *would* move close enough together to merge when they opened.

And then Dukat had offered them a way out—what O'Brien and the others had mistakenly taken to mean a chance to stop the nova detonation and save the universe.

But Dukat had had no intention of saving anything. He had only needed a crew to operate the *Boreth* long enough to keep Weyoun from entering either wormhole in the *Defiant,* so that the *Boreth* could enter instead.

O'Brien's mind pictured the destruction of Bajor as it had been shown on the main viewer of the *Boreth*'s bridge. Three Bajorans from DS9 had left their positions then, to charge Dukat in fury, only to be incinerated by the blasts of fiery red energy that sprang from the Cardassian's outstretched arms.

And now Dukat was holding out his hand to *him* just as he had to those three Bajorans. "Do not defy me, Chief."

O'Brien forced himself to remain calm. The last thing he remembered before waking up in the Dyson Sphere from hell was hearing Weyoun and Dukat scream at each other as the undulating mouth of the red wormhole grew larger on the viewer. Now he needed to know what had happened *after* that, to him and his friends, and to the *Boreth*. Not to mention the universe.

"I have no intention of defying you," O'Brien said. "But I'm not a mindreader. If you need me to do something, you have to *tell* me what it is."

Dukat's eyes flared red for a heartbeat, the betraying flash of unearthly energy uncomfortably reminding O'Brien of the events on DS9 which the Bajorans had called the Reckoning. He cautioned himself to remember that Dukat was still somehow possessed by a Pah-wraith, perhaps even the same one that had taken control of the captain's son.

"I need full power restored to this vessel," Dukat began calmly enough, though each subsequent word grew disturbingly louder and came faster. "I need weapons and sensors brought on line. I need to restore the Amojan for all eternity!"

O'Brien quickly looked around the bridge, taking what relief he could from the fact that Quark and the others sprawled by their stations still appeared to be breathing. Also, he noted, the Klingon displays and the retrofitted Bajoran control surfaces indicated that the ship was on standby reserve—the condition he would expect the ship to automatically establish in the event of the sudden incapacitation of its crew. That suggested that the *Boreth* was not heavily damaged. A positive sign.

But before he could act, there was still a major question he needed to have answered.

"Are we in the wormhole?"

"You just spent two thousand years in a sand-filled Dyson Sphere. What do you think?"

O'Brien hesitated, unsure. "Was that . . . an Orb experience?"

He flinched as Dukat reached out to him to put a heavy hand on his shoulder. "Chief O'Brien, what you experienced was your own personal hell. And now that I know what it is, I can put you back there any time I please. Do you understand?"

"I'll get to work at once."

Dukat lifted his hand.

O'Brien hurried to the main flight console where he called up the sensor controls. Swiftly, he reset the primary sensor net and ordered the ship's computer to reestablish an optical environment on the main viewer.

"Tell me what you are doing," Dukat warned.

"I'm making sure we're safe. No sense starting repairs if we're about to be attacked or—"

As if he were some primal beast, Dukat raised his voice in a bellow of rage as the viewer came to life.

"He's still there!"

O'Brien looked up to see the last thing he expected to see.

Deep Space 9.

Against a roiling red backdrop of twisting, glowing, pulsing verteron strings.

"We *are* in the wormhole," O'Brien said wonderingly. *But how did DS9 get here?* he thought.

"Of course we are," Dukat snarled. "The universe has

ended. This is the only reality that exists now. But *he's still here!*"

"Who?" O'Brien asked. He took a deep breath as he waited for Dukat's reply and then wished he hadn't. He could almost taste the acrid odor of burned flesh that still filled his nostrils.

"Weyoun," Dukat raged. "He's out there. I know it."

"On the station?"

"No, you fool!" Dukat swept over to O'Brien and angrily stabbed a finger at the top-right corner of the viewer. "There!"

O'Brien peered into what appeared to be a shimmering verteron node. But as the hyperdimensional energy artifact wavered in and out of view, he saw that there was another shape occupying the same area.

"The *Defiant,*" he said.

"Weyoun isn't supposed to be here," Dukat fumed, spittle flying from his mouth. "He was *supposed* to fade into nonexistence. Never to be. Never to have been."

O'Brien tried running a structural scan on the station in the center of the screen. "The ship must have entered the blue wormhole." It was the only explanation. At least, to account for the *Defiant.* As for what appeared to be DS9, its twin, Empok Nor, had been in orbit of Bajor. Perhaps that station had somehow been swept into the wormhole as well.

"Destroy the *Defiant!*" Dukat commanded.

O'Brien looked at the weapons status display. "Sorry, all weapons are off-line."

"Then we'll *ram* her!"

O'Brien pointed to the propulsion systems display. "Not like this, we won't. The warp engines are off-line, and the impulse engines need to be restarted."

O'Brien was yanked into the air as easily as if he were wearing an antigrav. Dukat had him by the front of his robes. The engineer tried to turn away from Dukat's foul breath as the madman whispered very softly into his face, "Then restart them."

Dukat abruptly released O'Brien, and he dropped awkwardly to the deck, almost falling backward over his chair.

"Look, Dukat, you need an engineer, and I'm willing to be that engineer—" O'Brien saw the telltale red flashes of light flicker in Dukat's narrowed eyes. He began speaking more rapidly. "—but for me to do my work, I have to know what I'm starting with. I don't know what the ship's been exposed to. I don't know how long we've been in here. I don't know how much longer we can last. So unless you want the *Boreth* to fall apart around your ears, let me do my job the way it's supposed to be done!" O'Brien stopped then, half expecting to be blasted by Pah-wraith lightning on the spot.

But Dukat stepped back. "Work swiftly," was all he said.

O'Brien pushed his luck. "It'd go faster if I had some help."

"Who?"

"Rom," O'Brien said. He searched Dukat's face for any sign of hesitation or resistance. Didn't see it. Pressed on. "And Garak, he can handle the computers." O'Brien saw Dukat's face darken. "That should do it," he said quickly. "For now."

"That's all there is in here," Dukat reminded him sharply. "The endless, eternal *now*. We are completely outside linear time."

O'Brien had never been able to accept that part of the story regarding the wormhole environment, and he still couldn't. As far as he was concerned, in a true realm of nonlinear time, even the simplest conversation would be impossible to conduct.

"If we're in nonlinear time," he asked daringly, "then why haven't I already finished my work?"

"You can be sure that somewhere in this wormhole, you

have," Dukat warned. "And unless you begin your work now, you can be equally sure that somewhere in this wormhole, I am already standing over your lifeless body."

O'Brien sensed he had gone right to the limit. He sat down at the main console and began queuing the diagnostic routines he wanted to run.

"Who do you need first?" Dukat asked harshly.

"Rom."

"Keep working."

O'Brien felt a sudden breeze disturb his robes, and when he realized he couldn't hear Dukat's ragged breathing any longer, he risked looking over his shoulder.

Dukat was gone. Rom must be somewhere else on the ship.

And though O'Brien wished nothing bad for the Ferengi, for the sake of the universe he found himself hoping Rom's torment was awful enough to keep Dukat busy for at least another thousand years.

Then O'Brien turned back to the viewer with renewed purpose: to restore the *Boreth*'s communications systems. Because, before he could do anything to change the situation, he needed to find out if DS9 and the *Defiant* were really in the wormhole with the *Boreth*.

And if so, who was onboard them.

CHAPTER 3

"THERE WERE too many hells," Jadzia said.

Sisko wasn't sure what she meant. He was still having difficulty concentrating, and the flickering emergency lights in the *Defiant*'s sickbay weren't helping. Beneath his Bajoran robes, his ribs continued to ache from the crushing and compressing that he—

"Benjamin? *Are* you all right?"

"I'm fine, Old Man." It was unimportant to Sisko whether or not he would ever find time to reflect on his own experience of hell. He had a ship. He had a crew. His duty was clear. "But for an illusion, the, uh, Venusian Firebeast . . . packed quite a wallop, as Mr. Russell might say."

Jadzia's smile indicated her commiseration. She had crossed into Sisko's illusion, and he knew she had seen exactly what he had experienced. In fact, when she had first appeared, she had been part of it, complete with a bizarre outfit that appeared to be comprised of an ex-

39

tremely abbreviated two-piece bathing costume incongruously made of hard, gleaming metal, in combination with a spherical, transparent breathing helmet. The mid-twentieth century had certainly given rise to some odd ideas about environmental suit requirements.

Sisko reached up a hand to the side of the diagnostic bed that had just examined him and pulled himself to his feet. "You were saying something about too many hells?"

"Think of it, Benjamin. You had to face the realization that you were only an imaginary character in a series of twentieth-century scientifiction stories. Julian felt responsible for the universe's destruction. Jake couldn't write. You all had a single worst nightmare hidden in your psyches, and that's what . . . what I presume the Pah-wraiths focused on and brought to life, creating an individual hell for each of you.

"But for me—" Jadzia placed her hand over her abdominal pouch. "—for *us*, there wasn't one hell, there were eight. One for each of Dax's hosts, plus one for Dax. And because we experienced our nightmares all together, all at the same time, it turned into one huge confusing jumble. Which reminded me exactly of what you and I experienced the first time we entered the wormhole six years ago."

Sisko understood at once. "Of course. That first trip. You saw a paradise . . . I saw a raging storm and barren rocks."

"Exactly. The wormhole was a completely subjective experience for both of us. And as soon as I made that connection, I woke up on the bridge of the *Defiant*, surrounded by the rest of you." She looked over to the main treatment bed and the patient still physically strapped to it—with the ship's primary power grid shut down, the confinement field generator was inoperative. "And him."

The patient, the prisoner, was Weyoun. Of the sixteen others onboard the *Defiant*, he alone remained in whatever subjective hell to which the Pah-wraiths had consigned him. The bed's diagnostic display indicated his lifesigns were within Vorta norms, except for the confused tracings of his brainwave patterns that revealed him to be in both deep sleep and a hyperalert state of consciousness at the same time.

"What do you suppose his nightmare is?" Jadzia asked.

"I don't want to know."

Sisko looked up as the sickbay doors scraped, then opened awkwardly as they were forced apart by powerful hands. The corridor beyond was almost pitch black, lit only by two palm torches.

Worf's tall form filled the doorway, moving stiffly. The Klingon was still suffering from the disruptor shots he had taken from the Romulans while on Admiral Picard's *Phoenix.* Immediately behind the Klingon was Ensign Ryle Simons, a young human from Alpha Centauri whose skin was as startlingly white as his hair was flame red. Sisko recalled that Simons had graduated the Academy two weeks before arriving on DS9 to await the arrival of his first ship, the *Destiny.* But only a few days later, the lost Orbs of Jalbador had been found and brought into alignment in Quark's bar.

Then, as the Bajoran system's second wormhole—or Celestial Temple—had opened *inside* DS9, destroying the station, the young human ensign had been one of the thirty-three Starfleet personnel, Bajoran militia, and handful of civilians beamed to the *Defiant* and subsequently tossed twenty-five years into the future. When Jadzia had entered young Simons' personal hell, she had found him floating in deep space, abandoned by his Academy classmates during a zero-G evacuation drill, his environmental suit improperly sealed, perpetually within three minutes of losing all life support.

Since Ensign Simons had taken a minor in Warp Theory, he had been the closest thing to an engineer the *Defi-*

ant had—which explained why Sisko had dispatched Simons with Worf to assess engineering.

Though it was at the very bottom of his list of priorities, in addition to restoring power, Sisko hoped the young ensign would also be able to do something about bringing the ship's replicators online. Sisko was more than ready to discard the Bajoran robes Weyoun had forced him to wear. He envied Worf, Jadzia, and Simons their Starfleet uniforms, even if they were wearing the versions adopted in the year 2400.

From the look on young Simons' face, it seemed to Sisko that the ensign had something to say. Simons was just as clearly waiting for Worf's permission to speak. Until the ship's internal communications system was restored, all reports had to be delivered in person.

Sisko turned to Worf, but the Klingon's attention was focused firmly on Weyoun.

"If we have indeed experienced the end of all existence," Worf said, "the Vorta must be killed."

Appealingly simple and direct as that Klingon approach to their situation was, Sisko did not agree with it. "He might be the only one who knows what's happened to us."

Worf kept his attention on Weyoun, took several cautious, shallow breaths as if even the slightest movement of his chest was painful. "Perhaps. But it might be that our fate is not in question. Under the circumstances, it is possible that we are in *Ko'th*. Limbo. A state of non-being between *Sto-Vo-Kor* and *Gre'thor*. In human mythology, it is the equivalent of being the damned."

Sisko was uncertain if Worf truly believed in what he was saying, or if he was just describing a Klingon tradition which held no special significance for him. "Is there anything that those in *Ko'th* can do to change their fate?"

Worf's tone and expression remained neutral though he held himself unnaturally rigid. "They must commit an act of vengeance, for right or for wrong, in order to proceed to one destination or another—*Sto-Vo-Kor* or *Gre'thor.* Killing Weyoun could be our act of vengeance. If we are the damned."

Sisko suspected that Worf himself did not know the answer to the question he had raised. "Are you that eager to proceed to eternity, Commander Worf?"

"If the universe has ended, Captain, what else awaits us?"

"But we don't know it's ended for certain," Sisko argued.

"Actually, Benjamin," Jadzia interrupted, "we do know. Our sensor net is still down, but I checked the logs for what was recorded just before we lost power. According to those logs, the *Defiant* entered the blue wormhole three point two seconds before it completely merged with the red wormhole. From the final readings of conditions outside the wormholes at that moment, subspace had already degraded by more than eighty percent. Basic astronomical observations showed wavelength disruptions entirely consistent with the emergence—the unraveling—of the hidden dimensions of space-time.

"While it's true we can't be certain that the incident of broken symmetry that triggered the vacuum fluctuation that became our universe was *initiated* by the splitting of this wormhole pocket we're in, it *is* certain that—based on the sensor logs and the Starfleet research I reviewed on Mars—when the two Bajoran wormholes were rejoined, our universe's originating vacuum fluctuation was *negated*. Space-time just . . . rolled in on itself, compressed to a singularity, and ceased to exist—returning to the quantum foam that underlies any concept of reality."

The elegant explanation might have made sense to his old friend Dax, but Sisko still felt a connection to reality. "Then why are *we* still here?" he asked, slapping his hand against the side of the diagnostic bed to physically emphasize his point. "This ship *exists. We* still *exist.*"

Jadzia nodded in understanding but not acceptance. "Only as an echo, Benjamin. Think of this ship as one last reverberation of mass and energy from our universe. In time . . . whatever time means now, we'll fade out, too."

Sisko thought of his son. "How much time?"

Before Jadzia could answer, sickbay was plunged into darkness as the emergency lights abruptly cut out, only to flash on and off and on again as the *Defiant* shuddered violently in the grip of some unknown new assault.

In the harsh, pulsing light, Sisko saw Jadzia grab hold of Worf's arm as the decks and bulkheads creaked and groaned, then fell silent as the ship steadied and the emergency lighting stopped flickering.

Sisko tried to focus on the impossible situation. "Does anyone know where Jake is?" The last Sisko had seen of his son had been on the bridge, just before entering the wormhole.

"He is on the bridge," Worf answered. "Working on restoring the computers."

"Thank you," Sisko said. He looked at Jadzia. The Trill had released her husband's arm. "What we just felt—a theory? Anything?"

The Trill sighed. "Benjamin, every wormhole Starfleet has ever charted, every wormhole for which records exist, is a *tunnel*. A tunnel that joins two separate points in four-dimensional space-time. What we're in now, it's not connecting anything. I can't even make a wild guess about how *verterons* can exist in an unconnected environment, let alone normal matter and energy."

"*Something* exists other than us, Old Man. For what we just felt, there have to be other forces at work on us."

Jadzia shook her head. "Until we restore some kind of sensor capability, we're blind."

Sisko turned to Simons. "What about it, Ensign? What shape are we in?"

Pale cheeks blotched with red, the young human was still staring upward at the sickbay ceiling, as if fearing it would crack open. He lowered his eyes, cleared his throat. "Uh, there's no warp core—"

"Weyoun had it removed so we couldn't slingshot around the red wormhole's maw and go back to our own time," Sisko explained.

"That makes sense, sir. Without warp capability, temporal relocation is impossible. But we still have all our power converters. And about thirty percent of our matter/antimatter reserves. If it's true we don't have anywhere to go in here and we can use all that power for life support for the eighteen people onboard, my, um, estimate is the *Defiant* can easily function for at least . . . twenty years."

Sisko grimaced at the thought that they were all trapped in a single hell now. Twenty years in a starship with nowhere to go and no hope. No crew could last that long under those conditions.

"Twenty years is out of the question," Jadzia said, making it clear that in her opinion Simons's estimate wasn't going to be an option. "Whatever bubble of space-time we're protected in for now will . . . evaporate. That's the best analogy I can think of. And then . . . then there won't be anywhere for us to exist, so . . ." She shrugged. She didn't have to finish.

But Sisko was tired of talk, anyway. "This isn't doing us any good," he said, starting for the sickbay doors. "We need to know what the conditions are out there. We need to know how long we have so we can look for a way out."

But Worf stood between Sisko and the doors.

Sisko halted. He faced the Klingon. "A question, Mr. Worf?"

"What if Jadzia is correct, and there *is* no way out?"

Sisko didn't want to even consider that question. But he

wasn't going to lie to Worf and suggest it wasn't possible. "I don't know."

"But if she *is* correct," the Klingon said slowly, as if considering each word before saying it aloud and bringing more pain to his chest. "And if our existence ends before we have killed our enemy—" He glanced at Weyoun's still form. "Then we will remain in *Ko'th* forever, knowing neither victory nor defeat." He held Sisko's gaze now. "Captain, even *Gre'thor* is preferable to limbo."

Sisko didn't intend to argue with Worf. But he also didn't intend to endanger Weyoun when the Vorta might be needed to provide information. So long as Worf remained true to his Starfleet oath, Sisko knew no officer more loyal, even in the face of death. But under the extreme conditions they faced now, Sisko also knew a point could come where Worf might feel he had to choose between his duty to an organization that no longer existed in any meaningful form and the needs of his Klingon heritage. Indeed, in the same situation, Sisko did not know if in all good conscience he could order his crew to place duty before their deepest spiritual beliefs. So he decided to make it a bit more difficult for Worf to choose to harm Weyoun, in case that conflict arose.

"Dax," Sisko said, "you're responsible for Weyoun."

"I'd be able to do more on the bridge," Jadzia replied.

Sisko glanced at Worf, whose expression remained neutral as he stepped outside, out of Sisko's way. "Commander, you will accompany Ensign Simons and me to the bridge." He looked back at Jadzia. "As soon as we're there, together, I'll send Commander Arla down to watch over Weyoun, and then you can join us. Until then, Old Man, whatever happens," Sisko concluded with a nod to Weyoun, "don't leave his side."

Jadzia pursed her lips as if to remind Sisko that if anyone had seniority in this situation, it was she with her three hundred years of experience. But all she said was, "Where would I go?"

"Maybe I'll find out on the bridge," Sisko said grimly.

Then the ship creaked again, and he wrenched open the sickbay doors and waited for Worf to switch on his palm torch and step into the corridor. The Klingon did so, without hesitation, though his heavy brow was more deeply furrowed than usual with thought.

"Um, what should I do, sir?" Simons asked, switching on his own palm torch as he followed after Sisko and the sickbay doors rattled shut behind them.

All three officers were now standing in the dark corridor, along which only the faint glow of emergency lights could be seen.

"First, get the lights on so we can restore the sensors." Sisko looked down at his Bajoran robes. "Then do what you can to get at least *one* uniform replicator working."

"Yes, sir!"

Simons's palm torch quickly disappeared around the curve to the left.

Worf led the way to the right, halting when he reached the first intersection. With only emergency power available, they would have to use the access ladder by the central turbolifts to get to Deck 1.

But Sisko stopped at Worf's side, not as his commanding officer but as a fellow being facing the same overwhelming, almost impossible-to-comprehend disaster.

"Worf, I do understand your concerns. I'm just not willing to admit defeat until we know more."

In the scattered uplighting from his palm torch, Worf's heavy features took on an ominous appearance. "I understand, sir. But if we discover that no other options are available, remember that there is no shame in accepting the inevitable, provided we behave honorably. And there is no honor in refusing to acknowledge that events have gone past our ability to control them."

"I'm not refusing to accept that. I'm just not convinced it's true."

Sisko sympathized with Worf. Starfleet protocol had little meaning in this era.

Because Starfleet—the epitome of life's best intentions—had come face to face with life's worst fears—total annihilation and meaninglessness. And in this future, in Starfleet's long deep stare into the abyss, those fears had won. Even the Prime Directive had been abandoned.

But in this future, Sisko had not been part of the battle that had raged during the past quarter century. As this time's Starfleet and its Federation had made concessions to the Ascendancy, small ones at first, only in the last years becoming an unstoppable movement toward appeasement and defeat, Sisko and his companions had been insulated—out of time—traveling in a single instant within their frame of reference from the year 2375 to the year 2400.

The optimistic hope for the future that had once been the cornerstone of the Starfleet known to him and the other temporal refugees from 2375 had been slowly crushed by 2400 during the war with the Ascendancy. But that dream still was alive within Sisko, undiminished. And he had to believe that in some way it still existed in his crew.

Even Worf.

"When the time comes, Worf, I will not stand in the way of you doing what your beliefs demand. But I will ask you to consider if the murder of a defenseless being is truly an act of honor, whether vengeance is required or not."

Worf studied Sisko for long moments in the darkness of the corridor, clearly wrestling with the difficult decision to place his fate for all eternity in the hands of an alien who could never truly understand his Klingon heart. "Captain, how will you know when that time has come?"

"I have faith that we will arrive at that decision together."

Sisko held out his hand.

"If we don't have hope, Worf, if we don't work together, then the Pah-wraiths really will have won for all time. The greatest battles demand the greatest risk."

Warrior to warrior, Worf reached out and clasped Sisko's hand.

"*Heghl'umeH QaQ jajvam,*" he said gruffly.

Then, together, through the darkness, Sisko and Worf ran for the bridge.

CHAPTER 4

ON THE *Defiant*'s bridge, Jake Sisko told himself his fingers did *not* hurt. The painful sensation was just something left over from the illusion.

But as he forced himself to concentrate on the basic task of resetting the ship's computers, he couldn't help thinking about how limitless the illusion was—had seemed—within the hell in which he had been lost.

One moment, he had been *there*—twenty-five years in the future, in the transporter room of the *U.S.S. Phoenix*, the monstrous starship conceived by this era's Admiral Jean-Luc Picard for travelling back twenty-five thousand years, to a time before the founding of the fabled Bajoran city of B'hala. And the next moment, he had been *here*.

In that nightmare future, the original mission for Picard's ship had been to place ultrastable explosive charges beneath those sections of B'hala that would not be excavated by the year 2400, A.C.E., guaranteeing that they would not be detected. Those charges were to be set to explode during the final Ascendant ceremonies on the day the universe was scheduled to end. The expected result was the death of Weyoun and most of his followers, as well as the destruction of a sizable portion of Bajor—a small price to be paid for the safety of all existence.

By setting the explosives to go off *after* the *Phoenix*'s departure, Picard's plan had ensured that the universe's timeline would not be altered and that no paradox would be created.

But unknown to Starfleet, a paradox had *already* existed. A team of Romulans had discovered the 25,627-year-old wreckage of the *Phoenix* and its explosive charges on the lifeless moon of one of the Bajoran system's gas giant planets. Thus, before the *Phoenix* had even set off on its mission, that mission could be proven to be a failure.

So Jake's best friend, Captain Nog, now twenty-five years older and Admiral Picard's assistant and supporter, had devised a *new* plan.

To maintain the timeline in which Nog and Deep Space 9 and Weyoun and the Orbs of Jalbador existed, Nog intended to travel back to Bajor's past and allow enough sections of the *Phoenix* to crash on the lifeless moon to account for the wreckage the Romulans would find.

Then just before the *Phoenix* had entered her temporal slingshot trajectory around Bajor's sun, Nog's programming activated the ship's advanced technology transporters, beaming Jake, Worf, Jadzia, Dr. Bashir, Ryle Simons, and their nine fellow refugees from the past to a starship near the opening Bajoran wormholes, so they could safely slingshot back to their own time.

That moment of transport had been unlike any other beaming experience Jake had ever had, even his most recent, when he had been plucked from his own time onboard the *Defiant* and taken twenty-five years into the future onboard the Vulcan ship, the *Augustus*. This time, he had felt a sudden chill, and at once the unfinished walls of the *Phoenix*'s transporter room had been instantly replaced by the corridors of the *Defiant*. He had felt no quantum-dissolution effect, nor any temporary loss of sight of his surroundings as his nervous system had been tunneled from one point to another. All Jake could remember now was that one moment he had been *there,* and the next he had been *here.* It had been like being in a dream.

And right now, he was still confused about just when it was that dreamlike experience had become his nightmare.

First had come the elation of being back on the *Defiant.* He'd quickly determined where he was in the ship and immediately raced for the bridge. The intensity of his excitement had been matched by the bedlam around him. On his run through the ship, he had heard shouting as all the *Defiant*'s alarms—collision and weapons lock and intruder alerts—sounded off at once.

Then the bridge doors had opened before him and he'd rushed in, caught sight of his father, called out to him.

Bajoran robes fluttering, Sisko had wheeled to face him, and he and his father had thrown their arms around each other, their embrace saying more than words ever could.

Then someone had called out, "Ten seconds."

And even if Jake had been able to explain why he and the others had come back to the *Defiant,* he'd known from the look of horror on his father's face that there was no time to follow through on the rest of Nog's plan. No time to follow through on their own escape.

They'd run out of time. Everyone had. Literally.

After that, Jake remembered hearing Worf report a supernova shockwave was approaching.

He remembered feeling the *Defiant* tremble. Hearing his father call out for some—any—explanation. Seeing Ensign Simons at the science station. Hearing the young

Centaurian identify the impact as a subspace pressure wave catching the ship.

On the main viewer, he'd seen the two wormholes about to merge, red and blue energy tendrils reaching out like the warring tentacles of two incomprehensible creatures.

He'd seen Weyoun, dressed like a Bajoran kai in blood-red robes, shouting out that the Temple was restored.

He'd heard Weyoun screaming just as Worf said, "Impact," as he himself . . .

At the *Defiant*'s computer station, Jake shook his head. He rubbed at his face as if he had slept for days. He remembered falling away from his father at that moment of impact. He remembered the lights going out, just for a moment, and then . . . he was in his room on the *Saratoga*, sitting hunched over his tiny, child-sized desk, inputting into his padd, seeing his words deleted almost as fast as he wrote them, somehow not questioning the sudden transition to a starship that in his frame of reference had been destroyed almost ten years ago.

Jake shivered. There had been *nothing* at the time that had made him even suspect the nightmare had not been real, not logical. Even now, he still couldn't shake the feeling that he had actually been on the *Saratoga*, fingers bleeding, absolutely certain that the moment he stopped inputting, the moment the cursor caught up with his words, it would be the moment he ceased to exist.

How long his nightmare had lasted, Jake didn't know. He couldn't even remember what he had been inputting. *Anslem,* he suspected. For all his detours had taken him into crime novels and thrillers and even Quark's attempts to talk him into a lurid collaboration about the Red Orbs, *Anslem* was the book he always came back to, always regretting ever having put it aside. Which is why, he decided now, it most likely *was* the book he had been frantically inputting in his personal version of hell.

But for however many years or hours or centuries he had existed within that room, his nightmare had ended the moment Jadzia's hand had slipped past his shoulder and her finger had lightly touched the POWER control on his padd.

At once, the all-devouring cursor had stopped moving, his words had been stored, and the padd's screen had winked out.

The next thing Jake could remember was staring at that blank screen until he'd finally become aware that Jadzia had stepped in front of him. He'd looked up to see that she had on the deep red sweater he remembered his mother wearing on the *Saratoga* that final day. He'd loved that sweater. It was the last real memory he had of his mother.

Dressed like that, her spots almost invisible against the dark hue of her skin, now the same color Jennifer Sisko's had been, Jadzia had held out her hand to Jake. "This is just a dream," she'd told him, "and your father's waiting for you to wake up."

An instant later, Jake had found himself in the *Defiant*'s sickbay.

And now he was here, on the bridge, desperately trying to dredge from his memory all the basic procedures Chief O'Brien had taught him in those years when everyone had expected Sisko's son to follow in his father's footsteps and attend the Academy.

A series of status lights turned green before him.

Jake sighed. Maybe his whole life was an illusion. Maybe the whole universe he lived in no longer existed. So what did the color green mean anymore, without suns to shine on plants that grew on worlds to be explored? What did anything mean anymore?

"Computer," a familiar voice suddenly said behind him, startling him.

Jake felt a hand pat his shoulder and looked up to see

Major Kira. He didn't know what the major's hell had been, but her eyes were still deeply shadowed, and he hadn't seen her smile since he had come to the bridge. Although he had heard her use a rather raw Bajoran expletive as she had ripped the sleeves off her Bajoran robes.

"Working," the computer replied, indicating that its most basic operating system had been reloaded.

"Good work, Jake. I'll get it up to speed now." From the way Kira looked down at him, it was obvious that she wanted him to get out of the duty chair.

"Right, sorry," he said. He moved out of the way as Kira took over.

For the moment, Jake realized, he had nothing to do but watch the others on the bridge take action while he stayed out of their way. Commander Arla was on her back under the combined flight and operations console, an access panel on the deck beside her. She was adjusting something inside the console's base with a pulsewrench.

"How's that power supply coming?" Arla called out, her voice echoing within the depths of the machinery she worked on.

The bridge lights suddenly brightened to full intensity.

"We're on-line," Kira announced. "Let's try internal comm. Bridge to engineering."

Jake heard Ensign Simons's high-pitched voice over the bridge speakers. "Simons here."

"Good work, Ensign," Kira told him. "Now . . . is it going to last?"

"It should," Simons answered. "We have plenty of antimatter, and we'll have the second power converter operational in twenty minutes. That'll give us full backup power, too."

"What about propulsion?" Kira asked.

"Um, you should probably talk to Captain Sisko about that. He's on his way up."

Jake's spirits lifted. He knew it probably wasn't the most mature reaction, but in a situation like this, he felt more secure when his father was nearby. Then the bridge doors opened and his father and Worf stepped onto the bridge.

Sisko nodded at him once, and Jake understood from that terse acknowledgment that his father was deep in his "Starfleet" mode. He wasn't anyone's father right now. Nor was he anyone's friend. Not even to Dax if she were here. For now, he was a starship captain whose only concern was his crew and his ship.

Sisko stopped by Kira's station. "What's our status, Major?"

"No significant damage. Jake reset the computer. Ensign Simons has restored power. And between me up here and Dr. Bashir in the replicator bay, full life support has been reestablished. All we need are exterior sensors and propulsion."

Worf was at his tactical station. "And weapons," he said.

"Sensors first," Sisko said. He went over to Arla. "Commander, how close are we to having the main viewer operational?"

Arla's head was still deep within the console and her voice was muffled. "Two more circuits to replace . . . one more . . ." There was a sudden spark of light from within the console. "Got it." The tall Bajoran commander pulled herself out of the console and sat up, shaking one hand as if she'd received a jolt of transtator current. "Major, give it a try now."

Jake watched as Kira left the engineering station and went to science to call up the ship's sensor operations system. The viewer instantly filled with a rippling pattern of blue light, bringing a cold glare to the bridge.

"Can you adjust focus?" Sisko asked.

"All the adjustment subroutines are functioning," Kira said as she studied her controls. "What we're seeing is what's out there. Or at least an optical extrapolation of the local energy environment. Seems to be mostly tachyon-based." She glanced up at the screen and said what Jake was thinking. "It looks like the inside of the Celestial Temple."

But Sisko didn't agree. "Not exactly. I don't see any verteron nodes. No energy strings." He scratched at his beard. "Commander Arla, go to sickbay and take over from Dax."

Arla was on her feet at once, no outward sign visible of the emotional after-effects of her own Pah-wraith-induced hell. Jake didn't know what type of subjective experience Arla had been trapped in, but, unlike the others, she appeared fully recovered.

"Take over how, sir?" With Starfleet efficiency, Arla asked the question as she headed for the doors, already on her way.

"Just standing by Weyoun."

At that, Arla stopped. "Sir?"

"We've left him in his . . . Pah-wraith experience. Just monitor his lifesigns, let me know if he shows any change or any sign of coming to. And tell Dax to get up here right away. The turbolifts are working."

Jake knew that his father had just ordered Arla to place herself in the same room as the man who had destroyed her people's world. But all Arla replied was, "Yes, sir." And then, without any other reaction that would betray her true feelings to Jake or anyone else on the bridge, she went through the open doorway in a run. Jake found her self-control astounding.

Then Jake saw his father's stern expression soften as he put a hand on Kira's shoulder. "How are you, Major?"

"Truthfully? I've been a *lot* better."

Sisko nodded, an understanding friend for one brief moment, before his Starfleet mission took control once more. "Run a full sensor sweep, maximum power and range. I want to find out if there's anyone else in here with us."

"You mean Dukat."

Jake saw the shudder that ran through Kira, just once, as she said that name.

Sisko confirmed the major's conclusion. "He was heading for the wormholes, too."

Kira's face hardened, but she began calling up the required controls to run the sweep.

Then his father's gaze finally fell on him, and Jake knew that Sisko was his father again. Saying nothing, Sisko walked over and hugged him again before making a point of tugging on the collar of Jake's twenty-fifth-century Starfleet uniform. "So this is what it took to get you to finally join up," he said, a half smile on his lips.

"Hey, this is a *civilian* specialist uniform," Jake said. Unlike the black uniforms given to Worf and the others, Jake's was gray. And where the other uniforms had single shoulders set off in a specialty color, Jake's shoulder was black. When he had first put it on, it had reminded him of a cadet's uniform.

"What kind of specialist?" Sisko asked.

Jake did his best to fill in his father about everything that had happened to him since he had been beamed off the *Defiant* right after the ship's arrival in the future. He recounted the story of Admiral Picard, Captain Nog, and Vash, and their mission to the past. And how Nog had hoped that he'd be able to send his friends back to their own time by beaming them to a starship near the opening wormholes.

"I'm surprised by that," Sisko said, frowning slightly. "There's no way any of us would have been able to return to our own time except by reversing the slingshot trajectory that brought us here. And that would have been possible only by being on the *Defiant* and looping around the red wormhole as it opened."

"Nog knew that," Jake said quickly. "We all did. But . . . because of everything else that happened, there was no way to save the timeline the way Admiral Picard had planned. So the best we could do was to create alternates. Wherever we ended up after our first slingshot around the blue wormhole, Dax was going to work out the trajectory that would bring us back to Bajor the day *after* DS9 was destroyed. That would've at least preserved *our* subjective timeline, and we could've stopped Weyoun's expedition into the red wormhole *and* given Starfleet enough time to figure out a way to destroy the Red Orbs."

Sisko's frown deepened. "Nog should have worked out a way to take the *Phoenix* back twenty-five years instead. Not risk trying to reach Bajor at the last moment."

"Dad, he had to make sure the wreckage of the *Phoenix* reached that moon twenty-five thousand years ago. Otherwise . . . well, I don't understand it all, but Dax confirmed the theory. Something about the paradox causing this timeline to collapse like a black hole, so that there'd be no one who could stop Weyoun in the past."

"In theory," Sisko said. "Does Nog have any way of coming back?"

Jake shook his head. "Vash said maybe . . . maybe Q would come looking for them."

Sisko's skeptical expression let Jake know how likely he thought that possibility would be.

Jake hadn't believed Vash, either. "I think she meant it as a joke."

"What did Nog think he and Admiral Picard and *Vash* of all people could accomplish that far in the past? Other than crash part of their ship?"

"I . . . don't know. We didn't have a lot of time to talk about it. Nog was mostly interested in what he missed on

DS9 the day . . . the day it was destroyed. Dax might know what he was thinking."

"Well," Sisko said, "whatever Nog thought he could do, it obviously didn't work. Not in this timeline."

Jake felt confused. "Uh, does this even still count as a timeline?"

Sisko's pain was obvious. Jake had always known his father would never lie to him, and he wasn't lying now. "I don't know, Jake. I—"

"Captain!"

Sisko and Jake instantly turned to Kira.

"There *is* someone else in here!"

"Onscreen, Major. Is it the *Boreth?*"

Jake saw Kira working frantically on her controls. "No, no. The mass is at least ten times greater. Whatever it is, it's huge, it's . . ."

She muttered something under her breath. To Jake, it almost sounded like she was praying. And then she simply turned her head to stare past Jake and Sisko at the viewer.

Jake turned to see what she saw. Felt the hair bristle on his arms, on the back of his neck.

For at the end of the universe, in the last pocket of existence that remained, Deep Space 9 was waiting.

CHAPTER 5

QUARK DRUNKENLY reached across the counter of his bar on the Promenade and his gold-pressed-latinum sleeve-binder caught the edge of the curved, leather-wrapped flagon of Saurian brandy.

Vintage Saurian brandy. 2215. One hundred bars apiece.

Behind the counter, by the sink, Rom watched in horror as the costly flagon rocked back and forth. Rushing forward, he slipped on the filthy floor and vainly stretched out the gnarled fingers of his injured hand full-length until his knuckles popped and shocks of pain skipped along his arm. But the instant before he could make contact with it, the flagon tipped over and shattered. The suddenly worthless amber-gold liquor swept across the bartop like a miniature tidal wave, taking with it what little remained of Rom's dreams.

Rom groaned as Quark reared back and cried out grandly, "Put it on my tab!" And then, whooping with laughter, he fell into his companion's arms.

"Oh, Quarky," Leeta giggled.

Rom stared in open-mouthed, abject despair as the beautiful dabo girl who had once been his wife pulled "Quarky" closer, then slowly circled his lobe with a single suggestive finger as she whispered something unintelligible that made Rom's brother giggle and lick his lips appreciatively.

"B-but," Rom stammered, "y-you never pay your tab, brother."

Quark merely grinned at him. "You were always telling me you could run this place better than I ever could. Here's your chance to prove it."

Just then, in the far corner of the bar's main floor, two outraged Klingons tossed a flailing, screaming Bolian through the air to land headfirst on the dabo table which promptly collapsed, the appalling damage clearly beyond repair.

Quark sniggered as he made a mock grimace. "Ooo, there go your dabo profits for the *month.* Ouch." Then he blew a farewell kiss to Rom as he left with Leeta hanging on his arm, heartlessly taking her up to the holosuites as he did every night, to enjoy the holocylinder for *Risian Ear Clinic—The Jamaharon Continues.* That had once been Rom's and Leeta's favorite, too.

Mournfully watching Leeta leave without him, Rom felt his chest ache almost as painfully as the deep cracks that furrowed the skin of his hands—the cracks that never healed anymore. Because he was forced to wash the dishes in scalding water every night now. Because he no longer had time to repair the sonic sterilizers.

"Hey! Ferengoid! Some service over here!"

A table of rowdy Nausicaans hurled their empty glasses at him—five at a half-slip each. One even struck Rom's bandaged ear where he had lost a lobe in the unfortunate altercation with Grand Nagus Nog.

"NOW!" the Nausicaans screeched, fangs nastily clicking to emphasize their threat.

Rom lurched forward to dab up what he could of the Saurian brandy with his already stained jacket, then quickly began pouring shots of steaming bile wine as more and more customers shouted out for immediate service.

But in the entire bar, there was only Rom to serve them. All the others who had once worked for Quark had walked out on strike, demanding such high wages that every day Rom bitterly wished he had never organized the union in the first place.

Even thinking about the union, Rom felt his hands tremble and he spilled more bile wine than he poured into the glasses, guaranteeing there would be no profit on this transaction. Even worse, there was no profit on any of the transactions he made these days, and his debt was growing faster than a black hole.

Then Rom jumped as the glasses on the bartop began to rattle rhythmically. Nervously, he looked up to see his absolute best customer—Morn—pounding his tankard, insisting on another round. Now!

Rom picked up a jug of draft Romulan ale. "H-how's it going, Morn? H-how're the brothers and, uh, sisters?" Morn had seventeen siblings in all. The question was a sure-fire conversation starter with the big guy. He usually went on for hours, consuming high-markup beverages all the while.

But these days, not even Morn was speaking to Rom. He simply sat in unnerving silence, as if he didn't have a word to say.

"I'm . . . I'm sorry!" Rom blurted, because in truth he was sorry for *everything*. He practically upended the jug into Morn's tankard, then winced as the ale's pale blue foam promptly bubbled upward and cascaded onto the bartop.

Morn's small dark eyes narrowed as he *growled* at Rom.

Rom shrank back, dropping the jug of draft on the counter. "S-sorry, sorry, sorry." The jug spun around in the foam and then slid off the counter, exploding spectacularly as it hit the floor beside Morn's feet.

Rom's voice rose high in a squeal. "Uh, I'll . . . I'll get you a bottle of *vintage* ale, all right? No bubbles?"

Morn growled again. Louder. Meaner.

"And on the house!" Rom squeaked, then rushed back to the replicator because dirty plates and platters were now raining down from the second-floor railing. The impatient Tellarites on the upper level were on a snorting, grunting rampage for more tribble pie.

"What kind of hell is this?" Dukat asked. Rom was so startled, he misentered the last digit of the tribble-pie code and then cringed as a hundred-count of brain-stuffed ravioli sprayed out from the mouth of the replicator. The filthy mess was an illegal dish his brother Quark had programmed years ago when a contingent of Medusan navigators had been onboard. The unsettling eating habits of the noncorporeal life-forms were a closely held secret known only to the top levels of Starfleet and a few select suppliers in the hospitality services. When Captain Sisko found out about the contents of that ravioli, Rom knew for a certainty he'd lose Quark's lease on the station. He was always losing Quark's lease.

"And what is that disgusting smell?" Dukat asked.

Rom's boots squished as he trudged through the mound of replicated pasta and Vulcan brain tissue that now covered the deck behind the bar. There were holes in the soles of his boots, so the body-temperature mass slurped up horribly between his toes.

"Uh, would you like some *kanar?*" Rom asked miserably. Then he blinked in confusion at the Cardassian.

Dukat was out of uniform. He was wearing what

seemed to be the robes of a Bajoran religious order. And his hair was white, his face deeply etched.

"Uh, Gul Dukat . . . are—are you feeling all right?" Rom asked, peering at him more closely. It was as if the Cardassian had suddenly aged a quarter century or more.

Dukat looked around the chaos of the bar. More fights were breaking out. Dishes and furniture were being destroyed at an accelerating rate. A group of Cardassian soldiers had just won their eighth consecutive dabo at the table that no longer seemed to be in pieces. And even more impossible, Quark and Leeta were locked in a seamless, impassioned embrace at a tiny table off to one corner.

"How is this *different?*" Dukat asked.

"Uh, different from what?" Rom couldn't be sure, but for a moment it seemed Dukat's eyes had glowed red.

"From the way it used to be. When all this was real."

Rom stared at the gul. His eyes *were* glowing red.

"This *is* real . . . isn't it?" But even as Rom said those words, there was something in Dukat's eerie eyes that made him doubt them.

Dukat held out his hand. "If you come with me now, I promise that when you return to . . . this realm, you shall be in whatever passes for Ferengi heaven, not this hell."

"I . . . don't understand," Rom said. He looked past Dukat and goggled at what he saw and heard. The crashes and screams of the bar's mayhem were rapidly fading. A Bolian was suspended, midair, about to crash headfirst into Quark's perfectly intact dabo table. All the other customers in the bar were similarly frozen in place, including . . . *Gul Dukat?* Younger, in uniform, treating those at his table to the most expensive *kanar* on the menu, just as he always did at this time of night, telling Rom to bill it to a Cardassian trade mission that had gone out of business years ago.

Rom wanted to ask how there could be two Dukats in

his brother's bar, but he didn't. He didn't want to say a single word to break the spell the bar was under. For the first time in . . . in centuries, in millennia, it seemed to Rom, the place was blissfully quiet.

"You don't have to understand anything," Dukat said. "Just take my hand, and promise to serve me."

Rom stared at that hand, hesitant.

"Rom," Dukat said, "really. How much worse could your life get?"

Rom considered the question seriously. "It . . . it couldn't. This is the worst it's ever been."

Dukat nodded once, held his hand higher. "So, what do you say?"

"I, uh, promise to serve you?" Then Rom took hold of that cold gray hand and at once—

—arose from the deck in the *Boreth,* in the engine room, hand in hand with Dukat.

Rom gazed around him in confusion, stared down at his hands, no longer cracked and gnarled. He lifted his one free hand, felt for his lost lobe, and found it intact. He looked up at Dukat, at last remembering what had happened.

"The universe?" he asked weakly.

"This fever called living is over at last," Dukat intoned. "There is no more universe."

"Then how . . ." Rom swallowed hard as he made his realization. "We're in the wormhole, aren't we?"

"Where else is there?" Dukat suddenly squeezed Rom's hand hard enough that Rom was sure he heard his own bones grate as the Cardassian hauled him into the air with one hand.

"And when I was in the bar?" Rom gasped.

Dukat's eyes flared with red energy as he excruciatingly tightened his grip on Rom's hand. "You were being toyed with," the Cardassian said. "Punished for no other reason than to satisfy those driven mad by their *own* punishment."

"Wh-who?" Rom hoped he wouldn't faint from the pain before he heard Dukat's answer.

"Chief O'Brien needs you on the bridge," Dukat said abruptly, dropping Rom to the floor. "If I were you, I'd do what he says. Otherwise . . ."

Rom nodded vigorously as he swayed on his feet and clutched his throbbing hand. He didn't want to go back to the bar. He would do anything to avoid that. He looked around the vast engineering section of the advanced-technology Klingon ship. "Uh, where is the bridge?"

Dukat dragged him toward the doors, never letting go.

Not that there was anyplace left for Rom to run to.

At the engineering station on the bridge of the *Boreth,* surrounded by the motionless bodies of the other temporal refugees, O'Brien stared at the displays on his sensor screens and tried to make sense of them.

At the least complex level of interpretation, there was little to question in the results he had obtained.

Just as the main viewer made clear, it was Deep Space 9—and not Empok Nor—which was within the wormhole environment in some sort of proximity to the *Boreth.* O'Brien could only conclude that instead of being gravitationally crushed by the opening of the red wormhole, the station had, instead, been swallowed by it. Judging from the fact that all its docking arms had been restored, Weyoun had apparently had repair crews in here to restore it.

In the same indistinct fashion, O'Brien could see that the sensors confirmed that the *Defiant* was also here, and also apparently without major damage.

But none of that solved O'Brien's key problem: In this realm, what did the term "here" mean anymore?

He touched a control that would give him access to the

Boreth's external communications array. As the comm keypads appeared on his board, he glanced again at the bridge's main doors. Dukat had been gone for ten minutes and there was no way to be sure how much longer O'Brien would have to work undisturbed. But if ever a situation called for taking a chance . . .

He set the communications transmit options to full subspace spread, no encryption, maximum power. "O'Brien to *Defiant*. O'Brien to *Defiant*. Come in, anyone." Then he put the message on automatic repeat and watched as the status lights showed it being transmitted up and down the subspace spectrum.

But there was no reply. In fact, the feedback sensors indicated that the message had not even been successfully sent.

O'Brien blew out his breath and called up a sensor diagnostic subroutine. And even allowing for the extra time it took to translate the controls and readings from their odd mixture of Bajoran and Klingon technical glyphs, it took less than thirty seconds to see what the problem was.

The message had not been transmitted because there was no subspace through which it could travel. The local environment was the equivalent of a subspace vacuum.

"Impossible," O'Brien muttered to himself. "We used to transmit subspace messages through the wormhole. We . . . oh." The chief engineer paused as he realized that the subspace environment that had allowed messages to be transmitted through the Bajoran wormhole was an artifact from the normal space-time metric which existed at each end of the wormhole.

But there were no ends here. Normal space-time no longer existed. The *Boreth,* Deep Space 9, and the *Defiant* were no longer in a wormhole tunnel, they were within a wormhole pocket. *Though how can you have a wormhole if there's nothing for that hole to pass through?*

Rather than torture himself over trying to answer the

maddening question, O'Brien decided then and there to accept the fact that he missed Dax. He could always count on her to come up with an equation or two to help give him a direction for his more practical, hands-on approaches to various problems.

But for this problem, without Dax, he was reduced to tapping his fingers at the side of the console, trying to think of what to do next. Then the ship trembled and the deck pitched as if the *Boreth* were an ancient ship at sea.

For whatever reason, the movement lasted only a moment. The lights didn't even flicker.

In fact, the only aftereffect the chief engineer could note was that the background of red energy and glowing verteron strings and nodes against which DS9 and, most of the time, the *Defiant* had been hung had changed.

Now it was blue. The same rippling, icy translucence that the chief engineer remembered from his trips through the first Bajoran wormhole.

O'Brien checked his sensor readings of the *Boreth*'s environment again but saw no appreciable change resulting from the switchover from red to blue. But the fact that color could change out there made him think of simple, ordinary photons. Unlike subspace transmissions which had to travel through a subspace medium as sound traveled through air, electromagnetic signals could propagate through a vacuum. O'Brien smiled in relief as he ran through a set of seldom-used Klingon communications settings until he found what he was looking for.

Radio.

The primary reason a ship like the *Boreth* even had that capability was in the event contact was made with an emergent, pre-warp technological culture. But in this case, primitive radio was just what he needed to conquer the unfathomable conditions of the wormhole pocket.

With a series of quick commands, O'Brien redirected

his spoken message so it was relayed over the simple electromagnetic spectrum. He even adjusted the *Boreth*'s transmitter arrays so that the message was aimed at the *Defiant*.

But, frustratingly, even though the feedback indicators showed that this time the message was indeed being transmitted, there was still no response.

O'Brien sighed, turned his attention to Deep Space 9. Under normal conditions, the station constantly transmitted automated navigational signals in a variety of energy spectrums, even radio. If he could measure how those signals were being transmitted from the station to the *Boreth*, perhaps get an idea of what kind of interference might be at work in here, he might be able to make adjustments to his own transmission to the *Defiant*.

He checked the bridge doors again. Still no sign of Dukat. "Keep 'im busy, Rom," O'Brien said under his breath. Then he scanned all frequencies he knew the station would be transmitting on.

Nothing.

"Bloody hell," O'Brien said. He looked at the viewer. Deep Space 9 took up the middle quarter. He knew it had power because he could see the glow of its fusion reactors and its running lights were . . . "Wait a minute." Tapping a finger each time the station's hazard-warning lights blinked on and off, O'Brien started to count off seconds out loud like a first-year engineering student. "One millicochrane . . . two millicochrane . . . three millicochrane . . . *that's it!*"

The hazard lights atop each docking arm were cycling on and off too slowly. "It's in a different temporal frame of reference!"

He ran a quick series of calculations based on how fast the lights should be blinking versus how fast they actually were. The offset was approximately twenty-eight percent.

Fortunately, Starfleet encountered enough antique space probes traveling at sublight, relativistic speeds that any junior engineer could handle the Hawking transformations necessary to bring timeshifted communications into synch. The realignment of the *Boreth*'s Klingon communications array took less than a minute.

O'Brien listened again, then smiled in triumph as familiar patterns of automated acquisition signals beeped over the bridge speakers.

"Ah, I've missed you, too," he said wistfully. Then he entered the transposition code that would translate the beeps into Federation-standard alphanumerics.

At that, his display screen changed to show three message windows. One was for DS9's Starfleet identification codes. One was for the codes required for in-system use by the Bajoran Transportation Commission. And the final one was a basic Cardassian location signal. One that Starfleet had elected to keep in operation for the benefit of any ships or automated probes that might have left the Bajoran system before the Cardassians withdrew and that might someday return to a different political situation.

But O'Brien's focus was on the Starfleet codes. These included time-alignment data, navigational positioning updates, and, of course, like any other Starfleet installation, local stardate calculations. He made some final adjustments in the selectivity of the *Boreth*'s electromagnetic receivers, then began working out his strategy for applying what he had learned to his next attempt to raise the *Defiant*.

As a final check of his calculations, he also applied the same adjustments to the radio channel on which the stardate information was being transmitted.

And then he sat back in shock, "No . . ."

The stardate was wrong.

That wasn't Deep Space 9 that faced the *Boreth*.

It was Deep Space 9 as it had existed on stardate 51889.4. Twenty-five years ago.

After having given up all hope of ever escaping his future, Chief Miles O'Brien found himself looking through a window into his past. And the first thought to burn through his engineer's mind was: *If light particles can pass through that window, then so can I.*

But before he could do anything about it, the bridge doors slipped open, and Dukat, red eyes ablaze, swept in, towing a baffled-looking Rom.

O'Brien erased his communications screens.

This wasn't the time, nonlinear or otherwise.

But soon it would be, and with that realization, hope returned to him.

Escape *was* possible.

But without Dax, it was all up to him.

CHAPTER 6

EYES CLOSED, Garak slumped down against the sharp rocks of unprocessed uridium ore piled by the slag cars. Each six and half hours, his labor cohort was permitted a ten-minute food break, and the last time the break signal had sounded, everyone in his group had rushed through the disk door like a herd of ravening *volekra*. But Garak hadn't joined them because he was conducting an experiment.

He no longer ate on any of his breaks. Neither did he drink water. And after more consecutive shifts than he could count, interrupted only when Gul Dukat made his regular appearance to take him to the Promenade to tailor a suit for Enabran Tain, Garak no longer even slept, though he was desperately weary.

For him to be able to withstand those deprivations, there was something wrong here. He knew it.

He just didn't know what.

The premonition took hold in him that soon he would no longer be able to even conceive of the notion of 'wrong.' That the sum total of his existence would be reduced to handling ore, half-making a suit, and then dying at his own father's hand. Again and again and . . .

Garak still retained one half-remembered idea that suggested dying was once the way all things were supposed to end, and that it only happened once. But for a reason that remained gratingly out of reach, life on Terok Nor seemed to allow no such escape. It continued forever in its bleakness, devoid of meaning or of hope.

"It's time for you to leave." The voice of the gul who commanded the station penetrated Garak's mental fog.

But Garak didn't even bother opening his eyes. "You're early," he murmured. "I've only been here for a shift. I remember too well what you're going to ask me to do. The same thing you always ask me. But you're supposed to let me work down here until I can't be sure what happened the last time was real, or a dream, so it can happen all over again."

"You think this is *real?*" Dukat asked. "Garak, I had thought that of all people, you might know better. Or, at least, have harbored some modicum of suspicion about its true nature."

Garak blinked, staring now at the high ceiling. Dukat had never said those words to him before. Usually, he simply escorted Garak along the station's corridors and discussed his dossier. At least, the dossier of a Bajoran resistance fighter who had once apprenticed to a tailor in Tohzat Province and with whom Garak had apparently been confused by the Cardassian bureaucracy.

Garak was honest enough with himself to admit that he couldn't really remember how he had actually come to occupy his current position on Terok Nor, or what he had been or done before coming here. But without question he knew he was not a Bajoran. And that knowledge did help him keep from accepting at least some of what he experienced here as unquestionable reality as Dukat seemed to suggest he should.

"Don't you wish to leave this place?" the gul asked.

Another question that had never been asked. Garak opened his eyes. Looked over at Dukat—

—and shot to his feet in surprise.

This Dukat was *different*. Not the same one who had been coming to him for . . . for centuries, it seemed. This Dukat was clad in the robes of a Bajoran religious order. His weathered features bore the mark of age. His hair was white. His strange eyes those of a fanatic.

And on his arm the red band of a Pah-wraith cult that—

Garak's breath came short and fast. "Of course! That explains it! This is an Orb experience."

"Close enough," the older Dukat allowed. He held out a hand. "But I can free you from it."

Fatigue lost its hold on Garak as relief unleashed a discomfiting torrent of memories. "Free me? Then there *is* something else that exists outside of . . . of this personal hell, I suppose we could call it." He gestured around him, at the ore-processing facility, its realization more detailed than the best Starfleet holodeck technology could produce. "I truly am impressed," Garak said. "Even I had no idea my issues with my father were so deep-seated. Here I had always thought that my personal hell would be to be confined in a narrow space with ravenous *marklars* gnawing on my flesh. But this *is* much more harrowing. On an emotional level, that is."

Dukat stared, wild-eyed, at him, hand still outstretched. "What are you talking about? I said, I can *save* you from this. Say after me: I will serve you."

Garak ignored the gul, or whatever rank this Dukat was. He really had no patience for such bizarre posturing. "This is most remarkable. Obviously, the *Boreth* entered one of the wormholes before the universe was destroyed."

He peered intently at Dukat. "The universe *was* destroyed, wasn't it?" He held up a hand to forestall Dukat's answer as he continued excitedly. "Forget that I said that. Of course it was destroyed. But somehow . . . somehow this ship must have maintained a small island of stability in the midst of . . . whatever conditions exist here. Wherever here is. And clearly—"

"Take my hand and serve me!" Dukat's voice rose in anger.

Garak nodded, not listening, as he linked his hands behind his back and began to pace beside the slag cars and their piles of unprocessed ore. "And since the Pah-wraiths came after me by subjecting me to this . . . this illusion of Terok Nor, in reality, or in whatever passes for it now, we somehow must be physically protected in the ship."

Garak stopped pacing and looked questioningly at Dukat, who still stood with outstretched hand. "Is everyone consigned to their own version of hell? Were you?"

A sudden wind set Dukat's robes fluttering as he withdrew his hand and then threw both arms open wide, declaring, "I am Kosst Dukat, ruler of this realm! And in Amojan's name I damn you to—"

"Oh, do be quiet and let me think," Garak said. "If you could do anything to me in here, you would have done it by now."

Dukat dramatically pointed both his hands at Garak, red sparks of energy flickering the length of his long blacknailed fingers.

"Dukat, are you really willing to throw away your one chance at eternal victory?" Garak asked, completely unintimidated.

The robed Cardassian stiffened, enraged, but he did not strike. "Why are you not afraid?"

"For the same reason you *are* afraid," Garak said, lifting his own hands before him, remembering in detail how they used to look. At once, his clear nails became black and pink skin that had been as repellently smooth as that of a gas-distended corpse became gray and lightly plated, neither black nor white but a perfect aesthetic balance of the two—the Cardassian ideal.

Garak put his restored hands to his neck, felt his proud dual spinal cords restored to their proper location.

"Consider what's happening here," Garak said with satisfaction. "This wormhole—or the Temple, if you prefer—is obviously a place with rules. A place with limits."

"I am without limits!" Dukat shouted. "I am absolute power—Amojan without end!"

"And if that were true," Garak said, "for my insolence, I would not exist, and you would not need me." He smiled pleasantly at Dukat. "Because that *is* why you're here, isn't it? You *need* me."

"O'Brien needs you!" Dukat sputtered. "As for me, I leave you here in your hell for all time!"

"Dukat, have you forgotten who I am? Is there anyone you have ever known who was better at . . . circumventing the rules? Finding exceptions to the limits?"

Dukat's eyes bulged as they pulsed with red energy, but none of that energy spilled out to strike Garak down.

"When you're ready to talk," Garak said, his argument confirmed by Dukat's inaction, "I'm certain you'll know where to find me."

Then, with absolute certainty about what would happen next, he closed his eyes for less time than it took him to blink, and when he opened them again, he was looking up at the ceiling of the *Boreth*'s bridge, less than a meter from the last place he remembered standing when the ship had spun into the wormhole and all the lights had gone out.

"How utterly remarkable," Garak said, getting to his feet. He nodded to the two people watching him: "Good day to you, gentlemen." He added a smile to his greeting, but the expressions on the faces of Miles O'Brien and Rom remained stern and slightly confused.

"Come now," Garak teased them. "We did survive the destruction of the universe. I believe that's worth a small round of self-congratulations, wouldn't you agree?"

"You'll pardon us if we don't join you," O'Brien said stiffly. "*We* were in our own personal hells."

"Indeed."

"Uh," Rom said as he looked back and forth like some type of agitated avian, "wh-what happened to Dukat?"

"Oh, the last time I saw him," Garak said, "he was in *my* hell." He shrugged at O'Brien. "It wasn't a very good one, though. No logic to it. I think . . . in fact, I'm sure I would have found my way out soon enough. How about you?"

"This isn't the time," O'Brien said. "Dukat might be back any moment."

Garak smoothed his robes, all that remained of his Bajoran captivity, then looked up at the main viewer and was startled by what he saw there. "The station? In here with us?"

"More than that," the chief engineer said. "According to its navigational time code, that's the station as it existed about the time it was destroyed."

"You don't say."

"This isn't a game!" O'Brien exclaimed with a nervous glance to either side of him. But except for himself and the two engineers, Garak knew there was no one else who was awake. The others, including Quark and Odo, were all unconscious.

"I assure you, Chief, I am quite aware of the situation. But given that the universe is gone and we can't possibly survive for long in . . . wherever we are . . . there really is little else to do but marvel at the fact that of all the trillions, perhaps quadrillions of sentient beings ever to have lived, it is *we* whom fate has chosen to be present at the end."

"Uh," Rom tried again, "I think what the Chief is trying to say is that this might not *be* the end."

Garak hid a smile. Ferengi were *so* amusing. Always trying to find an angle so they wouldn't have to admit defeat. "And how would that be possible?" Garak paused. *Unless—"Is* Dukat able to be about on the ship?"

"Yes," O'Brien said tersely. "He can be on this ship, *and* he was in my hell, and in Rom's."

"He . . . brought us out," Rom added. He peered at Garak suspiciously. "How did you get out?"

Garak hesitated, conducting his usual estimation of what he had to lose and/or gain by telling the truth and how he might alter that particular tradeoff one way or another with a judicious act of misdirection. But, he decided, in the end there was nothing to lose because everything was already lost.

"Yes. Dukat came to see me, as well," he said. "That visit was a change in the pattern that had been established, you see, and his presence fit with suspicions I had already entertained. After only a few minutes of conversation, it became apparent to me that he needed me more than I needed him, and I resolved to return here."

Garak enjoyed the way O'Brien and Rom exchanged a look of disbelief.

"It musn't have been much of a hell," O'Brien said, confirming Garak's long-held belief that humans had little resilience and even less imagination.

"Honestly, Chief," Garak replied amiably, "after the obliteration of my world, my people, my culture, and my universe, how could any concept of hell be worse than what I had already experienced?"

O'Brien grunted as he turned back to his engineering station. "Ask me when we're out of this."

"I would appreciate hearing what you're planning."

O'Brien turned around in his chair. "You mean you'll help?"

"When have I not?" Garak said.

Rom held up a finger. "Well, there was that time when—"

"*Since* the universe came to an end, I mean," Garak added.

O'Brien ignored them both as he got up and crossed from the communications station to what passed for a Klingon science station. As far as Garak could tell, the science station was about half the size of the flight console and, in true Klingon tradition, about one-fifth the size of the weapons station.

"The science of what's happened—and what's happening—is beyond me," O'Brien said bluntly. "But I've got a theory."

"I'm sure you do." Garak saw the flash of anger that passed through the human's features and realized once again that not everyone shared his ability to view adversity as an amusing diversion. A pity, really. "I'm sorry, Chief. That was uncalled for. Perhaps my illusion had more of an effect on me than I realized. Please, continue."

His apology, though insincere, had the desired result.

"All right," O'Brien said gruffly as he adjusted incomprehensible controls. "I think what we're seeing is some side effect of those bloody Red Orbs of Jalbador."

"The ones that opened the red wormhole in the first place," Garak said helpfully.

"Right," O'Brien agreed. "I think that . . . well, we're in nonlinear time, so one way to look at it is that in here, where we are, everything happens at once."

Garak nodded and tried to look interested.

"So," the Chief continued, "we're here, on the *Boreth*, existing in some sort of leftover bubble of space-time that originated in the year 2400. But Deep Space 9, as we see it out there, is in its own space-time bubble from the year 2375."

"I'm afraid I don't understand," Garak said kindly but truthfully. "Why from twenty-five years ago? Why not from last week? Or, for that matter, forty years ago?"

"It's the Orbs," O'Brien explained. "When they opened the wormhole, it's as if the maw *swallowed* a section of space-time. In 2400, the Orbs opened the wormhole, and it swallowed us on the *Boreth*. Back in 2375, the Orbs opened the wormhole, and it swallowed the station." He pointed to the viewer. "And see up there? Upper right-hand quadrant?"

Garak looked up as directed and reacted with appropriate surprise. "Is that the *Defiant?*"

"I'm certain of it," O'Brien said. "I just can't tell if it's the *Defiant* as it was when we entered the wormhole twenty-five years ago or as it was when it entered the wormhole with us at the end."

In spite of himself, Garak was intrigued by the possibilities. "As I recall, there was a great deal of confusion in those last minutes. Are you certain the *Defiant* did enter the wormhole with us?"

"Dukat seems to think so," O'Brien said. "He's convinced Weyoun's on her."

Garak chuckled softly.

O'Brien reacted crossly. "How can any of this be amusing?"

"Not this," Garak said quickly. "I was just thinking of a line from some old Klingon play. About 'the evil that men do' living after them. I mean, can *you* imagine continuing any sort of conflict after the *universe* has ended? What possible point could there be to it?"

"Uh," Rom piped up unexpectedly, "I think that the conflict Dukat and Weyoun are involved in actually started in here and not in our universe. But . . . I might be wrong."

"You are," Garak said. "The conflict isn't between

Dukat and Weyoun, it's between . . ." Garak waved his hand at the screen. ". . . whatever dwells out there."

"The Prophets and the Pah-wraiths," O'Brien said.

"Among others," Garak agreed. "Remember, Dukat says he represents those Pah-wraiths imprisoned in the Fire Caves, which I understand are different from those Pah-wraiths who dwell in the second Temple."

For just a moment, Garak allowed himself to sigh at the inconsequential wonder of it all. "Just imagine . . . is it possible that all of existence—*our* existence—was simply a random by-product of a war between beings we can never comprehend?

"To think that we were created by those superior beings, just as the religions of a thousand worlds maintain, but then to discover that those superior beings created us *accidentally.* Really, Chief, Rom, how can you not find amusement in that possibility? Surely, it's either that or madness."

O'Brien shook his head. "Garak, I'm a simple kind of guy. I leave science to the scientists and philosophy to the Vulcans. All I know is that I *liked* my existence. I *miss* my wife and children. And if there is one chance in a . . . a quadrillion that something I can do now might take me back to them, even for a minute, you can bet I'm going to do it.

"Now, are you going to help? Or are you going to stare into your navel and contemplate infinity?"

Garak allowed no offense to seep into his voice. "Seeing as how what passes for my navel is centered on my forehead, I believe my only choice is to help you. What would you like me to do?"

Then he listened carefully as O'Brien described his discovery that time was passing at a different rate on the *Boreth* than it was on Deep Space 9. The Chief's assumption was that the *Defiant* was also caught in a unique pocket of temporal progression, and that for communication to become possible between the two ships, that rate had to be calculated and compensated for.

Unfortunately, it seemed the *Boreth* was not able to create an image of the *Defiant* with enough resolution to measure the blinking of her navigational lights. Assuming, of course, that those lights were actually functioning.

Thus, what O'Brien needed Garak to do was to undertake a tedious set of scans of the *Defiant*. He was to look for any kind of timeshifted emanation from her, whether it was the venting of hydrazine from her station-keeping thrusters or the standard signals from her Starfleet automatic Identify Friend-or-Foe transmission.

"And how, exactly," Garak asked, hoping O'Brien took the question as seriously as he meant it, "will any of this enable you to return to your wife and children in the past?"

The chief engineer took a deep breath before answering. "Garak, when DS9 and the *Defiant* went into the wormhole the first time, none of us knew what was happening. No one knew how to take steps to reverse the process. But now the three of us do. So if one of us—" O'Brien looked over at the unmoving forms of Odo, Quark, and the others. "—*any* of us, can get over to the station or to the *Defiant*, or even transmit what we know to them, there's a chance we might be able to do something to change what happened."

"In other words," Garak said, "change the past to eliminate this future. Which means we won't exist." He didn't like the sound of that.

"Look at it this way," O'Brien said earnestly. "If you could save Cardassia Prime from being wiped out by the Ascendancy, would you do it, even if it meant you'd die?"

All sense of amusement drained out of Garak. "Without question."

"And I'd do the same for my family, my world, and my universe," O'Brien said. "And what might make it interesting is, considering we're in a realm of non-linear time, even if the past *is* changed, maybe we'll still exist anyway."

For a moment, Garak's mind fastened on the fascinating notion of being able to have dinner with himself. Then he recovered, bowed politely. "I am at your disposal, Chief."

O'Brien set him up at the communications console and showed him how to begin his scans. Garak hesitated before beginning his assignment, glancing over at Odo on the deck. "Is there anything we can do about them?"

"I don't think so," O'Brien said grimly. "Rom and I have both tried to wake them up. I don't know how Dukat does it, but he's the only one who can enter their illusions."

"It must be horrible," Rom said, shaking his head over his brother.

Garak smiled encouragingly at Rom. "If their illusions are crafted as mine was, they'll be more superficial than terrible. Your brother is probably in Ferengi Hell . . . what is it? Ah, yes, the Debtor's Dungeon. And knowing him, he probably thinks that *you* put him there. And Odo . . . well, wherever he is, you can be sure he believes he can't change shape. And he's alone."

"Those don't sound very superficial to me," O'Brien said. "And neither was mine."

"Chief," Garak countered, "I'll be the first to admit I don't have deep knowledge of Earth's religious beliefs, but how could you possibly think that you are important enough to the creator of the universe that he, she, it, or they would go to enough trouble to craft a hell specifically for you? Does the term, 'delusions of grandeur' mean anything on your world?"

O'Brien muttered something Garak couldn't decipher, then pointed at the comm console. "Just start your scans," he said.

Garak turned to the controls. And that was when Gul Dukat said, "Better that you don't."

As Rom squealed as only a Ferengi could, Garak spun around in his chair to see Dukat now on the bridge beside Odo. The changeling, conscious, was sitting up, rubbing at his neck, obviously disoriented.

"Welcome back," Garak said, his interest sharpening. Dukat had not arrived on the bridge through any door. Apparently his ability to enter others' illusions involved some sort of self-generating transporter effect.

"I know what you're doing," Dukat thundered at O'Brien. "And I will not allow you to continue."

"Look—you can do whatever you want in here," the Chief said with admirable defiance.

"You're right, I can," Dukat hissed.

"All we want to do is go back to our own time and leave the wormhole to you."

Dukat shook his head. "My realm can't be whole while your realm exists. So, you see, it's one or the other. And, understandably, as I'm sure you'll agree, I choose mine." His eyes flared with red fire.

O'Brien fell silent as if he had nothing more to say, and Garak waited, watching, wondering if the Chief would actually have the courage to charge Dukat and physically overwhelm him. But O'Brien made no such move.

Not surprisingly, Rom appeared to be in the same inactive, ineffectual mode. Though Garak could see that at least the Ferengi's gaze was frantically darting around the bridge, presumably seeking some kind of weapon.

But in the absence of the others' initiative, Garak could not deny his own role any longer: What happened next would be up to him. As it usually was when indecisive humans and calculating Ferengi were involved.

He stood up from his chair and started toward Dukat.

Beside Dukat, Odo was on his knees, staring at his own

hands as if he had never seen them before. Or had not seen them for centuries.

"What do you think *you're* doing?" Dukat demanded as Garak moved closer, until they were only centimeters apart.

"This," Garak said simply. And then he brought his open hand up to smash into Dukat's jaw, cracking the old Cardassian's brittle yellow teeth together and sending him tumbling back against the life-support station.

Even as Dukat regained his feet and stretched out his arms and the murderous power of the Pah-wraiths rose in his glowing red eyes, Garak stood his ground.

"I will crush your soul!" Dukat shrieked.

"Not likely," Garak calmly replied.

And then O'Brien finally acted, launching himself into the space between Dukat and Garak. *"Run!"*

Rom followed with an ear-splitting squeal.

But Dukat stepped back as he expertly flipped the Ferengi and deflected O'Brien's charge, knocking both of them over the life-support-station chair and onto the deck behind Odo.

Typical, Garak thought.

Then Dukat pointed his finger at O'Brien.

A halo of red energy enveloped his gray hand.

On the deck, O'Brien drew back, grimacing in expectation of what would happen next.

But nothing did.

Garak moved in on Dukat. "Don't you understand *yet?*"

Dukat backed up against the life-support console. He pointed both hands at Garak. Both hands glowed red, as did his eyes.

But there were no deadly discharges of red Pah-wraith energy. No attack of any kind. Dukat whimpered with incomprehension.

"You were only a *vessel,*" Garak said brutally. "A puppet for Kosst Amojan."

"He gave me power!" Dukat wailed.

"*Gave* you power," Garak agreed. "Certainly, while you were out there, in the universe of suns and planets and fragile linear beings and had something to offer him in a realm where he could not easily exist. But *think*, Dukat! What did Kosst Amojan want from you? What was his goal?"

Dukat looked at his outstretched hands and turned them both palm upward in a supplicating gesture. "To . . . to reclaim his realm."

"This realm?" Garak asked.

Dukat looked up, the first glimmer of understanding dawning on his time-ravaged face.

"And so what did you do?" Garak persisted. "You *brought* him here. Back into the realm from which he had been expelled."

Dukat nodded. Blood trickled from his slack mouth, a splinter of broken tooth adhered to his lip.

"So why does he need you any longer?" Garak asked. "Don't you see? This isn't your battle. It never was *your* battle. You were just . . . transportation. The real fight is out there!" Garak pointed to the viewer, to the pale blue glow of the non-linear realm. "The simple truth is, you have no power here. Not anymore."

Dukat swayed as he pulled himself upright. He spread his arms. "I *am* Kosst Dukat! I *am* the Emissary of the Amojan!" he cried.

Garak put a swift end to such nonsense. He grabbed Dukat's robes in both hands, hoisting the old man into the air. "You are *nothing!*" he shouted. And then he twisted around and hurled Dukat's frail form across the bridge to land by the empty command chair.

Garak looked down at O'Brien. The engineer seemed stunned by what had just happened. "Well, what are you waiting for?" Garak asked him. "The Prophets and the Pah-wraiths have their fight, and we have our ours."

Nodding wordlessly, O'Brien got to his feet.

Open-mouthed with shock, Rom followed suit.

"Gentlemen, it is time to go home," Garak told them.

Then he went back to his console to begin his scans, wondering if they had the slightest chance in anyone's hell of actually accomplishing what he had promised.

CHAPTER 7

Weyoun's storage tube was located at the far end of the main storage chamber on Rondac III. Since the nutrient-stasis fluid was colorless and the tube cover transparent, from his upright position he could stare out and see the entire facility. On one side, bank after bank of tubes just like his stretched out to the vanishing point. On the other side, the tube banks soared upward and plunged downward for kilometers.

There were so many storage tubes, he was unable to count them. But he did know what lay inside each one.

Another Weyoun.

Every few centuries, a team of Jem'Hadar would walk past his tube, usually escorting a Founder. Occasionally, Weyoun would see another Vorta in their company—an Eris or a Keevan or a Marklar. And always, he would see another Weyoun, freshly awakened, the nutrient fluid still dripping from his glistening body, his eyes bright with the prospects of the new life he was about to embrace.

But over the millennia that Weyoun had spent motionless, expectant, in his own tube, not one Founder, not one Jem'Hadar, not one other Vorta had come for him.

Slowly, in the sporadic bursts of thought that surfaced at random in a mind lacking stimulation, it occurred to Weyoun that though he had been brought to the brink of life in this cloning facility, it might not be his destiny ever to partake of it. Instead, he might spend eternity in his tube, neither dead nor alive, simply waiting ... forever ... without ever being—

Weyoun suddenly realized—a few decades later—that his view of the storage facility was blocked by a person standing in front of his tube.

No, not a person, Weyoun thought—eventually—*a female.* His eyes registered flowing dark hair and dangling ear jewelry. His artificial memory began piecing together disparate, disconnected images from half-remembered lives of all the decanted Weyoun clones who had preceded him.

Kilana. It was Kilana. Or, more precisely, a Kilana. A female Vorta whose third incarnation had once shared passion with Weyoun's sec—

The female Vorta placed her hand on his storage tube's cover.

Her hand *passed through* the cover.

The cover was gone!

The weight and thickness of the tube's nutrient-stasis fluid left Weyoun, spilling away from him, splashing noisily on the floor. The sound thundered in his ears. The overhead lights seared his eyes. He shivered as the slick coating of the fluid evaporated from skin that had never been exposed to a change in temperature.

Weyoun's lungs expanded and he drew in a huge gulp of air and he *lived!*

Driven by instinct, Weyoun stepped from his tube. But his legs were not ready and they buckled beneath him.

Kilana caught him, steadied him.

Weyoun heard his own voice as it moaned with delight. To be embraced by solid arms, to sense the delicious change of pressure and gravity bearing down on his limbs, to be in a position other than floating upright in his tube—it was so marvelous and so confusing and so overwhelming, all at the same time.

"Shhh," Kilana whispered, and Weyoun thrilled to feel her fingers gently brush his sodden hair from his forehead. "You're free now."

Weyoun stared into the face of the incarnated female who had meant so much to his own previous incarnation.

It was then that he noticed that something was wrong.

The female who held him was dressed like Kilana. Quite properly, she wore the standard deep-red gown of a Vorta negotiator—the color to imply the threat of violence. Quite properly, her shoulders were cloaked in the blue of authority—the color to imply the rewards of cooperation. And, quite properly, the gown itself was cut low and pulled tight to distract male eyes and attention.

But her ears—they were missing or mutilated. Weyoun saw no sign of Vorta amplifying nodes ascending from her jaw.

Instead, he saw what appeared to be some lesser form of sense-amplifying structure covering the bridge of her nose.

"Who are you?" Weyoun gurgled. Voicing that question made him cough up thick clots of nutrient fluid that he realized he must have been breathing during the millennia he'd spent in his tube.

"Arla Rees," the female said.

Weyoun gasped as the storage chamber melted away, replaced by the cold sterility of a Starfleet sickbay. In the same instant, his memory was restored, and he realized he was on the *Defiant*.

"How did you find me?" Weyoun asked. He tried to

pull his hand from hers, but she wouldn't relinquish her grip.

"The True Prophets guided me to you," Arla said, "so that I might give you your freedom, and you might grant me my release."

Weyoun knew exactly what she meant, why she wouldn't let go of his hand.

"Of course," Weyoun said. "I gladly share the gift of the Grigari."

He squeezed the flesh of her hand then, pinching it between two nails until the skin broke and blood welled.

She gave a small moan, then did the same to him.

And when their wounds met, blood to blood, the gift of the Grigari *was* shared.

"But what if *everything* that's happened since we entered the wormhole has been an Orb experience?" Dr. Bashir asked. "Including this conversation? Right now?"

In his command chair, and finally wearing a newly replicated Starfleet uniform, circa 2375, Sisko stared at the main viewer of the *Defiant*'s bridge. He couldn't take his eyes from the image of Deep Space 9 displayed there, now floating against a violent red background of rippling light, glowing verteron nodes, and shifting verteron strings.

No, that's wrong, Sisko thought. Despite Jadzia's discovery about why she couldn't receive any signals from the station and her subsequent adjustment of the *Defiant*'s communications systems to account for two different temporal frames, he still could not make himself believe it. *That is* not Deep Space 9. *Not yet.*

Sisko roused himself from his thoughts of the past. Returned to the present. Or to the future. "Doctor, this is *not* an illusion," he said firmly. He looked away from the screen and over at Bashir who was seated at the ship's auxiliary life-support station. Worf was at tactical, Jadzia at science, Kira at flight. Appreciatively, Sisko noted that Jake was sitting at the back of the bridge by the situation table, trying to stay out of the way. Off the bridge, Commander Arla was watching over Weyoun in sickbay, and Ensign Simons and the remaining eight members of the crew were on duty in engineering. "That you can be sure of."

"But how?" Bashir persisted. "The illusion I was trapped in was indistinguishable from reality."

Sisko knew each one of his crew was waiting for the answer to Bashir's question. After what they each had experienced, how *could* any of them be certain what reality was anymore?

Sisko knew his answer wasn't good enough as he gave it, but it was the only thing he could think to say. "This moment we're in, Doctor, it doesn't *feel* like an Orb experience." He held up a hand to stop Bashir's protest. "It doesn't *feel* anything at all like the individual illusion of hell I was trapped in. And if you think about it, I'm certain you can identify the differences between what you feel now and what you felt . . . before Dax came for you."

In the silence that followed his challenge, Sisko knew everyone was daring to revisit his and her own experience of hell.

Jadzia spoke first. "He's right, Julian. I remember my first Orb experience. Right in my lab on Deep Space 9. I opened the Orb Ark and the next thing I knew, I was with Curzon, in the transference bay, as Dax passed from him to me."

"That was an actual memory being replayed," Bashir argued. "Of course you knew it wasn't real because it had happened before."

Sisko intervened to take control of the discussion. They had decisions to make and, if Jadzia's estimates were correct, they would have to make them soon.

"Doctor, in your illusion, after the first time you . . . you fouled up the singularity containment field and the universe . . . ended, didn't you have some small question in the back of your mind when the experience began repeating?"

"Well, yes, but . . . it was more like an unsettling sense of *déjà vu*. It was nothing that made me think, 'Oh, right, this is just an illusion. Everything's going to be all right after all.' "

"But the point is, you *knew* something was wrong. When I had my first Orb experience, I found myself suddenly walking on the beach where I had met Jennifer. And I met her again, then and there, fully aware that I was in the past, even though I gave no thought to how I had arrived at that moment." Sisko spread his arms to encompass the bridge. "But *this* is different. Through the Orbs, or being in the presence of the Prophets, things feel altered. Time moves in fits and starts, back and forth. The . . . the light comes from outside *and* from within . . . the sound is something you feel as much as hear . . . the quality of *existence* is different.

"Having experienced the Orbs, having met the Prophets, and having been trapped in a Pah-wraith hell, I say what we're experiencing *now*, on this ship, is the *same* reality we all remember from our past. And I believe Dax's sensor scans bear me out."

Sisko looked to Jadzia, who nodded her agreement, then took up his argument.

"Julian," she said, "at some point we have to draw the line. Sure, maybe we're all still stuck in the wormhole from back in our first trip through it. Maybe everything that's happened to us in the past six years is an illusion. But if that illusion is indistinguishable from reality—*truly* indistinguishable and not just a convincing reproduction—then we have no choice but to *accept* it as reality and deal with it as best we can. Otherwise, we might as well sit in a corner, doubt the existence of everything, and just . . . do nothing."

"This is why I prefer medicine," Bashir grumbled. "Physics always ends up colliding head-to-head with philosophy."

Jadzia's smile was pointed. "Not quite. To test the postulates of physics, you can design experiments. Trust me: Domains of linear reality *can* exist within the nonlinear realm of the wormhole pocket." She turned to Sisko. "And Benjamin? My experiments show we really are running out of time."

"I'm convinced," Sisko said. He looked around the bridge for any other questions, but all attention appeared to be focused on what Jadzia would say next. For however it was that the *Defiant* and the station could exist in here at all, the Trill had clearly determined that they would not be able to exist much longer.

Then the ship pitched again and everyone on the bridge grabbed the closest chair or console to steady themselves. Sisko kept his eyes fixed on the main viewer. And just as before, by the time all movement stopped, the image on the viewer had changed. Now DS9 appeared before a background of undulating *blue* energy, with *no* verteron phenomena observable. Sisko turned to Jadzia for her report. "Old Man?"

"Another equalization wave. And it came . . . one hundred seventy-seven seconds faster than the last one."

"So they are accelerating," Sisko said.

"As predicted," the Trill confirmed. "Along a perfect geometric curve."

"Any change in the time required to equalize the pressure difference between the two wormhole fragments?"

Jadzia had discovered that when the wormhole pocket split in two, the resulting halves were not identical. The blue wormhole had extended from the Bajoran system through a hyperdimensional realm to emerge seventy thousand light-years away in the Gamma Quadrant. The red wormhole, though, had joined two regions of space more than one hundred thousand light-years apart, stretching from Bajor to the farthest reaches of the Delta Quadrant. To her, that implied that each wormhole contained a different energy density, so that when they were rejoined, that difference had to be evened out, just as when two spacecraft docked and their differing atmospheric pressures had to equalize when the airlocks were opened.

Sisko listened intently now as Jadzia read the displays at her station. "No change in my first calculation. Other than now I can be precise to five decimal places. The equalization waves will keep passing over us at an accelerating rate during the next . . . fifteen hours, twenty-seven minutes. Just like water sloshing through a pipe, trying to find its level. And after those nine hundred twenty-seven minutes, the delay between each pass will have shrunk to something on the order of the Planck interval so that the wormhole environment will effectively become homeostatic, and . . ."

Sisko completed her analysis. "The space-time bubbles containing the station and this ship will follow the universe into nonexistence."

"Exactly. The wormhole pocket will not only be nonlinear in time the way its two fragments were, it will also become dimensionless in space. And that, I'm afraid," the Trill concluded, "is as close to nothingness as the Heisenberg Uncertainty Principle will permit."

"Fifteen hours, twenty-seven minutes," Bashir repeated glumly. "So much for philosophy. And physics. And everything else."

Sisko stood up, alarmed by the doctor's sudden embrace of defeat, and also acutely aware of his crew watching him, looking to him for strength, and for leadership.

"That's enough, Doctor. It's not over yet." Sisko made his decision. *Their* decision. "We're going to cross over."

"What?" The startled response had come from Jake at

the back of the bridge. His son had obviously reached his limit for remaining a silent observer. "Dad, are we really going back to Deep Space 9?"

Sisko shook his head. It wasn't as simple as that. If Jadzia was correct, then, technically, that *wasn't* Deep Space 9 out there. In its current temporal frame, it wouldn't become Deep Space 9 for at least two more weeks. Because, according to the navigational signals that Jadzia had received from it, the station before them existed at a specific time in the past.

Like everyone else on the bridge, Sisko could not look away from the main viewer and the achingly familiar shape that was slowly turning on it, waiting. The home they had lost. Before it had become their home.

A time in which it had been known as Terok Nor.

Stardate 46359.1.

The Day of Withdrawal.

The day to which Sisko now had to return, to save his life, his crew, and his universe.

Odo, like almost all the others on the *Boreth* who had been "rescued" by Garak, didn't want to talk about the hell in which he'd been trapped, and O'Brien wasn't inclined to force the issue. Mostly because he had finally determined the nature of the periodic waves that had struck the *Boreth* and caused the huge Klingon ship to buck as if hit by a phaser volley. It appeared that the quantum structure of the blended wormhole fragments was equalizing, and as best as the chief engineer could determine, once equilibrium had been achieved, the space-time bubble containing the *Boreth* would no longer have any dimensions in which to exist.

By entering the red wormhole, those aboard the *Boreth* had *not* escaped the end of their universe. They had only postponed it, and not by long, either.

"*How* much time?!" Quark bleated, incredulous. Except for Dukat, who still lay unconscious, bound, and gagged on the deck beside the unused communications station, only the Ferengi barkeep among the twelve others on the bridge of the *Boreth* seemed not to have heard what O'Brien had just announced.

"I *said*, to our frame of reference," O'Brien repeated, "we have thirty hours and . . . some odd minutes. I can't work it out any closer than that."

Quark whirled to confront Garak, who as usual, O'Brien noted, looked unperturbed in the face of the Ferengi's extravagantly expressed emotions. "*You* should have left me in Debtor's Dungeon!"

"Believe me, if I had known how disagreeable you were going to be about being saved, I would have preferred to have left you there myself," Garak said.

"Then send me back!" Quark demanded.

O'Brien knew they didn't have the time for this. "That's enough, Quark. Settle down."

Almost comic in his bulky Bajoran robes, Quark drew himself up to shout at O'Brien. "You're not in charge!"

But any further protest from the furious Ferengi was quickly quashed as Garak clamped a hand on Quark's shoulder. "Yes, Quark, he *is* in charge. Chief O'Brien is the *only* one among us who understands the unique nature of our predicament. And I, for one, am content to hear his conclusions and act accordingly."

Indignant, the Ferengi shook off the Cardassian's hand. "Don't you understand?! You dragged us out of our afterlives! *Eternal* afterlives! To face absolute extinction in thirty hours!"

Odo, the only person on the bridge to be in proper garb—because he had formed his Bajoran uniform from his outer layers of mutable flesh—made a futile attempt to get Quark to listen to reason.

"Quark, we were not experiencing *real* afterlives," the changeling said. "The Pah-wraiths created illusions *for* us. Presumably because they couldn't get at us any other way."

"Uh, that does make sense, brother," Rom added.

"SENSE!" Quark all but screamed at Rom. "Have you grown points on your ears all of a sudden? What do *you* know about things making sense?"

O'Brien did not intervene in the exchange between the siblings. He was confident that Rom could handle himself.

"Well," Rom said, as if his brother had asked him a reasonable question, "according to the Chief, as long as normal matter and space-time exists in the wormhole pocket, the pocket's domain is disrupted. So it seems to, uh, make sense that if the Pah-wraiths, or whatever, didn't want to be . . . disrupted, they would have destroyed us when we first entered. But since they didn't, I agree with Garak. It's because . . . they can't."

"Well said, Rom," Garak added in an approving tone of voice; just to provoke Quark, O'Brien was sure.

"So how does that explain them putting us to sleep with illusions of the afterlife?" Quark asked acidly.

Garak took over. "Quark, it might help if you would start thinking less like a condemned prisoner and more like a Ferengi." The Cardassian ignored Quark's shocked, insulted gasp. "Why don't you consider what we're involved in as a business deal? What would your response be if you were trying to get the better of a potential customer—one who didn't realize he had some method of gaining an advantage over you?"

To O'Brien, it seemed clear that the glowering and dark-faced Quark knew the answer Garak was going after, but he didn't want to give the Cardassian the satisfaction of saying it.

So Garak did. "I believe," he said helpfully, "you would

attempt to *distract* your client. Perhaps provide him with an expensive yet potent bottle of bloodwine. Introduce him to a fetching dabo girl or two. Keep him occupied until the window of opportunity for exploiting his advantage over you has fled. And then, for the cost of a small distraction, you would no longer be at risk. At least, as *I* believe."

"So?" Quark said, surly.

"So," O'Brien said, impatient with the both of them, "the afterlife illusions we experienced were distractions. To keep us from attempting to get out of here."

His huge ears flushing perceptibly, the Ferengi lifted his hands up toward the ceiling in a dramatic gesture of frustration. "Am I surrounded by idiots?! There's nowhere else to go!"

O'Brien's displeasure with Quark's antics sharpened his voice. "Not *where*, Quark. *When*." He pointed to the main viewer. "That's not just Deep Space 9 out there. That's Deep Space 9 on the day it was swallowed by the red wormhole. If we can somehow get onto the station on that day, we can stop the Orbs of Jalbador from being opened in your establishment."

Quark's pale eyes bulged with shock. "That's—that's *time* travel!" he quavered. "And from the first *frinxing* day we popped up in this nightmare future, every one of you has said—" His voice now under more control, Quark adopted a high-pitched singsong voice, his impression of human, O'Brien guessed. "—'The only way we can go back in time is if the *Defiant* slingshots us around the red wormhole.' "

"In *normal* space, Quark," O'Brien said. "And we're not in normal space anymore. Normal space doesn't exist anymore. And under the circumstances, I don't think anyone here is terribly concerned about what the Department of Temporal Investigations has to say about avoiding the creation of alternate timelines."

Quark slapped his hands to his face. "How in the name of all that's profitable can you have alternate timelines if *time* doesn't exist?"

O'Brien was suddenly aware of everyone, even Garak, looking at him, waiting for his answer. For all the Ferengi's panicky, self-obsessed bluster, something in Quark's last outburst had resonated with the others on the bridge. And O'Brien knew that if he was to somehow keep this group together, make them capable of at least attempting his admittedly desperate survival plan, he had to come up with something convincing, and fast.

But for a moment, he just stared blankly back at them, the only thought running through his mind, *What would Captain Sisko do?* Followed almost instantaneously by, *What would Captain Picard do?*

Garak broke the silence. "Though I am loath to admit it, Chief O'Brien, our Ferengi friend does raise an interesting question."

And then, as if a phaser burst had struck him directly between the eyes to fill his mind with blinding light, O'Brien had it. Thanks to Captain Picard.

"Look, like I said, the multidimensional physics of what's going on here are completely beyond me. We'd be a lot better off if Dax were with us, that's for sure. But what I can tell you is that I *know* for an absolute fact that alternate timelines do exist."

By the silence that greeted his pronouncement, O'Brien understood that what he had to say next would be made infinitely easier by the fact that everyone *wanted* to believe him. Even Quark, it seemed, for all his negativity, was not yet ready to abandon all hope.

"Twice," the chief engineer began, deliberately making eye contact with everyone on the bridge of the *Boreth,* "when I was on the *Enterprise,* we had encounters with beings or technology from a time period beyond the year 2400. Once we picked up a time-transport pod from the twenty-sixth century. Another time, Captain Picard himself had a run-in with two unsavory types from the twenty-seventh century. And Vash was with him. So, *somehow,* in De Sitter space or the multiverse or some undefinable phase space in which time has more than two dimensions—and which Dax would be able to talk about for days—timelines exist in which the universe did *not* end in 2400.

"Now, I'm not Dax, so I can't tell you how. Or why. But I do know that it's possible the way one of those timelines came into existence is because some of us managed to get back to Deep Space 9 in 2375—and *stopped* the red Orbs from opening the red wormhole."

O'Brien stopped, having made his point as best he could, satisfied that he had done what every good leader was supposed to do: Show his followers a direction to go. And he was flattered to see that even if he had never delivered a speech like it before, this one seemed to have been effective. His audience was looking encouraged, even excited by his words.

Now only one last element remained to be put in place.

Captain Sisko and Captain Picard, O'Brien knew, would have taken care of it at once, out of instinct. The same instinct that likely had made them Starfleet captains in the first place.

But O'Brien wasn't working from instinct, but rather from his experience—first on the *Enterprise* and then on Deep Space 9, where he had observed great leaders in action, and those observed examples told him what he had to do now.

"*I'm* going to give it a try," O'Brien said in a ringing voice that sounded more confident than he felt. "Who's with me?"

He felt his face grow warm, and he knew his cheeks were red, as one by one every member of his crew stepped forward and vowed his or her support.

Even Quark.

His proud moment was brief.

"So it would appear," Garak said drily, "since we are all in agreement, that only one last detail remains to be worked out." The Cardassian nodded pointedly in the direction of the viewer and the tantalizing destination it still displayed. "How *do* we get over there?"

Relief swept through O'Brien.

"Now you're talking engineering," he said gratefully. "And that part I've got all worked out."

On the viewer, Deep Space 9 turned slowly, waiting, just as it had on the day it was destroyed.

The day to which O'Brien now had to return, to save his life, his crew, and his universe.

CHAPTER 8

THE TINY SHUTTLEPOD, designation Alpha, rose slowly from its landing pad in shuttlebay 2. Above it, the pressure door slid open to reveal the chaotic blue energy flux of the wormhole pocket. Capable of carrying up to six personnel, Shuttlepod Alpha, for this mission, was empty. Lifted by the expert manipulation of the shuttlebay's variable gravity fields, the shuttlepod continued its ascent until it was five meters above the *Defiant*'s ventral hull and well out of range of any localized, artificial-gravity fluctuations.

As precisely as if it were on a mechanical turntable, Shuttlepod Alpha then rotated in place until it faced its destination.

Deep Space 9.

On the bridge of the *Defiant*, Sisko gave the order and the main viewer switched from the optical view as seen from the starship to that seen from the shuttlepod's sensors.

"What's the distance?" he asked.

Ignoring the viewer, Jadzia focused her attention solely

on her science station. "Well, as we thought, no sensor ranging data are available. Not even a radar return. Going just by apparent size . . . Alpha's holding at fifteen kilometers from the station. Just as we are."

"All right, then," Sisko said. "Give her a nudge. Station-keeping thrusters only." The speed of the shuttlepod would be no more than thirty-six kilometers per hour. A cautious approach that would enable Jadzia to probe the structure of the space-time bubble in which the *Defiant*, for the moment, existed.

"First thruster fire," Worf announced. "Delta vee of one centimeter per second."

Sisko waited for the first report. It came in seconds. "I don't believe it," Jadzia said with a laugh.

"What is it, Old Man?"

"As soon as we stopped the thrusters, the shuttlepod stopped moving relative to us."

"*No* inertia?" Sisko asked, surprised.

"Not out there," Jadzia said, still sounding amused. "Absolutely incredible." She picked up a small padd from her console, then tossed it to a startled Dr. Bashir, who recovered quickly enough to clap two hands together to catch it. "At least we've still got inertia in here," the Trill scientist concluded.

"So what do we do?" Sisko asked. "Go to constant impulse? Or use the tractor beam?"

"Tractor beam," Jadzia said. "That way, we'll be able to measure any non-inertial resistance to the shuttlepod's motion, so it'll double as a measurement of the density of space out there."

Sisko nodded. They had fifteen hours, three minutes remaining until the pressure waves peaked and the *Defiant* ceased to exist. Time enough to transfer the eighteen passengers on the ship to DS9, provided they could determine a way to do so.

"Activating tractor beam," Worf confirmed.

"Let's see the shuttlepod," Sisko said.

The viewer switched over from the shuttlepod's sensors to display a new angle from the *Defiant*'s hull. The Alpha was suddenly bathed in a shaft of pale purple light.

"Start her forward, Mr. Worf."

As the angle of the tractor beam changed, Sisko watched the shuttlepod slip away from the *Defiant*, propelled by the gentle pressure of the tightly focused gravitons. When the tiny craft had cleared the bow of the ship, the viewer display changed again to a new forward angle.

"No resistance," Jadzia reported. "It's moving just as if it's in a normal vacuum."

"Speed?" Sisko asked.

"Twenty kilometers an hour," Worf said.

"Go to fifty."

"Aye, sir."

The shuttlepod grew smaller on the viewer.

"Still no anomalous readings," Jadzia said.

Sisko couldn't suppress his smile. "You sound disappointed."

"Just surprised that there're no surprises."

"Take her to five hundred kph, Mr. Worf, and stand by to bring her to a relative stop, fifty meters from the station."

"Aye, sir," Worf acknowledged. "Estimated time of arrival from current position is ninety seconds."

Just then, Sisko became aware of his son standing to one side of his command chair.

"It can't really be this easy, can it?" Jake asked.

"I think we're allowed to win one every once in a while," Sisko said with a smile. "How're we doing, Dax?"

"No distortion in the tractor beam. And no mass anomalies. Frankly, Benjamin, I'm at a loss to explain it."

"Maybe the shuttlepod's stretching the space-time bubble we're in," Bashir volunteered. "Dragging space-time with it."

Sisko glanced over at Jadzia, saw her thoughtful expression. "That's possible," the Trill said. "Certainly it would explain the fact that there are no detectable anomalies in the structure of space-time along the shuttlepod's path."

As Sisko returned his attention to the viewer, he caught sight of Jake's expression, recognized it.

"Go ahead, Jake. Ask your question."

Relief in his voice, Jake spoke hesitantly. "Well, . . . if we can see the station, can anyone on the station see us?"

"Unlikely," Jadzia said. "We're so far out of temporal alignment with the station's local frame of reference that at most we'd be showing up as a very faint chroniton shadow. Even then, someone would have to be specifically looking for that kind of phenomenon and adjust the sensors precisely. And I don't know why anyone would."

"But, then," Jake continued more strongly, obviously thrilled to be taken seriously, "how come we can see the station?"

"Good question." Jadzia smiled at Jake, pleasing Sisko by her encouragement of his son's curiosity, even under these conditions. "I think part of it has to do with the station's being much more massive than the *Defiant,* so in a way it's putting out a stronger signal. Not to mention the fact it's also still connected to normal space, which we're not." The Trill shrugged. "If I had to give a name to the phenomenon, I'd say the station had more temporal inertia, so it's easier to detect."

Jake nodded, but the confusion on his face suggested to his father that Jake had understood little of Jadzia's explanation. "I'll take your word for it," was Jake's only comment.

"Coming up on destination," Worf announced. "Fifty meters . . . and holding at relative stop."

"We're in good shape," Jadzia said. "Switching over to

shuttlepod sensors. We should be able to look right through the station's viewports."

The viewer flickered, changing from the optical view of DS9 from the *Defiant* at a distance of fifteen kilometers to a close-up from the Alpha at fifty meters.

Sisko leaned forward in his chair, expectant, but the viewpoint did not change.

"Old Man . . . ?" he said, turning to Jadzia.

Jadzia and Worf both made rapid adjustments on their controls, but the image on the viewer didn't change.

"It seems Jake was right," the Trill finally said. "It's not going to be easy. According to all our readings, DS9 is the same distance from the shuttlepod as it is from us. Fifteen kilometers."

"I won't even ask how that's possible," Sisko said. From the corner of his eye, he saw his son retreat back to his previous position at the situation table.

"Thank you," Jadzia replied.

Sisko stood up and walked over to the science station to see Jadzia's displays for himself. "How do we proceed?" he asked.

The Trill scientist didn't waste time. "Since we have full power reserves, I think we should take a few minutes to beam a test cylinder over to the shuttlepod, then retrieve it. We still need to know if we can actually establish a transporter beam in an environment without subspace, and now without inertia."

Sisko felt the unwelcome stirrings of concern. If they could not physically approach and board the station, the transporter would be absolutely critical to their plan.

"Do you foresee any problem?" he asked.

The Trill sat back in her duty chair with a sigh of finality. "I just don't know, Benjamin. When it comes to theory, I could spend the next week telling you all the ins and outs about what we're seeing here. But when it comes to implementing those theories . . ." She looked up at him, serious. "All I can say is I wish Chief O'Brien were here."

Sisko nodded. Jadzia was speaking for them all.

Odo stood by the empty command chair on the bridge of the *Boreth* and wondered what it was about Miles O'Brien that kept the engineer from taking his place there.

There could be no question the Chief was in command of this ship. Not by rank but by ability. Not even Quark questioned him anymore.

But O'Brien was adamant in his refusal to assume the trappings of command, even though such action would make it much easier for him to monitor the rest of his irregular crew.

"Odo, I think he's afraid," Quark said under his breath.

Odo was momentarily startled. He hadn't heard the Ferengi come up beside him at the engineering station.

"Who's afraid?" Odo demanded.

Quark impatiently gestured toward the side of the bridge. "The Chief. Who else?"

"Why would *you* say that?"

Quark stared up at him crossly. "I know you were wondering why Chief O'Brien wasn't taking the command chair. He's afraid, that's why."

Odo folded his arms. "I was wondering no such thing."

Maddeningly, Quark folded his own arms in mocking parody, the movement twisting up his Bajoran robes. "You can't fool me," the Ferengi smirked. "You think because you keep your face so smooth and . . . and unfinished, people can't see what you're feeling, or what you're thinking. But I've been watching you, Odo. Almost ten long years. I know you better than you know yourself."

Odo moved swiftly in verbal counterattack. "Quark, I've never seen you so nervous."

Predictable as always, Quark sputtered in immediate, indignant protest. "I'm not nervous. I'm never nervous."

Odo shrugged. "Aren't you? You're talking quickly. Your ears are flushed. And if you really were able to peer inside me and know what I'm thinking, you certainly wouldn't tell me about it."

Quark bit his lip, eyed Odo skeptically, then spoke extremely slowly. "And—why—wouldn't—I?"

"Because," Odo said with great satisfaction, "you're giving away a trade advantage. The next time I catch you smuggling something and haul you in for questioning, I'll stand behind you, and you won't have any idea what I'm thinking."

Odo enjoyed the way Quark's mouth fell open, then snapped shut. The Ferengi really hadn't been thinking clearly.

"Well," Quark stammered, "well, I don't care. Because there won't be a next time."

Odo smiled as coldly as he could. "I see. Your experience in Ferengi Hell has finally convinced you to change your ways."

"What ways? I don't need to change my ways. What I mean is, there won't be a next time because . . . because we're *doomed*. That's why. We're *doomed*. Not that *you* care." Quark gave a little sob and turned away, his back to Odo.

Odo grunted and took the chance to check again on Dukat. The aged Cardassian was still lying stretched out on the deck by the communications console, legs bound at the ankles, hands bound at the wrists. Someone had rolled up a blanket from a medical kit and compassionately placed it under Dukat's white-haired head, but Odo didn't think the Dukat of the year 2400 was someone who was concerned with physical matters, and certainly not with compassion. The Cardassian had remained unconscious since Garak's assault, and it was Odo's impression—or, perhaps, wish, he admitted to himself alone—that Dukat was now immersed in his own Pah-wraith-inspired hell. With any luck, he'd never bother his fellow passengers again.

Reassured that Dukat still posed no threat, the changeling walked over to watch O'Brien and Rom at the operations station as they worked with the crew members in the main transporter room to switch manual control to the bridge.

"Well . . . ?" Quark said.

Odo sighed. The Ferengi was right in front of him.

"Well what, Quark?"

Some of Quark's bluster appeared to be gone. His ears were definitely looking paler. "Well, I . . . I just poured out my heart to you. This is . . . this is when you're supposed to say something supportive."

Odo nodded in understanding. "Ah, of course. This is supposed to be a moment of bonding between us. Two old adversaries facing what might be their final hours. At last breaking down the barriers between them so they can finally admit their admiration for each other, reach some kind of common ground and mutual understanding in the face of oblivion."

"That's it, exactly," Quark said with a hopeful smile.

Odo returned the smile. "Good idea. I'll go talk to Garak right now."

The changeling walked away from the Ferengi, knowing precisely the sequence of emotions that would flash over Quark's face: shock, disappointment, and fear.

Garak had positioned himself at an auxiliary control console near to the entrance doors. Somehow, in the few minutes that had passed since Chief O'Brien had come up with his plan to cross over to Deep Space 9 of the past, the Cardassian had managed to find and change into an Ascendancy uniform—a poorly-fitting cross between Odo's own Bajoran uniform and a Starfleet design but a much more practical garment than the robes Weyoun had made them all wear in B'hala.

Garak looked up and gave Odo a slight nod of acknowledgment as the changeling joined him at his console. Then the Cardassian's gaze slid off Odo and settled on Quark, a forlorn and lonely figure standing in the middle of the bridge.

"Is he acting up again?" Garak asked.

"Nothing more than usual," Odo said. He peered over Garak's shoulder to see what was on his screen. But in a quick, careless gesture, Garak's hand brushed across the controls, erasing the screen before Odo could glimpse more than a fraction of its heading.

"Klingon Planetary Defense Analysis?" Odo asked. That was as much as he had been able to read.

Garak blinked at his console's blank screen. "Is that what was there? I was merely passing the time by randomly scrolling through the ship's library. And I appear to have lost my place."

Odo studied the guileless Cardassian. He quite understood if Garak wanted to find out how Ascendancy forces had defeated his world. Though he would never admit it to Quark, Odo thought, the Ferengi was right in thinking that in these final hours, some accounts should be settled.

"Is there something I can do for you?" Garak asked politely after several seconds of silence.

It was a difficult moment for Odo, but he forced himself through it. He cleared his throat. "I—I don't think I thanked you properly. For saving me from . . . from where you found me."

Garak held up a hand as if refusing a gift. "It was the least I could do."

Odo appreciated Garak's quick acceptance and desire not to exaggerate the nature of his gratitude. But he hadn't finished. "And . . . I was hoping that we might be able to come to an understanding that . . . well . . ." Odo wasn't sure how to continue.

But Garak was. "Rest assured," he said smoothly, "I will never speak of it. Where you were, what you experienced at the hands of the Pah-wraiths . . . that shall be a secret between us." The Cardassian allowed himself a small smile. "Indeed, considering the techniques that enabled me to enter into the Pah-wraith illusions of yours and the others, I could say that what I found comes under the heading of doctor-patient privilege."

Odo was puzzled. "What techniques?"

Garak regarded him in wide-eyed innocence. "Oh, this and that."

Odo rearranged his own expression into a stern glare.

"Well," the Cardassian said as he shifted forward in his chair, "if you must know, I once made a suit for a . . . person who I had reason to believe was a member of the—" Garak dropped his voice to a sibilant whisper "—Obsidian Order, Special Investigations Unit."

So it's like that, Odo thought. "I see. You made a suit . . . ," he said.

"A very nice one, as I recall. It took many fittings. And, as you may or may not know, a man has very few secrets from his tailor."

"And this . . . man, just happened to tell you all about the Obsidian Order's techniques for interrogating prisoners by entering into induced illusions."

Garak nodded gravely. "I was as shocked by his candidness as I see you are. But as things turned out, it appears that what little I remembered of the techniques he described did come in handy. Wouldn't you say?"

"Handy," Odo repeated. And all at once the changeling no longer felt disturbed that Garak had penetrated his hell to find him eternally wandering the barren world upon which the Great Link had once existed, forever fixed in his quasi-liquid state, unable to become any sort of shape or solid. Instead, he became concerned about any other secrets Garak might have obtained from the others he "rescued."

"I know what's worrying you, Odo," Garak said.

"You and everyone else, it seems," the changeling said gruffly.

"But you needn't worry. A mind is not something to toy with. Especially not those of one's friends and allies."

Odo didn't know whether or not to believe Garak, but for now, there seemed to be little point in thinking the worst. The worst was doing quite well on its own, and coming closer to them each minute.

"It worked!" O'Brien suddenly said joyously, and at once Odo, like everyone on the bridge except for Dukat, turned his full attention to the Chief and Rom at the operations console. "There are no more surprises about the structure of space in here."

Odo felt distinctly heartened to see the Chief smiling broadly. "We were able to beam equipment and biosamples to the probe we sent out to the station and beam them back with absolutely no loss of information."

"So what?"

Odo scowled as Quark dared challenge the Chief.

"Ten minutes ago," the Ferengi charged, "you told us it didn't matter how far that probe traveled. It was *always* going to be twenty-two and a half kilometers from the station, the same as the *Boreth*. There's *no* connection between the two space-time bubbles, you said. So what good does being able to beam out to a probe and back do us?"

"Quark, it's not important where we beam to," O'Brien explained, his good humor not diminished one whit by the Ferengi's rancor. "It's the fact that we can beam at all.

Since we can't get to the station physically, the transporter is the only way we can get from here to there."

"But *how?*" Quark demanded fretfully. "It could be a trillion light-years away for all we know."

Now Odo saw O'Brien's smile fade. But then, Quark could do that to anyone. "It's not a trillion light-years away, Quark. In absolute terms, its distance is probably only a few hundred-thousandths of a light-second."

Even Odo was surprised by that, though he left the questioning to Quark.

And Quark didn't disappoint him. "That's *impossible*. You said yourself you sent that Klingon probe five hundred kilometers away and that its distance to the station didn't change from our distance."

"Physically, no," O'Brien agreed testily. "But look at the viewer, Quark. We can *see* the station right there, plain as day."

Garak spoke up next. "Which raises an intriguing conundrum, Chief. Just how is it that photons are able to pass between the two bubbles of space-time if physical objects remain trapped in them?"

"Old-fashioned relativity and a bit of quantum physics, Garak." Regaining some of his previous elation, the chief engineer warmed to his topic. "You see, on average, all photons travel at the speed of light—the absolute top speed for a physical object in normal space. But individually, each photon is actually a probability packet—not an object, but a probability wave.

"Now, if you send out a thousand photons at a target at the *exact* same time, most of those photons will reach the target also at the same time—that time, corresponding to the speed of light. *But* it's been known for centuries," O'Brien said with a stern look at Quark, who shrugged and rolled his eyes to indicate his disinterest, "that a handful of those photons will arrive at the target slightly *ahead* of the others. That's because, when their probability waves impinge on the target and collapse into a photon, the photon, just by sheer quantum chance, is at the very front edge of the packet. So, there'll always be a few photons out of every bunch that manage to travel slightly faster than light.

"And *those*," O'Brien emphasized with a smile, "are the very photons our sensors are picking up to create the image on the viewer."

The chief engineer waved at the image. "And by exceeding lightspeed in their local frame of reference, those photons have popped out of their space-time bubble and entered ours. Just like a surface-launched space probe breaking out of the gravity well of one planet and traveling through space to another."

"Jadzia Dax could not have explained it better, Chief," Garak said silkily. "Yet you raise another intriguing possibility. Is it possible that whoever's on the station can also see us?"

But O'Brien shook his head dismissively. "No. First of all, this ship is much less massive, and second, our local rate of time is too different from the station's. If someone worked at it, reconfigured the main sensors, knew where to look, they might be able to pick up enough to know that *something* is nearby. But they wouldn't be able to resolve us with any greater detail than we can resolve the *Defiant*."

Odo turned to look at the viewer again to locate the small and indistinct gray disk that was the station's starship. Like DS9 itself, the *Defiant* was occupying its own space-time bubble, approximately forty-five kilometers away, judging just by its apparent size. But O'Brien had been unable to make any estimates of what era the ship was from. In fact, the Chief said it was likely they were seeing the ship as it was during one of its many trips through the blue wormhole. And since the *Boreth*'s sensors could not establish the ship's apparent position with the required accuracy, O'Brien had ruled out any attempt to beam to that craft.

The changeling was still studying the *Defiant*'s image when he heard the irrepressible Quark sound off once again.

"Would someone please tell me why all of you people are so pleased with yourselves?" Quark complained. "Even *I* know transporter beams don't travel faster than light."

Odo watched sympathetically as O'Brien took a deep breath before he answered. The changeling admired the Chief's resilience. "For our purposes, they don't have to," O'Brien said. "They just have to travel through something other than normal space."

Quark wasn't finished. "But even if they can go from . . . from 'here to there,' our time scales are *still* out of synch. You still haven't told us how can we possibly survive the trip."

"Uh, brother—"

Odo saw the grateful look that Chief O'Brien gave Quark's brother Rom. Quark just closed his eyes as if to ask, "Why me?"

Undeterred, Rom offered his own explanation. "Uh, almost every time someone beams from one place to another, the time frames are slightly out of synch. I mean, if you're in standard orbit of a planet, you're traveling more than thirty thousand kilometers per hour. And if you beam down to the surface? Suddenly, you're only traveling a few hundred kilometers per hour as the planet rotates."

Quark opened his mouth as if to say something, but Rom pressed on earnestly. "It's the transporters that do that, brother, by automatically compensating for changes in kinetic energy and temporal acceleration. I mean, Starfleet transporters can even manage near-warp transport at relativistic speeds. We might feel a bit dizzy sometimes, but the transporters have been doing what we need them to do for centuries."

"Thank you, Rom," O'Brien said. "Now, if there're no more questions?" The chief engineer looked around the bridge.

Beside him, Odo heard Quark mumble something that seemed to imply some natural connection between Rom and being dizzy, but that was the extent of Quark's effort. The Ferengi barkeep was back to looking glum and depressed.

"All right, then," O'Brien said, "let's go on to the next step."

"Uh . . . beaming a test pallet to the station?"

O'Brien gave his assistant a sideways glance. "Well, not really, Rom. That won't tell us anything."

Quark roused himself enough to snort at his brother's confusion.

"Uh, why not?"

"Because we won't be able to beam it back."

Odo saw Rom blink in surprise.

"No carrier wave," O'Brien said simply. He made his hand move up and down and forward like a small boat on rough water. "A transporter carrier wave propagates through subspace. But there is no subspace in here. So we're going to have to transport the way they did in pioneer days. Dead reckoning. One at a time."

"I knew 'dead' would come into it somehow," Quark sighed heavily.

"It's not that bad, Quark." O'Brien tapped a finger to his temple. "After six years, I've got all the key DS9 coordinates up here. There won't be any trouble finding a place to beam to. It's just that, well, without subspace, there's no way I'll ever be able to get a fix on anyone to bring them back. So it's going to be a one-way trip for all of us."

His panic revived, Quark's voice rose in a wail. "But . . . but what if you're wrong? What if that version of

DS9 is a mirage? Or it's only five seconds from being destroyed by the red wormhole? Or—"

Odo had had quite enough. He wheeled abruptly and placed a hand firmly over Quark's mouth.

"That's why we're going to send just one person first," O'Brien interrupted. "A volunteer. To see if—"

"Mmmmph—I'll go!" Quark cried as he tried to bite Odo's hand and the changeling jerked it sharply away from him. Even if he couldn't be bitten, Odo found the mere thought distasteful.

Everyone stared at Quark. Odo thought he heard a chuckle and knew it had to have come from Garak.

"What?!" O'Brien said, giving voice to everyone else's reaction.

"What's wrong with that?" Quark snapped. "I want to do my part, too."

"But . . . ," O'Brien said, almost choking, "you're a coward."

"I am not!"

O'Brien looked as if he were in sudden pain. "Well, not about some things," he conceded. "I'll give you that. But all you've been doing for the past half hour is complaining about how everything I've been saying won't work."

Quark held up his finger like an orator making a final point. "I've been . . . testing the hypothesis."

"You've been quaking in your boots, is what you've been doing," O'Brien said hotly.

Quark's face grew sober, as if he were trying to rise above his sense of outrage and hurt feelings. "I am sorry you feel that way, Chief, but your misperception of me, and, perhaps, of all Ferengi, in no way changes the fact that I am volunteering for this dangerous experiment in order to help my fellow. . . ." Quark looked around at the others on the bridge. ". . . uh, fellows," he concluded.

O'Brien ran his hand over his head, clearly nonplussed.

Odo snorted. This fiasco had to end. "I'll take care of this for you, Chief," he said. "You're not going, Quark."

"je SoH, Brute?" Quark said sadly.

"I beg your pardon?"

Quark waved his hand with a world-weary sigh. "It's Klingon. You wouldn't understand."

"No, but what I *do* understand is that you are *not* volunteering to be the first on DS9." Odo looked over at O'Brien. "Chief, think about it. The first thing he'll do if he actually shows up on DS9 twenty-five years in the past is to make sure he's safe and his bar is protected. And if the rest of us run out of time while he's attending to his own business—" Odo shook his head "—well, then, I'm sure he'll raise a toast to us on Ferenginar, or wherever he retires to after profiting from his knowledge of the future." He smiled grimly at Quark to let him know just who had won here. "How many years did you say we'd known each other?"

"You don't know me at all," Quark said in his most wounded tone, then spun around and marched away to sit by himself at an unused station, two down from Dukat's prone form.

Odo looked over at O'Brien. "I'll go," he said.

"You're sure?" O'Brien asked.

Odo nodded. He had no doubts. "When I get to the station, if time's of the essence, I can take on a liquid form and move more quickly than anyone else. And, perhaps most importantly, security won't be a problem."

"Why would it be?"

Seeing the worried look on O'Brien's face, Odo pointed out the obvious—at least, it was obvious to him. "Chief, what do you think Captain Sisko's response is going to be when what he'll take to be a duplicate Odo shows up and tells him to close Quark's, arrest Vash, and lock down the station until the Red Orbs are found and neutralized?"

O'Brien nodded, at once seeing the point. "You'll have

a better chance convincing him if we're *all* over there backing your story, giving Dr. Bashir DNA samples to confirm we're not a bunch of Founder spies." Then O'Brien gave an unhappy sigh.

"Chief?" Odo asked.

"We won't belong there, will we? I mean, Keiko will be married to the other me."

Rom's gasp was immediate. "Leeta!"

"Anyone think about *me?*" Quark whined. "I'm going to be a half-partner in a solely-owned business!"

"But we *will* be saving a universe," Garak said as he finally left his console to join O'Brien and Odo. "I daresay that will bring more than enough personal rewards to make up for whatever personal sacrifices we might have to make."

"Easy for you to say," Quark said. "With two of you, you'll make twice as good a spy."

"If I *were* a spy," Garak said pointedly, "I could see where you might have a point."

"So how do I signal back to you that the transport was successful?" Odo asked, to bring the discussion back to what was really important.

"Oh," Rom said, "I already worked that part out."

Odo waited patiently.

"When you get to the station, go to one of the upper pylon docking ports."

"Which one?"

"Uh, doesn't matter. Whichever one you can get to. Right by the manual controls for the airlock, there's a small control panel that activates the visual docking lights—for ships that have lost their guidance systems. There are three banks of three lights each—"

"How Cardassian," Odo said as Rom continued.

"—by the outer airlock door. All you have to do is turn them off and on by hand."

"Presumably in some sort of code?" Odo asked.

"Uh, I hadn't thought of that," Rom said.

"Idiot," Quark sneered. But no one was listening.

"Starfleet binary?" O'Brien suggested.

Odo recalled having studied it. "With the long and short signals?"

O'Brien now picked up a small Bajoran padd, input a command, then showed Odo the screen. It held a simple chart showing the long and short codes for the standard Federation alphabet. "Start with ten or so rapid flashes so we'll know which port to watch, then give us the local time. That'll let us know how quickly we have to get the rest of us over there."

It all sounded reasonable to Odo, which left him with only one final question. "What if I don't make it?"

O'Brien nodded at Rom, and the Chief's assistant held up another padd.

"I'm going to record a warning message for Captain Sisko," Rom said. "We'll store it in as many padds as we can replicate, then transport the whole lot to the Promenade ceiling *and* to Ops and let them rain down on whoever's there. One way or another, we'll get them—*us*—to do the right thing."

Odo was satisfied. Everything was covered.

"Then I'm ready anytime you are," he said.

"We'll transport you directly from the bridge to the target coordinates," O'Brien explained. "I'm sending you to that unfinished habitat area on Deck 4."

"Good choice," Odo agreed. He knew the location. It was a section in the lower personnel levels that the Cardassians had never completed as designed. In an area where up to ten individual living units might have been installed, a large room had been left instead. It was such a tempting storage area, so far from the cargo bays and the station's regular security patrols, that Odo had made it a point to inspect the area personally at least once a week. "The last time I checked it, it was completely empty."

"That's what I'm counting on," O'Brien said. "Without sensors or a carrier wave, none of the transporter's automatic positioning safeguards will be operational. I'm going to set your coordinates for a meter and a half above the deck, so brace for a drop."

"Understood," Odo said. "Shall I just stand here?"

"Maybe back up a bit," O'Brien suggested, "so we can get a clean fix. And I'd crouch down."

"Why don't I just do this?" Odo asked. He formed a picture in his mind, and became that picture, settling on the deck away from the others with a fluttering of coppery wings and feathers. Quark made a clucking noise but moved away hastily when Odo's form advanced on him with hissing beak.

"Perfect," O'Brien said. "Admiral Picard would be pleased."

Odo nodded his avian head in acknowledgment. He had taken the form of a Regulan phoenix, not much larger than a Terran hawk. In this form, a sudden drop would not be a problem.

He took advantage of the moment to enjoy the sensation of being in a different form, while O'Brien and Rom made the final adjustments to the transporter controls now accessible from their console.

"Ready?" O'Brien asked. "This'll be a slower transport than you're used to. Could be disorienting, the way they used to write about it back in the old days."

Odo spread his wings. He even enjoyed the odd way O'Brien's voice sounded to avian ears and how clear and sharply focused everything looked with avian eyes. He fixed his intent glance on Quark, who retreated even farther from him.

"Standby, then," O'Brien said. "Three-second countdown for the autosequencer . . . coordinates input . . . and energize."

Odo took a breath, thankful for the chance to finally be taking action, and only in the last second of the countdown did he realize that he was not the only one who had been waiting.

Because, just as the cool tingle of the transporter effect began to spread through him, with his heightened avian senses he felt the deck shake under pounding footsteps, heard ragged shouts of surprise, and then felt the tight grasp of powerful hands as he was lifted upward.

To stare directly into glowing red eyes.

And with that, the *Boreth* dissolved around him, and Odo beamed into the past.

Taking a monstrous demon there with him.

CHAPTER 9

THE *DEFIANT* SHUDDERED as the pressure wave disrupted its inertial dampeners and artificial-gravity generators, then forced both systems to reset. In the power surge that immediately followed, the ship's primary internal lights flickered, and everyone in the transporter room froze, expecting something worse to happen. Though what could be worse than the end of the universe was something beyond even Jake Sisko's imagination.

The young man's stomach lurched with the seeming rise and fall of the deck. But he really wasn't sure if it was because of the sudden physical disorientation or because in the midst of that disruption he had seen his father step up onto the transporter pad with Major Kira, ready to beam through whatever type of phenomenon it was that was only hours away from destroying them all.

Jadzia Dax, however, from her position at the transporter control console, sounded unperturbed as she announced, "Right on schedule. Next one won't be for another hour and three minutes."

Jake watched his father take his place beneath the dematerializer lens. "Dax," Sisko asked with a sudden thoughtful expression, "will we be able to feel the pressure waves on the station?"

"You shouldn't be able to," Jadzia answered.

"Shouldn't," Kira repeated with a small smile. "I've heard that before."

Once again Jake marveled at how, in the face of the ultimate disaster, everyone around him was still able to display a sense of humor, even confidence.

Jadzia returned the major's smile as Sisko gave Jake a nod of acknowledgment. They had already said what amounted to their good-byes, both maintaining that they would see each other again within a few hours.

Jake was well aware that his father and Kira were about to attempt something that had never been done before—beaming out of a pocket of space-time that was trapped in an unknowable domain of existence, into the past. And unlike any other Starfleet temporal mission he had ever heard of, Jake knew his father's stated goal this time was to *change* that past, *not* maintain the status quo.

For their mission, both Sisko and Kira were dressed in replicated costumes as Bajoran trustees. Since the *Defiant*'s historical records suggested that only a handful of humans might have been on Terok Nor at the time of the Cardassian Withdrawal—crew members of neutral merchant ships, for the most part—Jake's father also wore a stained bandage across the bridge of his nose, to disguise his lack of Bajoran epinasal folds. For expediency, Sisko had chosen the bandage over surgical alteration by Dr. Bashir. Besides, Starfleet Command was going to have a difficult enough time accepting the story that a duplicate Sisko would be telling them, and that difficulty might be reduced if his appearance was relatively unchanged. Though Jake had noted that his father hadn't elected to dissolve his beard or use follicle accelerators on his scalp to completely return to his appearance of the past.

"This is as ready as we'll be," Sisko told Jadzia.

"All right," the Trill said. "Benjamin, I'm sending you first. As ordered," she added pointedly. "You'll be materializing about a meter off the deck in Holosuite 2. After you drop, roll to the side and stay down. Major Kira will follow in thirty seconds."

Sisko and Kira nodded, but Jake saw that this time their smiles were absent. There had been a great deal of discussion about where to beam into the station. Without the system's subspace-mediated sensors and safeguards, it would be impossible for the operator to be certain the target coordinates weren't already occupied by a bulkhead, a piece of furniture, or even another person.

Jake knew that modern transporter technology had made all those concerns negligible, if not nonexistent. In fact, he couldn't remember a single transport he had ever experienced in which his feet had not rematerialized in perfect contact with the floor or ground.

Fortunately, the basic quantum-transporter effect itself created a weak repulsion force sufficient to clear the target volume of air molecules and dust particles. It just wasn't strong enough to clear away any denser matter.

Thus, based on almost everyone's recollections of Quark's complaints about how the Cardassian Withdrawal had almost bankrupted him because of a drop-off in business, Jadzia and Dr. Bashir had chosen the holosuites in Quark's bar as the safest possible beam-in point. Chances were good that the suites would not be in use. And, in the event they were, Bashir's surprisingly deep knowledge of holo systems made him confident that the suites' own safety subroutines that prevented the transport of replicated props into the same volume occupied by visitors would also deflect the incoming transport beam to a clear area, if necessary.

Whatever happened, Jake knew that he and all the others onboard the *Defiant* would have the answer within a few minutes. Both Sisko and Kira had radio communicators replicated from plans used by Starfleet in the first decade of its operation. Both were wearing shoulder straps to carry the bulky devices, each the size of a large book. To Jake, the communicators looked like antique tricorders, though considerably more awkward in design and size.

It had been Jadzia who had suggested the radios' use because, since photons could obviously travel between the pocket of space-time containing DS9 and that containing the *Defiant,* she believed it was likely other forms of electromagnetic radiation could as well.

However, the Trill had cautioned, for Sisko and Kira to have the best chance of sending a radio signal via the old-style devices, they would have to transmit from as close to the station's outer hull as possible. Transmitting through a viewport would give even better results. And if they had the time and opportunity, patching into the station's own radio transmission system would improve their chances most of all.

The moment had arrived. Jake held his breath.

"Get set for a drop," Jadzia warned Sisko. "Energizing . . ."

Jake watched as his father shimmered, then dissolved into a quantum haze of light. The process was much slower than usual, the result of Jadzia's having to coordinate the entire fifty-eight-step process manually.

Then Sisko was gone.

"No feedback fluctuation," Jadzia reported.

Jake slowly exhaled as he stared at the spot where his father had been. He knew enough of basic transporter theory to understand Jadzia's observation. It meant there was no sign the transporter beam had been deflected or dispersed. But again, in the absence of a subspace dimension, he also knew the Trill could not be sure if any transport fluctuation would feedback to the transmitters at all.

Jadzia tapped a control on her console. "Thirty-second countdown starts now."

The transporter room doors slid open a moment later, and Jake was surprised to see Commander Arla step in.

Kira spoke first. "Commander, who's watching Weyoun?"

"Ensign Simons," Arla said. "He and his team are finished automating the controls in engineering, so he's spelling me for thirty minutes. Has the captain beamed over?"

Jake saw but did not fully understand the flash of alarm that momentarily tightened Kira's face. The major continued to question the commander. "Does Worf know you're here?"

Must be something to do with the chain of command, Jake thought. In his father's absence, command of the *Defiant* had passed to Worf, who was now on the bridge.

Jake could see that Arla had registered Kira's concern, though she was controlling any defensiveness she felt. "I'm just stretching my legs, Major. I'm going to visit the head, get some soup, and go back to my station."

Ah, Jake thought, *that's why the major's upset.* Sisko had ordered Arla to watch Weyoun in sickbay, and by leaving her post, Arla was technically disobeying that order. For a moment, Jake speculated about what might have happened if Arla had come into the transporter room a few minutes earlier, when his father was still here. *Dad probably wouldn't have made a big thing out of it,* he decided. As long as Arla had made sure someone else was covering for her, his father was flexible enough to allow the commander her break.

Arla walked over to the console to look over Jadzia's shoulder. "You're doing it manually?" she asked the Trill.

"Fifteen seconds," Jadzia announced to Kira. Then she replied to Arla. "Just the first time. The major's transport will be easier because I'll just repeat the process, with a minor deflection to account for the station's rotation." She looked back at Kira. "Five seconds."

Jake saw the look of annoyance that Kira directed at Arla, but neither Bajoran said anything to the other.

"Energizing . . ." Jadzia said.

Jake watched as Kira dissolved into glowing light about twice as fast as his father had, though the process still took more time than usual.

A few seconds after the last sparkle had faded, Jadzia reported, "No feedback. It's a clean transport." She stepped away from the console then and bumped into Arla, who seemed to have been paying closer attention to the controls than to Kira.

"Sorry," the commander said to Jadzia. "I'll be back in sickbay in a few minutes. Should I send Simons up to the bridge?"

Now Jake sensed an undercurrent of tension between Jadzia and the commander, just as he had between Kira and the commander, and again he didn't understand it.

"I'll ask Worf," Jadzia said crisply. She glanced at Jake. "Let's go. I can use you at auxiliary communications."

Jake headed toward the doors. When they slid open, he continued through and into the corridor before he became aware that Jadzia was not behind him. He looked back to see her waiting for Arla to leave with her.

Then, as the transporter room doors closed behind the three of them, Jadzia turned to Arla and said, "All we can do now is hope for the best." The innocuous words were so unlike anything Jadzia might usually say that Jake stared at the Trill in puzzlement.

"Hope for the best," Arla said in agreement, "and trust in the Prophets."

The two women held each other's gaze for a moment, then Arla headed to starboard and the lift that would take her back to Deck 2. Jadzia and Jake took the corridor forward to the bridge.

As soon as he was sure Arla was out of earshot, Jake pressed Jadzia to find out what was really going on. "Since when does Arla believe in the Prophets?"

Jadzia waved his question aside as if it were unimportant. "Have you ever heard the Earth expression 'There are no atheists in a foxhole'?"

Jake shook his head, not grasping the connection, if any, between a small Terran animal's den and religious beliefs.

"Then how about what the Klingons say: The *bat'leth*'s blade always points toward *Sto-Vo-Kor?*"

"Oh, that one," Jake said. "Sure." He'd written the saying down as a useful example of tough-guy dialogue for the heist novel he'd been writing before the Orbs of Jalbador had come to the station. "Basically, it means people are more likely to turn to religion when they're facing death. You think that Arla—"

Jadzia nodded. "Arla didn't talk about her Pah-wraith hell, but maybe whatever it was she suffered through was enough to make her reconsider her interpretation of the Prophets."

They had reached the bridge and the door slid open before them.

"But Major Kira doesn't seem to have become more religious or . . . anything," Jake said.

Jadzia paused in the doorway. "On the contrary, that's what's made her so strong in all this."

Jake frowned. "She's always strong."

"Strong-willed, Jake. There's a difference. It's not inconceivable that some people might have had their faith diminished by what we've all been through. I mean, from a theological viewpoint, what's happened here could be interpreted as the final battle between good and evil . . . and evil won."

"Is that what Major Kira thinks?"

Jadzia shook her head. "Absolutely not. In fact, she doesn't believe this has anything to do with the Prophets at all. As far as she's concerned, the Prophets might test her people from time to time, but they would never be responsible for something as . . . as evil as the end of the universe and the deaths of so many innocent people."

Jadzia stepped onto the bridge and Jake followed her to her science station. "Then what does she think happened?" he asked.

"You know," Jadzia said as she took the seat facing her console, "the major doesn't have any answers, and she's comfortable with that." Then, the way the Trill shifted in her chair to look directly at him, Jake knew she wanted to emphasize the importance of what she said next. "Kira is a devout believer in the Prophets as her gods. And for all her . . . personal combativeness, when it comes to religious matters, she has a certain ease that comes from her absolute faith. That's why she never tries to force her religion on others, why she never judges those who don't agree with her, and why she's not troubled by what's happened—at least, in a religious sense. Faith is a wonderful thing, Jake, especially when it's pure like Kira's and not just a façade covering up unadmitted doubts—and fear."

Jake looked to the main viewer and the image it carried of Deep Space 9. "What do you believe?" he asked.

The Trill didn't hesitate. "That sometime in the next thirty minutes, we're going to pick up a time-shifted radio signal from your father and the major. That we're all going to be able to transport back to the station. And that we are going to be able to change our present so that the future we saw will never come to pass."

Jake regarded the Trill scientist as if seeing her for the first time.

"What is it?" Jadzia asked, but her compassionate smile told Jake she already knew the answer.

"Nothing," he said slowly. "It's just that, sometimes you sound like my dad. When he makes up his mind about something. And you just know that whatever he says is going to happen is *it*. You know?"

Jadzia placed a hand on his arm. "I think that's why your father and I are such good friends. We're a lot alike."

Jake blinked. "Yeah, but . . . you know . . ."

Jadzia smiled. "Right. Part of me's a three-hundred-year-old slug and—"

"No, no!" Jake said quickly, waving his hands. "I didn't mean—"

But Jadzia just patted his arm. "Jake, it's all right. I understand exactly. Admittedly, your dad and I do have differences, but in a lot of ways, well . . ." Her gaze fixed on the image of DS9 on the viewer. "What it comes down to is, out in space, *everyone's* an alien."

Now Jake did understand. "And if everyone's an alien, then—"

Jadzia completed his statement. "—then that's what makes us all the same."

Jake suddenly became aware of an imposing presence at his side. Worf.

The Klingon's deep voice rumbled. "I do not wish to intrude on this stimulating discussion of Vulcan philosophy, but is it not time to scan for radio signals?"

Jadzia winked at Jake. "Almost all of us." Then she swung her attention back to her controls and activated the ship's seldom-used Starfleet radio communication displays. "Jake, I'll need you to monitor the time scans on the auxiliary console."

"Right," Jake said as he stepped back to move carefully around Worf, who sported an extremely gruff expression and who was obviously still in pain from his Romulan disruptor wounds. He decided that if it was true what Jadzia had said about everyone being the same, then Worf's famously blunt manner was a lot like Sisko's "Starfleet mode"—just a specialized way of behaving when the situation warranted it. Jake hid a smile as he thought about how hard it would be even for Worf to maintain such an attitude for long in private with someone who liked to laugh as much as Jadzia.

As he sat at the console Jadzia had set up for him, Jake realized, odd as it seemed, that he was almost beginning to enjoy this mission. He was learning new things about people he had lived with for years.

But the realization was immediately supplanted by a feeling of horrible conflict. *What's wrong with me?* How he could possibly derive any sort of pleasure from such a terrible situation?

Jake's troubled gaze settled on his console screens as the ship's sensor net scanned for time-shifted radio signals, similar to the ones that might have come from a prewarp ship traveling close to lightspeed. Except, in this case, he thought, that ship was carrying his father, and it existed thirty-one years in the past.

The *only* thing that was making this whole mess bearable for Jake was his suspicion that, in some way, everyone else on the *Defiant* was feeling the same sort of apprehension and confusion he was. Even Commander Arla. That might even account for some of her newfound religious feelings.

Jake shook his head, tried to take control of his own emotions. It was essential not to think of the consequences of this mission. So he did what his father had so often taught him—he focused on the job at hand.

And his concentration became so intense, that when the transport alarm chimed and Worf rushed off the bridge, it took Jake several precious moments to realize that for some reason unknown, someone else had just beamed off the *Defiant* to follow his father into the past.

Sisko fell through a blizzard of light, its dying radiance lasting just long enough to reveal to him a familiar wall of banked holo-emitters, and then he hit the cold, hard deck in darkness and sprawled awkwardly onto his side.

Though there was now absolutely no light, Sisko didn't need to be able to see to know where he was. He could smell it: the faint undercurrent of overcooked popsnails that pervaded Quark's bar like methane in a swamp; the slightly acrid ozone twang contributed by Cardassian air filters; and the wholly artificial scent of the Bajoran industrial adhesive used to keep squares of friction carpet in place. Give most people a day in this unique atmosphere, and they would never notice any of those odors. But to Sisko, who had lived with them for so many years, then been away for weeks, their sudden reappearance was as welcoming as a fresh spring rain in New Orleans, as the salt air on Gilgo Beach.

He was home.

And then he remembered he wasn't the only one making the trip. Staying as flat as he could, he quickly crawled away from the point where he had fallen.

When he reached a bank of holo-emitters, he stopped, stretched out, head down, arms and legs flat, still in complete darkness. With his ear pressed against the deck, he could hear the thrumming of the station's air circulators and fluid pumps. The hum of the power system was there, as well, so it was unlikely the entire station was dark. And he was almost able to convince himself that he heard distant voices coming from the bar below, even though he knew the holosuites were heavily soundproofed.

Then golden light blazed in the room again, and Sisko relaxed as he saw the transporter effect take shape two meters away, a meter and half above. Moments later, Major Kira tumbled gracefully from mid-air, and the darkness returned.

"Major," Sisko whispered, "are you all right?"

"Nothing broken," Kira's voice came back softly. "How about you?"

Sisko let her know he was fine and that he was moving toward her.

When their hands made contact, they stood up together.

"Sure smells like Quark's," Kira whispered. "Probably the same pot of popsnails he was trying to sell the last time I was there."

Sisko heard her rustling in the layers of her Bajoran clothes. "Do *you* have a light?" he asked. For all their preparations, he hadn't thought to bring a palm torch.

"No, but maybe we can get something from the control panel on the radio. Unless . . ."

"Unless what?"

"Let's try the obvious first." Kira spoke normally. "Computer, restore room lighting."

Reflexively, Sisko half-closed his eyes, expecting to be blinded. But nothing happened. He opened his eyes. "Knowing Quark," he said, "if the suite isn't booked, then he's not about to waste power that someone else isn't paying for."

Sisko heard a soft click, then a blue glow appeared from the control surface of Kira's radio. The major held it facing up so they could see each other's face.

"Well," Kira said with a wry smile, "all your parts rematerialized in the right place. I guess Jadzia knew what she was doing." Then she aimed the pale blue light to the side, and slowly turned in a circle, dimly illuminating the suite. "Can you make out the door?"

Sisko squinted, saw a dark shadow between two panels of holo-emitters. "Over there." He moved toward it, and the major did the same, both of them walking slowly and quietly. But the door didn't open at their approach.

Kira frowned as she studied the door. "So how does Quark's security system work? If we open the door, is it going to trigger an intruder alarm downstairs?"

"It might," Sisko said. "But Quark is the least of our worries. We just have to avoid the Cardassians till they've all left, and after that . . . wait for Starfleet to arrive."

Even in the pale blue light, Sisko could see Kira was not convinced by his assessment. "So we open the door?" she asked.

"We have to," Sisko said. "We need to find out the date and time so we'll know how and when to proceed."

"Since we know the transporter works, couldn't we just beam everyone into the holosuite with us?"

In Sisko's opinion, that possibility had already been dealt with. "Major, what happens if Quark's is subjected to one last sweep by Cardassian security forces? We have to beam everyone to a place we *know* is safe. And we won't know what's safe until we know what time it is and how many Cardassians are still aboard."

Sisko sensed Kira still didn't agree with his reasoning, but she offered no further argument. She gestured to the door, inviting him to go first.

Sisko found the door control panel and pressed the 'open' control.

Nothing.

"Quark *really* likes to save money," Kira said drily.

Sisko was puzzled. "Why would he lock the door from the inside?" He tapped in his commander's override code which he had used in his first few months at the station, before the initial stage of the Starfleet computer retrofit had been completed. It had been Gul Dukat's code.

The door opened at once on the brightly lit corridor on Quark's top level.

And before Sisko's eyes had adjusted to the change in light levels, he heard the sounds of running feet charging up the metal staircase.

With identical movements, he and Kira instantly reached inside their clothes to withdraw their phasers—palm-sized Type-1s. Both weapons had already been set to stun.

"Only if they're Cardassians," Sisko cautioned.

Kira stood ready at his side as the footsteps came closer. Sisko heard their sound change as when the people approaching—two, at least—topped the stairs, raced across the metal flooring, and reached the corridor leading to the holosuites.

He held his breath, kept pressure on the phaser's firing stud, then—

—released that pressure and his breath as two Bajorans rushed around the corner with Cardassian hand phasers pointed ahead.

Sisko and Kira immediately raised their hands above their heads.

"We're with the Resistance!" Kira shouted.

But the Bajorans didn't seem to care what Kira said and continued their charge, unabated, as if they intended to run directly into Sisko and Kira.

"Wait!" Sisko said, then pulled Kira to the side as—

—*the Bajorans ran* through *her and into the holosuite.*

The emotions that swept over Sisko in that instant were too intertwined to make sense to him. Surprise at the impossible action he had just witnessed, relief that he and Kira had not been attacked. But also despair that his hopes for a quick solution were doomed because of some unexplained side effect of their travel into the past.

Kira's face betrayed her own shock. "What happened?"

"Did you feel anything?" Sisko asked.

"No, but . . . he ran through me?"

Sisko nodded, his glance darting back to the Bajorans who were sweeping the holosuite with phasers ready to fire.

"I don't understand," the taller of the two men said angrily, his voice deep and booming. "The computer picked up Dukat's code in use."

Then Sisko realized he had heard that voice before.

"Obanak," he said.

The prylar with the body of a plusgrav powerlifter looked directly at Sisko beyond the doorway, then turned away, clearly having heard nothing.

"He was in the Resistance with me," Kira said wonderingly. "But I never knew he was here for the Withdrawal."

"That's not important." Sisko was suddenly aware of the ache in his knees from his fall to the deck from the transporter effect. He pushed his hand against the doorframe. *Solid.*

"Of course, it's important," Kira snapped. "He's a member of a Pah-wraith cult. And the whole reason this version of the station exists in the wormhole pocket is because somewhere on it, someone's opening a Red Orb."

Sisko made the connection he'd been seeking. "So Obanak is looking for the Orb! We can work with him to—"

"No!" Kira said emphatically. "We don't know why he wants it. He could be here because he wants to open the red wormhole *now.*"

Now Obanak and the second Bajoran freedom fighter walked cautiously back to the holosuite's door, their Cardassian phasers concealed beneath their tattered clothing.

Sisko's natural reaction was to step out of the Bajorans' way, but he forced himself to stand his ground, and once again the two men passed through him, just as they had through Kira.

"Somehow," Sisko said, "we're not in phase with this reality."

In answer, Kira rapped her knuckles against the wall. Loudly.

Obanak and his companion stopped in the corridor and stared back, hands reaching for their weapons.

"We're in phase with part of it," Kira said. "Look at them!"

"Did you hear that?" Obanak asked.

Sisko raised his voice to a shout. "Prylar Obanak! Can you hear *me?*"

The two men gave no reaction to show they had heard anything.

Kira slammed a fist against the bulkhead.

At once, both men ran to the wall panel she had hit and pressed their ears against it. Needlessly, instinctively, Sisko and Kira jumped back to give them room.

"Any suggestions?" Sisko asked, perplexed.

"Other than we're *borhyas?*"

Sisko knew the Bajoran term for ghosts and rejected that explanation swiftly. "We're not dead, Major. This is a wormhole effect, nothing more."

Moving as if he were certain someone was hiding in the wall, Obanak edged slowly back, then subjected the wall to a wide-field phaser blast. Two ceiling lights winked out, but there was no other result.

"One of the Ferengi's smuggling tunnels?" Obanak's companion asked nervously.

The prylar shook his head. "Not in this wall. Maybe a service bay for the holo-emitters." He led the way back into the holosuite.

"So what do *we* do?" Kira asked Sisko.

"We have to get a message back to Dax. Maybe there's something she—"

"LOREM!"

Obanak's shout of warning came from the holosuite.

Sisko and Kira immediately ran into the suite to see the glow of a transporter effect shimmering in mid-air in the center of the enclosure.

Obanak and his partner could see it, too; they aimed their phasers directly at it.

Sisko didn't understand. "Why would Dax send—" And then he recognized the figure that fell from the light to the deck of the holosuite.

Weyoun. Still wrapped in his kai's robes of blood red— the same color as the Vorta's glowing eyes as he got to his feet to face Obanak and Lorem. And from their reaction to the sight of an alien whose species in this time had yet to visit the Alpha Quadrant, Sisko knew that the two Bajorans saw Weyoun. The Bajorans dropped their weapons.

"Serve me," the Vorta said to them.

And to Sisko's horror, Obanak and his companion fell to their knees and together whispered the one word Sisko did *not* want to hear in these circumstances.

"Emissary . . ."

CHAPTER 10

IN THE BLACKENED dust of his homeworld, Odo felt his wings melt and his feathers retract as he reverted to his true form, oozing like liquid despite all his efforts to create a solid form of any kind.

Dukat stood over him, his wild-haired, leering image repeated a thousandfold among the individual optical-perception cells that covered the changeling's amorphous body.

"That's right, Odo," Dukat said, and his harsh voice was multiplied by Odo's specialized acoustic cells, just as was his image. "We have returned to that place which you fear most."

Helpless, Odo could only watch as Dukat leaned over and scooped up a handful of him. Odo's essence dripped down Dukat's arm like thick, golden tar.

"Or should I say," the Cardassian sneered, "*you* have returned. Because *I* may leave any time I want."

Odo fought to create tentacles to wrap around Dukat's wide neck and strangle the Cardassian into silence. But physical control had left him. All he could do was to flow uselessly in the grip of gravity, powerless, just as when he had first experienced this personal and private hell—when the two wormholes had merged and he had flowed across the lifeless surface of this planet for millennia.

"Unless, that is," Dukat continued, "you make the right choice."

Odo felt tiny flakes of carbonized ash and debris adhere to his outer surface, and he knew those flakes were all that remained of his people after the Great Link had been incinerated by whatever disaster had struck this world.

But when the end had come here, Odo had been selfishly absent. His people had perished while he lived among the solids, adopting their ways, deliberately suppressing and ignoring his heritage. So that now he was even more alone than when he had been a solitary freak of nature on Terok Nor. Then, he hadn't known about his past or his kind. But now he knew exactly what he had lost, and he would know that loss forever.

"Do you have something—anything—to say?" Dukat asked. He shook the last of Odo from his arm. "Perhaps I can help." He gestured and a red glow of energy formed over the gray flesh of his hand. Suddenly, Odo felt reconnected to his form and to his abilities.

At once he pictured himself as a humanoid and within an instant his dispersed vision and sense of hearing coalesced into the localized regions of a humanoid head as he took shape and rose up from the ashes of his people.

"Is that better?" Dukat asked.

Odo controlled himself. He would not attack the madman. Not just yet. This experience was not real in any physical sense. But though Garak had not had any difficulty in extracting him from it, Odo wasn't certain how Dukat's manipulation of reality might have been affected by the process of their being beamed onto the changelings' homeworld. All Odo could remember of his transport from the *Boreth* was his shock when Dukat had leaped at him on the bridge.

"*Do* you have something to say?" Dukat asked again.

Odo cleared his throat, then spoke. "By adding your mass to the transport beam, it's most probable you've thrown off O'Brien's coordinate calculations. This time, we likely are dead."

But the Cardassian madman shook his white-haired head and his eyes glowed red with the fire of the Pah-wraiths. "Odo, really, can't you feel the difference? On the *Boreth*, it seems Garak was right. The Amojan had departed from me to do battle against his betrayers, leaving me with only a pitiful reminder of the power I once had." He held his hands before him, and weak scarlet sparks crackled from open palm to palm, sullying the dry air with the stench of burning flesh.

"But now," Dukat went on, "I exist in a temporal frame in which the Amojan has not yet returned to his Temple."

An almost dreamlike reverie come over Dukat, and Odo guessed the Cardassian was caught up in some memory of where he had been twenty-five years ago.

"At the time you and Sisko were tampering with the secrets of the Orbs of Jalbador, I was returning from my . . . sojourn in the Gamma Quadrant," Dukat said. "I was eager to meet with Weyoun and Damar, to retrieve the ancient fetish doll that had contained blessed Amojan's spirit. But now that I am returned to this time, the Amojan walks within me once again, needing no release." Dukat's eyes blazed with sudden red energy so searing in intensity that his features seemed to melt away and Odo was forced to shield his own eyes.

"He is a timeless being," Dukat chanted, as if reciting some ancient catechism. "All barriers fall before him. Accept this gift as you have always accepted him, now and forever, Amojan." The light faded and Dukat stared soulfully at Odo. "Can I hear an Amojan from *you*, Odo?"

"Why not?" Odo said.

Dukat blinked in happy surprise. "Truly?"

"Truly," Odo said. Then he morphed his right hand into a ten-centimeter cube of elemental iron and thrust it forward as fast as his nerve impulses could travel.

There was a satisfying crunch as the iron cube struck Dukat's face, and the Cardassian fell onto his back as if he were an android whose powerpack had been deactivated.

Odo knew this was an illusory realm and that nothing he could do would bring on Dukat's death. But even the illusion of pain might be enough to make the madman careless. And an enemy's carelessness usually brought with it opportunity. Odo changed his left hand into another cube of iron and swung it around like a hammer to crush Dukat's rib cage. The madman's arms and legs kicked out, twitched, then lay still.

Odo reduced the length of his arms, drawing the cubes away from Dukat's twisted body, savoring the illusion of dark blood that pooled around the illusion of a mangled face. He held his cubefists ready to strike again.

But the pooled blood faded as if evaporating and Dukat's face reformed from the battered ruins of his skull as if a melted statue had entered a pocket of reversed time. Then his chest reinflated, its ribs whole once again.

"Say hello to your eternity," Dukat spat at Odo, once his teeth had reformed.

Odo shut out all else as he concentrated on a critical alteration of his body, then sent out both fists—

—which missed Dukat because he was no longer there.

The Cardassian had vanished from Odo's reality.

But he had not vanished quickly enough.

For even as Dukat escaped the dimension within which this illusion existed, something else went with him—tiny barbed tendrils no thicker than a single human hair, identical to those of the Trelbeth grabber tree that had once flourished

145

in Keiko O'Brien's arboretum on Deep Space 9. Odo had projected then outward from each cubefist of iron to snare the robes covering the madman's still reforming body.

And Odo, whose morphogenic molecules shifted mass through other dimensions as easily as they altered their appearance and alignment, was suddenly in contact with both Dukat's position and his own. In one simple action, he now pulsed the bulk of his mass along those linking tendrils.

In that other location to which Dukat had fled, the changeling opened his eyes in his solid, humanoid body, just as the Cardassian ran from the large, unfinished storage room on DS9, exactly where O'Brien had beamed them.

Instantly, Odo withdrew the tendrils that connected him to Dukat. There was a momentary burst of disorientation as he puzzled over what had happened to him and where he had been—someplace that had been a psychic dimension for himself yet a physical one for Dukat. But the sound of Dukat's footsteps receding down the corridor made Odo quickly put the paradox aside.

His mission was plain to him. If the transport had gone as planned, and if Dukat's extra mass had not proved too disruptive, both he and Dukat were on DS9 twenty-five years in the past, at the time Sisko had returned from Jeraddo with two of the three Red Orbs of Jalbador. In slightly less than four hours, the third Red Orb would be discovered in Quark's bar, and the red wormhole would open, destroying the station and propelling the *Defiant* into the future.

Odo knew Dukat would do all he could to see that history played out exactly as it had before.

It was now up to Odo to prevent that from happening.

Odo rushed for the corridor, determined to use all the resources at his disposal. And as chief of security for DS9, his resources were considerable.

It only took him a few seconds to find a communications node at the intersection of two corridors, and he hit the emergency access control. "Odo to Security. Gul Dukat is on the station in the lower levels. He must be found and captured at once. Use heavy stun on sight. Acknowledge."

Odo paused, half expecting to hear his own voice in reply, demanding to know who was impersonating him.

But no response came.

He hit the control again. "Odo to Security, acknowledge." Nothing. He entered his personal ID code. "Computer, this is Odo. Put me in contact with the Security office." Again, nothing. "Odo to Ops, this is an emergency. Acknowledge!"

With a growl of frustration, Odo realized the node must be out of service. He was about to hurry to another intersection, when he took a closer look at the panel. Though he could not have articulated his suspicions—he was acting more on a feeling than any logical conclusion—he pressed the tab on the side of the terminal node and swung up the trapezoidal cover.

Inside, a tiny, isolinear status display screen glowed pale lavender; precisely, Odo knew, as a fully functioning node on this level should.

Recalling an action that seemed to be a habit with Chief O'Brien and Rom, Odo carefully held down the subsystem diagnostic key to the left of the display. Before anything else, the two engineers had always checked the status of the equipment they had been sent to repair, from the equipment's own perspective.

The self-check of the tiny terminal took less than three seconds. The Cardassian symbols that appeared in the display window indicated the device was operating at efficiency level 729—the Cardassian equivalent of 100 percent.

Yet the device had not transmitted his communications.

Odo tapped more controls, then stared at the new display line that appeared, this time in Federation alphanumerics.

O'Brien had miscalculated. Odo and Dukat had *not*

been beamed to DS9 on the day the three Red Orbs had been found and brought together.

The stardate was 51884.2—almost *five* days earlier.

"How is that possible?" Odo said to himself. O'Brien had been certain that the bubble of space-time containing the station existed in the wormhole pocket because it had somehow been 'swallowed' by the red wormhole when it opened in Quark's bar. The fact that the time signal the Chief had measured on the *Boreth* seemed to originate from a few hours before that event was easily explained by the nonlinear temporal nature of the wormhole. *But five days?* Odo thought. *What's connecting the station to the red wormhole in this time?*

As quickly as he had asked himself that question, he knew the answer.

With no time to waste this second time around, Odo stretched into a pseudopod of golden liquid and surged through a ventilation grille.

Before he could save the universe in the future, he would have to stop a crime in the past.

Sisko and Kira followed, appalled, as Obanak and Lorem reverently ushered Weyoun from the holosuite as if they were his acolytes.

"Why can they see *him* but not *us?*" Kira demanded. "Why can we interact with the station and not people?"

"There's an answer," Sisko said.

"For Dax, maybe," Kira replied worriedly.

They came to the metal staircase that led down to the main floor of Quark's where Sisko was surprised to hear a hum of conversation, even the familiar clacking of the dabo wheel accompanied by its usual chorus of cheers and groans.

Sisko looked over the staircase, down toward the main floor. Quark's was packed. Almost every customer was a Cardassian.

"Quark said business was dead in the days before the Withdrawal," Kira said.

For Sisko, there was only one explanation. "Then we're in the wrong time frame," he said.

"But how?" Kira asked. "Dax picked up the time signal for the Day of Withdrawal."

Sisko shook his head. "Maybe that's not the only day that connects the station to the red wormhole. Remember what Leej Terrell said. She studied the first Red Orb on the station. Hooked it up to some sort of device. Created what she called a 'wormhole precursor field,' and it allowed her to see *into* the red wormhole. It even allowed some of her researchers to step into it. That could be why we're here before the Day of Withdrawal—this might be one of the days Terrell conducted her experiments."

Sisko and Kira took the staircase down to the main floor. Weyoun had pulled up his hood to hide his features, and before him, Obanak and Lorem were moving politely through the crowd of Cardassians, heads bowed like nervous trustees grateful for even the small amount of freedom their position offered them. The three were heading for the main entrance. The Promenade beyond was bathed in cold blue light, heavily misted.

"We have to keep following them," Sisko said urgently. He started through the crowd, automatically trying to shift and twist to avoid colliding with the passersby who simply slipped through him without awareness of his presence.

Halfway to the entrance, Sisko looked over to the bar to see Quark serving drinks. The Ferengi, though younger in this time frame, paradoxically seemed older: his face haggard, his eyes deeply shadowed, his brightly colored jacket wrinkled and spoiled by a large stain. Sisko had forgotten how Quark had changed over the time the station had been home to a Starfleet presence. After six years, for all his complaints and occasional misadventures, the Ferengi barkeep

Sisko knew had become a successful businessman, obviously getting more sleep than he had in this time.

Sisko and Kira reached the Promenade, and now the changes between Terok Nor and Deep Space 9 became even more pronounced.

Half the storefronts were shuttered, closed for more than just the evening. They were out of business. And there were none of the small sales kiosks set up by optimistic entrepreneurs. This was a dying place.

"That way," Kira said, and she pointed to the right, where Obanak and Lorem remained to either side of Weyoun, walking toward the security fence that cut the Promenade in two—one side Cardassian, the other Bajoran.

Weyoun passed through the narrow gate without being troubled by the Cardassian guards, but Sisko saw a look pass between Obanak and a heavily-armed glinn and guessed that bribes were paid on a regular basis.

"I suppose we just walk through," Sisko said as he moved beside the lineup of Bajoran trustees returning to their quarters or carrying out assignments on the Bajoran side.

"Why not?" Kira said, and with a tight-lipped look of trepidation, stepped into the line and walked through the people ahead of her.

Sisko matched her movements, and the experience was definitely unsettling. He found it easier to only open his eyes every few seconds, to avoid the disorienting strobe-like flicker of darkness that accompanied each figure he passed through.

Penetrating the security gate required waiting for a Bajoran to approach it and then moving through the briefly open gate at the same time as the Bajoran. Kira went first, then Sisko.

"Did you see that?" Kira asked. She was pointing to a Cardassian in a security booth set back from the fence.

"See what?" Sisko asked.

"When we passed through, the guard monitoring the sensors couldn't see us but he acted as if he knew there was more than one person going through the gate."

Hope flared in Sisko that he and Kira might be able to use a computer terminal to transmit written messages. "Which confirms we're able to interact with the station's equipment at different levels. At least some of it." He peered around the darker and more crowded Bajoran side, trying to catch a glimpse of Weyoun's red robes. "Over there," he said.

Obanak was leading Weyoun into the Bajoran Temple.

"Not a good sign," Kira said flatly.

Sisko looked at her, waited for an explanation.

She gave one promptly. "The Resistance usually tried to avoid involving any temple in their activities, so the Cardassians wouldn't have an excuse to close them. So the one place on Terok Nor where you could almost guarantee there would be no Resistance members present is the Promenade Temple."

"But would the prylars have allowed it to be used by a Pah-wraith cult?"

Kira shook her head. "Until I saw Obanak go inside, I would have said no."

"Well, it won't do any good to try to signal Dax until time catches up with us and we're in the station on the same day the *Defiant* is observing it from the wormhole."

Kira understood. "So, first we follow Weyoun."

Together, they approached the Temple, and once they moved closer, Sisko noticed how threadbare the carpet was at the base of the steps leading inside. And how the elegant Bajoran carving which represented the gateway to the Celestial Temple appeared to be darker than he remembered, a result of the ore soot that the Cardassian filters couldn't totally eliminate from the station's air supply.

Kira paused at the entrance, also inspecting its tattered

condition. "We really made a difference here these past six years," she said softly. "We can't let it all have been for nothing."

Sisko regarded her somberly. "We won't," he promised.

They stepped through the doorway and entered the Temple.

And were instantly struck by a solid blast of blue light.

Sisko gasped as its impact crashed down upon him like a wave. But the force of it hit from all directions at once so that he remained on his feet.

He staggered as the light faded, leaned in toward Kira who had doubled over, trying to catch her breath. "What was that?" she said as she coughed.

"An explosion?" Sisko suggested. But there had been no sound to accompany the flash. He straightened up with some difficulty, to peer into the Temple's worship area, to see if Weyoun and his Bajoran followers had been similarly affected.

But the Vorta was gone, along with his acolytes.

The only occupant of the Temple now was a tall, distinguished prylar with a neatly trimmed white beard.

And his eyes were fixed on Sisko.

Sisko stared at the old prylar.

"Can you see me?" he asked.

The prylar bowed in acknowledgment. "I have been waiting to see you all my life, Emissary."

The way the prylar said that word brought a sudden memory to Sisko. The man before him was the *first* prylar he had ever met.

The first Bajoran to call him Emissary.

On the first day he had set foot on the Promenade when he had arrived on Deep Space 9.

And now the paradoxes begin, Sisko thought, fighting bewilderment. In his original timeline, he had met this prylar days, perhaps months from now, two weeks after the Cardassians had left the station. But now, when

Sisko's earlier self arrived on the station for the first time, this prylar would already have met him, in a way.

"Prylar Rulan," Kira said in greeting.

The Prylar nodded again. "Nerys."

"You know each other?" Sisko asked, realizing how foolish the question was as he said it. He forged on. "Prylar, there were three men just here. Two trustees and an alien in red robes."

A small smile played across Rulan's placid features. "There has been no one here today but me, Emissary. And there are no more trustees, thank the Prophets."

Sisko looked at Kira, about to ask if she knew of any hidden passages connected to the Temple. He knew of none.

But before he could ask his question, Kira had one of her own.

"Prylar, *why* are there no trustees anymore?"

"Not since the Cardassians left, my child. All of Bajor are free now." The prylar fixed his calm eyes on Sisko. "And you, too, are of Bajor now."

Sisko felt the skin of his arms rise up in gooseflesh. *The light,* he told himself. *That's what the light was.*

"Prylar," he asked, "when did the Cardassians leave?"

"Two weeks ago."

"We've shifted to a new temporal frame two weeks *beyond* the time we wanted," Sisko said to Kira.

"How?" she asked. Then answered her own question, just as Sisko had. "That light?"

"It has to be. I asked Dax if we'd feel the pressure waves on the station. We must still carry with us some connection to the *Defiant*'s frame of space-time so that each time an equalization pressure wave goes past, we get tugged along with it.

Kira took it to the next logical step. "So when the next one passes, we'll be tugged back into the past."

Sisko nodded. "Just not as far. Then we'll come forward again."

Kira looked at him. "What do you want to bet that the one place we'll finally settle is the Day of Withdrawal—the same time frame the *Defiant*'s observing."

Sisko rubbed his hand over his face. "And by then it'll be too late." He saw Kira's puzzled expression. "Major, if we're still linked to the *Defiant*'s temporal frame, when it ceases to exist, we probably will, too."

"Or else . . . the link will cease, and we'll be left here."

"Are you willing to risk that?"

Kira gave him a grim smile. "Do we have a choice?"

"The Emissary has many choices," Prylar Rulan said quietly.

In the back of his mind, Sisko tried to work out the difference in the rate of time passage between the *Defiant* of the future and this station in the past. Knowing that might give him some idea of how much longer he and Kira had before the pendulum of time swept them back into the past. But he had another, more personal question burning in him as well.

"Prylar," Sisko asked, "how do you know that *I* am the Emissary?"

The prylar smiled, as if to indicate he knew more than anyone could ever suspect. "You are the Sisko. You have just appeared before me from within the light of the Celestial Temple itself. There are those among us who have always known that just such a person will be the Emissary."

Sisko didn't understand how that could be possible. In this past, when he had first seen Rulan, Rulan had also called him Emissary at once, even though Sisko had merely stepped out from an airlock on the Promenade and not from a flash of wormhole radiation. But when Sisko had first met the Prophets, only a few days after that, those beings had seemed to not recognize him as anything except a disturbance in their environment. Indeed, at first they had seemed to have a difficult time even recognizing him as a corporeal being and had said they wanted to destroy him.

"You've always known?" Sisko asked, truly baffled. "How is that possible?"

Prylar Rulan shook his head as if the question had no meaning. "I know because those who came before me knew, because those who came before them knew, all the way back to the first writings of the great mystics in the time before Lost B'hala."

"The mystic Shabren?" Kira asked.

The prylar smiled. "And Eilin and Naradim."

Kira frowned. "But those are the mystics of *Jalbador.*"

Sisko was fascinated to see the serene prylar bristle at Kira's use of that term.

"Some have called them that," Rulan said sharply. "But they are mistaken. To those who *know* the Will of the Prophets, they are the mystics of *Jalkaree.*"

"But, Prylar, in all the lessons you've taught me," Kira said, "in all the lessons I've learned in all the Temples I've worshipped in, not you, not one prylar or monk, has *ever* taught me of Jalkaree. Or said the name of the Emissary."

The prylar's smile returned, this time like that of an indulgent parent. "Oh, my child, think what would have happened if those who knew the truth so many millennia ago had named the Emissary for all the world. Do you not think that every generation would then have hundreds, if not thousands of people coming forth to say that they were the Sisko? And do you not think that if the full prophecies of Jalbador and Jalkaree were known to all the world, if the history of the future were laid out for all with the mystics' precision, there would not be those who would attempt to change that future?"

The prylar stepped closer to Kira, placed a hand on her shoulder, looked directly and deeply into her eyes. "My child, I know your faith is pure and absolute, and as part of your faith, I ask you to accept that there is a reason the Will of the Prophets must sometimes be seen as difficult to interpret for the many, even while it is understood perfectly by the few."

"But who chooses those few?" Kira asked.

The prylar's expression revealed nothing. "In the end, who chooses the Emissary?" He looked over at Sisko. "I sense that you are not entirely accustomed to your role."

The prylar's understatement was overwhelming. Sisko held his true reaction in check, simply said, "That's true."

"Naradim spoke of that, in the same text in which Eilin states the danger inherent in revealing too much of the prophecies, that the revelation of the one direction of time might contain within it the seeds of another outcome."

"Another time," Sisko said.

The prylar studied Sisko carefully, as if looking through him, into the melee of thoughts that filled his mind. He reached out to Sisko's ear. "May I?"

"As long as you realize that Eilin is correct and some of what you learn must never be revealed."

Rulan nodded, then tightly, almost painfully, squeezed Sisko's left earlobe between his thumb and forefinger.

Rulan closed his eyes, turned his head up, opened his mouth—not in fear, Sisko thought—but in awe.

Sometime later, seconds or minutes, Sisko couldn't be sure, he felt the prylar's grip lessen, then his hand slipped away.

From outside the Temple, on the Promenade, Sisko heard a sudden clang of metal. He and Kira glanced back over their shoulders.

"The repair work," Rulan said. "But then," he added, "you know that."

Sisko nodded. A subtle though familiar tremor vibrated through the deck.

"That's an airlock cycling," he said.

Rulan nodded, as if hesitant to say much more. "Since the *Enterprise* arrived, there have been a great many comings and goings."

Sisko held Rulan's gaze for a few moments, knowing that the prylar would know—knew—or at least sensed—all that he did.

And then Sisko couldn't resist and spun around and walked quickly to the Temple's entrance.

He peered cautiously around the edge of the doorway. The Promenade beyond was even darker than it had been under the Cardassians. It was littered with debris and ruined components that had been too bulky to loot and so had been destroyed in place.

Fusion torches sent sparks through the shadows. Metal rang under the impact of molecular saws. And spinward, past Quark's, an inner airlock door opened.

A younger Chief Miles O'Brien stood before the disk door as it rolled to the side.

And Commander Benjamin Sisko set foot on the station for the very first time.

Captain Sisko, in the doorway to the Temple, was suddenly aware of Kira and Prylar Rulan at his side.

"This probably isn't the best idea in the world," Kira said.

"No, it's not," Sisko agreed. He stepped back; Kira followed. Prylar Rulan stayed in place, gazing out at the second Sisko now approaching.

"Remember, Eilin was right," Captain Sisko said.

Rulan looked back into the Temple. "Of that," he said, "I have no doubt."

Sisko understood the prylar's unspoken promise. Rulan would not tell Commander Sisko that he had just been visited by a future version of him. What would happen here on the Promenade in the next minute would be what had happened before.

"You must understand as well," Rulan said. "There can be no other time, or all is lost."

"*I* understand," Sisko said as he moved farther back into the protection of the Temple. "But *he* does not."

Rulan nodded as if to put Sisko's mind at ease. "Shabren is very clear about that in his text about the Emissary's first visit to the Gateway to the Temple. There were—there will be—many things the Sisko did not understand that day. This day."

Sisko thought back to his beliefs and his attitudes of six years ago. Had he ever been that naive? "In time, he will," he told the prylar.

"In this time," Rulan said emphatically. "Not another time." He looked back to the Promenade, then turned to bow his head to Sisko in the Temple. "If you will excuse me, I must go welcome the Emissary. For the *first* time."

Then Rulan left the Temple to await Commander Sisko, just as he had awaited him before. *Just as he will* always *await me,* Sisko thought.

And with an unexpected flash of insight, the concept of non-linear time became clearer to him. It wasn't that to the Prophets their realm of nonlinear time was without past, present, and future, it was that the past and present coexisted interchangeably within a third dimension of time, with only the future in flux.

"Are you all right?" Kira asked, and Sisko was surprised by the intense concern in her being. Then he realized that he could hear a conversation outside the Temple. A conversation that included his own voice.

"Fine," Sisko said. "I was just thinking that if I ever get the chance to see the Prophets again, maybe I'll have something *I* can teach *them.*"

Kira's voice sharpened. "Be careful who you say that to. Some might think it heresy."

"Believe me," Sisko said, "if I ever do get a chance to

spend that much time with the Prophets, I don't think I'll be too worried about what other people think."

Kira looked around the Temple as if searching for another way out. "Well, we can't stay here while . . . we're both out there."

Sisko didn't understand. "Why not?"

"You heard what Rulan said. The danger of changing time. We can't just walk out there and warn ourselves about the future. We have to let everything proceed just as it did the first time."

"Major," Sisko said, stunned by Kira's abrupt change of heart. "We will *not* allow the Pah-wraiths to win. I have no intention of allowing the universe to end, simply because that's what happened before."

Kira stiffened in anger. "That's not what I meant at all. I just mean, we can't change what happened *before* the Red Orbs were brought together. But we can *stop* that from happening just before we were pushed into the future—if we get rid of the one Orb hidden in Quark's right now. Nothing else would change for the next six years."

"But we'd still be changing the timeline." The nuance of the major's argument still escaped Sisko.

"If we stop the red wormhole from opening on DS9 in the last few minutes before we left on the *Defiant,* maybe we won't be changing time, we'll be restoring it."

At last Sisko saw what Kira meant. "Of course," he said. "Leave the past alone, but affect our present in order to create a new future."

"The same as we do every day," Kira added.

"So . . . all we have to do is get to Quark's and take the Orb from its hiding place inside the stained-glass portrait of the Tholian general."

The plan was just that simple. Its execution even simpler. At the back of the Temple, there was a wide selection of monks' attire, and in minutes, both Sisko and Kira were unrecognizable in large hoods and bulky robes.

Side by side, they crossed the cluttered Promenade, their passage met only by smiles from the Bajoran workers, clearly pleased to see religious figures using their newfound freedom to move about the entire station.

The noise and commotion all around him brought back to Sisko the heady sense of victory and celebration that had existed in the station's first days as Deep Space 9. At the same time, he remembered the tension that had equally been present, because no one had known how Bajor's provisional government would survive the next few weeks, let alone years.

But now, knowing that it *had* survived, Sisko continued with Kira to Quark's, easily resisting the opportunity to tell those around them that for the next few years, at least, their world would make great strides.

Once they were in Quark's, Kira brazenly stepped up to the bar and, with her head bowed and hood pulled forward, informed Quark in a low, muffled voice that they understood he was leaving the station and that the prylars were considering asking the station manager to have the Temple relocated to this larger area.

"We'd like to look around," Kira said.

Quark, still as careworn in this timeframe as when the Cardassians had been in charge, waved his hand dismissively. He was in the middle of packing up what few items remained that weren't broken. "Be my guest," he sighed. "You can even use the holosuites to guarantee mystic visions for the faithful. Ha." Then he turned his back on his visitors.

Kira and Sisko made their way slowly around the ruined bar, only gradually moving toward the large, yellow and orange glass mural that was about the only source of light at the moment.

Then they both stepped behind it where they couldn't be observed.

Sisko pointed at the access panel in the back of the mural's thick housing, flush to the floor. "There," he said.

Kira nodded, then knelt beside it, pulling out a small pulsedriver she had found in a maintenance toolbox at the back of the Temple.

Six years from now, Sisko knew that he had been led to this same spot by the glowing interior light from two Orbs of Jalbador, because hidden inside was the missing third Orb, protected from years of maintenance sensor sweeps by an unusual low-power Andorian sensor mask.

"Leave the sensor mask turned on," Sisko whispered. "Just take the Orb." What they'd do with it was something he work out later. The mostly likely possibility was to "borrow" a runabout and launch the Orb into the Bajoran sun.

The final fastener came out of the panel and Kira carefully pulled it free. From inside the service alcove, no larger than an Orb Ark, Sisko saw the pale blue glow of the sensor mask device.

He exhaled, abruptly aware that he hadn't taken a breath for the past half-minute.

Kira smiled up at him, then bent forward and reached inside.

She kept her hand in for a long time, methodically moving it back and forth, then leaning down close to the floor to peer inside.

She pulled back and stared up at him.

Before she could utter a word, Sisko knew what she would say.

"It's not there!"

Sisko even knew why.

Weyoun.

CHAPTER 11

LIKE A LIVING current of blood, Odo propelled himself through the *tiyerta nok,* what the Cardassians called the lifeflow of iron—the arteries of the machine.

But to Odo, they were DS9's complex, interwoven network of Jefferies tubes, air conduits, and even Quark's smugglers' passageways—a gift of the Obsidian Order.

Faster than a security team on turbolifts, the changeling unerringly flowed along those hidden paths through the vast station, their unrecorded layouts long memorized, a simple matter for someone who could effortlessly recall the three-dimensional molecular structure of virtually every solid object he had ever studied.

From the intersection where he had realized what was about to happen to the lower-level corridor where he knew Dukat was intending to go, Odo's swift liquid race took less than fifty seconds and ended when he streamed from a wall-mounted air vent, reforming into his familiar solid shape from his boots up, as if he were a wave of honey being poured into a transparent humanoid-shaped container.

At once, he looked around to be sure of his location: the side corridor leading to the false wall that cut off the long-concealed section of DS9. For six years, Leej Terrell's secret Orb research lab had escaped detection by Starfleet engineers and teams of retrofitters. Before that, not even Gul Dukat had known of its existence during his control of the station.

It had taken Jake Sisko and Nog, as boys playing in the Jefferies tubes, to accidentally discover the walled-off section of corridor and the hidden lab. The two youngsters had used it as their private holosuite, never suspecting that what seemed to them to be holographic environments were actually illusions created by the Pah-wraiths—illusions intended to tempt corporeal beings into the Pah-wraiths' realm.

But by the time the three Red Orbs of Jalbador had been brought to the station, the secret of the hidden section was known to Sisko's command staff. In fact, for Odo, only three mysteries had remained when DS9 was destroyed.

Why were his memories of the Day of Withdrawal, along with those of Quark and Garak, inaccessible?

Who had killed the two Cardassian soldiers in civilian clothes who had been discovered fused into the station's hull as if they had been deliberately beamed to their deaths?

And who had murdered Dal Nortron, the Andorian merchant of dubious ethics whose arrival on DS9 had preceded all the events leading to the destruction of the station?

Now, standing on the spot where Dal Nortron's body had been discovered—or would be discovered in just a few hours in this timeframe—Odo felt certain he was about to solve the third mystery. With luck, he hoped that he might even stop it from ever coming into being in the first place, simply by saving Dal Nortron's life before it could be taken.

He paused, listening carefully, but heard no one else nearby. Feeling confident he had arrived well before Gul Dukat, he moved to the false wall that hid the small intersection leading to Terrell's lab and pressed his hand to the seam between the false panel and the real one beside it. Taking advantage of the near-microscopic space between the two panels, Odo flowed through the crack and reformed on the other side like a crystal growing on a cave wall.

There was light in the hidden section, spilling out from the open door to Terrell's lab.

Odo temporarily changed his eyes from humanoid-normal to those of a nocturnal Vulcan primate, enabling him to see the dimly-lit corridor as if it were high noon.

The corridor was empty.

Odo returned his eyes to their usual size and construction as he moved quickly toward the open door. Pausing on its threshold, he beheld the laboratory's flawless recreation of an ancient village of the Bajoran moon, Jeraddo, as it had existed almost one thousand years earlier at the dawn of Bajoran space travel. It was the same illusion that Jake and Nog would discover two days from now, when Jake's research for his latest novel would inspire the two friends to revisit their childhood playground.

The details of the Jeraddan village were derived from the Cardassian memory rod that Dal Nortron had brought with him to DS9. But unlike the Andorian, who Odo knew was inside the lab's reconstructed village right now, convinced he was using a Cardassian holosuite, Odo understood that since the village was what Nortron most wanted to see, it was what the Pah-wraiths were showing the Andorian in order to bring him closer to their realm.

Stepping through the open door, Odo sensed the subtle changeover to the slightly weaker gravity of the moon as his foot crunched into gravel.

It was night here. To the west, the Bajoran stars formed

summer constellations like spilled jewels. To the east, the horizon was beginning to glow with the blue-green light reflected from Bajor itself, still unseen on the moon's dayside. A soft breeze blew, and in the village of stone buildings about a kilometer distant, Odo could see flickering candlelight in small windows.

But he saw no sign of Dal Nortron.

"NORTRON!" Odo kept his hands cupped to his mouth and shouted twice more. But not even an echo came back to him. He would have to go into the village.

Odo knew that Sisko had found the third Orb of Jalbador hidden in a mural wall in an underground chamber of a large structure in the village, as it really existed in this time: battered ruins on a world that had been transformed from Class M to Class Y as it had been converted into a seething power source for the hungry world it circled. Though the map had not shown the Orb's exact location, Odo decided the Andorian would be close to it. Because the map was incomplete, whoever had given or sold it to Nortron must also have given him verbal instructions for interpreting it. Otherwise, it would have been worthless.

Odo began to run, then leaped into the air and became a Kalari lightning hawk, flying the kilometer to the village in only a few seconds of hyperfast wingbeats.

Settling to the stony ground on the outskirts of the wide plaza at the center of the village, the changeling returned to his humanoid shape. The glow on the horizon was becoming brighter. Again Odo cupped his hands to his mouth and called Nortron's name.

Still no response.

But a shadow darted past a small building at the far corner of the plaza.

Odo recognized the rotund form of the stubby-antennaed Andorian in his bulky fur vest. Odo called out once more, but Nortron merely hurried on, head down, eyes fixed on what Odo took to be a small map reader, and then disappeared around a corner.

Odo sighed, thinking that solids could be so typical. *Try to save their lives, and what do they do . . .*

He began to run again, deciding against changing shape to avoid startling Nortron, or possibly offending the Andorian's solid sensibilities.

Odo raced around the corner where Nortron had disappeared, then skidded to a stop, sending small rocks flying. The Andorian stood facing him, the metallic blue gleam of a small, knife-shaped stinger gun clutched in one hand.

"What are you?" Nortron said shakily. Odo had encountered panic enough times to recognize its presence when he heard it.

"I'm Odo, Chief of Security for DS9. Your life is in—"

"I said, what are you?!" Nortron gasped in a thin, rising voice.

Odo realized that for whatever reason, the Andorian was in no condition to listen to reason. He had to be disarmed first, warned second.

"I'm here to help you," Odo said firmly as he took a step forward and—

An incandescent stream of relativistic ions shot forth from the Andorian's stinger, striking the ground where Odo's foot crunched into the gravel.

Sharp, glowing stone fragments sprayed up into the air.

Startled, Odo stared down at his foot, fully expecting to see his boot sliced in half faster than his restorative autonomic reflexes would have been able to act.

Instead, his boot was intact. But it rested in the center of a small glowing pit of melted rocks.

Odo snorted in exasperation. "Now we do it *my* way," he growled as he shot out his hand to cross the two meters to Nortron, to grab the stinger.

But then shock caused Odo's hand to snap back to him

like rubber. His hand had passed *through* the Andorian's. Suddenly, Odo understood why he had been unable to get a response from the communication node in the corridor.

His footsteps in the gravel prompted the Andorian to fire at him again, once at the ground, then once above the sounds of his footsteps, directly through his midsection.

But Odo felt nothing. The beam had no effect on him.

"Out of phase," Odo said to himself. Somehow, he could interact with the solid, nonliving elements of this timeframe. But for living beings, or anything directly connected to them like Nortron's weapon, Odo had no way of making his presence known.

As Nortron backed up, blue face glistening with sweat, short antennae fairly vibrating with tension, Odo wasted precious moments wondering how it was he could crunch gravel yet not make air molecules vibrate to produce the sound of his voice.

But, ever practical, the changeling abandoned the finer points of temporal physics to lean down and pick up a rock so he could scratch a message on the stone wall of the building beside him and Nortron. The Bajorglow was bright enough to allow such a message to be read, and surely the sight of a rock floating in air would hold the Andorian's attention.

But the instant he picked up that rock, Odo saw Nortron's eyes bulge and his mouth gape open, and the Andorian spun around and ran off screaming.

Odo tossed the rock away in disgust, then chased after him.

Panting and wheezing, the out-of-shape Andorian took almost five minutes to reach the improbable open doorway that hung suspended in midair a kilometer from the village, framing a corridor that was in distinct contradiction to the rocky landscape surrounding it.

Nortron scrambled up and into that doorway, then frantically twisted around to push the door sideways, sliding it shut in Odo's face.

But Odo liquefied to flow through the narrowing opening, reforming beside the Andorian even as Nortron, gulping for air, placed his shoulder against the door to seal it more swiftly.

Then the door closed, and Odo and Nortron were plunged into blackness. At once, Odo heard footsteps hastily scurrying away.

With a sigh, Odo altered his form to that of a Ferengi mudbat, his humanoid eyes merging to form a dark membrane of thermal-imaging cells, perfect for identifying prey on dark Ferengi nights when stormclouds cut off all starlight and perpetual thunderstorms had made the evolution of echolocation a rare event.

In the narrow, shimmering spectrum of infrared, Nortron was a blazing white blob moving rapidly away from Odo, toward the false wall. Odo glided after the Andorian, flying over him halfway. Peering down, the changeling caught sight of a dark band around Nortron's face and identified it most probably as a portable thermal viewer.

Then Nortron slid open the false wall and the heat spectrum of the corridor changed, as did Odo, back to his humanoid form. The amount of shapeshifting he had undertaken since arriving on the station was beginning to take its toll on his energy. Except when absolutely necessary, he customarily avoided switching from form to form as quickly as he had today.

The false wall slid shut again and Odo saw Nortron standing in the ordinary DS9 corridor, peeling a pair of thin, dark goggles from his eyes. The Andorian shook the goggles once, and they self-folded into a small, square packet which he stuffed under his fur vest. The stinger gun, though, he kept in his other hand.

Aware that Nortron had only a few minutes to live,

Odo came up with a simple but adequate plan. By using his limited ability to interact with the nonliving, mechanical parts of DS9, he would drive Nortron away from the site at which he had been or would be murdered.

As Odo fully expected, Nortron began hobbling on obviously strained legs toward the main corridor leading toward the turbolifts. The Andorian's free hand grasped his ample belly as if to help hold it up and make breathing easier. In his other hand, he gripped the stinger as if he were drowning and it was his lifeline. Every few steps, Nortron glanced behind himself, his fleshy blue face still streaked with sweat, no sign of his panic decreasing.

This time, Odo didn't need to change form to pass Nortron and stay ahead of him. Reaching the first intersection, the changeling stretched up to grab the overhead vent grille just beyond. When Nortron reached the intersection, Odo yanked the grille free and sent it crashing to the deck in front of the Andorian. Odo's expectation was that Nortron would wheel to the left, heading away from the site of his murder.

But instead, Nortron instantly fired his stinger. Unfortunately, he also fired without thought or aim and with his weapon pointed to the side. Instantly, an ODN conduit erupted in sparks and smoke and flung the doubly startled Andorian into a spin that made him stumble through Odo and continue on in the same direction he had been going before, only now wheezing horribly.

Odo kicked the useless grille to the side and ran past Nortron again to set up another diversion. This time, he decided not to drop the grille. He'd hold it up so that to Nortron it would appear to be floating. Then Odo planned to push against the Andorian with it, physically *forcing* him to go in another direction.

But before Odo could set his new plan in motion,

Nortron lurched to a stop in the corridor, staring ahead in even greater alarm.

"Did . . . did Atrig send you?" Nortron stammered.

Odo looked in the same direction Nortron did.

Dukat was there. Just as Odo had anticipated. Complete with robes and wild white hair. And for whatever reason, the Cardassian was in temporal phase, meaning Nortron could see Dukat, but Dukat, apparently, could not see Odo.

"Give me the Orb," Dukat said.

"I . . . I don't have it," Nortron stammered.

Dukat raised his left hand as if making an idle gesture. "You will be rewarded."

"No one else has arrived," Nortron explained in a shrill, anxious voice. "Quark says I have to wait."

"Or you will be punished," Dukat concluded. His left hand began to shimmer with red energy. "I should think it would be a simple choice."

"I have latinum!" Nortron pleaded. "I won three dabos! It's in a dimensional safe in my—"

Dukat's eyes sparked with red light. "Do I *look* like I want *latinum?*"

Nortron dumbly shook his head.

Odo thought furiously. As long as Nortron held his position, the Andorian was safe. His body had been found ten meters away, showing no obvious sign of having been moved. Odo just had to keep him from going that extra ten meters.

"Quark's little scheme was merely a smokescreen." Dukat held out his hand. "The Orb."

Nortron swallowed audibly. "Please . . . whoever you are, I *don't* have it. I was only given a map."

Dukat's face darkened with temper, puzzling Odo. The Cardassian apparently didn't know his history. Vash had brought the first Red Orb of Jalbador to Deep Space 9, while it was Nortron who brought the map that showed the rough location of the second Orb. And the third Orb had been hidden in Quark's bar since the Day of Withdrawal. So why would the Dukat of the year 2400 think the Andorian had one of the Orbs, when the historical record would indicate otherwise?

"You *are* Dal Nortron, are you not?" Dukat asked angrily.

The Andorian nodded.

Odo looked around for something heavy he could detach from a wall or the ceiling and use as a club.

"You have been in contact with Leej Terrell, yes?"

Nortron shook his head in denial.

Dukat's voice became acidic. "You spoke of Atrig."

"Yes," Nortron said hurriedly, frantic to please his interrogator. "Atrig came to me. Gave me the map. Told me to contact Quark to arrange an auction."

"Atrig works for Terrell," Dukat hissed.

"I . . . I didn't know."

"And she has the third Orb."

"I . . . I don't know about that, either."

Dukat advanced on the cringing Andorian. "Oh, she's had it since *I* ran this station. Right under my nose. Can you understand the betrayal I felt?"

Nortron backed up, nodding vigorously, clearly desperate not to do anything to further provoke Dukat.

Odo grunted with satisfaction as he spotted a section of an ODN conduit that hadn't been completely closed. It appeared he could rip down about a meter-and-a-half section of the composite, half-walled pipe that contained the optical cable. The pipe would make a good club to knock Nortron unconscious, so the Andorian *couldn't* move the ten meters to his place of death.

"You aren't what I had hoped for," Dukat mused in an almost dreamily singsong voice. "Of course, in this time, I wasn't hoping for much . . . only a chance to serve the Amojan. And so many years from now, when I found out about you . . . the summoning of the Orbs . . . your murder . . . the station's destruction . . ."

"Mmmurder?" Nortron gibbered.

"You're a shadow, my friend, a ghost of what was, never to be again. But I *was* hoping that this time around, you would tell me what I need to know to serve the Amojan . . . so I can retrieve the Orbs for his power and his glory. . . ." Dukat peered at the Andorian. "Can I have an Amojan from *you?*"

"Ama . . . Ama . . ." But in his horrorstruck state, Nortron couldn't form the name of Kosst Amojan, the Evil One, the Pah-wraith Dukat served.

"Last chance," Dukat warned. "Then I shall let history resume its flow, Amojan be his name. Who has the Orbs now?"

Odo decided he had waited long enough. He had hoped he might learn something useful, but he wasn't the only one who knew about Nortron's fate. Dukat did, and he was preparing to speed him to it. The changeling reached up for the loose ODN conduit.

"Oba—Obanak!" Nortron abruptly blurted.

Odo hesitated mid-reach at the mention of that name, looked back at Dukat, saw the Cardassian's dark eyes widen in surprise, a slight smile touch his gray lips.

"*Prylar* Obanak?"

Nortron wiped his face. His white hair lay in damp, flattened tendrils against his blue forehead. His antennae now twitched incessantly. "I . . . I don't know if he's a prylar. Just the name. That's the name Atrig used. Obanak—he's the one who . . . who gave the map to Atrig."

Odo held his hands over the conduit, ready to take action the instant before Dukat could strike but also alert to learn more, especially about the prylar. In this time, Odo knew, Obanak had been involved in a Pah-wraith cult. The prylar had come to DS9 at the same time as Leej Terrell and her associates, Atrig and Dr. Betan. Those three had proclaimed themselves to be humanitarians come to retrieve the bodies of the Cardassian soldiers found fused within DS9's hull plates.

But since Obanak had accused Terrell of being a mass murderer, a war criminal, why would he have provided Atrig, a member of Terrell's team, with the map that led to the second Orb?

Dukat loomed over Nortron. "I beg your pardon," he thundered. "But am I to understand that Obanak is *already* aware of the second Orb's location?"

Nortron almost gagged in his terror, clearly not knowing how he should answer such a question. "I . . . well . . . he had the map . . . so maybe he looked at it . . . maybe . . . I don't know." Then, in a single stream of fear, Nortron wailed, *"Pleasedon'tkillme!"*

Dukat reared back. "What can I say? To me, you're dead twenty-five years. And who am I to argue with history?" Imperiously, he raised his left hand. It began to radiate with red energy even as Nortron began to whimper mindlessly.

And then Odo snapped the conduit cover loose and in a single movement swung it through the air to impact not Nortron but Dukat, in a stunning blow to the side of his head.

The Andorian squealed like a stuck Tellarite and ran off, thick legs pumping like a prime athlete's.

Dukat was slammed into a bulkhead, then whirled around, dark blood running from his mouth, his red eyes literally afire.

"Too late, Odo!" he cried out, ducking. the changeling's second wild swing to charge down the corridor in pursuit of the shrieking Andorian.

Odo raced after him, joining the chase, rushing around

the next intersection in time to see Dukat direct a blast of red energy from both outstretched hands.

The double energy discharge struck Nortron square in the back, stopping him instantly.

Enveloped in a scarlet haze, the Andorian's corpulent body rose into the air, tossed violently back and forth in the grip of a power Odo had never witnessed before.

Odo raised the conduit cover above his head to swing it down again on Dukat.

But without turning, Dukat swung one hand away from his attack on Nortron and pointed it behind him to fire energy not at Odo but at his improvised weapon.

The conduit cover splintered, useless; shards of it dropped from Odo's hands.

Then the energy glow surrounding Nortron faded. The Andorian's body stilled, dropped to the deck, and lay there, unmoving.

Odo stared at Nortron's body. Its position exactly matched that in which Odo's security team had found it, when the Andorian was discovered killed by an energy blast of some unknown type.

The power of a Pah-wraith from an impossible future . . .

Now Dukat spoke directly to Odo, but without looking at him, letting the changeling know that his presence was suspected, although the Cardassian still could not see him.

"Don't you understand, Odo? You don't belong in this time anymore. So there's nothing you can do to change it."

"You seem to think *you* can," Odo muttered, not caring if Dukat heard him, as he looked about him for a new weapon.

"But," Dukat continued, moving his head back and forth as if addressing an audience of thousands, "I do belong here. Because the Amojan is a timeless being. Vengeance without end." Dukat sighed as if he still had more to say but had run out of time to say it. He looked down at Nortron's lifeless body. "From the few station logs remaining from the fall of Deep Space 9, I know you never solved this crime. But as you can see, it was *always* me. I hope you feel better now. Your perfect record will no doubt bring you much solace when you find yourself back in your own private *hell.*"

With that, Dukat's hands flared with energy as he abruptly lifted them and thrust them forward, and Odo barely had time to twist his body out of the way of the blindly aimed attack that sprayed along the corridor.

"Amojan, your will be done in the Gateway, as it is in the True Temple," Dukat vowed, then turned and stalked off down the corridor.

Odo slowly got to his feet, wondering if Dukat truly thought he had been successful in banishing him from this timeframe. But if that's what the Cardassian *did* think, then Odo wasn't about to object. He remained motionless so as not to make any sound, only moving when he was certain Dukat was gone.

Then Odo hurried over to Nortron. At the very least, he'd change the body's position to make it look more like the murder it was. *In fact,* he realized, *this is the perfect place to write a message to Captain Sisko.*

A long-missed feeling of relief came over Odo. All he needed to do was to find a shard of the shattered conduit cover, then use it to scratch a message into the bulkhead. Odo was certain his own security staff would notice it when they recorded the crime scene, and within hours, he could be communicating with Sisko—and even this timeframe's version of himself—over a computer link.

Odo picked up a shard from the conduit cover, judged the sharpness of it with his thumb. It was perfect, easily able to mark the soft decorative metal used in sections of the wall panels on this level.

He returned to Nortron's body, already composing his message.

Such a simple thing to change history, he thought. Then he held the shard to the bulkhead and—

—was struck by a flash of red light so powerful it felt distinctly like a physical blow.

Odo fought to keep his balance and then noticed with dismay that both his hands were pressed against the bulkhead for support, the shard gone.

He stepped back unsteadily, looking down at the deck for what he had dropped. And then he realized it wasn't the only thing now missing.

Nortron's body was also gone.

In its place, the telltale crime-scene seals and forensic markings of his security investigation of Nortron's murder.

"I've gone forward," Odo said aloud. It was the only explanation. But how far?

He stumbled as he ran through the corridors to the turbolift, too exhausted to propel himself in his fluid form.

He staggered off onto the Promenade, intending to go to his office.

But there was no need to search for his answer there.

It was right before him.

In the flickering, shifting bands of red-colored light that played across the Promenade's deserted expanse.

Odo lurched forward, bitter with the realization that he had come too far into the future, *past* the moment of DS9's destruction.

Through the overhead viewports on the Promenade's second level, he saw the energy displays of the red wormhole.

His mission had *failed.*

The Pah-wraiths had won.

Again.

CHAPTER 12

SISKO AND KIRA left Quark's, heads bowed, faces hidden by the robes they wore, to find a place to talk.

"The one good thing about the Orb being missing is that it tells us that the timeline *can* be changed," Kira said. "That means we can do it, too."

"But how?" Sisko asked her. "If we do get swept back to an earlier time on the station, then it's obvious we *don't* succeed, because if we had, the Orb would have been back in its hiding place." Hearing his own words, Sisko sighed. The grammar of Federation Standard was not equipped to deal with time travel.

He and Kira came to a tangle of fallen metal that was all that remained of the old security fence that once had bisected the Promenade into its Bajoran and Cardassian halves, and carefully stepped through it. The stores up ahead were dark, but at least the deck itself had been cleared of major obstructions. Sisko vaguely recalled that the initial clean-up crews wouldn't return to deal with the minor debris until the rest of the big pieces elsewhere had been cut up and carted away.

"Then maybe this is an alternate timeline," Kira said. "I mean, with the Orb missing from the place we found it, or will find it, six years from now, it's sure not the timeline we started in."

Sisko risked looking up to the viewports on the Promenade's second level. Bajor was bright in them, and close. Somewhere higher up, he knew, he himself, six years younger, was now in Ops, taking the stairs to his new office, listening to Kira give all the reasons why Starfleet's mission here wouldn't succeed, why Bajor would succumb to civil war in weeks, why . . .

He couldn't stop the ironic laugh that escaped his lips.

"We've had this conversation before," he said to her. "Except the last time, you were the negative one."

Sisko saw the major's confused expression, so he glanced up again, lifting a hand in the direction of Ops. "Remember what was going on about now?"

At that, startled, she gave a sharp laugh as well. But a tight one and only for a moment.

"So now I'll think positively," Sisko said. "Given current conditions, how do we accomplish what we set out to do?"

Kira shrugged. "Find Weyoun. Take the Orb from him. Put it back into its hiding place in Quark's."

"No, Major," Sisko said. "That *restores* the timeline. Somehow, we have to change it."

"All right. We put a message into the computer," Kira said. "Encrypt it, bury it in some database with a time-release code, so it . . . it shows up on your padd the day before those Andorians arrived and all this started."

But Sisko shook his head. "I thought about that, but remember all the work we've done on these computers in the past six years. More than half the components have been replaced. The programming has been lost and restored more times than . . . than I can remember. We can't count on anything we input today remaining accessible or executable when we need it to be."

Kira ran a hand through her short auburn hair. "So how else can we leave a message to warn ourselves?"

"Maybe," Sisko said, ". . . maybe we should just go up to ourselves now."

But even before he had finished uttering his suggestion, Sisko saw the major's objection register on her open face.

"Captain, you heard Prylar Rulan. Eilin was clear about the dangers of altering history."

"How could it be *history,* Major, if Eilin wrote his texts in the time *before* B'hala? That's more than twenty millennia ago."

"Twenty-*five* millennia ago," Kira corrected. "Eilin wrote his texts at the same time Shabren wrote the Prophecies. And the Fifth Prophecy came true, *exactly* as written."

"Not exactly," Sisko corrected her in turn. "The Prophecy said there would be a thousand years of peace if the Prophets defeated Kosst Amojan during the Reckoning."

Kira nodded vigorously. "That's right—*if.* The Prophecy said the confrontation *would* take place. It said *where* and *when* and *who* or *what* would be involved. And all those details fell into place precisely as foretold. But the one thing Shabren didn't say was who would *win* that confrontation. Don't you see? When the Prophets gave Shabren the gift of the Orb of Prophecy, they held back just enough to ensure that free will would still be the deciding factor. We're not their puppets or their playthings—"

Bridling, Sisko interrupted her. "I have never suggested that we are, Major."

"Maybe not said it. But you're feeling it now. I can tell by the way you're thinking about what we should do. As if . . . as if we should abandon the Prophets."

Sisko hesitated. He knew that at any other time, his instant response—and the response Kira would expect of him—would be to state emphatically that he would never abandon the Prophets. But this time, something held back his words, and he didn't know what it was.

"You see, you don't even know what choice to make, do you?"

Feeling overwhelmed, experiencing it again the way he remembered he had when first seeing it, Sisko looked up and down the Promenade. "Why . . . why would the Prophets make that choice so difficult?"

"You made a more difficult choice, once," Kira reminded him. "When you let the Reckoning proceed, even though your own son's life was at risk."

Sisko nodded. That day, that decision, still woke him from his sleep. "But that was different," he said slowly. "The conflict was clear-cut, well defined. I had no doubt what it was the Prophets wanted." He spread his arms to the ruins of the Promenade. "But this . . . how can linear minds comprehend what we're facing now? Isn't it easier to be a Starfleet officer? Because my duty here *is* clear-cut. To save Starfleet, the Federation, and the universe."

Kira raised a skeptical eyebrow. "By breaking every temporal translocation regulation in the book?"

Now it was Sisko's turn to remind her. "The regulations of *today*," he said. "Not of the future, Major. Even Starfleet recognized that drastic action must be taken. That's why they built Picard's *Phoenix*."

But Kira was already shaking her head. "They didn't build it to *change* the past. They wanted to put in position a weapon that would let them *save* the present. There *is* a difference, Captain. I believe Starfleet was being true to its ideals, even then."

"And if so, what did it get them?" Sisko asked angrily. "Nothing!"

Kira responded to his outburst with equal passion of her

own. "Which tells me that if you think there's a conflict between following the Prophets and being a Starfleet officer, then you're wrong! In this case, we know what being a Starfleet officer means: failure."

Now Sisko felt the touch of Kira's hands on both his arms, as if she worried that he might be getting ready to storm off, which he was. "I'm not saying that for you choosing the Prophets is always the right choice, or the only choice. Sometimes, I know you've *had* to choose Starfleet. And I'd argue that even those decisions ended up serving the Prophets eventually, in ways we couldn't foresee at the time. But here and at that moment. . . ." Sisko had never seen a look of such desperation or of such hope on Kira's face as she stared up at him at that moment. ". . . Emissary, if ever there was a time to trust the Prophets and their servants, this has got to be it."

Having delivered her speech, the major dropped her hands from Sisko's arms and stepped back, awaiting his answer.

Sisko looked away, unthinkingly adjusted the strap of the heavy radio he carried under his robes, trying not to think that the fate of the universe itself might rest on what his decision would be. Eventually, he turned back to face Kira.

"Major," he began, "my one hesitation, my one doubt that I just . . . can't overcome is that the *Bajorans* recognized me as the Emissary, but the Prophets did not."

"I know," Kira said. "Not at first. But it seems like the Prophets' acceptance of you . . . that changed, didn't it?"

Sisko nodded, not sure what her point was.

"Because, in time, the Prophets came to trust *you*."

"In time," Sisko agreed.

Kira stared at him fiercely. "The Prophets are *never* wrong."

"But is that the same as *always* being right?"

It was clear to Sisko that even Kira had no answers left

for him. Just as clear as his own knowledge that he would be asking no more questions.

It was time to take action. To exercise free will.

To save the universe, or destroy it.

Sisko made his decision.

Odo walked slowly to his office, still feeling disoriented by his latest transfer, shielding his eyes from the blinding blasts of red energy that lit up the Promenade's upper-level viewports. He had concluded that the flash of red light that had propelled him from the time of Dal Nortron's murder to this time in which the station existed within the red wormhole was related to the pressure equalization waves measured by Chief O'Brien.

Somehow, Odo thought, when those waves had washed over the *Boreth*'s bubble of space-time, they had affected him, as well, like flotsam on an ocean swell being pushed toward shore and then pulled away.

If that were the case, then there was hope that soon another flash of light—blue, this time—might shift him back into the past, before the station's destruction, when he could access a computer node to send urgent messages to Sisko and the command staff, telling them how they could change their present so this nightmarish future could never come to pass.

But as he walked around the Promenade's curve to see Quark's bar open and empty, and even his own security office apparently left unattended, the changeling realized the significant flaw in his reasoning.

When the Red Orbs had opened the red wormhole, he himself had seen the gravimetric effects rip apart the Promenade. Onboard the *Defiant*, he had witnessed the station's docking pylons buckle and the station's hub begin to deform like a wagon wheel twisting.

Yet everything here was intact. Perfect.

There had to be some explanation. But since he was a constable, not a temporal mechanic, if he was ever to find out what was really happening, he would need to contact an expert. Jadzia or O'Brien or—

"Hey, Stretch! Are you a sight for sore eyes!"

Odo whirled around in shock.

Shock that was multiplied a thousandfold as he said, "Vic?"

Vic Fontaine, a holographic representation of a quintessential Las Vegas lounge singer, circa 1962 Earth, elegantly clad in a formal tuxedo of his era, lifted a hand to wave happily at Odo as the singer quickened his approach.

Vic was a character in one of Dr. Bashir's role-playing programs. A clever combination of synthetic intelligence algorithms, holographic imagery, and micro-forcefields that could exist only within a holographically-generated environment. It was impossible for him to be on the Promenade, or anywhere else on Deep Space 9, except for the holosuites on the top level in Quark's.

"How . . . how can you be here?" Odo asked.

"I was going to ask you the same thing," Vic said. The holographic singer tugged on his collar and looked up at the viewports that seethed with red wormhole energy. "And I gotta tell ya, in person, space sure looks different from those photos in *Life* magazine."

"No, Vic, I'm serious. You're a hologram—"

"Thanks for noticin'."

"You can't be here."

"You don't have to tell me."

"So . . . *how* can you be here?"

Vic shook his head. "Okay, here's the story so far. I was doing my thing at a matinee. The power goes out. I find you and your pals locked up in some twenty-fourth-century hoosegow and spring the lot of ya. Then I amble back to my half of the program and let you guys take care of business."

"Yes, yes, I know all that," Odo said. That's exactly what had happened the day before the station had been destroyed. When Terrell had taken Sisko to Jeraddo to search for the lost Orb, she had imprisoned Odo and the others in a holographic version of Odo's security holding cells. Vic, perhaps the only holographic character with the ability to cross between programs of his own volition, had entered Terrell's simulation and set them free. "But what happened then?"

"Near as I can figure, one of those A-bomb tests the military runs out in the desert took a left turn. Big flash of light, thought it was an earthquake, then the power's out again and . . ." Vic's face took on an uncharacteristic grim expression. "Everyone sort of disappeared, Stretch. Like one moment I'm in the middle of panic city, telling the audience to walk not run to the nearest exits, and the next . . . I'm like Belafonte in *The World, the Flesh, and the Devil*, only there's no Inger Stevens, if you know what I mean."

"No," Odo said in bewilderment. "I don't."

"Everyone else *vanished*, Stretch. Everyone. And the other thing that's not kosher is that all of a sudden there's this crazy door in the middle of the casino that's got all these flashing lights and . . . where it leads to ain't exactly there, you know?"

"A holosuite arch?" Odo asked.

"Maybe it was the penthouse suite. How'm I supposed to know? But I step through it anyway. Y'know, maybe the little green men have come for me or something. But I figure, what've I got to lose?

"So, I step through, find myself on the top floor of what has got to be Ming the Merciless's favorite bar and grill, and when I ditch that joint . . ." Vic looked around again and shrugged.". . . I'm here in this circular shopping mall, with no doors to the parking lot. But with what's outside those big picture windows up there, I'm going to take a wild guess and say there *aren't* any parking lots. Am I right or am I right?"

From his reading of twentieth-century detective novels, Odo knew that a parking lot wasn't really a park of any kind. The hologram was right, and Odo told him so.

"So," Vic said, "my next guess is that this is that deep-space station you guys are always talkin' about."

"That's right."

"Whoa. Well, I can't stop now. I'll turn over all the cards and say, 'Something's gone haywire.'"

Odo tried to remember if that was a reference from a cowboy novel.

"You know—screwy," Vic said. "Messed up. SNAFU."

"Not right," Odo suggested.

"Now you're cooking."

Odo took that as agreement.

"So," Vic continued, "from what I remember, this station of yours is supposed to be crawling with crew members, visitors, a regular McCarran in space."

Odo understood what Vic meant if not his exact words. "Everyone's vanished from here, too."

"So . . . I'm no Einstein, but that makes me think that somehow what happened to your joint and what happened to mine are connected."

Odo nodded, remembered a phrase Captain Sisko liked to use. "You're batting a thousand."

Vic smiled and cocked a finger at Odo as if firing a phaser. "Good one, Stretch." But the smile was short-lived. "So, any twenty-fourth-century ideas about what we can do about the whole megillah?"

Odo suddenly had an unnerving thought. "Vic, how long have you been walking around the Promenade?"

"The mall?" Vic asked. "I don't know. Twenty minutes or so. Is it important?"

Odo didn't know the answer to that question. But he felt

confident that he hadn't been thrust into some Pah-wraith-generated hell concocted expressly for Vic Fontaine. Otherwise, the hologram would have thought he had been walking for centuries, if not millennia. Still, there had to be some explanation for how Vic managed to exist where there were no holo-emitters. Just as there had to be an explanation for how this once-ruined station was now intact and, judging from the lights and the breeze from the circulating air, fully operational.

Then Odo had it. "This is an illusion," he said.

"Hey, hold on, Stretch. A guy could get a complex from talk like that."

But Odo shook his head. He was beginning to make sense of his surroundings. "No, *you're* not an illusion, Vic. But everything around us . . . it's not what we'd normally call reality."

"Speak for yourself, pallie," Vic said. "My reality is Vegas. And this place is definitely not normal. Not that Vegas is all that normal to begin with."

Odo suddenly held out his hand. "Shake," he said.

Vic gave him a 'Why not' look, took his hand, and pumped it. "Was that supposed to prove something?"

"I think so," Odo said. "Let's go to my office."

"Lead on, MacDuff."

Odo knew things would be simpler if he ceased asking Vic to explain himself. So he just nodded at the hologram and continued on to the security station.

"You see," Odo said as they walked on together, speaking more to help himself understand his situation than from any expectation that Vic could follow his reasoning, "I was just in another version of this station. As it existed a week ago, more or less."

"Whatever you say, Stretch."

"And while I was there, I could touch the walls, I stood on the deck, I could even press controls on a communication node. But I couldn't touch anything that was alive or that was closely connected to anything that was alive. I couldn't even make anyone I saw or heard see or hear me."

Vic stopped at the entrance to Security. "I can tell you right now, I don't like where this is going."

Odo stopped as well. "I don't understand."

"Hey, you made me shake hands with you. And I can hear every word you say . . . even if a lot of them don't make all that much sense."

Odo stared blankly, waiting for some clue to what Vic meant.

"It's like you're saying because I can see you, hear you, and feel you, I'm not real—like I don't exist."

"Ah," Odo said, at last understanding Vic's concern. "You're seeing things from a twentieth-century viewpoint."

"Like I have a choice?"

"In this time, we recognize that life comes in many different forms. The majority of those forms are biological, and they're what I was referring to. You're a special case."

Vic looked skeptical. "Don't humor me."

"I'm not. You're what we call an isolinear-based life-form." In fact, Odo admitted to himself alone, he really didn't know if Vic actually *was* a life-form or not. At the one extreme, he knew there were artificial entities such as Lieutenant Commander Data of the *U.S.S. Enterprise*, who was unquestionably a living being under Federation definitions. At the other extreme, there were the Starfleet Emergency Medical Holograms, some of whom, like Vic, were prone to exhibit characteristics and behaviors that had never been intended by their programming. Dr. Bashir had told Odo of the debate raging within Starfleet Medical over whether or not the EMHs were evolving into true self-awareness, or were simply uncannily accurate reconstructions of the irascible Lewis Zimmerman.

But given current conditions, the changeling saw no need to hurt Vic's feelings, real or simulated as they might be.

"I was only pointing out," Odo said in conclusion, "that I seemed to have no connection to *biological* life-forms. But since your consciousness—" *If that's what you have,* Odo thought. "—arises from the station's computer system, it's as easy for me to interact with you as it is with this door." At that, Odo tapped his code into the door of the security station and it slid open. Then he gestured for Vic to step in first.

Vic maintained his skeptical expression. "You're pretty smooth, Stretch. So I'll take what you said under advisement. But the big question still remains: How come you and I are the only two cats on the station?"

To Odo, the answer was simple. "Everyone else was either evacuated or . . . or died, I imagine, when the station entered the red wormhole. I escaped on the *Defiant* and, to make a long story short, came back. In your case, well, obviously, since the station still exists and all its equipment is functioning, entering the wormhole wasn't harmful to you, either."

Vic blew out a deep breath, as if giving up. "You any relation to Rod Serling?"

To Odo, the name Rodserl had a Romulan sound to it, but he guessed he was safe simply shaking his head.

"Coulda fooled me," Vic said, then walked into Odo's office. "So where does all this fancy gobbledygook leave us? Are things ever going to get back to normal or a reasonable facsimile thereof?"

Odo sat down behind his desk, saw that all his computer systems were on-line. "There's a chance."

Vic sat on the edge of the desk. "Enlighten me."

"All right," Odo said as he began to access the station's main science logs, "we're in a wormhole."

"Let me guess. That's the twenty-fourth-century way of saying we're up the creek without a paddle."

"Exactly," Odo said, not knowing if it was or not. But

time was of the essence. "And the first time Sisko and Dax went through it, they ended up together but in two different realities." Odo glanced up at Vic, wondering if he was making any more sense to the hologram than the hologram was making to him.

Vic had tilted his head to one side and was regarding him with narrowed eyes. "You keep going. I'm just trying to imagine how'd you look with a beret and goatee." The hologram paused. "Ever think of playing the bongos?"

"Not . . . really." Odo looked back at his security screen, accessed the station's last hour of sensor logs. "Anyway, what Sisko's and Dax's experience seems to suggest is that a great deal of what we experience within a wormhole environment is subjective. But the fact that . . ." Odo hesitated, thinking of how Dukat had appeared to him on the desolate surface of the world that had once held the Great Link. How could he convey that to Vic? "The fact that you and I are both sharing this subjective reality of the station tells me that somehow there is an underlying reality to everything that's happening in here."

"Okay. Ya lost me back at that wormhole thing, pallie."

Odo called up the sensor log's gravimetric profile of local space and watched it play back at ten times normal speed. Keeping the record was a standard function of the station's sensors, one of the several dozen methods used to track and measure the opening and closing of the Bajoran wormhole. "Think of Las Vegas," Odo suggested as he watched the display.

"All the time," Vic sighed. "All the time."

"But where you live isn't really Las Vegas."

"Ooo, you don't pull any punches, do ya, Stretch?"

"But it's still Las Vegas to you. Just as it's Las Vegas to me when I go into the holosuite. And to Dr. Bashir. And Kira . . . it's a shared illusion. And the fact that it's shared means that something independent of the people visiting it is responsible for creating that illusion."

"Whatever you say, Stretch."

Odo persevered. "So the same principle is at work here in the wormhole. It's full of illusions, but because you and I can share this one, it must have some kind of independent reality."

"So basically you're telling me that we're just in some kinda big holosuite in the sky?"

"That's one way of putting it," Odo agreed. Then he saw what he'd been waiting for: The first gravimetric fluctuations that corresponded to the alignment of the three Red Orbs of Jalbador in Quark's bar. "Got it," he said.

Vic craned forward to peer at Odo's screen for himself. "Got what?"

Odo slipped a memory rod into an access port to copy the sensor log onto it. "This is how the . . . the doorway to this particular holosuite opened. It shows how the structure of local space-time was deformed when the station was swallowed by the wormhole."

"And that's a good thing?"

The moment the screen went dark, Odo held up the memory rod. "This is the equivalent of a map. It shows the way *in*, so if we can somehow reverse the deformations . . ."

". . . it'll show the way out," Vic concluded.

Odo nodded, inexplicably pleased that a hologram could follow his logic.

"So?" Vic asked after a few moments of silence. "How do you reverse the deformations and get us outta here?"

"I . . . don't," Odo said. "I have to get these data back to Chief O'Brien."

"Is he evacuated or . . . you know?" Vic asked.

"Evacuated." Odo stood up.

"So . . ." Vic pointed to the ceiling. "He's out there?"

But Odo shook his head. "Actually, he's in the past. Or in the future, I suppose. From this frame of reference."

Vic held up both hands and shook them back and forth. "Okay, that's it. Now you're being just plain nuts."

Odo smiled, then pressed the memory rod to his chest, concentrating on an entirely new modification to his humanoid body. The rod sank into him like a log disappearing into quicksand.

Vic's eyes opened wide. "Man oh man, if that's legit, you could give Blackstone a run for his money."

Odo knew he *was* in a race, though not the kind Vic might mean. At any moment, he suspected a new equalization pressure wave would strike the *Boreth* and somehow fling him back to the station's past. And if he was correct about the special nature of biological life-forms within the wormhole, then he was confident that the memory rod would survive the transition encased within the newly formed pocket inside his body as if it were a standard medical implant. He stood up.

"What happens now?" Vic asked, without moving from Odo's desk.

"We wait."

"For what?"

"For me to be sent back in time."

Vic stared at Odo. "Okay for you, but . . . what about me?"

"If what I'm planning works, you'll be fine."

"So what's 'fine' mean in the twenty-fourth century?"

"You'll remember rescuing us from the Security holding cells, just as you do now. Then you'll remember singing to the matinee audience. And then . . . we'll all come in, just like we usually do, and none of this will ever have happened."

Vic's eyebrows arched. "You don't say?"

"You should be happy," Odo said.

"Why? You think I don't know what happens to the

regular-type light bulbs around here? Push a button, and pow! Lights out, pallie. No memory. No life. Just reappearing back at the start of the program and carrying on like it's the first time all over again. Odo, that sort of thing . . . scares me, okay?"

"I had no idea," Odo said truthfully. "But you *do* remember what happens from one run of your program to another, don't you?"

"I do now. But if what you're saying is true and none of this will ever have happened . . . then I *won't* remember it, will I?"

Odo shook his head.

"Which is sort of like . . . being erased, wouldn't ya say?"

Odo nodded.

"I don't want that to happen to me."

Odo understood. "No living being does."

"Living." Vic's wistful smile was full of irony. "What a way to find out you're alive—the day you find out you're going to die."

"No, no. You won't die," Odo said hurriedly, trying to reassure the hologram. "Your life will continue—"

"But from back then. Not from now."

"That's right."

"So *that* Vic Fontaine will live." Vic tapped his chest. "But this one, *me*, the *putz* who stepped out onto your fancy space station, won't."

"That's right," Odo reluctantly agreed.

Vic took a deep breath, got to his feet. "You know, I probably shouldn't know this about myself, but, well, you know the guy who programmed me?"

"Felix."

"Yeah. He sort of . . . set it up so I could get away with a few things here and there."

"So I've noticed."

"So I figured out what these memory cylinders are." Vic

nodded at Odo's chest. "Like the rod you just 'disappeared' into your chest."

Odo was amazed by what he knew Vic was about to ask. But he also knew there was no answer he could give that would satisfy the hologram.

"Vic . . . I can't take you with me."

"But you're taking that map."

"Well, yes, but when I give the information on it to Chief O'Brien and *if* he's somehow able to use it to knock this station out of the red wormhole back in the past, then *none* of this will have happened. Not for you. And not for me."

Vic stared at Odo. "What? *You* get erased, too?"

"That's right."

"Well, ain't that a kick in the head." Vic sat down again on the edge of the desk and fixed his unfocused gaze on the wall.

"Are you all right?" Odo asked.

"Well, yeah . . . it's just that . . . well, I never really thought that you guys could, you know, *be* erased, or die, or whatever ya call it when you're biological."

Odo was thoroughly puzzled by Vic's sudden confusion. "Vic, exactly what do you think *we* are?"

Vic looked over at Odo with haunted eyes. "C'mon, Stretch. Ya come and go like ghosts. You're always talking about living in space, and in the future, and . . . well, between you and Spots and Worf and the little guys with the big ears, you sure don't look like any of the cats I grew up with back in Hoboken."

"So what does that make us?" Odo asked. He was absolutely baffled by the idea that any hologram might have a belief system that was different from the worldview created by its internal programming.

"You tell me," Vic said. "I mean, what do you and your friends think *I* am?"

Odo didn't even have to stop to think about the answer. "A friend," he said.

"I like that," Vic said. "Don't get me wrong—being erased really bugs the hell outta me. But being your friend, I can . . . I can live with that."

"I'm glad," Odo said. He checked the time readout on his desk. When he had beamed onto the station from the *Boreth* on the day Dal Nortron had died, he estimated he had spent approximately thirty minutes in that timeframe before jumping ahead to this one. Since O'Brien had noted that the waves would come closer and closer together, Odo had assumed he would have less than thirty minutes to spend in this timeframe, and he was almost at twenty-five minutes already.

"So, how do you go back?" Vic asked. Then he laughed as if it was the most ludicrous thing he could say. "In time, I mean?"

"I'll see a flash of light," Odo answered.

"Any idea what I'll see?"

"No."

"Will you be back?"

"Not to this timeframe."

"So, it'll just be me and . . . nobody."

Odo suddenly realized the paradox Vic had stumbled upon. Certainly, if everything worked out as Odo now hoped, and O'Brien *was* able to change the past, *that* version of Vic would have no knowledge of the events following the destruction of the station, because that destruction would never have occurred.

But in that case, *this* Vic would inhabit an alternate timeline, completely alone.

"Talk to me, Stretch. This just ends, right? I forget all about it? Go back to the ways things were?"

Odo didn't know what to say to comfort the worried-looking hologram.

Vic got back to his feet. "Hey, c'mon, pallie. This is Vic. Ya gotta talk to me. Ya gotta tell me this is going to work out."

"I . . . I really don't know," Odo said. "There're so many possibilities . . ."

"Are you telling me I might be stuck here by myself forever?"

"But there'll be other Vics . . ."

Odo winced inwardly as the hologram's voice rose with his concern. "I don't care about *other* Vics. Hell, Felix has probably sold copies of my program halfway to Timbuktu and back again. I care about *this* Vic."

"So do I," Odo said, struggling to think of a way to help the hologram. Could it be possible to copy him onto a memory cylinder? Was Vic's consciousness purely digital and totally transportable from computer to computer? Or was there an analog component to it that meant the hologram would not remain 'Vic' when copied from the computer system he inhabited at this moment?

"Stretch . . . ?" Vic said, plaintive. "Don't leave me here."

Odo opened his mouth to say something, anything that might ease Vic's growing fear of loneliness. But the instant he did, a flash of blue light of unbearable clarity struck him with a physical impact that shot pain through his body, focusing like a laser on the center of his chest.

When the light faded, Odo was still in his security office, but Vic was gone.

Odo checked the time display.

Stardate 51885.9. A day and a half after Nortron's murder. Three and a half days before the station would be destroyed.

Odo placed a hand on his burning chest, focusing on flexing muscles not naturally found in most humanoid bodies.

The memory rod passed through his simulated Bajoran tunic and into his hand.

He went to his security desk and slipped the rod into the access port.

The data—detailing an event that would not happen for another eighty-seven hours—downloaded perfectly.

But Odo knew that if he provided these data to O'Brien today, or to Dax, then the chances were that they wouldn't have need of them.

Instead, Sisko and his staff would make certain that the three Red Orbs of Jalbador would never be brought aboard this station, let alone brought into alignment.

"But what happens then?" Odo asked himself.

He thought of Vic stranded on an empty station in an alternate reality.

He thought of O'Brien and Garak and, yes, even of Quark on the *Boreth*. And the seven others with them, including Rom, waiting in a tiny bubble of space-time for a communication from him—for a sign that they would soon all be saved.

And in this time, Odo knew, they would all be saved. They would never travel into the future. The universe would not end in twenty-five years when the two wormholes were aligned and the Bajoran sun destroyed.

But in an alternate timeline, there would always be those whom he had consigned to an endless existence in an endless nothingness.

He stared at the gravimetric sensor log on his desk's display screen. Sometime in the next twenty to thirty minutes—however long it would be until the next pressure wave struck in a flash of red light—he could save the universe simply by inputting a warning into the station's computer system.

But if he did, then who would save his friends?

Odo struggled to think of a third possibility.

Because, for now, taking one path at the cost of the other was a choice he could not—would not—make.

CHAPTER 13

JAKE KNEW BETTER than to get in Worf's way, so he stayed in position at his auxiliary console while the Klingon thundered from the bridge.

But even though he had seen his father transport safely from the *Defiant* with Major Kira, Jake couldn't help imagining the worst.

"Dax?" he called out over the harsh staccato of the transporter alarms.

The Trill scientist had also remained at her station, and her eyes were fixed firmly on her displays. "It'll be all right, Jake. Worf can handle it."

"But handle what?"

"Someone probably got tired of waiting," Jadzia said reassuringly, "so they had themselves transported over on the same settings I used for your father and Kira."

"But what if whoever it is gets caught by the Cardassians or . . ." Since arriving in the future, Jake had learned more than he'd ever known about the potential consequences of creating new timelines. And what he'd learned was worrying him. What if his father and Kira set up one alternate past, and whoever had transported after them inadvertently set up another? That particular scenario could lead to the *Defiant's* being unable to maintain contact with *any* version of DS9.

But Jadzia didn't seem interested in leading him through another discussion of temporal physics. "Jake, right now, our job is communication. Just watch your board. Let Worf deal with security." As if to underscore her instructions, the alarms stopped just as she finished speaking, their cessation suggesting the situation had come under control.

Jake sighed, and for a moment his concentration diverted to his hand which he saw trembling above the controls at his station. It was time he got himself under control.

"Are you cycling for different time signatures?" Jadzia asked him.

Jake sprang back into action and input the sequencing code that would start the process. "Yes, sir," he said. *Focus,* he thought. Jadzia was searching for a radio signal from DS9, timeshifted by the same degree as the navigational timecodes the station was transmitting from the Day of Withdrawal. His job was to look for any other unexpected temporal perturbations generated by the wormhole environment that might obscure his father's attempt to communicate.

The overhead speakers hissed into life. It was Dr. Bashir from elsewhere in the ship. "Dax, I'm going to need your help in sickbay."

Jake looked over at the Trill, caught her eye. Someone was obviously injured. "Who is it, Julian?" Jadzia asked.

"Commander Arla. Weyoun came out of his trance or whatever it was. Beat her up badly. Then transported off the ship."

"Sorry, Julian. I can't leave my station."

"She has internal bleeding in her skull. I need an assistant."

"Then you've got at least nine other people to pick from." Jadzia did not look at Jake as the comm circuit went dead.

"Dax—Weyoun could change everything, couldn't he?" Jake asked nervously.

"I'm sure Worf is taking that under consideration." Jadzia's terse tone turned suddenly angry as Jake saw her hit her combadge sharply. "Dax to Bashir."

Bashir answered promptly, considerably calmer than before. "It's all right, Dax. I've got one of Simons's engineers to assist me."

But the Trill brushed his assurance aside. "I need to talk to you in private—immediately. Can you come to the bridge?"

Bashir's reply was indignant. "I'm not leaving my patient any more than you'll leave your station."

"Oh, for . . . Julian, step into the corridor."

Wondering what was going on but hesitant to interrupt Jadzia in her present mood, Jake studied his display, watching the spray of individual datapoints as they undulated up and down across the center screen. Out of the corner of his eye, however, Jake actually saw Jadzia's spots darken—he'd never seen her so upset before. But still, Jadzia kept her eyes on the console before her, and her hand moved rhythmically over the controls, continuing to carry out her duty.

"All right," Bashir replied a few moments later, exasperated. "I'm in the corridor. Now, what's this about?"

Jake's fingers continued to work at his own assignment, but his ears strained to catch Jadzia and Bashir's exchange for any clues to the Trill's concerns about Commander Arla.

"Arla came into the transporter room and watched me beam out Kira."

"So?" Bashir asked.

"So . . . she seemed too interested in the process," Jadzia said.

Jake immediately thought back to Arla's demeanor when she was in the transporter room, recalled the way the Bajoran commander had looked over Jadzia's shoulder with such close attention.

"As I recall," Bashir replied, "Arla's a Starfleet officer with limited starship experience. I would hope she would show some interest in procedures outside her field of—"

"Julian! Weyoun couldn't have beamed himself off the ship without help! There are no automated subroutines to handle transport in the absence of a subspace carrier wave."

Jake sat up straighter, not sure if he had heard Jadzia correctly.

"You're saying *Arla* beamed Weyoun off the ship?" Bashir asked.

"Well, *someone* had to have helped him."

Bashir didn't sound convinced. "So then who came up behind Arla and fractured her skull from behind *after* she operated the transporter?"

"I don't know," Jadzia admitted to Bashir. "I'm just suggesting you be careful with her."

"Suggestion noted," Bashir replied drily, then the circuit went dead again.

Jake heard Jadzia mutter something under her breath, knew it wasn't intended for him, but asked anyway to see if he could get her talking to him again. He had to find out if she had said what he thought she had.

"I'm sorry?" he asked.

"Nothing," Jadzia answered shortly. "I'm just surprised that given the situation, people aren't more concerned than they are."

Gathering courage for his next question, Jake visually tracked the sensor-scan advance to the limit of receptivity, then tapped in the sequence that told the sensor subroutines to begin again.

"Dax?"

"I'm here."

"The transporter . . . you said you couldn't set it on automatic?"

Jadzia's reply seemed unnaturally even-toned to him. "It's all right, Jake. I'm the most qualified transporter operator. I'll stay behind."

Jake stared at the Trill, unbelieving. "Does . . . does Worf know?" He couldn't imagine Worf allowing his wife to stay behind, to be lost with the ship.

Jadzia half-turned to meet his gaze. "What are you suggesting, Jake? That Worf would order someone else to stay behind and die so I could live?"

Put that bluntly, Jake knew she was right. There was another option. But Jadzia dealt with that one before he could even voice it. "And he won't stay behind, either. Worf knows he's not proficient enough to handle the beam manually under these conditions. If he even tried, he'd probably end up killing the last person to beam off. Besides," she said, "Worf has Alexander to think of. All my children—*Dax*'s children, at least—have already had full lives of their own. And I have lived seven lifetimes, while Worf hasn't even lived one. I know what I'm doing, Jake. So we don't have to talk about it anymore." She turned back to her console.

Jake looked back at his own display. A yellow spike flared out of the random noise.

"Dax! A signal on timeshift forty-seven!"

"What?"

Jake froze the sensor scan's progression before allowing himself to glance over at Jadzia, who was rapidly inputting a long string of commands.

"That's way out of bounds," she said. "Almost like it's a reflected signal instead of . . ."

The bridge speakers crackled with interference so intense that the computer couldn't remove it. But a new voice could still be heard within the cacophony.

"... *shifting with each ... lization wave ... days before Withdrawal ... weeks after ... Weyoun in phase but ...*"

A long hiss of static blanked out the rest of whatever was being said. But Jake had heard enough.

"Dax! That's my dad!" he said just as Worf entered the bridge.

"Have you made contact with the captain?" the Klingon asked.

"We're definitely getting something," Jadzia said. "But according to the timeshift on the signal, it's not coming from the time we sent him to."

Jake heard his father speak again through the harsh static. "*Repeating ... Major ... and I arrived safely ... on target day. At first, we ... phase ... on living ... to the day I arrived on ... first time. We're ... equalization wave through time. ... First arrival, several days before With ... then ... when Starfleet ... but doesn't get caught in the waves like we ... other time signals ... over at once ...*" Then interference swallowed the transmission again.

Worf stood beside Jadzia. "The captain said he was repeating his message. Have the computer overlay each transmission we receive to build a complete version."

"Already on it," Jadzia confirmed.

Elation and anxiety in equal parts filled Jake. He turned toward Worf and Jadzia, unsure if he could—or should—leave his own station now. "That means he made it, doesn't it?"

"And Kira *and* Weyoun," Jadzia said. "But it sounds as if each time the *Defiant* gets hit by an equalization wave, they get moved through time by a few weeks or days."

"What does that mean?" Jake asked.

"I don't know," Jadzia confessed. "Clearly, we can beam off the *Defiant* to the station, but if we're somehow still connected to this pocket of space-time when the wormhole environment finally stabilizes, I can't be sure we'll stay in the past. We might get snapped back here and . . . disappear."

"What will it take to make you sure?" Worf asked.

Jadzia looked up at her husband. "I'll need to have readings taken during a temporal shift on the station, then compare them to the readings I already have from this side."

"Then you will beam over now," Worf said. The short statement sounded a great deal like an order to Jake, despite what the Trill had said earlier about what her mate would do in these circumstances.

Jadzia stood up. "Sorry, Worf. I'm the best transport operator on the ship. Julian can take the readings I need and radio back the results."

From his own station, Jake tried to observe the two without being obvious. He understood they were dealing with something other than a Starfleet command decision. They were also a wife and husband. And perhaps the last hope the universe had of surviving in some form, in some timeline or another.

But for all the complexities of their conflict, Jake decided there must be advantages to their multilevel relationship as well. Because their argument ended before it had even begun.

"I will inform the doctor," Worf said gruffly. "Assemble whatever instruments you require him to take, then report to the transporter room."

Before Jadzia could respond, the main viewer flashed blue, and the *Defiant* pitched violently. Jake held on to his console to maintain his balance. Worf and Jadzia steadied each other.

The lights on the bridge flickered briefly before the ship's artificial gravity field returned to trim. And when

Jake next looked up at the viewer, Deep Space 9 now hung against a shifting field of red energy, not blue.

"The waves are speeding up," Jadzia reported. "Just as predicted."

"How much longer?" Worf asked.

"For the *Defiant*," Jadzia said as she glanced down at her console, "seven hours, three minutes. But the last twenty minutes are going to be rough, with waves hitting us every few minutes, then every few seconds."

"Then we will abandon ship before that happens," Worf said.

Sharing a brief, intense look at her mate, Jadzia nodded. "I'll . . . go get what Julian will need."

"And," the Klingon added, "when you have beamed him to the station, you will then work with the computer to automate the transport sequence so that—" Worf harshly cleared his throat before continuing. "So that . . . when the time comes, the last crew member will be able to beam off as well."

Jake could see that Jadzia wanted to argue about that, but again it was as if a burst of micropacket communications was exchanged between the couple, relieving them of the necessity of arguing with spoken words.

"I'll get on it," Jadzia agreed. She leaned down to tap some controls at her station. "Jake," she glanced over to his station. "The computer will continue to record anything your father transmits. But you stay here and listen for any changes we should know about right away."

Jake nodded.

Then Jadzia left the bridge, followed by her Klingon mate. Just at the door, Worf stopped and turned to Jake. "I must talk with Dr. Bashir." The Klingon looked around the otherwise empty bridge. "It would seem that you have the—"

"Oh, no, I don't," Jake said, though he knew his reaction differed from the one everyone else onboard the ship would give in his position. He pointed to the twenty-fifth-century uniform he wore. *"Civilian advisor, remember? I'll watch the viewer and monitor communications, but . . ."*

Worf nodded. "Carry on."

Then Jake was left alone on the bridge of the *Defiant*.

With its empty center chair.

Where his father belonged.

Where Jake *knew* he would see his father again.

As far as Jake was concerned, no other choice was possible.

Julian Bashir dropped easily from midair, rolled once, and was instantly on his feet in total darkness, knowing exactly where he was. The smell of Quark's was quite unmistakable.

"Computer, lights please."

At once, he found himself standing within a flickering pool of light coming from a series of wall-mounted torches, looking out through a dramatic marble arch at a set of wide stairs descending to a small garden.

Bashir's stomach tightened. The holosuite was in use. He wondered how close he had come to being beamed directly into one of the suite's occupants or replicated props.

A deep snorting sounded behind him, and he spun around to see who else was with him.

Bashir's mouth dropped open. "Morn?"

The big Lurian was sound asleep, huge mouth agape, in the midst of a mound of red pillows on which sprawled the softly breathing forms of four or five, perhaps even six, web-fingered Laurienton spa girls wearing . . . not much, as far as Bashir could tell.

"Computer," Bashir whispered urgently, "lights down, please. Intensity one."

Half the torches were suddenly extinguished and the others reduced to the glowing radiance of coals.

Undisturbed and unaware, Morn snored on in the arms of his holographic companions.

Bashir looked around the suite as he shifted his radio under the ragged Bajoran trustee clothes he wore and tried to guess where the holosuite's arch might be. It wasn't self-evident.

"Computer," Bashir said in a low voice, "please indicate the exit."

A green square of light flashed on the far side of the mound of red pillows. But at the same time, a computer voice warned, loudly, "Credit will not be given for any unused time."

Bashir cringed and began running for the flashing green light, but it was already too late.

Morn stirred, sat up, rubbed at his eyes. His movements woke the spa girls as well.

Bashir was almost at the hidden arch when the Lurian caught sight of him.

Morn's blank look of alarm betrayed no personal recognition, and the doctor realized that meant he had arrived in a timeframe before his first arrival on the station.

Bashir put his finger to his lips. "Shhh," he said quietly to Morn. "Don't say a word."

Morn's tiny eyes narrowed in brief suspicion, but then a mighty yawn struck him and the Lurian shrugged as if to say he had no argument with his unexpected guest's suggestion. Morn's eyes began to close as he sank back into his soft pillows and the giggling spa girls, who once more curled up against him, their holographic contentment a mirror of his own.

Bashir nodded with a relieved smile, hoping that the bandage he wore over the bridge of his nose had been enough to disguise him in the low light, so that the Lurian wouldn't recognize the younger Dr. Bashir when *he* arrived on the station.

Then, casting off any worry about what could not be changed now, Bashir approached the flashing green light and asked the computer to show him the arch.

Seconds later, he was standing in the corridor outside the holosuites, releasing a deep breath as the door closed behind him.

From what Jadzia had been able to piece together of Sisko's garbled message, the doctor understood that he had most likely arrived on Deep Space 9 in a timeframe different from the one seen by the *Defiant*, though still connected to it. However, from his current position, it was impossible for him to know precisely which timeframe he was in. Morn, for instance, had been a customer of Quark's before the Day of Withdrawal, as well as after it. About all he could be certain of, Bashir thought, was that this day was *not* one of those on which the station had been plunged into chaos.

Now he moved cautiously along the corridor, heading for the balcony overlooking Quark's main floor. Creeping up to the railing, he looked down and saw—

Cardassians.

"Wonderful." Bashir sighed.

He had arrived *before* the Day of Withdrawal. And judging from the raucous laughter down below, the station's Cardassians were in no hurry to leave.

He backed away from the railing, trying to remember if there were any nearby Jefferies tubes he could escape into.

But his thoughts of escape ended when he felt the emitter node of a phaser dig into his back.

Without being told to, Bashir slowly lifted up his hands to show he was unarmed. Rough hands efficiently patted him down, located his Starfleet radio and modified tricorder, relieved him of both.

Then a deep voice said, "Turn around. Say nothing."

Bashir did as he was told but couldn't hide a flicker of recognition as he saw Prylar Obanak.

"You know me, don't you?" the prylar said.

Though Bashir knew that each interaction he had in this time could cut him off from his own time, he also knew he had to reply. "You . . . look familiar."

Obanak regarded him doubtfully. Then he reached behind himself to a bulkhead panel, pressing something the doctor could not see, until the panel popped open a few centimeters, revealing an access port.

Obanak waved his phaser—a segmented Cardassian model, Bashir noted—to make it clear that the doctor was to go first.

Bashir complied and found himself looking into a narrow service-access tunnel. The node of the phaser again prodded him in the back. Obviously, Obanak wanted him to proceed.

Squeezing through the opening, Bashir could see the tunnel ran for about four meters to a poorly-lit Jefferies tube. Quickly guessing it would take the broad-shouldered prylar more time to squeeze through the tunnel behind him, Bashir began formulating a plan to escape. But the instant he poked his head into the Jefferies tube, another phaser node found his temple.

"Slowly," was all the second voice said. But that was enough for the doctor to put his plan on hold.

The Jefferies tube was unlike any other Bashir had encountered in his time on DS9. More than half its lights weren't working. Of the few that were, most were flickering on and off erratically. The customary, pristine ODN conduits installed by the Starfleet Corps of Engineers were nowhere to be seen. And somewhere off in the shadows, a liquid badly in need of recycling dripped noisily.

The Bajoran who held the phaser node to Bashir's temple pushed the doctor to one side as Obanak twisted out of the narrow access tunnel with surprising agility for someone of his bulk. Crouching down beside Bashir, the prylar handed his phaser back to his partner. Then, with shocking, almost unnatural, speed, he leaned forward and ripped the bandage from Bashir's face.

"Human," Obanak said. He made the statement sound like an accusation.

"I'm not here to make trouble," Bashir said quickly. If Jadzia's reconstruction of Sisko's message was correct, sometime in the next hour—adjusting that timespan for differing rates of temporal flow—an equalization wave would pass over the *Defiant*. All he had to do, the doctor reminded himself, was stay alive for that time, and the wave would snap him into a timeframe on the other side of the Day of Withdrawal. *If* Jadzia's reconstruction was correct.

"Does that mean you support the Cardassians?" Obanak asked sharply.

"Of course not!"

"Then what are you doing here?"

Bashir's genetically-enhanced intellect whirled through and considered all his options at an accelerated rate. Most of all, he knew, he had to be sure not to introduce any changes into the past. But he also had to find Sisko and Kira. And, Bashir knew, since Kira had said that Obanak was part of the Bajoran Resistance, his best strategy was to trust the man. The only question was how little information could he reveal and still earn Obanak's trust in return.

"Can you tell me the date?" Bashir began.

Obanak and his partner exchanged a look.

"The Third Feast Day of Tral," Obanak said.

"I mean . . . the stardate."

Obanak squinted at him, judging him. "Who is the Emissary?"

Bashir froze. How could he reveal that information in

the past, before Captain Sisko had been identified by the Bajoran people? "I . . . I can't tell you."

Obanak nodded as if he had expected that answer. "But you know him?"

"Prylar Obanak," Bashir said, "you have to trust me. For the good of your people, you—"

He fell back as Obanak lunged at him. The prylar's massive forearm shoved against his throat, under his jaw, pressing with shocking strength, cutting off his flow of air.

"What does a human know about what's good for Bajorans?" the prylar growled.

". . . I'm on . . . your . . . side . . . ," Bashir wheezed.

Obanak did not reduce the pressure. "Then tell me— Who is the Emissary?"

The light in the Jefferies tube became even dimmer to Bashir as his field of vision shrank and darkened. Bashir's hammering pulse filled his awareness. If he died here, then nothing would change. He had to take a chance. It was the only choice.

". . . Sisko . . ." he gasped.

The constriction on his throat was gone. Bashir gulped in a burning rush of air and his hands flew to his bruised throat.

Obanak rocked back on his knees. "You see?" the prylar said. "That's all we needed to know. To give us a common ground."

"For what?" Bashir coughed as he took another deep breath and flexed his leg muscles as best he could in the cramped space.

"This is what you need to know," Obanak said firmly. "In five days, the enemy will leave the Gateway abandoned. The Temple will be in disarray. The Prophets will weep no more. Fourteen days later, the Sisko will arrive from the stars. Three times he will deny that he is the Emissary. Then even the Prophets will deny him. But that will be a test. For the Emissary will come to the Gateway not once on that day but twice. And the Temple at last will open its doors for all to see."

Bashir staring intently at Obanak, saw only resolve in his eyes, heard only conviction in his voice. "How do you know that?" he risked asking.

Obanak stared back. "I know how I know. The question is, how do you?"

But Bashir had done with taking chances. "Truly, all I can say is that I will be gone in less than an hour. If you give me back my radio and tricorder, I'll stay right here, won't cause any trouble, and events will unfold just as they . . . just as they should."

Obanak's partner's glance went to the radio and tricorder on the floor of the Jefferies tube.

Obanak frowned. "I'm disappointed in you," he told the doctor. Then he shoved Bashir to the side, forcing him to start to crawl forward down the tube. "Turn left at the fourth intersection," the prylar instructed Bashir. "And remember, the moment you make noise is the moment you die."

The crawl through the Jefferies tubes took ten minutes at least, and by its end, Bashir couldn't be certain which level he was on. But Obanak knew. Shoving past Bashir, the prylar unlatched an access panel, then dropped through into a large room beyond. Bashir, then the prylar's partner, followed immediately after.

To Bashir, the room seemed to be a storeroom of some kind, smaller than a cargo bay, perhaps one of the supply lockers on the level directly under the Promenade where storekeepers kept their stock.

Two small emergency wall-mounted fusion lamps provided light. Bashir also noted a cot against the bulkhead between two stacks of shipping containers. Almost everything appeared to be labeled in Cardassian radians. Bashir guessed the most likely explanation was that this was a hiding place for resistance members on the station.

"I'd really like my tricorder and radio back," he said.

Obanak took them from his partner, held them out of Bashir's reach. "And I'd *really* like some answers."

"Look," Bashir said, "you've told me that you know about events in the future. How the . . . the enemy will leave the Gateway, how the Emissary will arrive from the stars. Is it really so difficult for you to accept that maybe I know something about what's going to happen, too? Can't you just accept that . . . that we both obtained our knowledge from the same source?"

"That is not possible," Obānak said, handing Bashir's tricorder and radio back to his Bajoran partner. "I know what my source is. The source of my people and of my order since time began. But you are not of my people. You are not of my order."

"Yet I know what you know," Bashir insisted, looking at Obanak's partner, wondering whether or not, when the pressure wave came, he would have enough of a warning at least to retrieve his tricorder.

"Only two types of beings know what I know," Obanak said. And now Bashir heard the conviction in the prylar's voice begin to turn into threat. "Bajorans and Prophets. Are you a Prophet, human?"

"No."

"And you're not Bajoran. So . . . I'm at a loss."

For all his superior reasoning powers and abilities, Bashir couldn't see how he was going to get out of this. "Prylar Obanak, I promise you, someday I will be able to explain everything to you. But . . . I just can't explain today."

"Because you don't know, or because you won't?"

Bashir struggled to project conviction equal to that the prylar had shown him. "For those of us who have . . . knowledge of what is to come, we know the danger of revealing too much. And that's what I face now. If I reveal too much, I might change what I know must come."

For once, Obanak did not have a ready reply. Instead, he simply contemplated Bashir with a thoughtful expression on his broad, weathered face.

"Will you," he asked at last, "at least reveal the source of your knowledge?"

Bashir shook his head. Even that information might be enough to change the history he knew. "I'm sorry."

Obanak looked over to a corner of the storeroom, and Bashir suddenly had the shock of realization that there was a fourth person with them in the storeroom.

A person who now stepped from the shadows into the cool blue light of the fusion lamps, his bright red robes the color of freshly spilled blood.

"I've heard enough," Weyoun said.

Obanak bowed reverently. "Yes, Emissary."

Bashir almost choked. *"He's* not the Emissary!"

"He is the Sisko," Obanak warned. "Even you knew his name."

"He's Weyoun! He's . . . he's possessed by the Pah-wraiths!"

Obanak took a step toward Bashir but stopped obediently at a gesture from Weyoun. "The Prophets are known by many names," the prylar said. "And dwell in many places. Reconciliation of all Bajor and her Prophets is—"

"Obanak!" Bashir said forcefully. "I'm from the future! Do you understand? That's how I know what will happen. And I'm telling you that *this* creature is *not* your Emissary. He is—" Bashir's tirade ended in a cry of pain as a bolt of red energy slammed into his chest, driving him back against the storeroom bulkhead.

"That, good doctor," Weyoun said softly, "is quite enough of that." The Vorta moved forward until he stood over Bashir, looking down at him with a pious expression of dismay. "Tell your friends, whatever they try to do, I will undo. There are no alternate timelines. There is only the one True Temple and those who dwell within it. And unfortunately for you, Dr. Bashir, you are not in their number."

At that, Weyoun raised his hand, and a nimbus of red energy crackled across his fingers.

"Damn you," Bashir whispered, still almost completely paralyzed by the first blow Weyoun had struck, knowing what the second blow was likely to do.

Weyoun smiled with real amusement at the doctor's choice of words.

Then a blast of light obliterated Bashir's consciousness.

And his last thought was to wonder why the light was blue, not red.

CHAPTER 14

O'BRIEN FLUNG HIMSELF at Dukat, but he was a second—a lifetime—too late.

The Cardassian wrapped his arms around the Regulan phoenix that Odo had become even as the transporter beam dissolved them both into their fundamental quantum essence.

O'Brien's arms wrapped around nothing, and he tumbled to the deck of the *Boreth*'s bridge, skinning his chin on the rough Klingon carpet, the air knocked out of his lungs.

"That was not a good thing," Garak said.

"No kidding," Quark muttered.

"But . . . Dukat can't win in a fight against Odo," Rom said hesitantly.

"It's not just Dukat," O'Brien huffed as soon as he could breathe again. "It's that Kosst Amojan thing, too." He rolled over and awkwardly pushed himself up from the deck, straightening the annoying robes he wore. Then, limping slightly and feeling every year of his age, he returned to his science console, where Rom was checking its display.

"No sign of beam dispersion, Chief," Rom informed O'Brien.

"So we may assume they survived transport?" Garak asked as he strolled over to O'Brien and Rom.

O'Brien thought about that for a moment, uncertain. Maybe it would be better if his coordinates *had* been off, or if smugglers had filled the supposedly empty room with supplies. Maybe it would be better if Dukat had been beamed into solid matter and—

Suddenly, he moaned. "Why didn't I think of that before?"

"Think of what?" Garak asked with interest.

But O'Brien didn't waste his time answering. He glanced over at the main viewer. Deep Space 9 was perfectly centered against a sea of shifting blue energy. The chief engineer focused his attention on the station's navigation lights. Each one he could see blazed without interruption or blinked on and off as it was intended to.

"Chief?" Garak prompted.

"Look," O'Brien said quickly. "Let's say the transport went wrong—"

"Why not?" Quark groused from the other side of the bridge. "Everything else has."

"What I mean is," O'Brien continued, "if Odo and Dukat had materialized in a bulkhead, there would have been a helluva explosion inside the station."

"Of course!" Rom said excitedly. "We'd see a power fluctuation in the navigation lights! Uh, *did* we see a power fluctuation in the navigation lights?"

On his console, O'Brien played back the last sixty seconds of the viewer's automatic recorded image. The lights didn't vary. "No, but that wouldn't have been the only effect."

"Uh . . . there'd be a minor subspace distortion caused by the superposition of fermions in conflict with the Pauli exclusion principle?"

Quark had stalked over to see whatever was on O'Brien's displays for himself. Seeing nothing that made sense to him, he shrugged, then rolled his eyes at his brother's suggestion. "*That* sounds reasonable."

But that kind of distortion wasn't what O'Brien was looking for. "No subspace out here, Rom." The chief engineer couldn't resist the opportunity to be a teacher. "But you're right—there would be a different sort of energy signature produced by a matter interference explosion."

"Uh . . . another signature which we could detect . . . ?" Then Rom suddenly shouted, "Electromagnetic pulse!"

Quark stuck a finger in his ear and shook it back and forth, as if he had been deafened by Rom's outburst.

"That's it, Rom!" O'Brien said. "If visible-light photons can jump out of their space-time bubble and cross the wormhole environment to reach us, then any type of electromagnetic radiation should be able to do the same. That's how we detected the navigation time codes in the first place."

O'Brien checked the broad-spectrum radio-scan subroutine he had set up when he had tried to communicate with the *Defiant,* still a blurry gray disk in a corner of the viewer. When the technique hadn't worked, he had put the idea of radio communication to the side. But now he realized that he should have sent Odo over with a radio communicator—it would have been a far easier way to receive a message from the changeling than by having him switch docking lights off and on in code.

"No spikes," O'Brien said. "They made it."

"Poor Odo," Rom sighed.

"Chief O'Brien," Garak said, "I think our next step is obvious."

O'Brien gave the Cardassian a curious look. "Are you volunteering?"

"Present company excluded, Chief, you have your choice of the seven Starfleet crewmen in engineering, only two of whom have experienced regular duty on Deep Space 9. I believe I am the most qualified for what needs to be done."

O'Brien took Garak at his word. "All right, you're next. Rom, see if you can coax a high-powered radio communicator from one of the replicators."

"Right away, Chief!"

"Excuse me," Quark complained as Rom hurried off to the back of the bridge. "But Garak's next for what?"

"Beaming to the station," O'Brien said.

"Why him? If it's safe," Quark protested, "why can't we all go?"

O'Brien paused, sternly regarding the Ferengi. "Quark, all we know is that it *looks* safe. We won't *know* it's safe until Garak goes over there and radios back a signal to us."

"And in the meantime," Garak added politely, "there is the small matter of Dukat allowing Kosst Amojan to run rampant on the station." He held out his hand to Quark. "But if you insist on going over first . . ."

"Never mind," Quark said, then walked away.

O'Brien lowered his voice. "What *will* you do about Dukat?"

Garak shrugged noncommittally. "At the very least, he'll have to deal with *two* Odos, so the odds will be in our favor. And I'm certain Captain Sisko won't have forgotten that little trick of flooding the station with chroniton particles to . . . persuade the Pah-wraith to move on."

"In case he has forgotten," O'Brien said, "remind him."

"Oh, I'll do more than remind him, you can be sure." Then Garak lost his usual expression of equanimity.

"What is it, Garak?"

"I take it that we are officially giving up on any plans

we had of trying to preserve the timeline in some semblance of how we remember it."

O'Brien nodded. "I know. That went by the boards when Odo beamed over. And Dukat cinches it."

Garak responded with an expression of sadness O'Brien couldn't remember seeing before. "While I'm no expert in these matters, Chief, I feel obligated to point out that with so many opportunities for changing the timeline in. . . ." The Cardassian looked over at the viewer and the station it displayed. ". . . that past, it is conceivable that at some point the *Boreth* will . . ."

"Disconnect from the Feynman curve linking it to the station," O'Brien said.

"Exactly," Garak agreed.

"A chance we'll have to take."

"No," the Cardassian said gravely. "It is a chance *you* have to take. I daresay the others—" Now he looked back at Quark and Rom arguing beside the replicator slot. "—have no understanding of the ramifications of what you're planning."

O'Brien knew Garak was right, but that didn't stop him from being surprised by the Cardassian's concern for the rest of his fellow temporal refugees.

"You're a decent man," O'Brien said.

Garak smiled with an expression of delight, quickly repressed. "How kind of you to think so."

"After you go, I'll explain it to them. If we hear from you, I'll beam everyone over."

"And if you don't hear from me?"

"I'll beam the rest over anyway. At least . . . at least they might have a chance at turning up someplace else. They certainly won't have one here."

Garak nodded, then paused, looking O'Brien directly in the eyes.

"Now what?" O'Brien asked.

"Just the way you said that, about beaming the *rest*. You *will* be able to beam yourself over, won't you?"

O'Brien chuckled, surprised once again by Garak's concern. "You're damn right. Now, if this had been a Starfleet ship, I wouldn't be able to take manual control of the transporter in the absence of a subspace carrier wave. But the Klingons, they don't see the need for the same sort of safety protocols we do."

Garak leaned forward conspiratorially. "Personally? I find it one of those traits that makes Klingons rather endearing."

Sometimes, when Garak shared opinions such as that, O'Brien found himself wondering if the man really saw things so differently. But this time, he realized that Garak was simply making a joke. So O'Brien just smiled, wondering how many other times he might have misinterpreted Garak's intentions.

Garak nodded graciously. "I'll just stand over there, shall I?"

O'Brien nodded back. "All we need is the radio," he said. "Rom?"

Over at the replicator slot, Rom and Quark jerked guiltily at the sound of his voice. They both looked flushed. "I almost have it, Chief!" Rom cried out.

"Is there a problem?"

Rom shot a sideways look at the replicator, where a Klingon device clad in a light-brown metallic casing suddenly materialized. "Uh, not really . . ." Rom grabbed the device and hurried over to Garak with it.

O'Brien joined Garak to check the radio. The chief engineer glanced back at Quark, who had remained beside the replicator. "What's he all worked up about?" O'Brien asked Rom.

"Uh, the replicator," Rom said. "I guess in the future . . . uh, they've figured out how to replicate gold-pressed latinum."

O'Brien groaned. Quark and latinum. But lacking the strength to yell at Rom's brother for delaying the replication of the radio, O'Brien turned his attention to the device. Like most Klingon technology designed for field use by warriors, the Klingon radio's controls were simple and intuitive.

"Just remember," O'Brien began.

Garak completed the warning. "Brace myself for a drop."

At his console, O'Brien called up the transporter controls. "Stand by . . ."

"I will see you all on the station," Garak said.

But before O'Brien could energize the transporter, an unexpected voice cut in over the bridge speakers, breaking up and full of static.

"Repeating . . . Major Kira and I . . . arrived safely, but not on target day . . ."

O'Brien stared at the sudden radio spike on his broad spectrum scan, afraid to say the words already on his lips, scarcely believing they could be true.

But in the end, nothing could stop him.

"That's the captain!"

Bashir wasn't frightened. He had experienced death uncountable times in his Pah-wraith hell. What more could Weyoun do to him?

But then he realized his chest hurt. And his head hurt. And the bare metal deck was icy cold.

He opened his eyes. A single fusion lamp, almost exhausted, provided the only light.

He was still in the storeroom.

But Weyoun and Obanak and the other Bajoran were not. They had vanished, along with most of the crates.

I've shifted, Bashir thought.

His aches and pains forgotten, Bashir jumped to his feet. If Jadzia had interpreted Sisko's message properly, then he should be on the station sometime *after* the Cardassians withdrew.

Bashir took the fusion lamp from the bulkhead and peered into the corners of the storeroom, searching for any sign of his radio or tricorder. Nothing.

But that couldn't stop him from creating a plan. First, he had to sneak up to Ops to set up a radio link. Then he had to beg, borrow, or steal a tricorder that he could set to record during the next equalization wave event.

Everything would be fine—as long as he didn't run into Obanak and Weyoun . . .

"Oh, no," he said aloud.

Weyoun would have had days, if not weeks, by now to alter events on the station. Bashir shook his head. For all he knew, with Weyoun present to reveal the existence of the Bajoran wormhole, the Cardassians might not have withdrawn at all.

Bashir headed straight for the storeroom's door, put his ear to it, then tapped it open.

The corridor beyond was also poorly lit, but empty. Judging from the corridor's size and the tight curve it followed, Bashir decided he was correct in thinking he was in the shopkeepers' storage area, one level down from the Promenade.

Entering the corridor, he turned to his right for no particular reason, then set off at an easy run until he came to a Cardassian radian indicator. The sign revealed he was beside Turboshaft 3, which told him exactly how far away his Infirmary was. Bashir decided to go there first. Homeground was always best.

During his tenure on the station, he hadn't used the storage area beneath the Infirmary, primarily for security concerns. But Bashir knew there was a narrow stairway that led up to a supply locker off his small back office, and as he climbed it now, he was relieved to see the narrow doorway hadn't been sealed. That meant that he hadn't arrived on the station *after* he had first arrived on it, because one of the first things he had had the work crews do was to block off this doorway, which they hadn't yet done. Despite the seriousness of his situation, Bashir couldn't help smiling: The confusing thought actually made some sense to him, in a time-bending sort of way.

Bashir reached the top of the narrow flight of stairs. The small door before him operated by means of a manual lever, and he pushed against it, making the door squeak open.

What would eventually become his office was littered with debris, and all the lights were out. But light from the treatment areas filtered in through the half-opened main doors.

Bashir carefully picked his way over the mounds of trash on the deck and peered out through the doors, trying to catch a glimpse of who might be on the station. If he saw any Cardassians other than Garak, he'd know he'd have to stay hidden.

But all he saw was another blinding flash of light. Not red or blue, but white.

"What're you doing back there?"

Bashir realized that he hadn't been shifted through time again. He still had twenty minutes before that could happen. Shielding his eyes with his hand, he tried to look past the blinding light to see who was addressing him.

"Get out of there," the annoyed voice repeated. "Hands where I can see them."

Bashir squeezed out through the inoperative doors and felt a moment of unreality as he found himself standing in the middle of his Infirmary as he had never seen it before—looted, trashed, and not yet even marginally cleaned up as he had seen it on his first day.

"I said, who are you?"

Relief flooded through Bashir. The Cardassians *had*

left. His questioner was a Bajoran wearing an old-style militia uniform.

"Are there any Starfleet personnel onboard?" Bashir asked, blinking in the glare of the Bajoran's palm torch.

The Bajoran moved closer, keeping his torch centered on Bashir's face, specifically on the bridge of his nose.

"You're human?"

"I'm with Starfleet." Bashir guessed that would be a safe enough admission to make.

"Dressed like that?"

Bashir looked down at his trustee's rags. "I was . . . undercover."

The Bajoran muttered something that was obviously a curse but which Bashir didn't hear clearly enough to understand.

"Don't you people have any sense?" the Bajoran growled. "The Provisional Government is tying itself in knots trying to decide whether or not to invite the Federation in as observers. And the biggest thing you've got going for yourselves is that you've been neutral through the whole Occupation. But if the opposition finds out there are Federation *spies* in the system, the next thing you know, we'll be inviting the *Romulans* in to keep the peace."

Bashir's mouth went dry. If his presence here could lead to such a profound change in the timeline . . . if the *Romulans* discovered the wormhole . . . made contact with the Prophets . . . with the Dominion . . . the whole history of the galaxy and of the universe would change. And if the Romulans and the Cardassians formed an alliance and shared what they would undoubtedly learn about the wormhole and the Tears of the Prophets, it wouldn't take six years for the Red Orbs of Jalbador to be brought into alignment. It would take months.

"I'm not a spy," Bashir protested, but even he could

hear the tension that thinned his voice. "I only just got here. On a . . . a fact-finding mission."

"Dressed like a Bajoran slave?" the Bajoran said suspiciously. "We all burned those clothes a week ago."

A week, Bashir reasoned rapidly. *The* Enterprise *hasn't arrived yet. Starfleet is making contingency plans in case the invitation to observe the peace is actually made.* His mind raced as he thought back to where he 'was' in the week after Withdrawal: at the medical conference on Vulcan, torn between attending a lecture to be given by Admiral McCoy himself or contacting everyone he could think of back on Earth to lobby for the position of Chief Medical Officer on the mission to Bajor, should it come to pass.

"Is there any way I can at least *talk* to someone from Starfleet?" Bashir asked, urgent. "I know I can straighten this out without . . . without harming relations between Bajor and the Federation."

Obviously, the Bajoran was a Federation sympathizer, because he now took a moment to consider Bashir's request.

"Well, they've got some huge starship standing by outside the system."

"The *Enterprise?*" Bashir asked with hope in his voice. Captain Picard would be the perfect person to tell his story to. Starfleet would listen to him.

"I think so," the Bajoran said. "It's been sending in shuttles with humanitarian aid. I could maybe talk to one of the pilots."

"That would be best," Bashir agreed quickly. "And the quieter we can keep this, and the faster I can talk with someone, the less disruptive my presence here will be."

The Bajoran lowered his palm torch. "I'll see what I can do. But I'm still going to have to take you to Security. The constable has to—"

"Odo?"

"You know him?"

Bashir didn't want to give away more than he had to. "We . . . have friends in common."

"Maybe that'll help." The Bajoran gestured with his palm torch. "Walk ahead, and don't try anything."

"I won't," Bashir promised, thinking once more that everything might still work out after all.

Until Major Kira blocked his exit, dressed in her old uniform, hands on her hips.

"What the hell is going on here?" she demanded.

"Major," Bashir said in resignation, knowing the paradox he was about to create, "my name is—"

"I don't care who you are," the major interrupted. "You keep your mouth shut until I deal with *him*." She pointed at the startled Bajoran militiaman. "Is this human your prisoner?"

"Uh . . . yes, Major."

"I don't see any restraints. I don't see your weapon drawn. I don't recall having heard anything over the security channels. Is this your idea of an arrest?"

The Bajoran's face flushed. "I thought . . . he said he was with—"

"I don't *care* what he told you. You're on security patrol. *You* round up suspects. *I* do the thinking. Is that *clear,* Mister?"

"Y-yes, sir."

Kira waved her hand at the door. "Then you go do your job, and let me do mine."

The Bajoran nodded vigorously, then bolted for the doors leading out of the Infirmary, halting abruptly when Kira put a hand on his shoulder.

"We're all new at this," she said in a low voice. "So I'll let this go without a formal report. If you don't talk about it, I won't talk about it. I don't want anyone thinking I'm getting soft. Understood?"

"Understood, sir," the Bajoran said as if he couldn't believe his good fortune. A moment later, he was gone.

"How long have you been here?" Kira asked Bashir.

So many complications filled the doctor's mind that he remained silent.

"Julian, it's me," Kira said. "I'm *your* Kira, from the *Defiant*. Six years from now. From the end of the universe."

There was only one thing to do, and Bashir did it. He reached out and hugged her. Hard.

But Kira pushed him away. "Things are very complicated. We have to talk quickly. How long have you been in this time?"

"Ten minutes?"

"How much longer do you have?"

"At least ten more," Bashir said, still marveling at the sudden turn of events. "I came in before the Withdrawal. Weyoun told Obanak that he was the Emissary."

"I know," Kira said with a grimace. "Weyoun is somehow anchored in this timeframe. He doesn't shift back and forth, so he has a lot more time than we do."

"Time to do what?"

"To get the Red Orb from Terrell's lab. The captain and I are trying to get it, too. But . . . in the past, before the Day of Withdrawal, the lab is under heavy guard, completely unapproachable. And in this timeframe, it's abandoned."

"Then we'll have to get in *on* the Day of Withdrawal!" Bashir said. "That's the key time signal we're getting on the *Defiant*. So that's when the Orb effect must be strongest—the timeframe we're all settling toward."

"You've been talking with Dax?" Kira asked.

Bashir nodded. "Look, I need a tricorder and a radio. Jadzia needs readings from a timeshift event, and then I have to be able to radio back the results."

Kira frowned. "I've only got about five minutes left before I go back." She hit her communicator. "Major Kira to Ops. I need emergency transport for two from the Cardassian Infirmary to Cargo Bay 4. Lock on my signal."

A Bajoran voice answered. "Did you mean emergency transport *to* the Infirmary?"

"I meant what I said!" Kira snapped. "There might be Cardassian saboteurs still on the station. Now, *energize!*" She gave Bashir a rueful smile as she took his arm. "Back then, I really was a b—"

But the transporter effect muffled whatever else she was about to say.

A moment later, Bashir and Kira materialized in Cargo Bay 4.

"—wasn't I?" Kira concluded.

Merely smiling, Bashir offered no comment. Instead, he directed his attention to the gleaming shipping containers that surrounded them, containers marked with the Seal of the Federation. He found what he was looking for at once. General science kits designed to help in the construction of emergency shelters, to dig for water, to check for unexploded ordnance.

Kira helped him shift the crates and tear open the science kits. "You find a tricorder," Kira told him. "I'll check out the communication gear."

Bashir located and pulled out a Mark VII tricorder, which he hoped would be a satisfactory replacement for the Mark X Jadzia had given him. At the same time, Kira cracked open a communications package and brought out a Vulcan radio wand. She passed the thin green cylinder to him. It was no more than ten centimeters long. "This is intended for ground-to-ground communications, but since you only have to broadcast for under a hundred klicks . . ."

"It'll do," Bashir said, satisfied. "Where's the captain?"

Before Kira could reply, a familiar voice crackled from her combadge.

"This is Major Kira to Cargo Bay 4. What the hell is

going on down there, and who the hell is saying she's me?"

Kira looked at Bashir, grabbed hold of his arms to emphasize what she had to say. "Julian, this is important. We will *not* change the timeline. Understand? It is crucial that you do nothing that will change how events took place the first time."

Bashir was puzzled. He didn't understand.

"I said," the other Major Kira demanded, *"who's down there?"*

"But Weyoun must be changing things," Bashir said.

Kira shook her head. "As far as we can tell, he's keeping a low profile, too. All he wants is that Red Orb in Terrell's lab."

"That's it," the other Kira said over the combadge. *"Whoever you are, you are now encased in forcefields and under transporter lock. If you have weapons, I'd strongly advise you to throw them away and put your hands on your head."*

"Why can't we change the timeline?" Bashir asked *his* Kira. "What do you know?"

With a troubled look, the major gave Bashir's upper arms a squeeze. "Julian, trust me. It's the Will of—"

She looked to the side. Three columns of transporter light sparkled into being.

"Just trust me!" Kira said.

Then, once again, Bashir was blinded by light. And this time, it was red.

CHAPTER 15

THE UNIVERSE SEETHED, chaotic, and for Garak, there could be no greater pleasure than to study that confusion for the sole purpose of teasing out such random bits of order as the cultivated mind might discover.

The stuff of a sublime opera here. An intricately crafted novel there. The delicate composition of a landscape captured on an unknown artist's canvas. Even the meticulously orchestrated sequence of political upheaval following a flawless assassination.

All order was fleeting, which is why, Garak supposed, it brought such joy to civilized beings. And joy without despair was, of course, utterly meaningless, for one could not exist without the other.

That was why each snick of his scissors was as deeply satisfying to Garak as the pruning he had undertaken in the gardens of Romulus—pruning both that world's indigenous flora *and* fauna, as it were. To take a formless plane of cloth, each portion of it identical to the rest, and by a precise series of cuts and stitches create a three-dimensional structure that would, for a moment at least in the affairs of Cardassians, define his world's epitome of style and culture and civilization, was, for Garak, a way to achieve profound personal peace. Surely the ancient explorers of Cardassia's past could have felt no greater happiness upon first glimpsing the beacon of a lighthouse on the shores of the homeland to which they returned. So it was with Garak and the simple craft, the exquisite art of the tailor.

Thus, it was with contentment that Garak was engaged in cutting a particularly fine bolt of Remarlian wool to make a handsome hunting jacket when the chime of his tailor shop's door sounded, and he rose from his work to meet whatever new visitor, customer, perhaps even appreciator of art, whom chaos had selected to cross his threshold this day.

At first glance, the stranger was commonplace, as from the plain cut of his traveler's robe it was apparent he was a Cardassian civilian of limited means. But that was not surprising, given that fully eighty percent of Terok Nor's inhabitants were of Garak's species. It was only on rare, fortunate occasions that a glinn made arrangements to bring by one of the slight, pale-skinned Bajoran females that the Cardassian command staff seemed to hold in such high regard. It was always a particular challenge for Garak, and one he enjoyed for its novelty, to fashion flattering gowns for beings with such pathetically thin necks, unsettlingly smooth skin, and ill-hued complexions that warred with any reasonable color palette, so unlike the universal harmony of pure Cardassian gray.

"Welcome to my shop," Garak said with a gracious bow despite the poor amusement value the stranger offered. "May I offer you some refreshment? A cup of Linian tea, perhaps?"

Most delightfully, the stranger did do something quite

surprising then. Without removing his hood, he glanced furtively over his shoulder, as if looking out to the Promenade to see if anyone were following him.

Garak felt a flash of anticipation. He did appreciate a day that began with an unexpected touch, and actual intrigue would go a long way to brighten his mood.

Eager to make his mysterious visitor at home, Garak moved quickly past him to lock the door and tune the windows to their holographic display mode.

"As a matter of fact," he said cheerfully, "I was just going to close for a mid-morning break. Perhaps you might be more comfortable if you knew no one could disturb us. Or see into the shop, for that matter."

Garak turned his back to the sealed door and smiled in welcome to his visitor. And then it took all his powers of self-control to keep that smile in place as his visitor lifted his hood to reveal his identity.

"You're right," the second Garak said, "it would be best if we weren't disturbed."

Garak the tailor paused for the briefest of moments and then asked the most obvious question. "Odo? Is that you? If it is, I am most impressed with your new mastery of fine detail."

"Alas," the new Garak replied, "that *would* be the simplest explanation. Unfortunately, in this case, we are facing something much more complex."

"And that would be?"

"Exactly what it seems to be," the new Garak explained. "I *am* you."

"If that's the case, then you'll understand my skepticism."

"Oh, absolutely. I know exactly how I would respond to such a situation, so I am certain that is exactly how you are responding."

Garak the tailor felt his heart rate increase. It was most unlikely that the duplicate across from him was really himself, but what if he was? What a thrillingly puzzling conundrum *that* would be.

"If you know how I will respond," the tailor said carefully, "then you must know what my first suggestion will be."

The visitor returned the tailor's smile. "In the back room, third shelf, beside the tea jars. There is a dimensional safe with a . . . shall we say, medical kit."

The tailor beamed. "I *am* impressed. Though, of course, there is a flaw in what you're proposing."

"Correct," the visitor said. "If I know about the medical kit, then it's very likely I have altered its contents in order to return a false DNA match."

The tailor nodded, entertained beyond measure. "And is there a way out of that difficulty?"

"I believe so. For I am not just you, I am you from the future."

Outwardly, Garak gave no reaction. But his heart wasn't just racing now, it was fluttering. "You'll forgive me for taking a moment to try to organize the . . . the . . ."

"Possibilities?"

"My thought exactly. The possibilities of the situation that has brought you here. *If—*"

"What I'm saying is true."

"Of course."

"Naturally."

The tailor regarded the visitor with narrowed eyes, secretly hoping that he truly was who he said he was and not some tired psychological gambit initiated by the—

"And no," the visitor said, "this has nothing to do with the Obsidian Order."

The tailor grinned as he held up a finger. "Which is precisely what someone from the Order would say!"

"Which is why I must insist you check my DNA and my chroniton levels. And in the meantime, I can think of a few questions which only I could answer, and I suggest you ask them."

Finding the visitor's suggestion to be reasonable, Garak the tailor led the way to the back room of his store. He paused on the threshold of the doorway. "But then, if you're me from the future, you must already have a memory of this meeting."

Garak the visitor shrugged. "That is, shall we say, where things might get confusing."

"I certainly hope so," Garak the tailor replied. Then he entered his back room and went directly to his dimensional safe, withdrew the interrogation implements which could also, in a pinch, double as a fairly complete emergency medical kit, and began the analysis of his visitor's molecular and temporal structure.

During the procedures, the two Garaks continued to test each other. They began with the memories of a certain young upperclassman at the Bamarren Institute who had been most generous in her enthusiastic initiation of Garak into certain adult pleasures. Then, on a more somber note, there were the hurtful contents of the final encrypted communication from his father. And on the professional side of things, the exact and inspired molecular modification to the untraceable poison used on the Gentleman Usher to the Romulan Assembly.

Before ten minutes had passed, Garak the visitor was rolling down the sleeve of his tunic, having not complained about any of the necessary tissue excisions. "*I* would be convinced by now."

Garak the tailor nodded, even as he struggled to think of any detail or additional test he might have overlooked. "Transporter accident?" he asked. "I have heard such things are possible."

"But would that explain the chroniton levels showing I am from six years in your future?"

Garak the tailor sighed, accepting defeat—for the present.

"That's the right decision," Garak the visitor said. "Reserve final judgment, but go along with the moment, see where it leads."

"I must say I find it tremendously refreshing to speak with someone—"

"—who understands exactly how you think?"

Garak the tailor offered his visitor a chair as he took one himself. "As your host, you must allow *me* to begin," he said. "Frankly, I must admit, as I try to think of what might possibly inspire me to travel back into my past and speak to myself, I can only imagine the most grave of events."

Garak the visitor nodded, his mood now one of deep sadness.

"The survival of Cardassia?" Cardassia's defeat was the gravest event Garak the tailor could imagine. Nothing meant more to him than his world and his people, despite the flawed leadership that currently blighted both.

"Even graver, I'm afraid," the visitor replied. "Though I have seen . . . I have seen Cardassia Prime laid waste and our people . . . our people erased from existence."

The tailor leaned forward, eyes wide. "All this, in six years?"

"Longer than that," the visitor allowed. "But six years from now, I—you—*we* will be afforded a chance to look even further into the future. And it is a future that cannot be allowed to come to pass."

"And the answer is here?" the tailor asked, greatly curious. "In this time?"

"In a sense."

"*Do* you have any memory of this meeting in your past?"

The visitor shook his head.

"I'm no expert in such things," the tailor said, "but does

that not mean that you are setting in motion an alternate timeline?"

Now the visitor leaned forward and lowered his voice conspiratorially. "There are those with whom I am working today—*my* today," he added, "who have despaired of saving the . . . the universe—"

Garak the tailor felt the unfamiliar thrill of shock at that first mention of the catastrophe that lurked in his future.

"—*without* changing the timeline."

"But you have not despaired of that?" the tailor asked, matching his visitor's low voice and intense manner.

"As long as I see that I have a choice in the matter," the visitor replied. "For example, I'm sure that if you think of it, the very fact that I have returned to you from six years in the future informs you that you will survive the next six years."

The tailor nodded, grateful. "I have taken heart from that."

"Not that there haven't been a few close calls," the visitor warned.

"Then I will have survived *and* not have been bored," the tailor said with a smile.

"And six years from now, our Cardassia is not in the finest state it could be."

"War?" the tailor asked, not the least bit surprised.

"Several, I'm afraid."

"With what you know, couldn't we stop them before they start?"

"But that's my quandary," the visitor said with a slight frown. "I *know* how the next six years transpire. I *know* that if I am successful in undertaking an extremely difficult task in this time, the next six years won't change, yet the future I have seen beyond that will. And Cardassia and the universe will be saved."

"I think I understand," the tailor said slowly. "On the other hand, you could take drastic measures now, change the outcome of the next six years, and by your knowledge of the future make Cardassia stronger and more secure than it ever has been before. Yet if you choose that course of action, you can't be certain that the disaster you saw even further in the future might not come to pass through some other means."

Garak the visitor nodded appreciatively. "I couldn't have said it better myself."

Then both Garaks laughed lightly, together, in perfect synchronicity.

The moment passed. Then the tailor asked, "Six years from now . . . are we happy?"

The visitor folded his hands, looked down. "When have we ever been?"

"But we do live in hope, do we not?"

The visitor nodded. "Always. How can we do anything else?"

"A final question, then," the tailor said. "If we make no changes in this time, six years from now, as best as you can see the new future you'll create, will Cardassia survive?"

The visitor studied him before answering, truly considering the question.

"Yes," he said at last. "Our people face a most challenging set of circumstances, led by rulers who have lost their way, who have chosen the path of expediency. But . . . over the next six years, we will make many new friends. And . . . quite unexpectedly, in their way, they will care for Cardassia's fate as well. With the help of those friends, I do believe that Cardassia will return to her rightful glory in time. Though at great cost. Great cost."

The tailor studied the visitor, carefully considering him and his story, then got to his feet, his decision made. "So what may I do for you—for us?" the tailor said. "Bearing in mind that I trust your judgment as much as if it were my own. Above all else, Cardassia must survive as a *great* world, not merely survive."

The visitor got to his feet, his decision apparently made as well. He reached into the open interrogation kit, withdrew an ampule of straw-colored liquid, and held it out to the tailor.

The tailor understood at once. "I had already guessed that was the other possible reason you have no memory of this meeting. Not because it takes place in an alternate timeline but because . . ." The tailor accepted the ampule from the visitor—from himself. ". . . because the memory of it no longer exists."

"But you're not to take the inhibitor yet," the visitor said. He slipped a hand into his robe and withdrew a padd. "I've recorded a series of instructions I would like you to follow in the next few days."

The tailor studied the padd, didn't like what he saw. "This is Klingon, is it not?"

"I arrived here from a stolen vessel," the visitor explained. "One makes do with the tools at hand." He pressed the padd controls that accessed his instructions. "Try your best to accomplish everything, but whatever else happens, take the inhibitor *before* the Withdrawal begins."

"So we *do* withdraw?" The tailor had seen the signs of Cardassia's unrest, but to his understanding, those signs might just as well have foretold a further escalation of the noble attempt to bring peace to the fractious Bajorans.

"We withdraw," the visitor confirmed. "Very soon, now."

"And what happens then? The Bajorans destroy themselves?"

"Let us just say that your life—our life—will become more interesting than you could possibly imagine. For the first year, I promise you, you will live in a state of perpetual delighted surprise."

"How pleasant." The tailor looked at the ampule. "Tell

me, six years from now, will the technique exist to reverse the inhibitor? I would enjoy having some memory of this encounter."

The visitor seemed never to have considered that possibility before. "I'll look into it. You will come to make a very good friend in the weeks ahead. A human, of all things."

The tailor rocked back in surprise. "A human? A *friend?*"

The visitor held up a cautioning hand. "Now, now. He has been genetically engineered to enhance his intellect. I assure you he is the equal of any Cardassian—a condition which I must say puzzled me for the first few years of our acquaintance, until I learned the truth. However, he is quite clever in medical matters, so I shall put the task to him. I, too, share your desire to remember this meeting."

"How fascinating to remember it from both sides." The tailor started for the door, then stopped as he saw that his visitor did not follow. "Am I wrong to assume that you will have to leave soon?"

"I'll take my leave another way," the visitor said.

The tailor guessed his counterpart referred to a transporter of some kind. "Soon?"

"Any minute, I think. Neither the process nor the timing is completely under my control."

The tailor nodded. "I look forward to the day I will understand what you mean."

"It's well worth the wait," the visitor assured him. "I envy you your—"

And the visitor was gone. Simply and abruptly. Without so much as a flash of quantum dissolution or even subtle harmonic hum.

"How absolutely fascinating," Garak said. Whatever had happened, it was not a transporter that was responsible.

He looked down at the padd he held. He pressed the activate control.

On the small device's display, an image of himself appeared. An image that spoke to him.

"There is a hidden laboratory on Terok Nor," his future self said calmly, "and within it is a most remarkable artifact. An artifact that represents the gravest of dangers to our world and our people . . ."

Once again, Garak the tailor sat down to listen in his empty back storeroom. He had his own complete attention. Six years from now, it was obvious, he still knew how to tell a story.

But what Garak was about to find out from himself was whether that story could have a new ending.

CHAPTER 16

ODO STOOD AT the door of his office in Security, gazing out at the empty Promenade. The station was on its night cycle, so the lighting was subdued, and the only indication of activity was coming from Quark's across the way.

It was peaceful, Odo thought, and he liked Deep Space 9 this way. The station was, in a very real sense, his adopted home. And he knew from the time display on his desk that in less than a week it would be gone, destroyed by the red wormhole.

Unless he took action in the next thirty minutes. But what action?

His brief peace vanished suddenly as a small cloaked figure stepped out from a turbolift, looked both ways, then quickly ran for Security.

Odo felt a momentary twinge of panic. Right now, he knew, the Odo of *this* time was in Kira's quarters but would soon receive an urgent call from his second-in-command, delivering the preliminary findings on the cause of Dal Nortron's death. Odo remembered that only minutes after that, he had come up to check on his 'prisoner,' Quark.

The Ferengi barkeep, for now under protective custody, was in a holding cell behind him. But before morning came, he would be under legitimate arrest for Nortron's murder. Odo's specialists had just not been able to identify the Pah-wraith energy Dukat had used on the Andorian for what it actually was. So Quark had been left as the only likely suspect in the murder.

Odo knew it would be simple enough to make a similar call to his other self this evening, to rouse his other self out of Kira's bed and tell the whole story of the Red Orbs, one of which, even now, was hidden in Quark's, awaiting its discovery by Sisko in just a few days.

But just where would that leave Vic, Odo asked himself, *and all the others stranded in the wormhole pocket?*

For their sakes, at least until he had had more time to consider all the possibilities, he did not want to make that call and set in motion an alternate timeline. And for the same reason, right now, he didn't want to be caught in Security by whoever was running toward it. Since the other Odo had not been in the office at this time, history might change if he were found here now.

With nowhere to run without drawing attention to himself, Odo stepped back against the textured security wall and spread himself over it, careful to duplicate every feature and still leave openings through which the security scan lights could continue to shine. Only the most observant eye would notice that the texture on one wall was a centimeter thicker than that on the others.

The small cloaked figure raced up the steps to Security doors, pressed his face against a transparent section, hands cupped to either side.

Then the figure whispered a single word: "Odo?"

Odo was puzzled. Whoever this was seemed to be in urgent need to find him. Yet the changeling had no memory of anyone having sought him out at this time. As he recalled it, Dal Nortron's murder investigation had been the only business of concern that he had undertaken that final week.

"Odo," the figure said more loudly, barely muffled through the doors. "It's me!"

With that, the figure pulled back his hood for just a moment.

But the moment was long enough.

Odo poured from the wall and reformed into his humanoid shape, swiftly opening the doors and hauling Quark inside.

"What do you think you're doing?" the changeling said harshly. He began dragging Quark toward the holding cells. "You're supposed to be under protective custody."

But Quark struggled and slapped both hands against Odo. "You moron! That was a month ago! I'm *me!*" He pointed ahead through the door leading to the cells. "Not *him!*"

And Odo stopped abruptly, one hand still gripping Quark's arm, as six meters away another Quark slept in his holding cell.

"Why did they send *you?*" Odo said in disgust, letting go of Quark's arm.

The Ferengi backed off at once, indignantly straightening his cloak. "Garak's at another version of the station, six years back, trying to get Sisko and Kira and everyone from the *Defiant* back to this time."

Odo stared at Quark, as if having to translate from the original Ferengi traders' tongue himself, and not rely on a universal translator. Quite clearly, other things had been going on while he had been swinging back and forth through time.

"Are you able to explain *any* of this?" Odo demanded, not really expecting a useful answer from the Ferengi.

But just then, from across the holding room, the other Quark suddenly cried out, *"Moogie!"* and sat up in his Cardassian sleeping ledge so suddenly he slammed his head against a utility shelf.

Odo started as he heard the dull thump echo in the bulkheads. From his experiences when he had been imprisoned in solid form, he knew that had to have hurt.

The Quark of the past sat up on the side of his ledge, rubbing his head, cursing colorfully to himself.

The current Quark tugged on Odo's arm. "Unless you want to ask *yourself* what's new, let's go!"

Quickly comprehending their situation, Odo grabbed Quark's arm and pushed the Ferengi out of Security onto the Promenade. The changeling understood that his own past self must already be on his way up here. He remembered walking in on Quark as the Ferengi stood in front of the replicator slot.

At the same moment as the doors closed behind him and Quark, Odo heard the hum of a turbolift arriving. Though he could not recall having seen anyone suspicious that night as he returned to his office, the changeling took no chances on untimely discovery. Slightly changing his form to something more feminine, he slipped an arm around Quark and strolled onto the quieter half of the Promenade without looking back.

As soon as he and Quark had passed by Garak's shop, closed for the evening, and were beyond the Shipping Office, out of sight of Security, Odo felt Quark twist out of his grip. The Ferengi stared at him in equal parts fascination and horror as Odo returned his body to its usual male form.

"Odo, sometimes you frighten me."

"I assure you," Odo said, "the feeling is mutual. Now, how much time has passed since I left the *Boreth?*"

"An hour, maybe. Garak was all set to beam over and help you out with Dukat—" Quark suddenly looked up and down the Promenade. "Where *is* Dukat, by the way?"

Odo scanned the Promenade as well. The last thing he needed was for one of his security officers to come across him talking with Quark here, while he was also talking with Quark in his office. He pointed over toward the barber shop. "This way. And I don't know what happened to Dukat. He beamed over with me, tried to put me back in an illusion of Pah-wraith hell, then murdered Dal Nortron."

"Ah ha!" Quark exclaimed. "I told you so!" The indignant Ferengi jabbed a finger into Odo's chest for emphasis.

Reflexively, Odo lessened his molecular cohesion in reaction to violent contact and Quark's finger sank deep within the changeling's torso.

"Ewww, I keep forgetting," the Ferengi said, cringing at the sucking sound that accompanied the reemergence of his finger.

Odo pulled the barkeep into the entrance of the barber shop and punched in his security override code on the doorplate. "Keep it down, Quark."

"Anyway. Told you so," Quark said sulkily as he needlessly shook his finger to cleanse it. "Arresting *me* for murder . . ."

The door to the barber shop slipped open, and Odo shoved Quark inside. As a general rule, there was little in the station's barber shop and beauty salon that was worth stealing, so it had one of the simplest security setups on the Promenade. Most important, Odo knew it had no interior sensors that would record his presence.

"Then what happened?" Quark demanded. "*After* you found out that I was innocent—just like I told you."

"Look," Odo said, "I don't have much time in this . . . timeframe, and I'm guessing you don't, either."

The Ferengi scowled. "Oh, right. Sisko's radio message

talked about that, all of us jumping back and forth in time whenever one of those waves goes over the ship. I think O'Brien's just about figured out what the captain was talking about."

"What do you mean, 'figured out'?"

"Figured out whether or not we'll be yanked back to the *Boreth* when the last wave hits or left where we are in the past." Confusion twisted Quark's face. "I mean, in the present. Or . . . or . . . oh, wherever it is we are when it—"

"Quark, just tell me what O'Brien *thinks* will happen."

"Well, supposedly, we'll be okay *if* no one changes the timeline for the places we're in. The Chief mentioned something about more 'temporal inertia' or something . . . I don't know. But the important thing, Odo, is if we change anything and an alternate timeline splits off, we're in trouble. O'Brien says we won't stay with the new timeline."

Odo frowned. "We'll go back to the ship?"

"Not exactly. I mean, we do, but we get there just in time to . . . to evaporate into *nothingness*. No, it's even worse than that. The Chief says if we somehow cause that new timeline, there won't even *be* any more nothingness. Talk about the story of my life."

Odo checked out the silent, darkened shop. Past the hair dryers, scale buffers, and cosmetic replicators, the narrow windows offered a restricted view of the still-deserted Promenade. "Does the Chief have a plan?"

"He thinks he does." Quark sighed heavily. "Unfortunately, my idiot brother is helping him with it, so—"

"Quark, what *is* the plan?"

"Okay, see if this makes sense to you." The Ferengi reached under his cloak and brought out a padd. As Quark rattled off his explanation, Odo listened carefully, trying to find the pattern in the events.

"When the *Boreth* fell into one of the wormholes, just before they merged, it somehow established a link with that moment just when the wormhole opened on the station. In my bar, I might add. And from what the Chief got out of the captain's message, he says it looks like the *Defiant*'s also got a timelink to DS9, back around the time when the Cardassians withdrew from Bajor."

"Terrell must have been conducting experiments with her Red Orb back then," Odo said.

"Whatever," Quark said, hurrying on with his account. "Anyway, Sisko and Kira have to deal with Weyoun, so O'Brien sent Garak to the timeframe they're in to help them out."

"Are you saying O'Brien can beam us back to another time?"

"Not *us*, Quark said in a tone suggesting the changeling was a Pakled. "Anyone on the *Boreth*. The Chief . . . triangular . . . ized the hyper-something-or-other radio whatsit from Sisko. And that let O'Brien lock onto . . . another DS9. The one that's linked to the *Defiant*."

Inwardly, Odo marveled at O'Brien's ingenuity. Outwardly, in the interests of time, he confined himself to a simple question of Quark: "So what happens next?"

Quark rechecked his padd, ran a black-nailed finger over the text until— "Here it is. Garak gets word to Sisko and Kira. Sisko and Kira transmit messages to the *Defiant*." Quark looked up. "We can only communicate in one direction, y'see."

"Believe me, I get the point, Quark. Go on."

"So everyone from the *Defiant* beams to *this* station, the one that the *Boreth*'s linked to, and—"

Odo interrupted the Ferengi. "What about Sisko, Kira, and Garak?"

"*And* Weyoun," Quark said, picking up where he left off.

"Well? What happens to them in the past?"

"O'Brien's still working on that. I believe that if all else fails, they turn themselves into the Department of Temporal Investigations and . . . sit out the next six years. Which, I don't mind telling you, is a real waste of an opportunity in the interplanetary futures market. I mean—"

"That's enough, Quark. Now, specifically, what are you and I supposed to do?"

"Well, the first thing is, you and I don't change a thing. We have to stay linked to this timeframe."

"Up to what point?"

"Uh, O'Brien's still working on that, too."

"And then what?"

Quark looked down at his padd again. "Second thing . . . second thing . . . oh, here—make sure Dukat doesn't change anything, either."

Odo turned away from the Ferengi, looked around the shop for a time readout, concerned that he didn't have much more time here. "That might be difficult. Dukat doesn't seem to be affected by the equalization waves. I can't be sure what he's been doing here while I've been bouncing back and forth."

Quark looked at him anxiously. "*Is* anything different from what you remember?"

"Not so far."

"Then . . . maybe . . . maybe he's gone off to Cardassia or something."

"*Two* Gul Dukats," Odo said darkly. "I'm sure *that* won't affect the timeline."

"I'm just the messenger," Quark said, self-pity etched on his broad face. "None of this would have happened if—"

A flash of red light blinded Odo. By now, the changeling knew what it was and what had happened.

When his vision returned a few moments later, he was still standing in the barber shop, which now appeared to have been abandoned during business hours. All of its lights were on, Bajoran music played softly in the background, and the strong, acrid aroma of overbrewed *rakta-*

jino cut sharply through the shop's varied chemical scents and perfumes.

Odo stepped out of the barber shop onto the Promenade, looked up, and saw the blazing cauldron of red wormhole energy beyond the viewports. Once again, he had jumped forward to a timeframe *after* the station's destruction. The changeling hesitated, tempted to go to the other side of the Promenade to see if Quark's had been completely restored by this time, but just as quickly thought better of the idea. It wouldn't do to encounter Vic before the moment the holographic singer met this timeframe's Odo for the first time.

Instead, the changeling sought out the nearest turbolift and selected his next destination: Ops. As the turbolift rose to the deck of Ops, Odo discovered that it, too, was abandoned, though every piece of equipment appeared to be in perfect working order.

Odo stepped out of the turbolift and headed for Jadzia's science station. Its sensor display was frozen at the moment the first gravitational anomalies were recorded in Quark's. Seated before the console, Odo studied the fixed display for a moment, then decided that the sensor's readings described DS9 as the station had existed the moment *before* it had begun to deform. But why that should be, Odo had no answer. During his earlier conversation with Vic, which would actually take place *later,* the changeling recalled concluding that there was an underlying reality to this destroyed version—this illusion of destruction—of the station. But who or what had created that illusion, Odo did not know.

It took a few minutes more of silent contemplation before the changeling abruptly remembered that in twenty minutes or so, he'd swing back through time again and reappear at this spot *before* the station's destruction. The realization spurred him on to setting his next priority: finding an out-of-the-way place to wait, so that when he reappeared in the past, he would do so without witnesses who could then ask bothersome, perhaps potentially history-changing questions.

Returning to the turbolift, the changeling reviewed what Quark had told him, and he felt inordinately pleased that his own purely emotional reluctance to change the timeline had been backed up by O'Brien's careful consideration.

He halted before entering the turbolift again, remembering something else Quark had mentioned: Sisko and Kira had used radio to communicate with the *Defiant*, and it was those signals O'Brien had intercepted.

Odo turned back into Ops, approached the equipment replicator, and entered his security codes to order a Bajoran militia ground-to-ground radio communicator. The replicator obediently produced and delivered a device the size of a padd, though about twice as thick. Included with the device was an equipment belt and holster. Odo retrieved the radio and its accessories and carried them back to a library terminal, where he called up the setting for a Starfleet emergency-channel radio frequency. He adjusted the communicator accordingly.

Two minutes later, the changeling was safely ensconced in a dead-end Jefferies tube above the main habitat ring, waiting for the next wave to strike. Only then did Odo begin his transmittal to tell his story.

He wondered who might be listening—not just in space but in time.

On the bridge of the *Defiant*, Jake turned to Jadzia, and though they both opened their mouths to speak at the same time, Worf beat them to it.

"That's Odo!"

At once, the Klingon was out of his command chair, heading for Jadzia's communication console. Since receiving Sisko's first message, the Trill had made refinements to the *Defiant*'s antenna simulators, and the message Jake heard was the clearest one yet, with far less static and interference than the first.

"*. . . right now, I am in . . . as it exists after being swallowed by the red . . . I have been here once . . . later time. I have also been in the station prior to its . . . first visit, Dukat killed Dal Nortron, but . . . not seen him since. In my last visit to . . . Quark, who told me Sisko and . . . on the station around the time of the Day of Withdrawal. From what they've said and from . . . O'Brien has concluded that as long as we do not change the timeline, we . . . on the station when the final equalization waves destroy what pockets of space-time remain in the wormhole pocket. . . . Garak back to Sisko and Kira's time, . . . wants everyone from . . . Boreth to beam over to the station of this time at once.*

"*This is Odo. Right now, I am . . .*"

The speakers went dead. A moment later, the *Defiant* shuddered as another equalization wave passed over it.

Jake saw Jadzia and Worf exchange a glance.

"I think we got the whole message," Jadzia said.

"Does that mean everyone else is all right?" Jake asked her. "I mean, everyone on the *Boreth?*"

"Sounds like it," the Trill said. She made further adjustments to her console. "And it sounds as if O'Brien's making more headway than I am."

"Does his hypothesis sound reasonable?" Worf asked.

"That we not change the timeline?" Jadzia said. "I'm not sure. I mean, if we do absolutely *nothing* to change the past, then the future will unfold as we saw it, and everything will come back into this same endless loop. So, assuming that we *can* all get back to the station before it was destroyed, we're going to have to do *something.*"

To Jake, it was as if a small photon torpedo had burst in front of him. The answer was that clear to him. At least, it seemed to be. "This is the same thing that Nog and Admiral Picard faced!" he said excitedly.

Jake's sudden assurance wilted in the blast of intense scrutiny that Worf and Jadzia now directed at him.

"Uh, you know," Jake faltered. "Time traveling to the past to make a change that won't show up until *after* the point at which the journey to the past took place. So the past won't be changed, only the future."

Jadzia and Worf turned their attention from Jake to each other.

"He's right, Worf," Jadzia said. "If we can do something that results in history unfolding just as it did up to the point at which we traveled into the future, and then see to it that we return to that timeline even an instant later, we won't have changed *anything* in the past. So if Chief O'Brien is right—and he usually is—we'll stay in 2375, and not in the wormhole."

"But the station will still be destroyed?" Worf asked.

Jadzia nodded reluctantly. "We can't press the reset button on that one, I'm afraid. If we change the past, we die."

Worf looked as dejected as his mate but for a different reason. "But if we do *not* change the past, then the universe dies."

"Which is why," Jadzia concluded, "we'll have to choose the moment we change something with . . . great precision."

"You know, . . ." Jake suddenly said aloud without thinking, then stopped as quickly as he had begun.

"Continue," Worf said, the suggestion issued Klingon-fashion, as an order.

But Jake only shook his head, feeling foolish, struck by the ridiculousness of what he had been about to say. "It's nothing. Really."

Jadzia gave him an encouraging look. "Jake, this isn't the time to hold back. The worst that can happen is that we'll listen to you, then go on to another idea."

Jake sighed and steeled himself for ridicule. The Trill scientist was right. How could a minute's worth of embarrassment compare to the end of the universe? "Okay. Before . . . before any of this happened, the Orbs and . . ." He saw Worf's brow begin to furrow, and he picked up the pace. "I was working on a new novel. *The Ferengi Connection?*"

"Time *is* of the essence," Jadzia advised calmly, even as Worf grunted his impatience.

"The point is, for the heist to work and Quark and Morn—uh, for Higgs and Fermion, the bad guys—to get away, they had to set up a diversion. So what they did was, they rigged a runabout to take off into the wormhole, so that Odo—uh, Eno—would chase after them, but they actually hid under the runabout pad and didn't go anywhere until after Eno had gone into the wormhole, too."

"And your point would be?" Worf asked.

"We do the same thing. Get back to the station just before it's destroyed, then hide." Jake held up his hand to cut off Worf's almost immediate rejection of his idea. "Not on the station, Commander Worf. On a *ship*. And we don't come out until *after* the station's been destroyed. That way, the timeline we're connected to now doesn't change, but we'll be in a position to stop the future we saw by warning Starfleet about the Ascendancy."

Jadzia and Worf looked at each other once more, and again Jake sensed the strange current of unspoken communication between the two.

"Check our logs to see if you can find a suitable ship in range of DS9 on the day it was destroyed," Worf said.

Jadzia nodded, then glanced up at Jake. "A fallback plan," she explained.

Not being privy to the secret mode of communication Jadzia and Worf appeared to share, Jake didn't understand. "Why a fallback?"

"If it is in *our* best interests not to change the past,"

Worf said, "then we must assume that it will be Dukat's and Weyoun's intention to do the opposite."

"Which means," Jadzia said as she completed Worf's assessment, "we have to be prepared for making drastic changes of our own. Assuming we can actually figure out how to get ourselves into the *Boreth*'s timeframe."

Jake felt Worf's and Jadzia's eyes upon him, measuring, wondering if he truly understood now.

He did. He met their gazes unflinchingly. If the only way to save the universe was to change the timeline, then change the timeline they must. Even if the result would be their own deaths.

Jadzia had already faced that decision when she had chosen to remain aboard the *Defiant*.

Jake hoped he could face his own decision as bravely.

He also hoped he wouldn't have to make it.

CHAPTER 17

BASHIR GRUNTED as he slammed his shins into a dark shipping crate.

He was still in Cargo Bay 4, though it was almost empty now, without a trace of Starfleet supplies.

The woman still gripping his arms, squeezed them, twisted him around.

"Julian?"

"Major!"

"I was holding on to you," Kira marveled, staring at her hands on his arms. That's what must have done it." She beamed at him. "We're in phase! The two of us!"

Bashir wasn't certain what she meant, but Kira dispensed with his confusion as she told him about the first trips back and forth which she and Sisko had taken. "The captain started thinking about what was happening to us as if we were on a pendulum, swinging back and forth," Kira said. "In the beginning, we were so far out on the end of the swing that we weren't keeping in step with everything that was around us. So the first time we arrived, people couldn't see us. But the more often we got caught in the back-and-forth, the more in phase we became. And that just continued until it was as if we finally belonged here."

The major's last words provoked a sudden memory in Bashir. He looked down at his tricorder—it had accompanied him on the transport through time as well.

Even better, he had remembered to switch it to record mode.

"I've got the readings!" He held up the green cylindrical Vulcan radio. "I've got to send them to Dax!"

Kira's response was to hold out her hand. "Give me your jacket." She pointed to her uniform. "We've gone back. I can't wear this out there."

"Of course," Bashir said, and quickly slipped out of his tattered trustee's coat. "But wouldn't you be better getting rid of the uniform?"

Kira pulled the jacket over her shoulders. "In twenty minutes or so, I'll need it again, when we get swept back to the other side of the Day of Withdrawal." She started for the main cargo bay doors. "Let's move it," she said, without waiting to see if he would follow. He did.

"Move it where?" Bashir asked.

"Dax thought the original radios we had would work best if we used them by a viewport. We should be able to get over to one of the ore-transfer docks from here without running into too many Cardassians."

Bashir preferred not to think what running into *any* Cardassians might mean to the timeline. Nor did he wish to think of how his and Kira's presence here and now could do anything *except* change the past. But then it hit him, and he stopped in mid-stride with one thought churning his stomach: *They had already failed.*

"Major, wait!"

Kira stopped just as she was about to open the main cargo bay door.

"We might already have altered the timeline," Bashir said.

"How?" Kira demanded, alarm widening her dark eyes.

"Just a moment ago, when you called yourself on your combadge. Do you remember that having happened? That someone impersonated you?"

Kira looked troubled, as if Bashir had brought up an unwelcome memory. "Julian, that week before the *Enterprise* was finally invited to the station, this place was a madhouse. Sabotage. Impersonations. At least five people claiming to be in charge of the station under the orders of the Provisional Government. I was just getting over Lake flu. I don't think I slept for a week once I came up here. I was beaming everywhere, trying to do everything at once—at least, whenever the transporters were working. Which wasn't all that often."

"But do you remember someone claiming to be you, requesting transport from the Infirmary to Cargo Bay 4, and then you beaming in to find that two people had escaped from forcefield confinement?"

Kira took a quick breath. "I don't know. Maybe. I can't remember exactly."

"Because you've forgotten? Or because it never happened?"

"What's the difference? Either way, the event couldn't have had any effect on the timeline."

"What if *our* presence in the cargo bay just then made you spend time in it investigating our disappearance, when you should have been doing something else that *would* affect things?"

Bashir could see the major struggle to control the same agitation he was experiencing. "Look, Julian, either we altered the timeline or we didn't. All we can do now is get those readings to Dax!"

Bashir abandoned his argument. The major was right: They had failed, or they had not. Time, like everything else in the universe, was quantum. "Let's go," he said.

Kira opened the door, checked both directions in the corridor beyond, then ran off to the left. Bashir ran after her. Much to his surprise, they almost made it to a docking port before they met their first guard—a gorr, one of the lowest of the named ranks in the Cardassian military. Her uniform, though, clearly showed where two insignia had been removed, indicating that up till recently she had held the rank of glinn. That act of discipline, Bashir decided, could explain the grimace of ill humor that twisted the guard's face as she caught sight of what she probably thought were two Bajorans on the loose outside a designated work area.

"Transit forms, *now!*" the gorr barked at Bashir and Kira. For emphasis, she brought out her phaser.

Bashir quickly ducked his head, holding a hand to his nose as if he were in pain, hoping that the major would know what to say.

"We were robbed!" Kira wailed, cringing as she edged closer to the soldier, both hands held up to make her plea, blocking the Cardassian's view of Bashir. "A glinn took our ration rods, our idents, *and* our transit forms. He said he'd sell them back to us, but—"

The gorr shoved Kira to the side, ignoring her. She pointed her phaser at Bashir. "You! What's your problem?"

"The glinn beat him!" Kira cried. "I think his nose is broken! If we don't get to sick call, our cohort will miss its quota! And you know what Gul Dukat said last—"

"*Quiet!*" the gorr commanded. She stepped closer to Bashir. "Look at me."

Bashir gingerly bobbed his head up and down as if moving it was excruciatingly painful.

But the Cardassian soldier didn't seem to care about

what a Bajoran might feel. "Put your hand down or I'll phaser it off your wrist."

Bashir lowered his hand. The gorr's attention fixed on the bridge of his nose.

"The glinn must have *crushed* his nose!" Kira sobbed. "We'll never make it back in time!" Then she rushed to Bashir to try and cradle his head in her arms.

But the gorr grabbed Kira by her hair and yanked her back, throwing her to the deck.

"You're *human?*" the Cardassian asked Bashir in amazement. She looked down at Kira, whose coat had opened in her fall. "And you're in *uniform?*" The gorr sounded as if she were about to start laughing. "I think I just won my rank back."

Bashir rapidly considered the odds. No one else was in the corridor. If he and Kira both took action at once, the guard could only get one of them. But if they were arrested and then disappeared in front of their captors, it was anybody's guess what the temporal ramifications would be.

His eyes met Kira's. He saw her almost imperceptible nod.

They would have to take the chance and—

"Oh, good, you found them," a familiar voice suddenly said. "I'll take over now."

The gorr jerked her head to the side. "What?"

Garak had just rounded the intersection and confidently approached the gorr with a pleasant smile. "You have done excellent work. These two have been eluding security patrols all day. And as you might imagine, they are wanted for questioning."

Bashir was confused. Had he and Kira previously been spotted on another swing through time? Or was Garak actually trying to save them from the gorr? The doctor quickly glanced at Kira, but from the surprised expression on her face, it seemed she was just as bewildered as he.

"Garak," the gorr said tersely, "you have no authority here."

Garak's smile faded, becoming an expression of stern reproach. "Oh, but I'm afraid I do. You see, this is not a matter of concern to the *military*."

The gorr narrowed her eyes. "Then who is it of concern to?"

Garak locked his eyes on hers. "Do you really want to know the answer to that question? Or would you rather I report that you were most cooperative and deserving of a return to your rank?"

Bashir could see the Cardassian soldier hesitate, and it took no great insight to guess exactly what she was thinking: Of course, Garak was only a civilian tailor, but what if the rumors about him were true?

The gorr backed down. "Do you . . . do you require any assistance, sir?"

Garak's contented smile returned. "No, thank you. But I do appreciate the offer, and I will make my appreciation known. And now, if you would be so kind . . ."

Realizing she was being dismissed, the gorr promptly holstered her phaser and left.

Kira was the first to speak. "Garak, how long have you been here?"

But Garak shook his head as he produced a Cardassian tricorder from his jacket and directed it at Kira and Bashir. "I'm afraid that your chroniton levels indicate I am not the same Garak with whom you're acquainted."

Bashir was shocked and knew his voice revealed it. "But . . . you know about us?"

"As little as possible. Suffice to say that two days ago, I had the most remarkable experience of being visited by myself."

"Oh, no," Kira said. "That's it."

"Now, now," Garak admonished her. "I am well aware

of the dangers of changing anything that you remember as the past. I assure you, precautions have been taken."

Bashir didn't know whether or not to believe that assurance, given its source. "What kind of precautions?"

But Garak was in no mood for conversation. "I am also aware," he said briskly, "that you are both pressed for time. I believe you will have a radio communication to make? Yes?"

Bashir nodded.

"Very good," Garak said. "If we go this way, we won't be disturbed."

Garak led them along a short corridor, then up a service ladder to a level just above a docking port. A series of small, square viewports ran along the outer bulkhead. "I believe this should be suitable," Garak said.

Kira opened her mouth to ask a question, but Garak interrupted. "Please, the less information exchanged between us, the less we will have to fear that the 'precautions' are not entirely adequate."

Because it was the simplest decision to make, Bashir had no difficulty in accepting Garak's suggestion. He took up a position next to the center viewport and had the tricorder relay its data to the Vulcan radio, which, in turn, transmitted them to . . . wherever, whenever, the *Defiant* was.

After a minute, Bashir sensed Kira's presence beside him and felt the touch of her hand on his arm once again. "Just in case," she said in a low voice.

"This is all you need to do?" Garak asked Bashir.

"That's right," Bashir said. "We need information about exactly what's—"

"Ah-ah-ah, but I don't," Garak interrupted.

Bashir smiled. "Sorry, Garak." Then he noticed the Cardassian tailor's puzzled and curious regard of him. "Yes?"

"Nothing," Garak replied pleasantly. "I was just . . . tell me, by any chance, are you involved in medical matters?"

Bashir couldn't think what harm that innocuous information might cause. "Yes, I am. Why?"

Garak smiled, shook his head. "No reason. But I do wish you good fortune. For all our sakes."

"Thank you," Bashir said.

"No, thank *you*."

Bashir laughed, then added for Garak's enlightenment, "Well, at least, *you* haven't changed."

"How reassuring."

Before Bashir could say anything more, a blinding flash of red light erased the scene before him, and when the brilliance had faded, Garak was gone.

Someone else stood in his place, though.

"It's about time," Prylar Obanak said. "I've been waiting for you."

"Nonlinear time!"

On the bridge of the *Defiant*, Jake looked up from his auxiliary station to see to whom Jadzia was talking. Worf was at the ops console, and three of Ensign Ryle Simons's *ad hoc* team of engineers worked at the life-support, engineering, and science stations. Off the bridge, three other crew members were on duty in main engineering, and two civilians stood watch over Commander Arla in sickbay. The commander was still recovering from Dr. Bashir's treatment of her subcranial bleeding, and Worf had ordered that no crew member be alone until he could determine who had helped Weyoun beam off the ship—though given everything else the crew faced, that was a mystery that seemed destined to remain unsolved.

But Jadzia, who was still at the communications console, was only talking to herself.

"That's it!" she said, more loudly than before, and Jake could hear real excitement building in her voice. "Worf, look at this." Then, surprisingly, she added, "Jake, you, too."

On Jadzia's main display, Jake saw an unusual graph that to him looked something like a spider's web with its center point pushed off to the right. The skewing of the rectangular segments that the crisscrossed strands defined made it seem as if he were looking at a net made of rubber. About a dozen of the strand intersections were marked by blue Starfleet symbols; about half as many others were tagged with yellow Klingon tridents. At the center of the warped web was a single red Bajoran emblem.

"I was trying to trace the Feynman connections among our bubble of space-time, the *Boreth*'s, and all the other bubbles that hold different versions of DS9," Jadzia explained to Worf, and to Jake. "But I couldn't find any pattern that made sense, especially—"

A pressure equalization wave enveloped the *Defiant* and disrupted the ship's gravity generators. Like everyone else on the bridge, Jake lurched as the deck seemed to pitch, but he managed to hold on to the back of Jadzia's chair. He also felt Worf's large hand on his back, helping keep him in place. The faster the waves came now, the more powerful their impacts were. At least with the extra crew manning key bridge stations, the *Defiant* was recovering more rapidly as well.

At the same moment the deck felt level again, Jake became aware that the constant background chorus of voices coming from the bridge speakers had once again increased in number. Over the past hour, as Jadzia had begun reconfiguring the sensors to respond to greater timeshifts in any detectable radio signals, the *Defiant* had begun to pick up multiple messages being transmitted from all the different temporal versions of DS9.

Jake's ears caught the repetition of his father's first message, as well as his second and third, together with Bashir's spoken messages and data transmissions, all of them layered in with Odo's and Quark's and even Garak's multiple transmissions. Fortunately, the ship's computer was capable of extracting all the pertinent information from each message, because with each new wave that swept over the *Defiant*, even more transmissions became detectable, and the old ones invariably repeated as if some eddies of time were caught in a loop.

On Jadzia's console, Jake saw that the center of the web was now distorted to the left, instead of to the right as before. He guessed the change was in response, somehow, to the passage of the wave. There also appeared to be even more Starfleet and Klingon symbols at additional web intersections.

Jadzia picked up her wave-interrupted explanation where she had left off. *"Especially* because those equalization waves keep changing temporal conditions. Until I realized my problem was that I was trying to include too much information."

Jake was lost, so it was a great relief to hear Worf say, "Explain."

Jadzia pointed to her display, touching the Klingon tridents first. "According to the time signatures on the radio transmissions we've been receiving from Odo, and Odo and Quark, these are all the relative positions of the *Boreth*. Both from *before* the station's destruction by the red wormhole and *after* it.

"And these," she said, indicating the Starfleet emblems, "according to the time signatures of the transmissions from Captain Sisko, and now from Julian and Major Kira, and Garak, are all the relative positions of the *Defiant*—from before the Day of Withdrawal and after."

Once again, Worf asked the question Jake thought. "I do not understand. How can the *Defiant* be in so many different positions when movement is not possible?"

"At the risk of sounding old-fashioned," Jadzia grinned,

"it's all relative. You see—" She tapped the central Bajoran symbol. "—this is the station, the one unchanging element in the wormhole pocket."

"But shouldn't there be many stations," Worf asked, "each accounting for one of the timeframes experienced by the personnel that we and the *Boreth* have beamed to it, and from which we are continuing to receive radio transmissions?"

"That's just what I thought," Jadzia said. "And *that's* what made it impossible for me to connect all the different Feynman connections, even using Mannheim transformations."

Jake sighed. He hoped the discussion did not become so technical that he would be unable to follow it. He really wanted to understand what they were in the midst of.

"But then it hit me," Jadzia went on. "In this wormhole pocket, Deep Space 9 *itself* is the object, the location, the timeframe . . . whatever you want to call it . . . that's most strongly connected to the wormhole environment. And the wormhole itself is a domain of nonlinear time! So I took all the hypermaps I had been trying to assemble and compressed them so that all the different versions of the stations occupied the *same* coordinate positions, making station time nonlinear. And there it is." The Trill's smile of triumph was bestowed equally on Worf and on Jake. "A complete hyperdimensional map of all possible space-time interconnections between the station and the two ships, reducible to only two dimensions."

Jake felt like the odd man out. It was clear that Jadzia was incredibly pleased and relieved at her breakthrough, and Worf might know why. But Jake certainly didn't.

Then Worf's next question made Jake feel much better. "Does this knowledge provide an advantage to us, or is it simply interesting?" Worf's tone left no doubt about what the Klingon position was regarding applied versus pure research.

"An incredible advantage," Jadzia said. "The *Boreth* is an advanced-technology ship, twenty-five years ahead of the *Defiant*. I had no idea it was in here with us, but according to Odo, they can see the *Defiant* on their viewer. And one of Garak's messages said that Chief O'Brien will be able to set the *Boreth*'s transporter for automatic use."

This time, when Jadzia smiled up at Worf, Jake felt certain he understood the meaning of the unspoken message that passed between them: If everyone from the *Defiant* could get to the *Boreth* as Chief O'Brien had requested, then the crews of both ships could be saved. Without requiring an operator to stay behind and sacrifice himself—or herself—for the others.

With new hope, Jake listened closely to Worf's next query.

"Jadzia, can the personnel on the *Defiant* be beamed to the *Boreth*?"

"With this map, yes," the Trill said. "We just have to get the information to the Chief, and he should be able to lock onto us."

Worf completed the plan. "Then, to get the information to O'Brien, we must send it with someone to DS9. So it can be transmitted from the station."

"Exactly," Jadzia said. "And we still have four hours and—" She checked her console. "—twelve minutes. More than enough time."

But Jake thought he saw a flaw. Reminding himself that fear of embarrassment could not stand in the way when so much was at stake, he spoke quickly. "Hold it," he said. "The *Boreth*'s connected to the day the station was destroyed. So . . . what happens to my dad? And Major Kira and Dr. Bashir? And Garak? Do they just get left in the past?"

His heart sank as he saw the compassionate look that

settled on Jadzia's face. "If they can contact the Department of Temporal Investigations, they can be relocated to an isolated community to wait six years before rejoining the timestream."

"*If?*" Jake asked. "What if they can't contact the Federation in time? What if the Cardassians get them? What if . . . if *anything* goes wrong?"

"Then the past *will* change," Worf said.

The Klingon looked at Jadzia, and Jake once again understood the question that was being asked.

Jadzia sighed. "The transporters on the station—*if* they properly reconfigured to resonate with the gravimetric distortions of the Red Orb hidden in Quark's bar—*might* be able to transport our people from the station in the past to the station the *Boreth*'s linked with in 2374."

"Might?" Worf repeated.

"It would depend on the skill of the operator," Jadzia said.

Worf folded his arms. "Could *you* make the necessary modifications?"

"Yes," Jadzia admitted, then quickly began to add, "but if I beam over, there won't be anyone here to—"

"Then you *will* beam over," Worf said, cutting off all further discussion. "You will then transmit the dimensional map to Chief O'Brien, so that he may attempt to rescue us from the *Defiant*. And then you will reconfigure the station's transporters in order to send Captain Sisko, Major Kira, Dr. Bashir, Garak, and yourself six years into the relative future."

"And if O'Brien can't rescue anyone from the *Defiant?*" Jadzia asked tightly.

"In the end," the Klingon said firmly, "there will be less disruption to the timeline if this ship is lost with all hands than if the captain and the others remain in the past. It is a risk I am willing to take."

"What if I'm not?" Jadzia said with more than a trace of challenge in her voice.

"In this case," Worf growled, and Jake shivered at his tone, "your concern is not of importance. I am the commander of this vessel. You will beam to the station at once."

But Jadzia didn't give up easily. She shook her head. "No one can operate the beam manually the way I can."

"Jadzia, I have reviewed the procedure you have followed for the three previous transports. *I* can handle the beam manually."

"Worf! I am the only—"

"That is the end of the discussion," Worf interrupted, sharply. "You will accompany me to the transporter room."

The tension between officer and crew, husband and wife, was so explosive, Jake didn't know where to look, and he was sure everyone else on the bridge felt the same. Right now, more than anything, Jake wanted to know his father would be safe with the others. Just as strongly, he wanted the timeline to remain unchanged. But he couldn't see any way both situations could come to pass. If the decision were his, Jake didn't know if he'd be able to make it.

But his problem was not Jadzia's. She *could* make the decision that was required, however much it troubled her. She took a tricorder from the utility compartment under her console, downloaded her map, then stood up. "Let's do it," she said curtly.

"Good luck," Jake said, knowing it was not enough, but it was all he could think of in the time that was left.

"You, too, Jake," Jadzia told him. Then she and Worf were gone.

Jake turned back to Jadzia's communications console. He focused his attention on the multiple time displays showing estimated elapsed time on the *Defiant*, the *Boreth*, and the most recently contacted versions of DS9.

The closer the waves came to one another, the smaller the time distortion became among the different timeframes, and Jake saw that in two hours and two minutes, all the different rates of temporal flow would become identical— at the exact same moment as the temporal pressure between the two wormhole fragments equalized and all time stopped.

Jake decided to return to his own station because he didn't know what else to do. But then a new thought came to him.

Thinking back to what Jadzia had said about Arla's renewed interest in her people's religion, Jake found himself wishing he knew more about the Prophets, too. Because all too soon, it seemed, his fate and the fates of everyone he cared about would be in their hands.

Jake made a new decision: to see if Arla was awake.

He wanted to know how Bajorans prayed.

CHAPTER 18

EACH TIME SISKO was swept into the relative future, past the Day of Withdrawal, he took the opportunity to rest, and he had found the perfect site to do so.

Cannibalized over the years by Cardassian engineers, an antiquated fifty-year-old Cardassian ore hauler had remained undisturbed beside an unused ore-processing bay in Deep Space 9's outer ring for six months after Sisko had originally arrived to take command of the station. In a timeframe several days prior to the Withdrawal, Sisko had located the hulk again and saw that its condition *then* was no different from what it would be six months later, when Chief O'Brien would finally arrange to have it carted away as scrap.

Since nothing had disturbed the hauler in all that time, Sisko felt secure hiding in its cargo hold, in no danger from departing Cardassians searching for plunder or—depending on which timeframe he was in—zealous Bajoran militia searching for saboteurs.

Now, on this latest transfer into the future, Sisko carefully set down the two cases he had brought with him that held his work. He had learned from experience that he could carry through time anything he could hold that was not in direct contact with the station. Next, he recovered the Cardassian tricorder he had concealed behind a loose baffle plate in the past and checked the local time and date. Once again, he had been swept past the actual events of the Day of Withdrawal, though not as far as on his previous jumps.

According to the tricorder's readout, he was now approximately fifty hours past the departure of the last Cardassian from DS9. From the reports he had read when he had taken command, he knew that confusion would still reign on the station. In the next few hours, a minor general from the Bajoran Resistance, whose name Sisko could no longer remember, would declare the station the Star of Bajor and begin to organize the transport of orbital weapons to its cargo bays, in order to enforce what he termed a just peace on the planet below. That general's term of office would last a little more than one day before he was taken into custody by an assault team sent from the hastily-formed Provisional Government, whose hurriedly-elected members even now were struggling to make their way across their ruined world to hold their first assembly.

As for himself, Sisko recalled that he had been on Earth at this time, his visit to Rutgers University cut short by an urgent recall order from Starfleet Command. He had been considering a teaching position, and when the recall had arrived, he was standing in the backyard of a quaint mid-twenty-second-century cottage on Moravian Lane, smiling as he watched his son Jake eye the towering maple trees, already imagining himself climbing them.

With that, Sisko's thoughts inevitably turned to Jake in this present, a young man now, off somewhere in time with the *Defiant.* Though Sisko knew he couldn't be sure that the action he had decided on would result in his own individual survival or Jake's, the certainty at least would exist that *a* Ben Sisko and his son would live on in another timeline without the threat of the Bajoran Ascendancy and the end of the universe it would bring.

The decision itself had not been an easy one for Sisko to make, but he felt that somehow Jake would understand. If their positions were reversed, he even thought there was a possibility that his son might make the same choice.

In Sisko's last face-to-face exchange with Kira, after the two of them had left Quark's knowing that the Red Orb had already been removed, the Bajoran major had not supported his decision. Kira was convinced that they had to follow the admonitions of Eilin, the ancient mystic of Jalbador, and of Prylar Rulan, who had first welcomed Sisko to the station: No change in the timeline was to be permitted; everything was to be left in the hands of the Prophets.

Sisko had told the major he thought her choice *was* the better one, and the one he would prefer to see prevail, but that even if he put his duties as Emissary first, he could not stop thinking like a Starfleet officer, and that every aspect of his training was demanding that he consider what might happen if the Prophets remained silent to their plight.

"If faith fails us," Sisko had argued, "then science must not."

He and Kira had agreed to separate. Kira told him she would do all she could to establish further communication with the *Defiant,* to track down Weyoun, and to obtain the Red Orb of Jalbador from Leej Terrell before whoever stole it from Quark's hiding place was able to take it from the station.

"You know," Kira told him in that last conversation, "maybe the people who stole the Orb were *us.* I mean, if we took it two days after Quark hid it, that would explain why it wasn't there when we tried to find it two *weeks* later. Right?"

Sisko allowed the possibility of that scenario but pointed out that if he and Kira *were* responsible for the Orb's disappearance, then surely they would have left some sort of sign to themselves, so they would know what actually happened.

"Maybe not," Kira said. "That would be like telling ourselves the future, and that might mean we'd be careless and miss the opportunity to steal it. Or maybe we intended to leave a sign or message for our future selves to find, but we were being chased and didn't have the time."

"The truth is," Sisko said, "this is like every other life-or-death situation we've been in. We have no idea what will happen next."

"I believe the Prophets do," Kira said.

"I hope you're right."

Then a flash of light had swept the two of them into the past, more than a week before the Withdrawal.

Fortunately, they materialized in the Bajoran half of the Promenade, and their sudden appearance in a shadowed alcove was barely noticed by the exhausted slave workers who huddled together during the station's night, the fabled Cardassian efficiency having failed to provide them with berths.

Sisko and Kira had gone their separate ways then, Kira steadfastly determined to do what she had to do, telling Sisko that if—when—she succeeded, she would seek him out where she knew she could find him, no matter the timeframe, in the abandoned ore hauler. On his own, Sisko managed to steal a Cardassian tricorder and reach the hulk within a half hour, after which he was swept ahead into another post-Withdrawal timeframe.

By now, Sisko was spending less than ten minutes in each timeframe, and it had taken him multiple timeshifts to nearly complete building the device that, if necessary, could take the place of Kira's faith: a chroniton pulse-emitter which he now carried with him through each new timeshift, along with his assorted borrowed tools. To assemble the simple emitter, he'd made use of various components left behind in the Cardassian ore hauler, as well as key isolinear circuits and a spare sensor-resonance chamber which he liberated from the Starfleet materiel that had arrived from the *Enterprise.*

He knew the emitter would be a crude device, unlikely to operate for more than a few minutes once the power supply was attached. But Sisko was betting that at the appropriate time, even the brief cascade of chronometric particles the emitter produced would destroy the wormhole-precursor field that Leej Terrell had created with the Red Orb in her secret lab deep within DS9. That destructive cascade would have the added benefit of driving whatever entity possessed Weyoun from his body—presuming, of course, that Weyoun was still on the station. As yet, Sisko had seen no sign of the Vorta, other than when Weyoun had been greeted by Prylar Obanak as the one true Emissary, the first time Sisko had arrived with Kira.

Weyoun, however, was not all that important now. The actions Sisko planned to take would still change all of the history that unfolded from the Day of Withdrawal, with or without the Vorta's presence on the station.

Sisko knew the chroniton cascade would be easily detected on Cardassia, only five and a quarter light-years distant. Undoubtedly, the Science Directorate of the Obsidian Order would ask pointed questions, and Terrell, in particular, couldn't help but suspect a connection to wormhole phenomena. That could lead her to return to the station more quickly than she had in Sisko's original timeline. If she did so, Sisko thought, at worst, the Red Orb would be discovered years earlier, perhaps when the Cardassians were destined to retake control of the station at the beginning of the Dominion War. At best, the Orb would remain hidden, and there would be no secret 'Cardassian holosuite' for young Jake and Nog to discover. The consequence of that would be that it would take more time for the Sisko and Odo of that day to realize what Quark and Vash and Dal Nortron, among others, were planning almost six years later.

In the end, Sisko knew, the new future he would bring into being was unpredictable. After all, from the moment he and Kira discovered for themselves that the Red Orb had been moved from Quark's, the timeline had already changed. At least, Sisko reassured himself, the strategy he had decided upon would introduce a *different* set of changes and would thus create a greater chance that the three Red Orbs would not be brought together.

Beyond that, Kira was right. All their fates would be in the hands of the Prophets.

Sisko carefully replaced the Cardassian tricorder behind the baffle plate, picked up his cases with his tools and his almost-completed emitter, then stood expectantly to one side in an area of the cargo hold he knew he had left clear in the past.

When the next equalization wave struck, Sisko estimated he'd be arriving in the past about the time the first troop transports had left Bajor. At first, he knew, those departures would seem to be no different from a normal troop rotation. But as soon as word began to spread that fresh troops had not arrived to replace those who had left, the first uprisings would begin among the Bajorans, and battles for the Cardassian-controlled spaceports would rage across the planet. Since the first uprising had occurred about two days before the Cardassians evacuated the station, Sisko guessed it would take him another three or four more time oscillations to reach that specific timeframe. When he did, he would activate his emitter. Then, one way or another, the nightmare would end.

Sisko was prepared when a flash of blue light blinded him. He had learned that closing his eyes did nothing to lessen the light's intensity. At least, he thought, wincing, repetition served to blunt the physical shock of timeshifting.

But this time, the moment his vision cleared, Sisko was struck by a shock of a different kind.

Kira was in the cargo hold, and so was Dr. Bashir, and both were bound and gagged and kneeling before their captor.

Weyoun.

In the *Defiant*'s sickbay, Jake nodded to the two crew members watching over Arla. Each was a civilian, garbed in the same style of gray and black advisor uniform he wore. Briefly over the past few weeks, Jake had talked to both of them. They were agricultural technicians, human, from Deneva, who had been returning from a Federation exchange program to Ferenginar. When the red wormhole had opened both had been on DS9 waiting for transportation because they had lost all their personal belongings and equipment in an all-too-common misunderstanding of Ferengi hotel laws. Neither had been aware that those laws equated the offer of shelter with imputed ownership of whatever was then placed in that shelter unless money changed hands first—a minor detail Ferengi hoteliers regularly neglected to share with off-worlders. Since the technicians were the only personnel onboard the *Defiant* with anything close to training in biology, Bashir had deputized both of them as his nurses.

"How is she?" Jake asked, looking down at Arla's still form on the sickbay treatment table.

But Arla herself replied before the technicians could. "Jake?" The Bajoran commander lifted her head and looked over at him.

Jake went to her side as she slowly sat up on the treatment table. "I wouldn't move too much. Dr. Bashir said you might be dizzy for a few days." At the time, Jake had considered the diagnosis optimistic, considering they might only have a few hours of existence left.

But Arla merely stretched her neck from side to side, arched her back, and a moment later slipped off the table to stand unaided, without any unsteadiness. "Actually, I feel fine." She looked around sickbay. "Where *is* the doctor?"

"A lot's happened," Jake said. He enjoyed the novelty of talking with someone who was almost his height. Arla was definitely one of the tallest Bajorans he had ever met.

"Um, excuse us," one of the technicians interrupted. "But Commander Worf . . . he wanted to be informed the moment Commander Arla woke up."

"Why?" Arla asked.

"You should let him know," Jake told the technicians. To Arla, he said, "Do you remember who hit you?"

"Hit me?"

"Your head," Jake said, repeating what Bashir had told him. At the same time, the technician who had just spoken with Jake fumbled with his combadge, achieving contact with Worf only after several false starts.

As the technician informed Worf of her condition, Arla gingerly touched the top of her head. "What happened?"

"What do you remember?" Jake observed her action, puzzled. Bashir had said Arla had been struck on the back of her head, not the top. Couldn't she feel the injury? Or was the doctor's treatment that good?

Arla wrinkled her face in concentration. "I . . . I went on a break. Ensign Simons sent someone up from engineering to watch Weyoun." She snapped her fingers. "I saw Major Kira beam out to the station. Are she and your father all right?"

"So far," Jake said. "What else?"

"Well . . . let's see . . . did I come back in here?"

"The engineer who spelled you said you did."

Arla nodded. "That's right . . . that's right . . . I did come back. I was carrying a coffee . . . Weyoun was on the table . . . and . . ." She shook her head in frustration. "All I remember after that is a red flash." She smiled apologetically at Jake. "Do you think there's any coffee left?"

"Sure," Jake said with a shrug, deciding she wasn't used to starship food replicators. The coffee was always on.

Then, after asking the technicians to tell Worf that he and Arla would be in the mess hall, he left sickbay with her.

On the short walk to the mess, Jake filled in Arla on what she had missed. But the best news of all was that Jadzia had managed to contact O'Brien and that the crew of the *Defiant* were already being beamed to the *Boreth.*

But as they entered the mess hall and went straight to a replicator, Arla didn't seem particularly interested in their pending rescue.

"So all the times are converging?" she asked, then instructed the replicator to give her coffee, black, New Berlin blend.

Jake nodded, watching as a gray mug of steaming dark liquid appeared in the replicator bay. "Dax said it's inevitable. These pockets of space-time we're in, they're the last remnants of linear time, and basically they're going to dissolve into the nonlinear environment of the wormhole."

Arla picked up the mug. "How much more time is left?" she asked.

"It's different for each pocket," Jake said. He gestured to the closest table and accompanied her to it, taking a seat directly across from her. "As if we were all traveling at relativistic speeds, back before inertial dampeners. Dax set up a time display at her station. We've got about three hours. The *Boreth* has about two and half. On the station, they have just over two."

Arla stared down into her coffee, warming her hands around the mug.

Jake didn't know if there would ever be an easy time, so he decided to be blunt. "How do you feel about the Prophets?" he asked, mortified by the sudden betraying catch in his voice.

He thought he saw a brief smile lift Arla's mouth at the corners. "You mean, do I believe in them?"

"Yeah. I guess that's it."

"I didn't used to."

"I . . . I know. That's what Dax said."

"You were talking about me?"

Jake flushed. "Well, I heard what you said about, you know, hoping for the best and trusting in the Prophets."

Arla again raised her coffee mug, but it seemed only to touch her lips. She set it down again without drinking from it, as if just going through the motions.

"I heard what the Pah-wraiths did to you," she said. "The hell they put you in."

Jake shivered, recalling the whole all-too-real experience of inputting as if his life had depended on it.

"Do you know what my Pah-wraith hell was?" she asked, stroking the side of the coffee mug.

Jake shook his head, said, "No," almost too softly to be heard.

"I didn't have one."

Jake stared at her, not understanding. "But . . . everyone else did . . ."

"I didn't believe in Pah-wraiths, either." She looked up at him then, so suddenly Jake was startled. Her large eyes were bright, gleaming. She gave him a half-smile. "My parents didn't even tell me stories about them to scare me when I was a child. They were very practical people. No Prophets. No Pah-wraiths. No absolute good. But no absolute evil, either. Funny how that works."

"So . . . so what happened to you?" Jake asked. "Did you experience anything?"

Arla nodded. "Oh, yes. I *was* punished."

Jake was startled by the intense pain in Arla's voice. "But . . . not by the Pah-wraiths?"

"By the Prophets." The Bajoran spat out the last word as if it were the foulest substance in the universe. "They put me in a camp. With Cardassian soldiers. I was their . . ." She shook her head, unable to continue.

Jake waited. He thought again of what the doctor had told him, about how people were the product of their experiences, and he knew how much of life was still before him. At least, he hoped it was.

Arla spoke again. "There was only one way out left to me. One way. The Prophets. And I begged for them to help me. I prayed to them. And the soldiers . . . when I was no more use to them, they'd throw me in a pit and bury me alive with all the others, and then I'd wake up and I'd be crawling through the battlefield again, and the Prophets . . ." Arla bent over her mug of coffee, and her voice became little more than a whisper that Jake could barely hear. "The Prophets *would* come to me then. And they'd say, 'Sorry, Arla. You had your chance. Now this is what you get.' And then the soldiers would come again, and . . ." Arla's hands tightened around the mug until Jake could see the bones in her knuckles. "We *all* had our chance."

Jake sat silent, unsure what reassurances a nineteen-year-old could offer a Starfleet commander. If Arla had been his age, maybe he would have put his hand on hers, to try to tell her that things would be all right, that she had had a Pah-wraith experience after all, that the Prophets wouldn't abandon Bajorans. But he didn't know if any of that were true. All he did know was that he was as confused as she was.

"But . . . you said, 'Trust in the Prophets,' didn't you?" Jake finally asked.

Arla let go of her coffee mug, pushed back on her chair, stood up. "I should go talk to Worf."

Jake quickly got up to follow her. "Uh, Worf says we should all go around in pairs."

Arla stared at him, frowning.

"Until . . . until we know who beamed Weyoun out."

"Don't worry," Arla said with a brief laugh that made the hair on the back of Jake's neck bristle. "I'm sure we'll see him again."

Then the ship seemed to drop out from beneath Jake's feet as the lights brightened and dimmed and everything about him shifted abruptly to port. *Another pressure wave.* The violent movement slammed Jake's head—which was level with Arla's—directly into hers, his forehead smashing into her upper lip, the recoil of the collision tossing them both to the deck.

A moment later, Jake was sitting up, a hand to his head, looking over at the Bajoran. "Are you all right?" he asked over the ringing in his ears.

Arla was sitting up as well. She had lifted one hand and was touching two fingers to her already-swelling split lip. A bright red smear stained her teeth; a trickle of blood ran down her chin.

"Commander—I'm sorry," Jake said. He got unsteadily to his feet. "I can get a medikit and . . . and . . ."

"No need," Arla said, her speech slurring as she licked the blood from her fingers.

Then her split lip knit itself back together and deflated until it was its normal size. Unbelieving, Jake watched as the trickle of blood on Arla's chin broke into small, distinct beads which then disappeared as if they were being reabsorbed into her skin.

"Now you know why I don't have to believe in the

Prophets," Arla said as she came for him. "I have something even better . . ."

Jake didn't even have time to scream.

On the bridge of the *Boreth*, Rom delivered his confirmation: All transporter settings had been realigned according to Jadzia's specifications.

The transporter was ready to energize.

But energize what? O'Brien thought. He knew he was dealing with a more sophisticated transporter technology than he was used to. He knew that Jadzia understood the theory of temporal mechanics much more thoroughly than he did. But as far as the chief engineer could see, the coordinates to which he had set the transporter contained *imaginary* numbers. Frankly, he was surprised the computers—even Klingon ones—had even allowed him to do so.

"Uh, Chief?" Rom prompted. "We're ready to . . . go."

"All right," O'Brien said, feeling a touch apprehensive and not too proud to show it. "You might want to stand aside, because I have no idea what we're about to bring in here."

Rom and the two other crew members—Starfleet personnel who had just happened to be on DS9 between assignments when the red wormhole had opened—immediately moved to the back of the bridge.

Though the main transporter rooms were on other decks, it still remained easier for O'Brien to keep transporter controls switched to the bridge because wormhole conditions continued to limit targeting to one person at a time. With the *Boreth*'s warp engines unusable in an environment without subspace dimensions, the massive Klingon vessel had power to spare for such energy-intensive, point-to-point beamings.

"Energizing," O'Brien said.

Because the coordinates didn't seem to correspond to

any physical location in local space, on his display O'Brien saw no gravitational deviation in the transport beam's propagation. Instead, as the Chief expected, it remained as coherent as a laser, until it snapped back as quickly as if he had initiated an intraship transport.

Then, to O'Brien's complete surprise, the resulting cylinder of sparkling light in the center of the bridge resolved into a form, and that form became solid—a living, breathing, redheaded Starfleet ensign whom O'Brien hadn't seen since the battle with Tom Riker's ship, when the ensign had been transported from the *Defiant* in the midst of the action.

"I see it, but I don't believe it," O'Brien marveled.

Ensign Simons looked down at his hands as if to count his fingers, then said excitedly, "It worked! It really worked!"

"Rom—set the controls for another go."

"Aye, aye . . . Chief."

It took O'Brien only ten minutes more to beam over all but five of the *Defiant*'s remaining crew, with the chief adjusting the coordinates of each transport in precise accordance to the detailed instructions that Jadzia had transmitted from the station, along with her remarkably simple dimensional map.

Ensign Simons had made the process even more efficient by providing the up-to-date figures Jadzia needed to compensate precisely for changes to the *Defiant*'s navigational deflector shields—changes that had been brought on by the ship's fall into the wormhole.

"Uh, that only leaves Commander Worf," Rom said happily as he checked off Jadzia's manifest, "Commander Arla, the two agricultural technicians, and . . . Jake."

O'Brien frowned. He was having a hard time believing that beaming through *time* and space—as he had once done in Earth orbit—could be this simple. Not to mention accepting that in only about two and a half hours, if his calculations were correct, even a truly amazing accomplishment like this might amount to nothing. What good would it do to rescue people from the *Defiant* if the end result was merely that everyone then died together instead of alone? The chief engineer shook off his dark thoughts. There was nothing to be gained by dwelling on what might go wrong. Beam everyone to the *Boreth,* then beam everyone to the station. Those were his orders, so that was what he would do.

"The transporter has recycled," Rom announced.

"Here comes the next one," O'Brien said crisply. "Energizing . . ."

On O'Brien's transporter display, the beam shot out once more to the new, impossible coordinates, but this time it didn't snap back.

O'Brien watched, unconcerned at first. The beam was showing no feedback ripple to indicate it had dematerialized anyone, so no immediate danger existed. To compensate for target drift, the chief engineer did what usually worked. He increased the power by eight percent and widened the focus by two.

Nothing happened.

"The coils will time out in ten seconds," Rom called out in warning.

After first making sure the beam was still clear, O'Brien forced it back to rematerialize anything it might have found but that might not be showing up on the display.

But nothing appeared. O'Brien didn't understand. He had Rom reset the system.

The hum and pop of the Heisenberg compensators echoed through the deck as O'Brien rapidly worked out the new degree of Jadzia's coordinate drift, basing his calculations on this minor delay alone, then energized the beam again.

Still nothing.

Beads of sweat began dotting the Chief's brow as he tried five more times until the coils timed out for quantum-phase realignment.

O'Brien swore under his breath. He had no choice but to shut down.

"What happened?" Rom asked, worried.

O'Brien had no answer other than the most troubling one—the one now shown on the *Boreth*'s main viewer.

"The *Defiant*," O'Brien said. "It just . . . isn't there anymore."

CHAPTER 19

"IS THIS *EVERYONE?*" Odo asked.

Rom looked around the crowded storage room with Ferengi exactness, then rattled off the count. "Uh, not yet. There are still five unaccounted for on the *Defiant*. Chief O'Brien's on the *Boreth*. And . . . five people on the station back at the time of the Withdrawal: Captain Sisko, Major Kira, Lieutenant Commander Dax, Dr. Bashir, and . . . Garak." Rom gave the constable a quick, nervous smile. "That means *we* have eighteen out of twenty-nine possible retrievals, or sixty-two percent . . . rounded."

Odo was not pleased with the news about the *Defiant*. When the first of that ship's rescued crew and passengers had started arriving on the station from the *Boreth*, he had thought it would only be a matter of minutes before everyone was finally reunited after their harrowing trip through time. Everyone, that is, except Vash and the three Bajorans killed by Dukat on the bridge of the *Boreth*. Those four absences were responsible for the reduction in the number of temporal refugees from thirty-three to twenty-nine. Still, the changeling decided, the combination of Jadzia's scientific skills and O'Brien's engineering expertise had worked better than he, for one, had dared hope.

"Any idea what's happened to the *Defiant?*" he asked.

Rom shook his head. "Not really. The wormhole conditions are changing so rapidly now, the ship might have experienced a phenomenon we've never even seen before. Or else . . . well, the Chief thought it might even be cloaked."

Odo looked sharply at Rom for an explanation. "Why?"

But the Ferengi could only shrug. "Equipment failure, probably."

"Constable Odo?" Ryle Simons broke into their discussion. "You asked for a one-minute warning." The red-headed Starfleet ensign held up his tricorder.

Odo nodded, then turned to face the seventeen others who were sheltered in the storage room which now existed in a timeframe just over a day after the station's destruction by the red wormhole. It was the same storage room into which he and Dukat had first timeshifted. "Everyone, your attention! We're going to transfer again."

Most of the rescued crew and civilians had already been through enough time transfers to know what to do, and within the space of ten seconds, each held the hands of those to the right and left, until all eighteen people were linked in a circle. No more than thirty seconds later, a flash of red light engulfed them, and they found themselves still in the same storage room, but now *before* the station had been destroyed.

At the moment of their materialization, a murmur swept through the group as everyone stumbled, losing their footing, shuffling a step or two forward in the direction of the far end of the room, which was now decidedly downhill.

Odo knew at once that in this timeframe, DS9's gravity generators were still unbalanced, a direct result of their infection by the Bynar computer virus. The virus had been introduced into the station's computers by Satr and Leen, the two Andorian sisters who had accompanied Dal Nortron.

At a nod from Odo, Simons switched on the handheld Klingon communicator O'Brien had beamed from the *Boreth,* which the chief had modified so it could eavesdrop on Deep Space 9's internal communications network. The first words Odo heard this time were especially welcome. They came from Kira, though it was the Kira of this timeframe.

"—from the Rio Grande. *They found the captain!"*

Bashir's voice answered. *"What's his condition?"*

"Exhausted," Kira replied. *"But he's uninjured. And he found the Orb!"*

Those events were very clear in Odo's memory, and they told the changeling that he and his group were now approximately twenty-six hours away from the red wormhole's opening.

Odo glanced around the storage room. "Everyone still here?" he asked.

When he received no reports of anyone's missing the transfer, Odo concluded that once again the mere act of remaining in physical contact had been enough to keep everyone—with all their initial individual time differences—in joint phase.

"We should stay here about nine minutes, ten seconds," Simons advised.

"Thank you, Ensign," Odo said. "Give us a one-minute warning as before."

"But what do we do for . . . eight minutes?" Rom asked hesitantly.

"How about saying hello to your brother?" Quark said indignantly, pushing Simons aside.

Rom turned and smiled happily at Quark. "Hello, Brother."

Quark snorted. "Good to see you, too. Well, so much for family reunions. Now, here's *my* plan—in eight minutes, we can get to a runabout and get off the station."

Odo sighed as he shook his head. "Quark, we've been through this. All the runabouts were employed in the evacuation when the red wormhole opened. If we take one now, the people who originally used it to evacuate won't get off the station, and that will change their timeline. *And* when *we* jump through time again, we'll have no guarantee that the runabout will still be around us when we reappear."

"Odo, really," Quark snapped. "The station and this room are always around us!"

"Because this station and this room are linked to the red wormhole. And O'Brien doesn't know how far that linkage extends."

"He's right, Brother," Rom added quickly. "If we try to fly away from the station, why . . . there's a chance we might be snapped back to the wormhole, or to the *Boreth*, or to . . . nothing."

"Which is what's going to happen to us in—" Scowling, Quark turned to Simons. "You, how much 'relative' time do we have now?"

"Altogether? Maybe ninety minutes," the ensign said.

The red blotches mottling the young ensign's pale face were the result of simple exhaustion, Odo knew, but continued exposure to Quark might make them permanent.

Odo frowned as Quark pointed at the communicator. "Odo, c'mon. One lousy message to Major Kira, telling her not to take the Orbs into my bar. That's all it would take."

"You heard what Ensign Simons told us about O'Brien's and Dax's conclusions, Quark. That's all it would take to shut down our timeline and snap us back to the *Boreth*, too."

"So we just wait here till we *die*, is that it?" Quark asked incredulously.

"No," Odo said for at least the thousandth time, it seemed. Surely no amount of timeshifting could be as bad as the endless repetitions Quark required. "We wait here until the red wormhole begins to open, and then we leave with all the rest of the evacuees. Then, once the station is swallowed by the red wormhole and the wormhole closes, the Chief and Dax both agree that we'll be stable in this timeframe, and we can do whatever we want to change the future we saw. And that's exactly what we're going to do, Quark—*when* the time comes and *not* before."

Quark's barrel chest began to swell, and his enormous earlobes darkened dangerously. "*Frinx* time travel!" he sputtered.

Rom nodded brightly. "That's pretty much what Chief O'Brien thinks, too."

And as if he had heard his name spoken, O'Brien's voice was the next to come over the communicator. "*O'Brien to Odo.*"

Odo's first thought was that O'Brien's modification to the Klingon device had made it very sensitive. The Chief had taken part in the search for Sisko on Jeraddo, while Odo had remained on the station. Thus, whatever they were hearing now had been a long-range transmission. Though Odo couldn't recall having spoken to the Chief until he had returned with the search parties.

But then his confusion cleared as O'Brien said, "*This is O'Brien on the* Boreth *to Odo in the storage room. This channel is encrypted, so reply using the communicator I gave Simons if you can.*"

Simons instantly thrust the communicator at Odo, and the changeling touched the transmit control. "Odo to O'Brien, we can hear you!"

Everyone else in the storage room ceased talking. Until now, all communication had been from the station to either the *Boreth* or the *Defiant*, but neither ship had been able to transmit messages back.

"Wonderful," O'Brien's voice said. *"I'm picking up a bit of timeshift distortion, but we're almost in phase now, so the channel will get clearer. What's your status?"*

"Eighteen safe and sound," Odo reported. "Any word from the *Defiant?"*

"Nothing yet," O'Brien said. *"But in about five more minutes, the phase difference between the* Boreth *and the past version of the station should reach the point where Dax can contact me directly, so I'll put her to work on it, too."*

"What about you, Chief?" Odo asked.

"Not much I can do except stand by here till you get closer to the opening of the wormhole. I'll . . . transport in at the last minute so . . . I can join you."

But Odo had registered the hesitation in O'Brien's voice and understood with sadness that the engineer intended to stay at his station until it was too late to save himself. Just for the chance of making contact with those still on the *Defiant.*

"Whatever you think is best, Chief."

"Well, I'm going back to sensor sweeps," O'Brien said. *"Every time you transfer into a timeframe before the wormhole opens, contact me so we can keep everything synchronized. The next time we talk, I should have a report from Dax."*

"Thanks, Chief," Odo said. "We'll stand by. Odo out."

"And cheerfully wait to die," Quark muttered, "like good Starfleet soldiers."

Odo looked past Quark to Simons. "Time, Ensign?"

"Three minutes and counting."

Then hammer blows of pounding shook the storage room's main door—the one connecting it to the corridor.

All heads turned toward the closed door. Odo immediately gestured for everyone to remain silent, and everyone had the good sense to comply, even Quark.

Rom caught Odo's eye. "Is that you," he whispered, "making a security check?"

Odo shook his head. He had last inspected this room for contraband the day before he had placed Quark in protective custody. Someone else was pounding on the door.

The changeling held out his hand, palm up, to Simons, and the ensign promptly passed him the tricorder. Odo switched it over to detect life-forms and aimed it at the door.

Nothing.

The pounding stopped, then started again.

Altering the soles of his boots to air-filled pockets of soft, spongy flesh, Odo soundlessly made his way to the door, then used the tricorder again.

But even as another sequence of heavy blows rattled the door, the device detected no lifesigns. In frustration, Odo set the tricorder to register any energy phenomenon, and the small display screen suddenly turned bright red as all intensity bars filled their scales.

Two more blows hit the door, this time deforming it.

Odo backed up, just in time to avoid being struck by the door as a final, immensely powerful blow burst it from its tracks, and it spun forward, clanging as it skidded across the bare metal deck.

But Odo's attention had already shifted from the door to the creature who had dislodged it.

Dukat.

The madman whose white hair twisted away from his gray scalp as if charged with electricity, whose wild eyes pulsed with red energy. Who rushed into the storage room as if his bare scaled feet no longer were in contact with the deck and whose scarlet robes floated around him like the trailing fronds of water plants caught in a boiling ocean's currents.

"*I want QUARK!*" Dukat roared. And as he raised his

hands encased in red fire, all Odo could hear was the high-pitched squeal of a Ferengi.

"Emissary," Weyoun said amicably in the hold of the old cargo hauler. "It's been such a long time." He smiled at the chroniton emitter that Sisko grasped in one hand. "And I see you've been busy."

Sisko's other hand dropped his tool case, and he quickly reached inside the emitter to close the circuit that would set it off, knowing full well that because the device wasn't yet complete, the resulting explosion would probably kill him. But with any luck, it would also kill whatever entity possessed Weyoun, ending this here and now.

But the Vorta merely flicked his hand as if waving off an airborne pest and the emitter flew from Sisko's grip, sailed over the heads of Kira and Bashir, and shattered against the bulkhead.

"But I'm afraid it was a waste of time," Weyoun said. "Especially when there is so little of it left."

"What do you want?" Sisko asked through gritted teeth.

Weyoun folded his hands back inside his blood-red robes and smiled. "I'm sure you can guess."

The Vorta paused, expectant, a solicitous expression on his face, but Sisko did not intend to play his game.

"Or perhaps not." Seemingly untroubled by Sisko's refusal, Weyoun looked down at his two captives—Kira and Bashir, on their knees before him, wrists and ankles bound with red cloth. Mouths gagged with narrow strips of the same fabric.

It took Sisko a moment, but then he recognized the strips. They were the same as the arm- and headbands worn by adherents of the Pah-wraith cults.

"That's right," Weyoun said, apparently noticing Sisko's gaze. "I am not without supporters here." He raised his hand. "Allow me." Red sparks haloed one upraised finger, and the gags dropped from Kira and Bashir at the same time.

"Obanak!" Kira gasped.

"He was waiting for us," Bashir added. "After Withdrawal! He took us to an airlock, and when we jumped back, Weyoun was waiting for us."

"Obanak thinks Weyoun is the Emissary," Sisko told them.

"Because I am," Weyoun said serenely. "True Emissary to the True Prophets, as Obanak and his people believe. As they have always believed. As has always been true, I might add, Benjamin."

Sisko took a step toward the Vorta, hands becoming fists.

But Weyoun stood his ground, smiling. "Do you really think you can accomplish anything like that?"

"Afraid I'll break your nose again?" Sisko taunted him. He had struck Weyoun when they had been together on the bridge of the *Defiant*—before the universe had ended. He had savored Weyoun's look of shock and pain as the Vorta had gingerly touched his flattened nose.

But this time, Weyoun merely placed two fingers alongside his own nose, no longer damaged, and laughed. "A *human* actually hurt the *Emissary?* Never."

Whatever the reason behind Weyoun's denial of their last encounter, Sisko understood from the eerie glow of red energy now animating the Vorta's dead eyes that attempting another physical attack on him was impossible. In any case, in a little more than eight minutes, Sisko knew he'd be shifted again into the future and would be able to escape the ore hauler. Beyond that, he wasn't sure what to do. But he was ready to do anything—*anything*—before he'd let Weyoun win. And right now, that meant keeping the Vorta talking. For at least another eight minutes.

Weyoun studied Sisko like a disapproving parent. "You're being unusually quiet, Benjamin. I have come to expect a more spirited response from you."

"You won't win," Sisko said.

"But you forget, I already have. You were there, remember? The year 2400. The joining of the Temples. The battle between the True Prophets and the Pretenders at last under way." Weyoun shook his head as if overcome by the wonder of it all.

"I don't mind admitting to you, especially, Benjamin, that I do regret not being present for the culmination of eons of effort. Those 'pressure equalization waves' you're experiencing? What they really are is the waves of battle. True Prophets surging forward for the attack. Pretenders desperately struggling to push back the assault. The True Prophets regrouping and charging forth again. That's what your ship was caught in. A war beyond your comprehension. A war that can have only one conclusion. Victory. The end to all conflict. Forever."

"I don't believe you."

Weyoun pursed his lips. "I never took you for the masochistic type. Do you enjoy suffering? Do you know how many *billions* of inhabited worlds were in your universe? Do you know how many more billions of intelligent species arose, looked at the stars, felt the pain of that enormity they would never conquer, faced the bleak, meaningless prospect of not only their own individual deaths but the deaths of their cultures and their worlds?

"Is that kind of torture humane by your standards, Benjamin? Would you truly prefer to allow the universe to continue without end, condone another *trillion* races to such pathetic despair, all for the sake of your personal continued existence for, at best for a human, another few *decades?* How petty of you. How selfish. In fact, how perfectly *evil* of you."

Sisko did not reply. *Another four minutes,* he thought. *Keep talking . . .*

Weyoun nodded as if Sisko's failure to respond was not

unexpected. "I can see I'm making some headway. The old headstrong Captain Sisko would have engaged me in a scintillating argument by now, forcefully renouncing my statements, trying his best but in vain to establish that he speaks for all living beings on behalf of the stalwart Starfleet and the venerable United Federation of Planets. But your silence tells me you're finally beginning to understand. Aren't you?"

"Whatever you say," Sisko said curtly.

Weyoun shook a finger at him. "Now, now. When I hear that tone from you, I know you're thinking about something else. But believe me, Benjamin, there is *nothing* else to think about. You can do nothing to stop me now, because this moment has already come and gone in your history.

"That's what I want, you see. Nothing. I want the Cardassians to withdraw from the station, Leej Terrell to shut down her secret lab within it, the Red Orb to find its way to its safe hiding place in that Ferengi's bar, exactly as it happened before."

Sisko tried but couldn't completely contain his surprise at what Weyoun had just said. For whatever reason, it seemed the Vorta had not experienced any oscillations into the future just beyond the Day of Withdrawal. He didn't realize that Kira and Sisko had discovered that the Red Orb was not in its hiding place where it had been found in the hour before the station's destruction.

The Vorta's voice continued on, in response to Sisko's sudden spark of interest. "Ah, I see I've intrigued you at last. What did you think? Surely not that I came back to this time in order to *change* the past? To find the Orbs ahead of schedule? To try to bring on the joining of the Temple earlier than 2400? Oh, Benjamin," Weyoun chuckled, wiping a false tear from his red eye, "I will miss you, you know."

Sisko had only half listened to the Vorta, caught up in thought about his one advantage over Weyoun. Between this moment and a time two weeks after Withdrawal, the Orb upon which all of Weyoun's mad dreams depended had been stolen—and without Weyoun's knowledge. History had already been changed. But by whom?

"Weyoun, if the end of the universe is such a good thing," Sisko began, trying his utmost to keep his growing excitement hidden from the Vorta, "why *not* end it early? Think of all the suffering that would never take place."

"Ah, but that would add variables to the equation, don't you think?" From Weyoun's relaxed manner now, it appeared that the Vorta was in no hurry to do anything. And Sisko wondered why. Surely, Weyoun had to know about the swings through time, despite all that talk about the equalization waves being only the waves of battle. The Vorta had been waiting in the ore hauler for Sisko to appear, after all.

"I don't know what you mean," Sisko said, guessing he had fewer than three minutes left in this timeframe.

Weyoun snickered as if he had thought of a private joke. "Why change perfection?" he asked airily. "If things proceed as they did, unchanged, then we know what happens for a certainty: The universe ends. All sentient beings are freed from the suffering of their existence. But if I were to take the Orb from Leej Terrell now, try to locate the one hidden on Jeraddo, somehow locate the Orb that Vash secured before she originally obtained it . . . well, who knows what might happen? Perhaps the Bajoran Ascendancy would arise more quickly and the Temple would be restored a few years earlier. But perhaps not. At best, we would gain six years. At worst, we would lose everything. So why risk it?"

"Six years times trillions of beings is a lot of suffering," Sisko said, keeping up his mental count of the time remaining in this timeframe. *Less than two minutes now.*

Weyoun walked over to a dented, unpainted bulkhead, leaned against it nonchalantly. "Benjamin, I can see your interest waning. Perhaps it's time we changed the topic of our conversation."

Sisko shot a glance at Kira and Bashir, made eye contact with both. But there was no information they could communicate to him in a glance. Just their frustration.

"A good choice," Weyoun said approvingly. "Let's talk about Dr. Bashir and Major Kira. Temporal refugees, I believe was the term they used. Like you, Benjamin. Caught in time, thrown backward and forward in the wake of the Prophets and the False Prophets. Tell me . . . as you sit there now and plot your escape, did you take a moment to ask yourself how it is these two came to be my prisoners for longer than the few minutes they might otherwise stay in this timeframe?"

The effect of Weyoun's question was as strong as if Weyoun had struck Sisko. Since Kira and Bashir had been here before Sisko had appeared, of course they should have vanished to another timeframe by now. But they hadn't. Why?

"Oh, Benjamin, really," Weyoun hooted. "Stop it. You'll make me die of amusement. You're so transparent. You honestly thought that you would simply *vanish* like a character in a child's morality tale?"

Sisko tried to think of some reason he wouldn't. Rapidly, he scanned the cargo hold. Had Weyoun installed some kind of forcefield?

"Here. Let me explain," the Vorta said, and suddenly he was at Sisko's side, one hand gripping Sisko's arm, the other Sisko's neck.

Sisko fought against Weyoun's grip, struggling to strike back, but in the starburst of red energy that lanced forth from Weyoun's eyes, his body went rigid, unmoving.

"It's all about being in *phase*," Weyoun crooned, his face only centimeters from Sisko's. "About being in harmony. Remember how, at first, you didn't belong in this time at all? How no one could even see you? And how, later you could stay a few minutes now, a few minutes then, as you searched to find the one time in which you would finally belong?

"Trust me, Benjamin. You've found your time. You belong here, and you belong now. With me. No more oscillations. No more chances for escape. You will stay in here with me, and with your friends, for a few more hours. And then, when Leej Terrell runs her final experiment and the barest glimmer of the one True Temple opens on this station in her lab, all times will become one, and you will return to your ship in the restored Temple, and there even you will melt into oneness with the final oblivion."

Weyoun suddenly released Sisko from his grip and paralysis. Sisko staggered but stayed on his feet, swaying from the draining residual effects of Weyoun's red energy.

He could only watch as Weyoun began walking away from him, returning to the bulkhead. The Vorta's smug voice floated back to Sisko. "It's over, Benjamin, and it was over before you were even born. In the realm of nonlinear time, the end of the universe was always there, always waiting for you. You saw it happen once. And you will see it happen again."

There was no logic to the fury that erupted in Sisko then, freeing him from his stupor, and finally propelled him into action. Without a sound, Sisko rushed not at the departing Weyoun but at the hatch leading to the hauler's command cabin.

Sisko leaped up the short ladder and had rolled into the small cabin before Weyoun had even turned around.

The cabin hatch cover had been removed long ago, and Sisko jumped through its opening, dropping two meters to the deck of the ore-processing bay. All his concentration and all his energy were focused on crossing the ten meters to the main corridor exit before Weyoun could scale the ladder behind him and get within striking range.

Sisko ran across the deck as if he were possessed himself, not looking back, seeing only the exit.

He had to find Cardassians or Bajorans or anyone to whom he could shout out his story. Thirty seconds would be all he would need to alert someone—anyone—to the traitors, the saboteurs, the spies, whatever, hiding in the ore hauler. All he had to do was to cause enough chaos to bring on what Weyoun did not want at any cost—a change in the way things had been in the past.

Sisko reached the exit and its half-open disk door. Breathing hard, he twisted sideways and lunged through it, not quite fitting, ripping his jacket and badly scraping his chest and back in his haste.

He stumbled forward into an airlock, tripped, slapped the deck to break his fall. He kicked his legs free of the disk door behind him, then began rolling back to his feet.

The next disk door opened onto the corridor. Sisko only had time to give the airlock status panel one fast look. But that was enough—it was not locked. He threw himself at the controls, slapped his hand against it.

The door began to roll open.

In the agonizing seconds the door's movement took, Sisko risked a half second to look behind him, which is when he learned that he had lost.

Weyoun was nowhere in sight.

Sisko's heart sank.

The only reason Weyoun would not pursue him was that no pursuit was necessary.

The disk door was open enough that Sisko could run through it.

But it was also open enough for Obanak and Lorem to enter, weapons charged and aimed.

"We serve the Emissary," Obanak said.

And then he fired his phaser.

CHAPTER 20

JAKE FELT as if he were twelve years old again, running with his mother through the shaking corridors of the *Saratoga,* with no comprehension of the nightmare playing out around him. He felt that helpless, that useless, as Arla held an emergency medikit protoplaser to his neck and pushed him onto the *Defiant's* bridge, shouting out her warning: *"Move away from the controls or he dies!"*

At the ops console, Worf instantly jumped to his feet, but Jake could tell the Klingon's action was not in response to Arla's threat. Worf was preparing to attack.

"Don't even think about it!" Arla ordered. "The plaser's set on high, and that means his head comes *off.*"

"There is no need to harm him," Worf said, his voice level and controlled. "We can all be safely on the *Boreth* within the next five minutes."

"Nothing can change," Arla said as she moved to the back of the command chair. "Nothing *will* change. All we're going to do is remain on this ship until the war comes to an end."

Jake could see Worf's confusion at Arla's mention of 'the war.' "She must have been infected by Grigari nanomachines," Jake said to Worf. "She's—"

The swift, increased pressure of Arla's arm against Jake's throat ruthlessly cut off the air to his lungs. He gasped for breath.

If Arla had had no weapon, he knew he would have had at least a chance of breaking the grip she had on him. Nog had shared with him several good Vulcan self-defense moves from his Academy lessons. Even if Arla had just been holding a knife to his throat, it would have been worth the risk to struggle to escape. But not against a protoplaser. All Arla had to do was touch the device's activation switch once, and the resulting force beam would shoot out faster than Jake could move to deflect it. Realistically, that left him with only one choice: remain passive.

"Commander Arla," Worf said firmly, "you are a Starfleet officer who has been infected with an alien contagion. The contagion is affecting the performance of your duty. You must fight its influence and—"

"*Be quiet!*" Arla shouted. "I am Bajoran! And I will serve the True Prophets *before* I will be a slave to Starfleet!"

"Arla," Worf tried again, this time making his appeal more personal, "what has happened is not the Prophets' doing. You—"

Arla jabbed the tip of the protoplaser deeper into Jake's neck. "I will kill him!"

Worf issued his own ultimatum. "Then you will have no protection against my attack. And I promise you I will rip your heart from your chest."

But Arla did not give way. "Spoken like a true Starfleet officer, Commander. Now, cloak the ship."

Jake caught Worf's questioning look, obviously trying

to understand some reason for Arla's wanting the *Defiant* to cloak. But Jake could only stare back, mute. He had no idea what Arla wanted or why.

"That system is off-line," Worf bluffed.

"I might not know starships as well as I know starbases," Arla said, "but I know how to read status displays. The cloaking device works. You will activate it."

"I am unqualified, and there are no cloaking specialists left aboard," Worf said stonily.

"In five seconds, I will take off the boy's head, and then you can try to take the protoplaser from me. Five seconds . . . four . . . three . . ."

Jake braced himself for the assault. He had to give Worf a chance. Maybe the Klingon could—

But Worf gave in. He started for the cloaking console. "I will require approximately twenty seconds. We are not at battle stations."

"Twenty seconds, then," Arla said. "Nineteen . . . eighteen . . ."

When her countdown hit three seconds, the ship's cloaking device switched on.

"We are cloaked," Worf said. "Release Jake."

Arla shifted Jake to the side, and he realized it was so she could see Jadzia's console. The action caused her arm restraining Jake to relax by a fraction. His breathing steadied and Jake began to think more clearly again.

"Not for another eighty-two minutes," she told Worf.

Jake stared at the time displays on the console. Eighty-two minutes was when all the pressure waves would achieve equilibrium. When everything would end.

"Now, move away from the console," Arla ordered.

The Klingon did as he was told, until he was facing her from the front of the command chair.

Despite her control of the situation, Arla's anxiety was making itself felt to Jake. He could hear the shallow rapidity of her breathing, feel the sporadic tremors that struck her body. He quickly reassessed his situation. He might still not be able to do anything physical against her, but that didn't mean he was *completely* helpless. Especially if all Worf needed was about a second—more than enough time for Klingon reflexes to act.

Jake decided to give Worf what he needed: a diversion.

He twisted his head around to look at Arla. "You beamed Weyoun over to the station, didn't you, Arla?"

"I serve the True Prophets," Arla said automatically. "They gave me the power to save the kai from his unjust punishment. Their will is my will." The Bajoran commander's attention was still on Worf. Obviously, she did not consider Jake a threat.

"And that head wound you got—that was Weyoun, because—"

Arla's arm pressed harder on Jake's neck. "*Kai* Weyoun, Emissary to the True Prophets."

"Right." Jake coughed and rolled his eyes in warning at Worf, to let him continue without interruption.

Arla's arm lessened its pressure. Jake went on. "Kai Weyoun . . . he's served by the Grigari, so the Grigari also serve the True Prophets. I bet it was their nanites that worked on your head—made it look as if you'd been attacked when you hadn't. You've probably got millions, maybe billions of tiny machines inside you right now. Pushing around your individual brain cells. Changing you."

Arla said nothing, and Worf held his position, so Jake pressed ahead, hoping Arla's silence meant there was some part of her unchanged that still remembered being part of Starfleet.

"So you can see why Worf thought you were like someone who'd been infected by an alien contagion. A natural mistake. I mean, because you have things in you that can change the way you think. Maybe even put thoughts in your head."

Arla's thumb flicked on the protoplaser's adjustment setting, and the device hummed. Jake stiffened.

"I know what you're trying to do, Jake, and this is what I think of it!"

"Owww!" Jake cried as an electric jolt of pain shot through his cheek. He twisted away from her in a reflex motion and surprised himself by suddenly discovering he had slipped out of her armhold.

In the same instant, Worf let out a roar that shook the bridge and Jake dropped and flattened, making himself dead weight just as Nog had taught him.

Jake's practiced fall threw Arla off balance when she didn't let go of his jacket. And just as she stumbled sideways, Worf hurtled over the command chair, one forearm expertly deflecting her hand holding the protoplaser, his other slamming into her throat.

Now Jake felt Arla's grip release on his jacket and he immediately rolled to the side to stay out of Worf's way, then scrambled to his feet and ran to a weapons drawer under the closest console.

But the *Defiant*'s computer didn't recognize him as an authorized crew member and the drawer would not open.

Only then did Jake look back at Worf and Arla wrestling on the deck. The Klingon's face was awash in bright blood, his left arm flopped uselessly, his one good hand still strained to hold both Arla's arms in check.

Then Jake saw the protoplaser's force-beam shoot out to a length of at least ten centimeters. Arla had obviously decreased its reach to inflict the warning cut on his cheek, but now Worf faced the glowing equivalent of a Romulan fusion blade.

Untrained to react instinctively to battle situations, without any real experience in the tactics of hand-to-hand combat, Jake did the only thing he could think to do: He asked himself how Nog would respond.

As if he were writing a scene in one of his stories, Jake visualized Nog's probable actions then carried them out, charging across the deck with an earsplitting roar of his own, and kicking Arla's shoulder where it touched the deck as hard as he could.

Arla cried out and Jake fought down the automatic urge to apologize for hurting her. *The whole idea is to disable to win,* he told himself. He spun around, prepared to strike again.

But Arla was on her side now, Worf right above her. And just as the Klingon brought his huge fist down on her face, she swung up with the plaser.

At one and the same moment in time, Jake heard the dull crunch of breaking bone and the sizzle of plased flesh.

Arla's body arched and went limp, the protoplaser rolled from her hand. The left side of her face appeared to have been crushed by the force of Worf's blow.

But Worf, too, fell to one side, moaning.

Jake ran to Worf, remembering to kick the protoplaser away from Arla.

Then he stopped and stared in shock at the gaping wound in Worf's chest. The plasing beam had sliced deep into one of Worf's hearts, and every beat sprayed more blood from the wound.

Worf looked up at Jake with clouded eyes. Tried to speak. But then slumped, head down, as if dead.

"No . . ." Jake protested, furious at his inability to help. A simple wound was something any medic could treat in seconds. But what could a writer do?

Jake slapped at his combadge. He called the agricultural technicians in sickbay, told them to get to the bridge with a full medikit at once.

They arrived within a minute, and by then Jake had

used the bridge's emergency supplies to spray a coagulant into Worf's wound and hypo him with electrolytic stabilizers, metabolism blockers, and the three other drug ampules marked for emergency use in cases of BLEEDING, MAJOR: KLINGON.

The agricultural technicians helped Jake apply a self-constricting pressure bandage to Worf's chest, and with only a brief bout of squeamishness, Jake found he was capable of following the moving illustrations on the medikit's instruction padd to assist in setting up intravenous delivery of TRIOX FLUID REPLACEMENT: KLINGON in a vein in Worf's inner elbow. But the instruction padd ended with the warning to get the patient to medical facilities at once.

"The *Boreth*," Jake said. "O'Brien's got to beam him over." Then he remembered the cloak. As the technicians assembled an antigrav stretcher for Worf, Jake went to the cloaking console. But the console was unusable. Half the controls were in Romulan, and when Jake asked for translations to be displayed, the computer asked in turn for his command authorization codes. He couldn't shut it off.

Desperation impelled Jake to think back to everything O'Brien might have told him about the *Defiant*, about cloaks—which was nothing—about anything at all that might—

"Emergency transporter beacon!" Jake said. He turned to the technicians, told them to float Worf to the transporter room.

"Uh, what about her?" the bald technician asked. He looked over at Arla's still form.

Jake couldn't even look at the Bajoran, remembering the way Worf's fist had crushed her skull. "She's dead."

The technician held up his medical tricorder. "Not according to this."

"Oh, man," Jake said, forcing himself to look again at Arla. He frowned—her injury didn't seem as bad as he had first thought. He looked back at Worf, on the stretcher. *Make a command decision,* he thought, remembering a lesson from his father. *In the heat of the moment, when people are depending on you, don't waste time trying to think of the* best *decision, just make any reasonable decision and be open to correction.*

"Stay here," Jake instructed the technician. "Uh, stabilize her. And . . . tie her up or something, just in case."

The technician knelt beside Arla. "Okay, but I don't think this one's going anyplace soon."

Jake nodded without really listening. His mind was already one step beyond his next task. He gestured to the second technician to lift Worf with the antigravs and then hurried from the bridge to the transporter room.

"Can you even beam through a cloak?" the technician skeptically asked as he floated Worf's stretcher onto the transporter pad.

Jake bit his lip as he stared intently at the transporter control console, knowing just enough to bring up the printed menu of command options—the sort of information that was built into the system primarily for instruction and diagnostic purposes. "I don't know for sure," he said. "But I do know that my dad always said that a cloaked ship couldn't risk making any transmissions. So if O'Brien's still trying to find us . . . and I can get this thing to put out an emergency transport beacon . . . *yes!*"

He had found the command line. And, he noted gratefully, it wasn't dimmed, which would have indicated he'd need to input a command code to access that function. But the emergency beacon was something that was used for disasters, when a ship's crew had to be evacuated. And in cases like that, the system had to be accessible to anyone—even civilian advisors like him.

"I don't know if this is going to work," Jake cautioned, "but you should probably move off the pad."

"Right," the technician said, then jumped down, away from the stretcher. "What now?"

Jake looked at the console and the display that showed the emergency transport beacon was in operation. "I don't know," he said truthfully. "I guess we just have to wait."

That was when his combadge came alive with a call from the technician who had stayed behind on the bridge with Arla.

The technician was screaming.

The crowd in the storage chamber scattered before Dukat as the crazed Cardassian pushed through them.

Odo repeated the tactic that had worked before and changed his arms into heavy battering rams. But before the changeling could make contact with Dukat, a sphere of red energy pulsed around the Cardassian's robed form and Odo was thrown back as abruptly as if he had tried to breach the security field of a holding cell.

By the time Odo regained his feet, Quark was within Dukat's energy sphere, stubby legs kicking as the Cardassian held him up by the throat, his airway squeezed shut. The Ferengi's lavender-rimmed eyes goggled and bulged outward as his lungs ran out of air.

"Where is it?!" Dukat demanded.

A handful of others threw themselves against the glowing sphere and were repelled with the same crackling flares of red energy that had attacked Odo. Most gave up after two or three tries. But Rom kept mounting his charge over and over again with heartrending squeals of despair.

Odo quickly and gently blocked Rom, who was half-dazed by now, to discourage him from attempting yet another useless charge, then passed the distraught Ferengi over to the care of others. Only then did the changeling begin to circle Dukat's shimmering forcefield, searching for any sign of an opening.

Within the forcefield, Dukat loosened his grip on Quark's throat and lowered the frantically, flailing Ferengi to the deck, to give him a chance to answer the question.

"I don't know . . . what you're . . . talking about," Quark wheezed as soon as he had sufficient breath to speak.

"Wrong answer," Dukat said. His gray-scaled hand closed around Quark's neck and the hapless Ferengi was swung high again.

Odo didn't think Quark could last a minute more without air. But with the thought of that time limit came another. The changeling turned to Simons, silently mouthed his own question: *How long?*

Simons looked at his tricorder, held up one finger.

One minute, Odo thought. That's all it would take, and Quark would survive to disappear from Dukat's grip as everyone else in the room swept into the future again. Odo was sorry he wouldn't be present to see Dukat's face when that happened.

But another thought occurred to him. Although Quark had been in phase with the rest in the group for so many oscillations already, what if, because he was in Dukat's grip, he did *not* sweep ahead with all the others?

Just to ensure that the proper transfer took place, Odo decided that Dukat should release his grip on Quark.

"Dukat!" Odo shouted, his voice echoing against the bare metal bulkheads and deck. "Put him down!"

Dukat whirled to glare at the changeling.

"I know where it is," Odo said.

Dukat suddenly grinned. "Tell me, or he dies."

"Let him go, and I'll tell you."

Dukat vigorously shook his head, and Quark. The Ferengi's eyes were closed now. Odo doubted Quark would survive much longer.

"Let me into your forcefield; let Quark out," he quickly said. "Then, if I don't tell you, you can kill me instead."

Odo stood steady as the section of the spherical force-field directly in front of him flickered, then winked out.

He stepped forward, knowing there could only be seconds left. The forcefield reformed behind him.

"Now I can kill you both," Dukat crowed as he reached for Odo. "Tell me where the Orb is, because it's not in Quark's bar!"

But before Odo could even think of a new bluff with which to respond, blue light flashed around him—

—and he was in the storage chamber, the gravity gradient perfectly level, with everyone else but *one*. Quark hadn't made the transfer.

Odo called out to Simons. "Get me O'Brien!"

The young ensign switched on the Klingon communicator and called for the *Boreth*.

But there was no response. Odo felt Rom's pleading eyes upon him.

"It could be the Chief can't reach us when we're in the wormhole environment," Simons suggested.

"Odo," Rom pleaded, "what are we going to do?"

"The only thing you and the others can do is wait to go back," the changeling said gruffly. Then he started for the door.

As a changeling, Odo had other options.

CHAPTER 21

"Now, where were we?" Weyoun said.

Sisko opened his eyes. He focused blearily on the stained metal plates that formed the roof of the ore hauler's cargo hold.

"Ah, yes," Weyoun said. "Back to the *beginning*. Where everything *ends*. Poetic, don't you think?"

Sisko sat up, queasy. A wave of post-phaser nausea rumbled through him, though he couldn't remember when he had last eaten.

"Captain, how are you feeling?" Bashir asked.

Sisko looked away from Weyoun and saw Kira and Bashir, still tied up, sitting with their backs to the far bulkhead.

"I'll survive," Sisko said.

"Now, now," Weyoun cautioned him. "Let's not have that conversation again."

Sisko took a deep breath and slowly registered the fact that his own arms and legs weren't tied. He wondered why Weyoun would trust him not to make another escape attempt.

Then he heard a slight scraping sound behind him, looked over his shoulder, and answered his own question.

Obanak and Lorem were there, phasers in hand.

"*I* am the Sisko," Sisko told them. It was worth a try.

But Obanak looked unimpressed. "*A* Sisko, perhaps. Not *the* Sisko."

"That would be me," Weyoun explained for Sisko's benefit.

Then all the loose baffle plates in the ore hauler began to rattle at once.

"So," Weyoun said with great satisfaction "it really has begun. That will be the transports leaving. We're in the final hours of the Day of Withdrawal."

Sisko made an attempt to construct a list of what few options remained to him but came up with none. Rushing Weyoun, or Obanak and Lorem, was out of the question. Before he even got to his feet, he'd be blasted by Pah-wraith energy or by phaser fire. And even if the blasts were meant only to stun, Sisko estimated that in the hour or two remaining before all time would end, he might never wake up.

"Are you satisfied yet, Benjamin?" Weyoun asked solicitously.

"How can I be? You're not dead."

"Droll, Benjamin. Droll. I was referring to your escape options. Are you satisfied that you have none?"

"Oh, I have at least one."

Sisko enjoyed seeing the brief flash of apprehension on Weyoun's face. "And that would be . . . ?" the Vorta asked.

"All I have to do is to convince one of you three to turn against the other two."

Weyoun chuckled in relief. "You are a rare and singular being. The twenty-five years in which you were missing from the universe were dull indeed."

Sisko looked back at Obanak. "How well do you know your texts, Prylar?"

Obanak shook his head. "This discussion isn't necessary."

"But it is. I want to know what your texts say will happen in the next thirty-one years. I'm from that time. I experienced the Reckoning. I can tell you about—"

"Benjamin!" Weyoun said sharply. "You can be conscious for the end of the universe, or you can be dead. The decision is yours. And the way you're talking now is one way to make it."

Sisko was encouraged that Weyoun didn't want him describing the future to Obanak and Lorem, who still had to live through the next thirty-one years. If he could say the right thing, maybe these two could make changes in that time.

"You won't kill me," Sisko challenged Weyoun. "You need an audience. And when the three Red Orbs of Jalbador were opened in Quark's bar six—"

A bolt of red energy crackled against the deck plate beside Sisko.

Weyoun glared at Sisko.

"It's all right, Captain," Obanak said unexpectedly. The prylar's thick-soled boots rang on the bare metal deck of the ore hauler as he walked around Sisko so they could see each other clearly. "If you think about it, there is nothing you can say to convince either Lorem or me to act against the Emissary. After all, in five days, we will capture your friends—" He glanced over at Kira and Bashir. "—and deliver them to Weyoun. If you *had* changed anything with what you say here, then they wouldn't be captives."

Sisko fought the growing surge of desperation swelling inside him. "Not in this timeline. But in another! Another time!"

Weyoun sighed. "Benjamin, Benjamin, Benjamin . . . haven't you realized it yet? There are no other times. No alternate realities. No mirror universes. Everything is interconnected and intertwined—like tributaries branching off from the main river. Some fall over escarpments, some dry up in thirsty ground, others rejoin the river again. But in the end, all that water, all those different ebbs and currents of cause and effect, they all spring from the same source and empty into the same sea.

"What we're about to experience isn't the end of just a *single* timeline in which the True Prophets have just happened to win. It is the end of *everything*. Oh, I grant you, other timelines might have arrived at the same moment with different timing, some sooner, some later. But just as all the pockets of space-time in the restored Temple will finally converge on the same exact eternal moment, rest assured, Benjamin, that *every* universe that ever was or ever might be will reach that moment at the same time, too."

Obanak respectfully moved to one side as Weyoun came forward until he stood over Sisko. The Vorta's gaze was full of pity. "You really must accept it, Benjamin. You simply must accept there is nothing you can do, nothing you will do, and nothing you might have done to change the inescapable fact that *this* is the *end* of *everything*."

Sisko kept his eyes locked on Weyoun's. "I don't believe you."

Weyoun clapped his hands together in frustration. "Honestly. The one negative aspect of the end of everything is I won't be able to see the expression on your face when you realize I was right."

Sisko made up his mind then. Attack Obanak. Even if Weyoun struck him with a lethal blast of energy. Perhaps the blast would also be lethal to the prylar, and that would certainly prevent his capturing Kira and Bashir five days from now. That, along with the fact that the Red Orb would go missing from Quark's, still might be enough to change everything.

"May I stand up?" Sisko asked, then started to get to his feet anyway.

"No, you may not," Weyoun said crossly.

With a gesture from the Vorta, Sisko felt his legs go numb and he fell backward, to the deck.

"Accept it, Benjamin," Weyoun said with finality. "Who knows? You might even find it enjoyable."

Sisko vigorously rubbed his legs to bring back feeling. He wouldn't give up. There had to be something . . . something he could do, or might do, or had done . . .

And then he looked up as a transporter harmonic chimed in the close air of the cargo hold and a handheld communicator resolved from quantum scintillations in the middle of the deck.

Obanak and Lorem stepped forward and aimed their phasers at the device.

"It's Klingon," Weyoun said, perplexed.

Then the communicator buzzed to life. And with that sound and the voice that followed it, new life—and hope—took hold in Sisko.

"O'Brien to Sisko. Can you hear me, sir? I can't beam you off the station, but we have figured out a way to shut down the wormhole in Quark's before it can open. All I need from you are your personal computer override codes. Are you there, sir?"

Weyoun gave a soft laugh, leaned down to pick up the communicator, then turned it around in his hand until he found the transmit control.

"Miles O'Brien," Weyoun said sweetly, "however did you survive the destruction of Bajor, you clever, clever man?"

"Is that Weyoun?" O'Brien asked in shock.

"I prefer that you think of me as the last voice you'll hear," Weyoun said with a chuckle. "As for Benjamin, he won't be giving you any codes, because he never gave

hem to you in the first place. Don't *any* of you understand that—"

And then Weyoun looked up in indignant outrage as he
began to dissolve into a stream of sparkling light.

Sisko was on his feet in seconds. He wanted to cheer
even as Obanak and Lorem rushed forward but were unable to do anything but watch their leader disappear.

Except he didn't disappear.

For just as the transporter effect reached the final moment when all within it should have vanished, the glittering light began to intensify again.

Sisko didn't wait to see more. He jumped Obanak and
fought for the phaser. If he could fire one blast through
Weyoun's still forming body, it would be enough to disrupt his rematerialization.

But Obanak would not relinquish his grip and even as
Sisko wrenched the powerful prylar's arm around to try to
force him to fire the shot that would kill Weyoun, Sisko
abandoned the struggle.

The figure in the beam was not Weyoun.

It was O'Brien.

"Chief!" Sisko shouted in joy. Then he remembered the
Bajorans. "Look out!"

But the two prylars with phasers did more than alarm
O'Brien. They rushed to Kira and Bashir. And untied them.

"What's going on here?" O'Brien asked Sisko as the
prylars helped Kira and Bashir to their feet.

"I'm . . . not sure, Chief."

Obanak approached Sisko. "The events that are occur-
ring," the prylar said, "are exactly those which are supposed to occur."

"I don't understand," Sisko said, now completely baffled, convinced that more than physical timeshifts were
responsible for the utter confusion in this nightmare existence he was in.

"Your understanding isn't necessary, Captain." Obanak beckoned to Lorem. "You merely have to play out your role and do exactly what the false Emissary wanted us all to do—make no changes." Then the prylar left Sisko to go with Lorem to the hatch that led up to the hauler's flight cabin.

"The false Emissary?" Sisko called after Obanak. "Then you *knew* he wasn't the Sisko?"

The prylar paused before ascending the hatch's short ladder. "Of course," he said. "But in case you're wondering, neither are you."

As Lorem started up the ladder ahead of him, Obanak delivered a last message to Sisko. "Your friends will be with you soon. Leave this time; make no changes." Then he followed after Lorem.

But Sisko didn't want them to go. He still had so many questions for them. "We *will* meet again," he called up after them.

He could see the prylar pause in the opening to the flight cabin. Obanak was in shadow, and Sisko couldn't be sure, but it almost seemed as if the grim prylar was smiling as he said, "Another time, Captain." Then he and Lorem were gone.

"What was that all about?" O'Brien asked as Sisko turned away from the hatch and walked toward him.

"I don't know," Sisko said. He gave in to impulse and gathered the engineer into a bear hug. "Where's Weyoun?"

Clearly discomfited by Sisko's show of emotion, O'Brien mumbled, "Um, Dax did a sensor scan that told us he was here. So I made up all that nonsense about stopping the wormhole from opening so he'd pick up the communicator. And as soon as he did, I did a transport swap, used the same beam pathway. He'll be on the *Boreth* now, all by himself, and . . . the transporter coils . . . they should be shorting out right about now."

Sisko beamed. "Chief, you're a genius!"

"Thank Dax. She talked me through it."

"Where is she?"

"She's up in Dukat's hideaway, right under the Prefect's office, still shifting through time. You know how the transporters were always so touchy when we first got here?"

"Yes?" Sisko said encouragingly. He was so pleased to see O'Brien, he just wanted to hear him talk, even if the Chief's timing for reminiscing was not entirely appropriate.

"I think it was because of all the modifications Dax is making to them now. I didn't understand it back then, but it's starting to make sense."

"What kind of modifications?" Sisko asked sharply, his attention now firmly on O'Brien, whose ramblings had suddenly become much more relevant.

"Well, software changes, mostly. And if it works the way Dax says it will, she'll be able to adapt to the wormhole distortions and beam us six years into the future, to just before the station got destroyed. Then we can all evacuate, and as long as we don't interact until after the station's swallowed by the wormhole, we'll be stable in this timeline and be able to change the future."

"We can *all* evacuate! Even Jake?" Sisko's heart soared with the unexpected change of fortune.

But his all-too-brief exhilaration was quickly crushed as O'Brien painfully added, "I lost contact with the *Defiant*, sir. Jake, Worf, Arla, the two agritechnicians from Deneva. They were still onboard."

O'Brien continued his explanation, but Sisko had already begun walling off his heart again. He barely heard the Chief's next words.

"Captain—Dax is still scanning for them. I . . . would have kept trying from the *Boreth*, too. But Dax ordered

me to get rid of Weyoun and not risk being on the sam
ship with him."

Sisko nodded like an automaton. "You did the rig
thing, Chief. Dax knows what she's doing. And we di
need Weyoun off the station." He turned to Kira. "It
what you wanted, Major. What we both wanted. No
nothing will change but the future."

But Kira's haunted expression stopped Sisko and he re
membered then the one detail he had forgotten in the ex
citement of seeing O'Brien and the torment of losing h
boy once again.

"Six years from now," Sisko said, "the red wormhol
won't open."

"Why not?" O'Brien asked, looking from Sisko to Kir

"The Red Orb in Quark's bar," Kira said quietly. "Tw
weeks from now, we went looking for it. But it was gone.

O'Brien couldn't accept that. "Well . . . we have to fin
it. Unless *everything* goes as it originally went, we'll g
snapped back to the wormhole when all the different time
frames converge."

"Where's the Orb now?" Bashir asked. "In this time
frame, I mean?"

Sisko had the answer, but it wasn't reassuring. "This
just about the time Terrell told me she sent her men lookin
for a Ferengi—to enter her lab and retrieve the Red Orb."

"Quark," Bashir exclaimed, his eyes alight with realiza
tion. "He doesn't remember anything that happened o
the Day of Withdrawal. And neither do Odo or Garak."

Sisko was getting used to thinking in terms of effec
and *then* cause. "Then let's hope it's because the three c
them were helping us," he said.

O'Brien checked his tricorder. "Well, if they are goin
to help us, they've only got fifty more minutes to do it,
he said.

Sisko looked over at the ladder that led out of the or

hauler. "Then let's give the Cardassians a hand leaving our station," he said.

The last day of the Occupation had begun.

Quark was awash in *déjà vu*.

A mad Cardassian was dragging him through the crazily tilted, deserted Promenade. By his throat. Which was almost crushed. He could hardly breathe. And worst of all, there was absolutely nothing he could do except wait for the final darkness to descend. So he would once again bribe his way to the doors of the Celestial Treasury and—

The sudden memory of the Pah-wraith hell in which he had seen the face of the Divine Nagus inspired Quark to struggle anew. He *couldn't* die. Not if it meant he'd spend eternity charting profit-and-loss statements for Rom.

"Settle *down!*" Dukat snarled at Quark, digging his long, black-nailed fingers even deeper into Quark's bruised throat.

"Ehcanbreef," Quark gasped.

Dukat's exclamation of disgust was still ringing in Quark's ears as his cruel captor threw him to the steps in front of his own establishment.

"My bar. It's still here." Quark nearly sobbed in relief.

"For seven more hours." Dukat sneered. He kicked Quark as if to keep his attention focused. "Now, show me where the Orb is hidden."

Wincing, Quark stood up, looked up and down the Promenade, but saw no one. It was the middle of the station's night, and all the excitement with Dal Nortron and the Andorian sisters had inspired his idiot brother to close early. *Just when people needed a chance to relax most,* Quark thought, still indignant at the lost opportunity for profit.

"Now!" Dukat commanded.

Quark pushed slightly against the closed doors of his bar. "Oops. Locked. We should come back—"

A bolt of red energy traced the frame of the doors, and they slid open noisily.

"—or go in right now," Quark said.

He stepped inside, looked around his beloved bar, so peaceful, so quiet, almost everything in it paid for. "Can I offer you a drink?" Quark asked cheerfully, desperate for any type of delay that might help him think what to do next.

But he was suddenly looking into eyes like dying suns and breathing the air of a charnel house.

"O-on the house," he added weakly.

Dukat's slap hurled Quark five meters across the main room, until he collapsed in a heap beside the covered dabo table.

Quark sat up more slowly this time, heart racing, limbs trembling, unsure how much longer he could keep up this foolhardy attempt to laugh in the face of danger, and absolutely furious at Rom for squandering latinum on a new cover for the dabo table when the old one was perfectly serviceable as it had been for the past eleven years. But for the matter at hand, Quark was sorry for everything bad he had ever said about time travel. More than anything, he longed for a blue light or a red light or any color light the Prophets might choose to scoop him up and put him down in any time other than *now*.

"Are you that eager to die?" Dukat shrilled at him angrily.

"Of *course* not," Quark snapped back, surprised anew by his own impressively inexhaustible temper. "But . . . but I don't know what you want from me!"

Dukat advanced on Quark, forcing the Ferengi to back up until he hit the dabo table and could go no farther.

"In approximately six and half hours," Dukat thundered, "history records that your Captain Sisko discovered the third Red Orb of Jalbador in a hiding place in your bar. When that Orb was found, it was brought into alignment with the other two, and the doorway to the Second Temple was opened."

"I'm with you so far," Quark whispered nervously, holding his hands over his ears.

"That cannot happen," Dukat hissed, spraying spittle. "That *will not* happen. Do I make myself clear?"

Quark turned his face away, closed his eyes, and nodded.

"Because the denizens of the Second Temple don't deserve to be free," Dukat intoned. "When the time came to battle the False Prophets in their Temple, when the Pah-wraiths rose in vengeance, where were those of the Second Temple?"

Eyes still tightly shut, Quark shook his head, not wanting to do anything but agree with the madman, wishing he knew how.

"They *hid,*" Dukat spat at Quark, who distinctly felt drops strike him but was too frightened to wipe them away. "Cowered in their Temple as Kosst Amojan fought the good fight and *lost. Lost* for the many because of the cowardice of the few." Dukat put a hand on Quark's shaking shoulder. "So there's really only one thing left for us to do, isn't there?" he asked.

"What-whatever you say," Quark agreed tremulously.

"We find the third Orb. We destroy the third Orb. And the Second Temple will never open." Dukat leaned in close to Quark, his frightful breath hot in Quark's ear. "Can I have an Amojan from *you?*"

"Amana-Amana- . . . what you said."

Quark moaned as Dukat's hand began crushing his shoulder. "Then tell me where you hid the third Orb, Quark. Because I've already looked in this timeframe, and it's *not* where Captain Sisko will find it."

And that, Quark told himself, *is that.*

There was nothing more to say. No other options to explore.

A mad Cardassian from the future, possessed by who knew what kind of evil alien being, was set on killing him, and there was nothing more Quark could do to save himself or the universe.

There was only one last thing to do, and that was to go out like a Ferengi.

Quark opened his eyes and faced his adversary.

"Dukat," Quark said, beginning to recite the traditional last words of a Ferengi facing certain death. "This is my final offer . . ."

Dukat stared at him as if he had no idea what Quark meant.

And then, with pure Ferengi aplomb, Quark brought up his hand, extended two fingers, and poked Dukat in his red glowing eyes as hard and as fast as he could.

Dukat's otherworldly screech of shock and rage stung Quark's ears as the Ferengi ducked down and dove away from the dabo table, not sure of where he was going but determined to run away till the end.

Ahead of him, a hellish red glow crept up the walls and was reflected in all the glasses and bottles on the shelves behind the bar. Feeling most ill used, Quark braced himself for a final bolt of energy, and then—

—as quickly as if a curtain had been drawn, the red glare faded, disappeared.

Quark had bolted to the entrance but sighed, unable to help himself, and looked back.

"Huh?" Quark said.

The brand-new dabo table cover now fully covered the fallen form of Dukat's body.

And then the cover rose up by itself.

Quark drew back in horror.

But the cover reformed into Odo.

The changeling ran at Quark. "Hurry! We don't have much time!"

"Tell me something I don't already know!" Quark wailed, horridly confused and upset.

But as usual, Odo didn't show any concern for how Quark felt, and Quark groaned as the changeling grabbed his arm to drag him back along the Promenade. Uphill against the slope of the malfunctioning gravity generators. In the opposite direction from the way he had just come.

As far as Quark was concerned, it was *déjà vu* all over again.

Jake had one last hope.

He looked up at the ceiling of the transporter room and called out, "Computer! This is an emergency!"

"Please state the nature of the emergency," the calm computer voice replied.

"The commander of the *Defiant* has been attacked by an intruder."

"No intruder alert has been authorized."

Jake struggled to think of some way to get through to the system that had the ability to control almost every piece of equipment on the ship.

"Can't you hear the screaming on the bridge?" He could. The vibrations from the tiny speaker in his combadge were awful.

"No request for specialized security functions has been received from an authorized member of the ship's crew," the computer replied.

Jake looked at the technician by the transporter pad on which Worf lay in his stretcher. The technician looked even more frightened than Jake felt.

Jake pounded his fist on the side of the transporter console, as if that might make it easier to get the computer's attention. "There *are* no more authorized members of the ship's crew! Worf's dying! Arla's infected by nanites. And everyone else is a civilian!"

"Civilians are not permitted in the transporter room without authorized personnel. Please leave at once."

The screams from Jake's combadge stopped. "If we go out there," Jake said, "Arla will kill us!"

"No request for specialized security functions has been received from an authorized member of the ship's crew."

"Because they're all *dead!*" Jake shouted. "Now, help us!"

"Please state your command authorization codes."

Jake uttered a strangled cry of rage.

"Your response was not understood. Please state your command authorization codes."

"Jake?" It was Arla on the combadge now. "Are you still there?"

"Computer, please . . ." Jake pleaded. "Use your scanners or your sensors or whatever you have to examine Commander Arla for yourself. She's infected by nanites! She tried to kill Worf!"

"Bioscan facilities are not available on the bridge of this vessel."

Suddenly, a curtain of sparkling blue energy sprang up around the transporter pad, cutting Worf's body off from the technician.

Jake stared at the shimmering blue barrier. "Computer—what did you just do?"

"A class four security screen has been erected around the transporter pad."

"Why?"

"Authorization codes were received from Commander Arla Rees, now in command of this vessel."

Jake didn't want to give up. He couldn't just sit down and wait for Arla to kill him. But what was the point of trying anymore when not even the ship would back him up?

In desperation, he looked down at the transporter console. At least the emergency transporter beacon was still operating. If O'Brien was out there, maybe he could—

"Jake! Look!" the technician cried out.

Past the security screen, Worf's prone body was dissolving into light.

Jake looked back to the console. None of the *Defiant*'s transporter systems was in use.

"It's the *Boreth!*" Jake said. "O'Brien saw the beacon!"

"What do we do now?" the terrified technician asked.

Jake thought wildly, knew they couldn't get through the security screen to the pad where O'Brien could find them. He caught his breath. There was another option. "Transporter room 2!" he said. "Deck 3, forward!"

The technician started for the door, but Jake ran to him, stopped him, pulled off both their combadges. "This is how the computer tracks us!" He sprinted back to the aft bulkhead, pulled open the Jefferies tube access hatch, then leaned in and threw the combadges as far down the tube as he could.

"Now," he said. He raced back to the doors. They opened. Jake looked directly to the left and saw the aft ladderway that linked all decks. He waved the technician down first, checked for any sign of Arla in the corridors, found none, then followed.

They reached Deck 3 in seconds. Transporter Room 2 was only a few dozen meters ahead. Breathing hard, Jake slowed as they ran past the escape-pod hatches.

"Go ahead!" he urged the technician. He had just thought of the perfect diversion to distract Arla. Just in case she saw the second emergency transporter beacon switch on and decided to try to stop it from the bridge.

Working as fast as he could, Jake armed three escape pods with two-minute countdowns, then raced off to catch up with the technician.

Jake saw him waiting outside the transporter room, clearly afraid to even try to open the doors.

Jake ran up to them. They opened. He rushed in first.

"Get on the pad," he ordered the technician, then

called up the same basic command menus as he had before.

Jake held his finger over the control that would activate the second beacon. He sent his thoughts to Chief O'Brien on the *Boreth*. *Keep scanning for the beacon . . . keep scanning . . .*

Then the deck thudded with the launch of the first pod. Then the second and third. Jake hit the control. The beacon began transmitting.

"Get up here!" the technician called out in a panic.

But Jake shook his head. "Worf said the Chief could only handle one at a time. I'll jump up as soon as—" Jake whooped with victory. The technician was already dematerializing. The Chief had come through again!

Jake ran for the pad as soon as it was empty.

And fell back as the security forcefield hit him.

"Very clever, Jake," Arla said from the overhead speakers. "I can see that you know this ship better than I do. Unfortunately, I have the command codes, and you don't."

Without stopping to argue, Jake was out of the transporter room before Arla could think to seal it off as well.

He ran aft again, remembering the time-honored truism every Starfleet officer he had known had insisted on quoting: *Whoever controls engineering controls the ship.* Chief O'Brien called it Scott's First Law.

By the time Jake reached the antimatter storage facility and ran between the frost-covered, supercooled magnetic field generators, Arla's voice was coming over every speaker in the ship. But that only improved Jake's spirits. It told him Arla had no idea where he was. With any luck, she might even believe he had already beamed off with the technician.

But luck was not completely with him.

"I know you're still onboard, Jake," Arla's voice echoed around him. "Worf got away. But I raised full shields in mid-transport—only half of the technician got through to

Chief O'Brien. I ran a DNA analysis on the other half. It wasn't you."

Jake found another ladder, took it up a deck and crossed into the Jefferies tube that connected with engineering.

"You can't stop what's going to happen, Jake. So why be alone?"

Jake squeezed through the last hatchway, then shut the cover behind him and ran to the master console.

"I was alone," Arla said. "But then I found out I didn't have to be."

Small droplets of sweat fell from Jake's forehead to spatter on the glossy control surface. At least these controls were familiar to him. Thanks to O'Brien and Nog, he knew at least half a dozen different tricks to disable a starship—until now, strictly research for his novels. The Chief had cautioned him that any good engineer could work around the tricks in a minute or two. But Jake was confident that Arla wasn't any kind of engineer, good or bad.

"Ah," Arla's voice said. "I see excess computer activity in engineering. Is that where you are, Jake?"

Jake hit the controls that activated trick number one and vented a small amount of radion isotope gas into the air feed for engineering. The gas was slightly radioactive, used for calibrating the engineering tricorders that tested for leaks. The gas was also harmless, but in the words of Chief O'Brien, the safety systems onboard a Starfleet vessel jumped to warp first and asked questions later.

"Warning!"

A siren began wailing, and red flashing lights appeared on the room's cavernous ceiling.

"Radiation leak detected in engineering. All personnel must evacuate."

Within seconds, all possible entry points into engineering had been sealed, and Jake knew they would remain that way until the ship's Chief Medical Officer instructed the computer that there was no more danger of contamination. Now Arla couldn't come in after him.

"Jake?" Arla said over the sirens. "What have you done? What sense is there putting yourself in danger so close to the end?"

Jake initiated trick number two: He forced a primary bus overload.

A heavy shipwide thud announced the initial cutoff of direct power to every part of the ship except engineering. Jake knew that batteries would instantly provide backup power and could do so for days. But he also knew that a side effect of the process was that the bus overload had to be reset manually. And until it was, Arla would not be able to switch engineering control to the bridge.

Unless she knew exactly which Jefferies tube to go into, and exactly how to manually reset a bus, Jake had just effectively cut off Arla's control of propulsion, weapons, and life support.

Arla's voice was almost plaintive on the speakers. "Jake? What are you doing? It doesn't matter if you have control of the ship. There's no place to go. Nothing to do with it."

But listening to her, feeling breathless, exultant, determined, Jake knew Arla was wrong. Everything he had just done had a very specific purpose—to protect him from her. And now, undisturbed, he intended to do everything he could to figure out how he could create an emergency transporter beacon. So Chief O'Brien could find him in engineering instead of a transporter room.

And from this console, Jake had the resources of one of the most powerful starships ever built by Starfleet and access to the ship's complete engineering library.

He knew the answer he needed was in there.

Somewhere.

But he had less than one hour to find it.

CHAPTER 22

It HAD BEEN years since Sisko had been on the emergency escape stairs that led from the lower levels of the station all the way to Ops. He had almost forgotten the enclosed circular staircase existed. But he flew up it now, with Kira, Bashir, and O'Brien close behind.

"Fifty-five minutes," O'Brien panted. "Dax should just about—"

Sisko swung to a stop on the stairs, held on to the railing, looked down past Kira and Bashir. "What was that, Chief?"

"He's gone," Bashir told Sisko. "The timeshift!"

Sisko groaned. *Of course,* he thought. O'Brien hadn't been "grounded" in this timeframe by contact with Weyoun. So as the pressure waves swept over the *Boreth,* he'd still be subject to being drawn back and forth through time.

"He's probably gone two hours ahead," Sisko said. "Major, the Bajorans didn't know about this escape passage, did they?"

Kira shook her head. "Not till O'Brien started looking for a place to put new ODN conduits."

"Then he'll be safe in here till he gets swept back. Maybe eight minutes or so," Sisko said. "Let's go." He began running up the stairs again, up the final levels to his intended destination: Gul Dukat's private safe room, just below the Prefect's office overlooking Ops.

When Sisko had first seen the secret chamber—just before O'Brien had turned it into a secondary computer installation—his first thought had been that Dukat must, at some level, have lived his life in constant fear.

The small enclosure, nearly the equal in size of the office above it, contained resources suggesting someone with great concerns for his own safety: a sensor-masking generator, a month's supply of food and water, a chemical waste-disposal unit unconnected to the station's main plumbing lines, a cot, encrypted communications gear, and a single emergency transport pad for rapid evacuation. In the event of a real emergency—or slave worker uprising—Dukat would not even have to risk running to an airlock or runabout pad. He merely had to duck through a panel in his office upstairs and conceal himself one level below until a suitable Cardassian ship came within transporter range.

Sisko had often wondered what the gul's reaction had been when, upon regaining control of the station under the Dominion, he had discovered his secret escape route had been jammed full of backup computer cores.

At this moment, though, Sisko expected the hidden chamber would be as Dukat had left it—with the exception now that it was Dax, and not the Chief, who had claimed it for a workroom.

But as Sisko entered the safe room through the half-height door at the top of the emergency stairway, he saw something unexpected.

At the far end of Dukat's private chamber, the single

transporter pad that rested on a small raised platform was covered in bright pink blood.

"Worf's been hurt!" Sisko said as Kira and Bashir pushed in behind him.

"The Chief said Worf was unaccounted for on the *Defiant*," Kira said.

"But look at the blood. It's Klingon." Sisko scanned the empty room. "And where's Dax?"

"She's still shifting, too," Bashir said. "Her schedule will be slightly different from—"

"Julian!" The Trill's cry came from the transporter platform as she and Worf suddenly appeared on it.

Bashir sprang toward Worf, lowered the unconscious Klingon to the deck, and quickly told Jadzia what to bring him from the medical supply cabinets on the wall.

Without any hesitation, the doctor tore through Worf's already gashed jacket, grabbed a Cardassian scalpel to remove an improperly applied pressure bandage, and exposed a badly closed wound even now spurting blood. Sisko had never seen Bashir work so swiftly.

"He was treated by a butcher," Bashir said tersely as he turned away from Worf to rifle quickly through the contents of a Cardassian surgical kit, looking for supplies he could use.

In less than sixty seconds, Worf's wound was securely sealed, and from the combination of drugs Bashir had employed, the Klingon's deep brown skin was no longer ashen.

Bashir complained to himself as he studied the intravenous fluid pack on Worf's arm. "Well," he allowed, "maybe I was too hard on his first doctor. This fluid replacement pack saved Worf's life." He looked up at Sisko. "And it came from the *Defiant*. He must have been treated there."

"That's right," Jadzia said, her face still unnaturally pale from her ordeal. "O'Brien said the *Defiant* had disappeared from his sensors—almost as if it had been cloaked. So I kept scanning for it, and I finally picked up an emergency transport beacon. And then . . . on my first try . . . I got Worf . . . like this . . . and . . ." She stopped to take a steadying breath, still shaken by discovering her husband moments from death. "A few minutes later, I got a second beacon. But . . . it wasn't a successful transport."

Jake. Sisko steeled himself. "Who was it, Old Man?"

"Not Jake. Not Arla. It had to have been one of the two agritechnicians from Deneva."

The words *not Jake* echoed in Sisko's mind. But his profound gratitude was dampened by the death of another. "Was Worf able to tell you what happened?" he asked.

Jadzia shook her head as she looked from Sisko to Bashir, her own need to know etched on her face.

"He'll be fine, Jadzia," Bashir said as he got to his feet. "But I can't risk speeding up his metabolism to wake him. He's lost too much blood to survive that." Bashir looked at Sisko. "Sorry."

"Is that transporter set for beaming ahead?" Sisko made himself ask.

"Yes." Jadzia looked down at her husband's blood on her hands. "Yes, it is." She looked up again, at Sisko. "This pad doesn't exist six years from now. But I *can* send everyone from here ahead six years to the transporter in the *Rio Grande,* the night before the second wormhole opened. And if the first person I send uses the right override code on the pad airlock, we won't alert security."

"And everyone else is present in that timeframe?" Sisko asked.

"Everyone," Jadzia repeated. "Everyone except whoever's left on the *Defiant.* And Garak . . . can't seem to find Garak anywhere . . ."

Sisko saw how Jadzia was struggling to maintain her

self-control. He had never seen her so upset. "Old Man, are you going to be all right?"

She nodded. "It's just that Worf . . . he was always afraid that I would die first, and now . . . now I know what he meant . . ."

Sisko put a hand on her shoulder, gave it a squeeze. "He'll be fine. You heard Julian. We've all got long lives ahead of us."

Jadzia gave him a smile, and Sisko saw the old fire in her eyes. "You're right. We do." She wiped her hands on her jacket. "So—who goes first?"

"Send Bashir," Sisko said, "so he'll be there when you send Worf through. Then Kira. By then, O'Brien should come wheezing up those stairs. Can you set it for automatic?"

"First thing I programmed into it," Jadzia said. She held up a tricorder. "Just set the timer on this."

"All right, then you go next."

Jadzia stared at him. "Benjamin, what about you?"

"I have to go find out what happened when Terrell sent Quark in after that Orb."

One look at his friend's face told Sisko that wasn't answer enough. "It's missing, Dax. Somehow, I have to make sure the Orb gets put back where I'm supposed to find it six years from now, or . . ."

Jadzia continued his statement. "The timeline's changed, and the instant we create an alternate history . . ."

"This history's over," Sisko said in conclusion. "And so are we."

"Isn't this risky?" Quark whispered far too loudly.

But Odo was in no mood for either argument or explanation. "I know what I'm doing, Quark." He dragged the Ferengi through the doors of Security.

At once, Artran Mage—the young Bajoran security officer on night duty this week—jumped to his feet behind Odo's desk. "Constable!" Artran quavered. "I thought you were taking the night off."

"So did I," Odo growled. He pushed down on Quark's shoulder to let the Ferengi know he shouldn't budge from that spot if he valued his life, then went behind his desk to the storage drawers.

Artran vainly tried to change over a computer screen before Odo could see the tongo cards displayed on it, but he was too late.

"Slow night?" Odo asked as he entered his code for the enforcement equipment drawer.

"Uh, I was just taking a break, sir."

"Mm-hmm," Odo said, not really caring one way or another. Right now, in this time he knew, he was in his quarters, meditating. And Quark was in his own quarters, snoring, most likely. So everything around Odo and Quark at this moment could almost be considered a dream of the past.

The drawer slipped open and Odo took from it the equipment he needed, safely packaged in a hard-composite shoulder case.

Artran's eyes widened at the sight of it. "Trouble, sir?"

"Not yet. Carry on, Artran."

The young officer nodded, quite confused. "Y-yes, sir. Thank you, sir. Good night, sir. Good night, Mr. Quark."

"Whatever," Quark said as Odo dragged him through the door again.

Once outside his office, Odo got a more secure grip on the Ferengi and then broke into a run as he started back toward Quark's bar.

"I—thought—you—didn't—want—to—change—anything," Quark complained as Odo's long strides bumped him up and down.

"I didn't," Odo said as he charged through the bar's doors, dropped Quark, and stopped in front of Dukat still prawled on the floor. "You and I are both sound asleep in his timeframe."

Quark straightened his jacket grumbling. "And what appens when you take over from that kid tomorrow morning and find out you paid him a visit tonight?"

Odo knelt by Dukat and opened the case. "That's just it, Quark. I didn't. Tomorrow morning, I'll have breakfast with Major Kira, go up to Ops to see how the computer repairs are coming, then get called back down here when he Orb is discovered. I never find out that I was in two places at once, and neither do you."

"Oh, you think you're so smart," Quark snorted.

"You'd better hope that I am. Now, stand back." Odo napped confinement forcebands around Dukat's ankles, hen pulled the Cardassian's arms together to secure another set of bands around his wrists.

Dukat stirred, mumbling.

"He's waking up!" Quark warned.

"I can see that, Quark." Frankly, Odo was surprised at Dukat's premature recovery from the concussive blow he had given him. The changeling had used a technique he'd earned in the Great Link. First, he had swiftly flowed around Dukat's body like a rubber membrane, then instantly compressed against every square centimeter of the Cardassian at once. To a solid, the changeling had been instructed, the effect was similar to being caught in the blast wave from an explosion.

Odo pulled another, wider forceband from the restraint kit, tuned it to half strength, then slapped it over Dukat's eyes. Even if the Cardassian came to full consciousness now, he wouldn't be able to see a thing. Odo hoped that might reduce the effectiveness of whatever Pah-wraith powers he could wield while restrained.

Quark didn't look impressed by Odo's elaborate precautions. "Why don't you just kill him?"

"Because he doesn't annoy me even half as much a you do."

Next, Odo chose a clear cylinder from the kit an snapped it in half, activating the tiny device inside— general-purpose neurocortical stimulator, preset to induc deep sleep, authorized for application only by law en forcement officials. As a further safeguard against misuse Odo knew, the device would only remain active for half day after opening. It was an extreme, though safe, metho of capturing potentially dangerous suspects and mucl more humane than even a phaser stun in Odo's opinion.

The moment the stimulator was fixed on Dukat's tem ple, the Cardassian ceased his restless muttering and la still again.

Odo allowed himself to sit back with a sigh. "I think did it."

"You did it?! What about me?!" Quark said.

Odo straightened up with a sigh. "You know, Quark when it comes right down to it, none of this would eve have happened if it hadn't been for you."

"That's not true," the Ferengi protested.

Odo bent down, hooked his hands under Dukat's arms and hoisted him up with a grunt. "Get his feet, Quark And yes, it is true."

Scowling but complying, Quark lifted Dukat's feet an began backing up toward the bar's entrance. At the sam time, Odo began walking backward in the opposite direc tion, with their opposing actions threatening to tug Duka in half. But Odo had the advantage of height an changeling strength.

Quark promptly dropped Dukat's feet with an exclama tion of disgust. "Aren't we taking him to Security?" Quar demanded. "And if you ask me, this is all Vash's doing."

"Pick him up, Quark," Odo growled so fiercely the Fer engi instantaneously obeyed. "If I take him to Security then as soon as I wake up tomorrow morning, the report will be on my personal padd. And since it wasn't on my padd, we're not taking him there. Besides, it's a bit crowded with all your friends and business partners already locked up in it. Base and Satr and Leen. And aren't you ashamed, blaming your shortcomings on a woman who's no longer here to defend herself?"

Quark huffed in his struggle to keep his end of Dukat in position as Odo directed them toward the bar's backroom. "We're not putting him into *my* storage room?!" Quark gasped.

"As a matter of fact, we are," Odo said as he shouldered open the storeroom door.

Having lost the battle, Quark was anything but gracious in defeat. "Well, anyway, don't forget Sisko brought the other two Orbs in here. It's his fault if it's anyone's."

Odo lowered Dukat to the deck. Once again, Quark simply let go of Dukat's feet, and they fell with a thud.

"Now what?" Quark sighed.

"Now we let time catch up with us," Odo said. "Any moment now, we're going to be swept into a timeframe after the station's destruction—"

"Speak for yourself, Odo. You all disappeared last time, remember? But *I* stayed put with Dukat."

Odo paused and thought about that. Quark was right. Everyone in the storage chamber had shifted to the future timeframe, leaving only Dukat and Quark behind. Odo himself had hurried through the empty station to become a cover for the dabo table, so that when he had been swept back to the same timeframe Odo and Dukat occupied, he had been ready to attack in the bar, where he had strongly suspected Dukat would come.

Could it be possible that Quark was permanently in phase with this timeframe now?

Odo reached out and took Quark's arm.

"Now what?" Quark exclaimed in total frustration as he tried to wriggle out of Odo's grasp.

"Now we find out if—"

A flash of red light burst around the changeling, and when it faded, Odo was alone in the backroom of Quark's deserted bar.

Poor Ferengi, Odo thought.

It had happened again.

Quark and Dukat were alone in the past with each other. It was a toss-up to Odo which one would be more dangerous.

Jake looked up from the main display screen on the master console in engineering and checked the time readout.

Forty-seven minutes.

And he still hadn't found what he needed.

"Think, Jake," he said aloud. "Think!" Still talking to himself, pacing back and forth by the console, he suddenly came up with an approach. "What would Higgs and Fermion do?!" He shook his head, quickly chose another scenario. "No! What would . . . Marauder Mo do?!" At least he knew the answer to that one. Mo would call for help from Nit, his comic sidekick, and Nit would come bumbling in, crash an aircycle into the villain's warship or, better yet, stumble and knock poison into the vat of slicerfish his partner was slowly being lowered into, or otherwise end up freeing Marauder Mo by accident.

Mind racing, thoughts tumbling, Jake discarded the idea of an accident—that was too much to hope for now.

He stopped pacing. *Then again, the idea of calling for help . . .*

He brought up the emergency communications screens on the master console. Everything he wanted to do was already built into the ship's comm system!

"Jake? Are you still there?"

Arla's voice was huskier, as if she'd been shouting. Or coughing. Or weeping. Jake didn't reply to her. There was no reason to.

"If we're together when the end comes, Jake, then maybe we can end up in the next realm of existence together. Would that be so bad? We wouldn't be alone then."

Great offer, Commander, Jake thought. *That's just how I'd like to spend eternity. In a Pah-wraith hell with someone infected by nanites.* He pressed his hand to the large red square that appeared on the console and immediately a new screen confirmed that he was transmitting a Starfleet general distress call on all subspace and electromagnetic frequencies.

The response was almost immediate, as if someone had been listening specifically for his signal. Jake almost whooped in his excitement, in his relief.

"Dax to *Defiant!* I am receiving your distress signal. Come in, *Defiant!*"

Jake leaned forward, staring at the screen, almost unable to believe that after all he had been through, the solution to his nightmare had been so simple. But the emergency comm system was designed to be used by people with no experience with starship procedures. Now all he had to do to reply was touch the command line indicating the preferred mode of communication—in this case, ordinary radio.

He touched the control with one trembling finger. "This is Jake! Dax, where are you?"

"Jake, we're all on the station."

"Is my dad there?" Jake held his breath as he waited for Jadzia's reply. As he waited to hear if his nightmare was really over.

And it was. Sort of.

"He's here," the Trill said, "but . . . you know about the timeshifts. Right now, he's back at the Day of Withdrawal.

But the rest of us, we're back full circle, Jake. Right on the day the red wormhole opened."

Now Jake needed to know why his father was alone in the past. "Can you bring him forward? Are we going to make it? And what about Worf?"

"Worf's stable," Jadzia answered. "Julian says whoever treated him on the *Defiant* saved his life. But Jake, now we have to get you and Arla and the last tech off the ship. Can you get to a transporter room?"

"Can't you beam me off from here?" Jake asked, his voice rising, unwilling to let hope slip so soon from his grasp. Quickly, he filled Jadzia in on what had happened to Arla. What she had done to the tech. Why he couldn't leave engineering.

Jadzia's answer was heartstopping. "I can't beam you out while your shields are up, Jake. Can you drop them?"

"I don't know," Jake said, despairing. "Can I?"

A new voice came on the circuit, and Jake's spirits rose again at its capable, practical sound. "Jake, it's Miles. Where are you exactly?"

Jake told him *everything*. What was on the displays. The tricks he had used to seal engineering and block Arla from taking control of most of the ship's subsystems— most but not all.

On the bridge, Arla still controlled the shields.

"And I'm not going to let them down," Arla's voice suddenly said as she intruded into the circuit. "If that's what it takes to make you people accept the inevitable, I am *not* going to let them down."

Jake heard something else on the circuit then. Something he had never ever heard before.

Chief O'Brien swearing.

And that told Jake there was no use in struggling anymore. If the Chief couldn't get him off the ship, no one could.

CHAPTER 23

FROM THE second level of the Promenade, Sisko stared down into the hell Terok Nor had become—a tumultuous pocket universe of heat and noise and anarchy.

The security gates that had bisected the Promenade were collapsed, twisted by hammers and wirecutters and the frantically grasping hands of slaves set free. The glowing restraint conduits that once had bound the gates now cracked and sparked and sent strobing flashes into the dense blue haze that choked the air, still Cardassian-hot.

Hull plates resonated with the violent release of multiple escaping shuttles and ships. A thrumming wall of sound sprang up as departing soldiers phasered equipment too heavy to steal.

Decks shook as rampaging looters forced internal doors and shattered windows. Turbolifts whined and ladders rattled against their moorings. Officers shouted hoarse commands. Soldiers cursed their victims. In counterpoint, a calm recorded voice recited the orders of the day: "Attention, all biorganic materials must be disposed of according to regulations. Attention . . ."

But the only response to that directive that Sisko could hear was the high-pitched shriek of a Ferengi in fear for his life. A Ferengi whose shriek Sisko recognized.

"A compelling display, wouldn't you say, Captain?"

Sisko jerked away from the safety railing as another familiar voice whispered unexpectedly in his ear.

"Garak! Where have you been?"

The Cardassian knelt beside Sisko, the mangled decorative wall panel that leaned against the railing providing the two of them a semblance of cover from the combatants one level below. Sisko saw that Garak wore a uniform obviously replicated from the *Boreth*—an odd combination of Starfleet and Bajoran militia designs that was completely out of place in this time.

"Oh, here and there, reliving history, as it were."

Sisko had no patience for Garak's infamous perversity right now. "Get up to Dukat's personal shelter, beneath his office. Dax set up a transporter that will beam you to the *Rio Grande,* six years into the future."

"Ah, good," Garak said. "Then everything's working out."

"What do you mean?"

But Garak ignored the question and pointed past Sisko to the level below. "Look, there's Quark and Glinn Datar."

Sisko looked down to see Quark's struggling form being lifted by an ODN cable that was wrapped around his neck and attached to a rising antigrav cargo lifter. All around Quark's suspended form, a crowd of angry Cardassian soldiers chanted and jeered.

Sisko's automatic reaction was to try to do something to stop the outrage. But Garak put a hand on his shoulder.

"Don't do anything foolish, Captain. You know as well as I that our Ferengi friend survives this day."

So Sisko forced himself to remain hidden, flinching as

Quark kicked so desperately hard that one of his boots flew off.

"The soldiers didn't like Quark," Garak explained. "They decided to use the absence of the command staff to obtain some justice of their own."

Sisko was appalled by the treatment Quark endured. No wonder the Ferengi had been packing up and eager to leave when Sisko had arrived on the station.

Then a lance of blue phaser fire sliced into the antigrav. The machine burst in two and fell, dropping Quark flat on his back in the middle of the Promenade. At the same time, another round of phaser bursts killed Datar and scattered the soldiers who had gathered to see Quark punished.

"What now?" Sisko asked, sickened.

"Ah," Garak said, "this is where it gets interesting. I believe you know the group approaching just down by the gem store? Leej Terrell's associates?"

Sisko caught a glimpse of three Cardassians through the haze, and though he couldn't recognize them at this distance, he remembered Terrell had told him what she had sent three Cardassians to do on this day.

Right now in this timeframe, the Red Orb that the Cardassian scientist had studied was in her hidden lab in the station's lower levels. And whatever equipment she had connected to the Orb to amplify its powers was at this moment creating a precursor field that would eventually lead to the opening of the red wormhole. Sisko knew that several of Terrell's scientists had already stepped through that field and had disappeared, tempted by the red wormhole entities themselves.

So, to retrieve her Red Orb safely on the Day of Withdrawal, to keep it from the Bajorans without sacrificing any more of her staff, Terrell had decided she needed a Ferengi to fetch the Orb, because Ferengi brains were resistant to most forms of telepathy—including, Terrell hoped, the influence exerted by wormhole entities.

More phaser beams shot forth below. Sisko peered down through the railing. A Cardassian soldier was crouched protectively by Quark, but he was drawing heavy fire from Terrell's three cohorts.

"Now someone's trying to *save* Quark," Sisko told Garak.

"Glinn Motran," Garak said with an unconcerned nod. "One of Dukat's personal bodyguards. There is considerable bad blood between Terrell and Dukat. And many others, I might add. In any case, from the communications I've managed to intercept today, it appears Motran's assignment is to delay Terrell's departure by any means possible."

"Why?"

"So she'll still be on the station when the self-destruct countdown reaches detonation."

Sisko turned to Garak in amazed alarm. Terrell had told him that Dukat had set the station to self-destruct. But why the system had failed was still unknown.

Garak misread Sisko's reaction. "Why so surprised, Captain? Of course Dukat set the self-destruct timer when he left. I believe there is something on the order of slightly less than two hours remaining."

"Who stops it?" Sisko asked.

"Ah," Garak said with a smile. "That remains to be seen. *So* many mysteries to be solved this day." He pointed down again as if commenting on a passing parade. "Oh, look, there goes Motran . . ."

Glinn Motran was suddenly hit by multiple shafts of disruptive energy and his body flew backward across the Promenade. At the same moment, Quark scurried into his bar and out of sight of the second level.

But Sisko knew the Ferengi barkeep wouldn't remain there for long. The three Cardassians who served Terrell were marching forward, shoulder to shoulder, along the ruined Promenade toward Quark's bar.

"I can handle it from here," Sisko told Garak. "Go up to the transporter and get out of here."

But Garak shook his head. "Remember, Captain, you're on my station now. For the next few hours, this is still Terok Nor, and I would be most remiss if I did not do all in my power to see that you survived your visit."

Six years after the Cardassians withdrew from Bajor, in the back room of his bar, Quark stared at the empty space where Odo had been just an instant before. Then he looked down at Dukat, sprawled on the floor at his feet.

Gingerly, Quark rapped his foot against Dukat's arm.

No reaction.

Quark escalated from a tap to a kick.

Still nothing.

With a sigh of relief, Quark realized he could walk out of his storeroom, leave Dukat behind, and not feel the slightest bit guilty. The insane Cardassian had been removed from the equation by DS9's own constable. If he woke up later and caused any trouble, then it definitely would not be Quark's fault.

"Thank you, Nagus," Quark said softly, then returned to the main room of his bar.

He knew exactly what he was going to do.

First, he was going to clean out his floor safe. True, the Quark of this timeframe might be upset at losing his working capital so mysteriously, but it belonged to Quark as much as it belonged to Quark. "Or . . . however that works," Quark told himself. "It's all mine no matter how you calculate it."

Then Quark planned to open up the long-hidden, long-forgotten alcove behind his towering, stylized, stained-glass portrait of what Gul Dukat had once believed to be a

Tholian general but Rom had identified as that part of a Tellarite not to be mentioned in polite company. And *then* he was going to take out that *frinxing* third Red Orb and . . . and . . . throw it into Bajor's sun.

That way, the red wormhole would never open. The station would not be destroyed. And everyone *and* the universe would be saved. All because of one selfless Ferengi, Quark.

Quark repeated the description to himself, relishing the sound of it. Really, he mused, it was a mystery how the people on this station could ever think they could get along without him.

Cleaning out his floor safe was a simple matter. He had rehearsed the operation often enough, and he always kept inside the safe a variety of belts and a vest with custom pockets for latinum bars and slips so he'd be able to carry as much as he could.

The only unfortunate thing, Quark thought as he now retrieved his vest and belts, was that he could carry a lot more than he had in the floor safe.

But what he did have would be enough to put him on an equal footing with the second Quark who already inhabited this timeframe. Perhaps they could even become partners. Quark filled his vest pockets to bursting with latinum and then paused for a moment before fastening his belts. It was an absolute certainty he'd make a much better brother to himself than Rom had ever been.

With that self-satisfied thought, Quark closed the empty floor safe. Then he leaned behind the bar counter and took out a small deconnector tool and ran—actually, with the tightly belted, latinum-stuffed vest, it was more like waddled—over to the large frame that held the orange, yellow, and red mural that was the centerpiece of his main room. Making his gait even more awkward was the slant of the deck caused by the still-unrepaired gravity generators.

Quark awkwardly squatted down behind the mural's

frame and removed the connectors holding an access panel in place. The opening it revealed and the space it protected within were no larger than those of a typical Bajoran Orb Ark.

"Marauder Quark *saaaves* the universe," Quark cackled as he reached inside, past the sensor mask.

He reached a bit farther, hit the back wall.

Moved his hand back and forth. Hit the side walls. The deck. Even the top of the compartment.

"I know you're in there," Quark said. "I saw Sisko find you six hours from now."

But even as he frantically waved his hand back and forth until it moved like the clapper of a bell, no Red Orb was found or magically materialized.

"Odo," Quark said in growing outrage. The changeling was the only one on this station who would deliberately change history in order to make life more miserable than it already was for Quark.

"When he comes back . . ." Quark vowed hotly. "I am—"

He heard someone move behind him. Froze. Cringed. Turned slowly, barely breathing, expecting to see the mad Dukat reaching out for him.

But it was someone else.

Quark let out his breath. He patted down his vest to be sure that none of its precious cargo showed.

"I'm sorry, but I'm not open yet," he said politely as he got to his feet, never one to annoy a customer—unless the customer deserved it. "But I'm sure the cafe just down the—"

Quark never finished his sentence.

Because the third Red Orb of Jalbador, swung like a club by his unexpected visitor in prylar's garb, smashed against his head much too fast and too hard.

Quark's body hit the floor and stayed there, every bit as limp as yesterday's *gagh*.

* * *

Jake read the master console's time display.

Thirty-two minutes.

O'Brien had thought of nothing that could be accomplished in the time remaining. Not that the Chief hadn't been trying, endlessly suggesting ways to gain control of the *Defiant*'s shields.

If Jake had been elsewhere on the *Defiant,* the Chief might have been able to induce a minor matter-antimatter explosion, disabling the ship's entire power grid so the shields would drop and Jadzia could attempt to blindly beam Jake from the unprotected vessel. But even Jake knew that while he was sealed in engineering, any attempt by O'Brien to explosively damage the *Defiant*'s generators would prove fatal.

Even Bashir had tried to save him. The doctor had provided his authorization codes so Jake could report to the computer as the ship's chief medical officer. But that hadn't worked, either. The computer was not that easily fooled.

"How's my dad?" Jake asked, needing a short break from the relentlessly hopeless attempts.

"He and Garak still aren't here," Jadzia radioed back. "But we've got a little time."

Then Kira's voice came over the channel. "Commander Arla, are you still there?" she asked firmly.

"Major Kira," Arla answered breathily, her voice continuing its gradual decline that Jake had noticed earlier but could not explain.

Jake was guessing that Arla was still on the bridge. Though with a combadge, he knew, she could be anywhere else on the ship. He shivered.

Kira's voice was commanding, persuasive. "Arla—why won't you let Jake go? You've heard what's going on. If Sisko and Garak don't return to this time, history will change. You'll have won."

"And what if they do return?" Arla asked.

Jake was troubled by Arla's deep, rough tones. It was as if her throat had changed in size or configuration. He didn't want to think about what the Grigari nanites might be capable of doing to her. And perhaps, soon, to him.

"Then Jake's death accomplishes nothing but to add to the sorrow of the universe," Kira argued. "I know there's enough of you left inside, beyond what the Grigari have done, to know I'm right. Let him go, Rees. Please. As a Bajoran. For the sake of our people."

"You are the dead," a new voice said.

Jake jerked back from the console in a reflex action.

Weyoun was back. But where?

"Oh, yes," Weyoun continued in a voice that froze Jake's ability to think. "I'm still here. On the *Boreth*. Exactly where you placed me against my will."

Jake heard the change in Kira's tone. "Is that what this is going to take?" she demanded of Weyoun. "A trade? Your life for Jake's?"

Jake stared at his communications screen, listening, hoping, dreading. He didn't want to die on this *Defiant*. But he didn't want Weyoun to go free because of him.

"What life, Major?" Weyoun said over the comm link. "There's less than an hour remaining by whoever's timeframe you measure it. Arla is doing the right thing." Then he added for Arla's benefit, "You *are* doing the right thing, Commander."

"It is the will of the True Prophets," Arla chanted tonelessly.

Jake leaned over his console, rested his head in his folded arm. He'd been right before. There was no way out of this.

"Weyoun," Jadzia suddenly suggested, "I could beam you from the *Boreth* to the *Defiant*. You and Arla could be together at the end."

Jake did not lift his head, but he listened in spite of himself.

"What a splendid idea," Weyoun answered. "Then, when the *Defiant*'s shields drop to let me beam onboard, why, you could beam Jake off, too. Do you really think that's going to happen?"

Jake lifted his head. He had heard that tone of voice before, back in his school days on Earth. It was the sound of a bully. Someone who enjoyed creating pain because he drew strength from it. "You're not talking about the will of the Prophets anymore," Jake said accusingly to Weyoun. "You're just mad at my father."

"I assure you, Jake, I am quite beyond such petty emotions."

"You want me to die out here because you want to hurt my father."

"Jake, it doesn't matter to *me* where you die. The whole universe is coming to an end."

"But not because you want it to!" Jake said. He sat up in his anger.

"Jake, it is the will of the True Prophets. I am sorry that—"

"It's *not* the will of the Prophets!" Jake cried out. "Don't you understand, it's the will of those lousy little nanites in your skull. Rearranging your brain cells. Making you think whatever the Pah-wraiths want you to think."

Weyoun's voice hissed with menace. "If you were within my reach, Jake, I would settle this now. You would die for your blasphemy."

"Blasphemy," Jake muttered. "Ha! Don't you remember anything about the 'discussions' you used to have with me on DS9 when you were in control? You never used to care if I didn't agree with you. You might have clamped down on what I could write, but you never had a problem just listening to me!"

"That was another time," the Vorta said. "And another Weyoun."

"Why? Because the Grigari nanites have . . . have reconfigured you! Just like they crushed Arla's skull and rebuilt her brain in their image!"

"Jake, I can tell you're working yourself into a regrettable emotional state. It would be a shame if you were to miss what is likely to be the defining moment of your life's experience."

"You know what my defining moment is?" Jake shouted at the console. "I love my father! Who the hell have you ever loved?!"

There was no reply on Weyoun's channel. Nor anything from Arla on the intraship link.

Jake rocked back and forth as he breathed deeply to steady himself.

He checked the readout.

Twenty-four minutes.

The end wouldn't be so bad, Jake thought, if only he could talk to his father one more time.

If he was a condemned man, that was his last wish.

CHAPTER 24

"OH, LOOK," Garak said with satisfaction. "Now I'm here, too."

Sisko looked in the direction Garak indicated and saw— Garak.

This timeframe's version of him, dressed in civilian clothes, huddled behind the twisted wreckage of a collapsed air channel on the second level of the Promenade.

"It would appear all the players are now in the game," Sisko's Garak said.

"Do you know what you were doing here?" Sisko asked. He looked down through the railing to the main level, to see Terrell's three agents marching Quark and Odo out of Quark's bar. They were heading for a turbolift.

"No doubt the same thing I'm doing now," Garak said. "Trying to make sense of a very confusing day for the Cardassian people. Oh, look again—Quark's seen me!"

Sisko saw the Ferengi below look up in their direction,

his attention caught by something he saw on the second level—Sisko's Garak, in his hiding place.

But atypically silent, the Quark below walked on without giving any other reaction.

"We should go down," Garak said behind Sisko.

Having already made up his mind to accept the Cardassian's lead, Sisko now followed him, quickly reaching the first level via a winding metal stairway.

With Sisko close behind him, Garak edged out onto the Promenade, then ducked a moment later into a half-opened airlock. Once again, Sisko stayed with him.

Garak stayed a step back within the shelter of the airlock's entrance. He held up a cautioning hand. "Well, that should confuse the poor fellow," he said. "I believe Quark just saw me again."

Sisko peered past Garak. But if the Quark of this time had seen the Cardassian, again he was not giving any reaction to confirm the sighting. All Sisko could confirm for himself was that Quark and Odo had stepped into a turbolift car with the three Cardassians, then descended.

"Now where?" Sisko asked his guide.

Garak gave him a look of reproach, and Sisko realized how obvious the answer to that question was.

Over the next few minutes, Sisko and Garak's task of following Quark and Odo and their captors was made immeasurably easier by knowing where they were going—to Terrell's hidden lab.

The most delicate aspect of the operation for Sisko and Garak was ensuring they wouldn't be spotted by Garak's past self, as he also followed the other Cardassians for reasons of his own.

"This is all so new to me," Sisko's Garak said as they ended up crawling through a Jefferies tube on the same lower deck as Terrell's lab. "I must have already been suffering from some sort of memory lapse—because of the inhibitor I had asked myself to take. Afterward, since I undoubtedly suspected that I had been subjected to a memory-altering drug developed by the Obsidian Order, I, of course, must have suspected Terrell."

Sisko attempted to make that causal loop make sense. "So . . . you followed Terrell's agents in the past," he reasoned, "because you came from the future to give yourself a memory inhibitor, because you couldn't remember why you followed Terrell's agents."

Garak paused for a moment and looked back at Sisko with a good-natured smile. "Isn't time travel remarkable? Such an invigorating challenge!"

A minute later, Sisko and Garak hit the end of the same dead-end conduit that Sisko recognized as the one Jake and Nog would discover a year or so from now, when they first located Terrell's lab and believed it was a Cardassian holosuite.

Through the air mesh of the conduit's cover, Sisko had a direct view of the door to that lab. The door itself was pulsing in and out in what Sisko recognized was a manifestation of Pah-wraith energy—something that Terrell had not yet learned to identify, quantify, or fear.

But because of the rumble of other sounds that now echoed deep within the conduit—explosions, alarms, the thrum of departing shuttles—Sisko couldn't hear what Terrell was saying about Odo and Quark, who were right beside her. He could see her face, though, and its expression revealed to him that she wasn't happy. Sisko's assessment was confirmed as in the next moment Terrell shot Odo.

Sisko tensed as the changeling collapsed, but Garak only whispered, "Easy. Remember—Odo survived this day, too. Though I'm afraid the same can't be said for those two young men in the brown suit and the blue."

All three Cardassians with Terrell were civilians—at least, their clothes were.

And the tailor was right. Sisko had seen those two suits before.

They'd been on the two soldiers whose bodies would be found fused into the hull plates of the station—at the same time as Odo investigated Dal Nortron's murder.

And Terrell's three agents weren't the only Cardassian civilians in the corridor below. Because now, the blue-suited Cardassian held onto a third captive—Garak.

"I must say, it's beginning to make some sense to me now," Sisko's Garak said.

Sisko watched and tried to listen through the conduit cover's air-mesh as Terrell said something to the Garak held captive before her, then turned and had a separate word with Quark.

"She's telling him she wants him to go into the lab and get the Orb," Sisko said.

Quark's reluctance was apparent.

Tendrils of red energy had begun to snake out all along the doorframe, as if outlining a miniature wormhole that was already beginning to form inside.

"That must be what's linking us to this day," Sisko said in a low voice. "And what's linking the station's time-frame to the wormhole six years from now. Terrell almost succeeded in opening a wormhole just with one Orb and her equipment."

"A sobering thought," Garak said quietly beside him.

Suddenly, in the scene beyond the conduit air-mesh, Sisko saw Odo come back to consciousness and then begin to shout out something. Almost immediately, the changeling was drawn to the distorted, pulsing door to Terrell's lab, moving toward it as if compelled.

"A telepathic summons," Sisko whispered to Garak. "That's what Terrell said happened to some of her scientists."

Now the third Cardassian—perhaps Atrig, Sisko thought, younger and unscarred—jumped between Odo and the lab door. He pointed a weapon at the changeling, then stunned him again, preventing Odo from entering the lab.

Meanwhile, Terrell pushed Quark closer to the door.

Sisko instinctively recoiled as a huge strand of red energy unfurled from the opening upon the door and then lashed out at Terrell, who was saved at the last moment when Atrig leaped in front of her. This time, the Cardassian was struck by a tendril on his back and was hurled forward across the corridor, falling facedown on the deck, red energy snapping over the length of his body.

Then two more coils of energy darted out and Sisko saw Quark duck as they shot over him to strike the two Cardassians—the same two who would be found six years later, merged halfway into the DS9 hull.

Sisko and Garak watched as red light crept over the Cardassians' flailing forms as if it were alive and ingesting them. Then, like a whip being cracked, the coils snapped back to the door, and the bodies of the two Cardassians were pulled through solid metal.

Terrell's small phaser was now pressed against Quark's temple.

Sisko saw waves of indecision sweep over the Ferengi's face and could almost guess at his thoughts: Accept a clean death here? Or face whatever lay beyond that door that might be worse?

But as Sisko knew Quark must, the feisty Ferengi gathered up his courage, wrapped his head in his arms, ran straight at the door, and—

—disappeared.

"A remarkable display of character," Garak commented. "I wonder what convinced someone like Quark to make the attempt?"

Sisko didn't know. He accepted that he never might. Whatever had driven the Ferengi forward, though, Sisko knew it hadn't been cowardice.

"And now we wait?" Sisko asked Garak.

The Cardassian nodded. "There can't be much time remaining, but if we wish to know how Quark obtained the Orb, then wait we must."

A moment later, though, the waiting was over for the versions of Odo and Garak who stood below in the corridor. Two more red coils whipped out from behind the door and pulled them both back into the realm of the red wormhole, even as Terrell finally gave up her vigil and shouted for her people to withdraw.

Sisko's eyes tracked the Cardassian scientist's retreat, not to return for six long years, abandoning her research and her lab. Without ever learning what now transpired behind its pulsing, glowing door.

Sisko's eyes remained fixed on the door.

He wondered if he would ever learn its secret.

And if so, who would tell him.

In a timeframe six years later, Quark awoke. And wished he hadn't. His head throbbed as if Morn was performing his favorite toe-tapping, crowd-pleasing Lurian fertility dance directly on Quark's skull.

He tried to get up, but something—someone—held him back. Someone behind him.

Quark groaned as he twisted his neck to look back over his shoulder.

Then he squeaked to see Dukat's unconscious form slumped behind him.

He and the mad Cardassian were tied together, back to back.

Quark lurched forward in his desire to get away, but his legs were tied together, too. He struggled to do more than squeak, but he was gagged.

He took a deep breath to quell his panic, forced his racing heart to settle down, exactly as Odo would undoubtedly instruct him. He looked around.

Wherever he was, the dim light was coming from a single fixture overhead. Slowly, his eyes adjusted to the insubstantial light and then, with a start, he realized he knew where he was: tied up in his own storage locker under his own bar.

And from the sounds of the footsteps overhead, his bar was opening up for business.

Quark's eyes widened. If whoever had hit him had placed the Red Orb in the hiding place where it belonged ... He began to struggle against his bindings again. In only an hour, maybe two, he knew the red wormhole would open and the station would be destroyed, exactly as it had been before.

Except this time, *he'd* be trapped on it, bound and gagged and facing certain death with his only company a madman.

There was only one way out.

Even as Quark sent a silent entreaty to the Divine Nagus, he knew how utterly ridiculous he was being.

Yet what else could he do?

So he said the words he would never in a millennium have believed he would ever utter.

Squeaking full volume through his foul-tasting gag, Quark cried out: *"Dukat! Dukat! You have to wake up!"*

On the *Defiant*, Jake leaned with his back against the master console, arms folded, thinking about Mardah. Thinking about all the things he had left undone, the books unwritten, the secrets never shared.

"Still there?" Jadzia asked over the comm link.

"Yeah," Jake said. "Any word from my dad?"

"Not yet." Jake could almost picture the Trill's smile as she spoke. "But you know your father, Jake. He likes to push his deadlines to the very last second."

"Yeah. Maybe he'll surprise us." Jake shook his head at his own words. A surprise was about the only thing that *could* save him now.

He twisted around to look at the time readout.

Nineteen minutes.

Jake turned back.

Just about time for the universe to end.

Again.

CHAPTER 25

"FIFTEEN MINUTES," Garak said as he looked at his tri
corder. "Ah, well. Perhaps there are some things we are
not meant to know."

"Five more minutes," Sisko said. He had peeled off his
ripped jacket in the close confines of the conduit. It was
enervatingly hot in here. The air circulators were off-line
along with most of the other equipment on the station.

"It will take five minutes for us to reach the transporter
in Ops," Garak reminded him. "And then there will be two
of us to beam out. Even for you, that is leaving precious
little time."

"Do you want to go ahead?" Sisko asked.

But Garak declined the offer. "What I might do, how
ever, is move back to the Jefferies tube. I find the conduit
is a bit . . . closed in for my liking."

Sisko shifted out of the way and Garak crawled back to
the Jefferies tube to which the conduit connected.

Quark, Odo, the past Garak, and the two Cardassian

soldiers had been gone from the corridor outside Terrell's lab for almost ten minutes. If time in the red wormhole was nonlinear, anything could have happened by now, Sisko knew.

Then Garak called out in an urgent whisper, "Captain! Quickly!"

Sisko slid along the conduit to join Garak in the Jefferies tube.

"Quark!" the Cardassian whispered. He pointed ahead. "He just crawled through that intersection. And he was carrying the Orb!"

Sisko immediately began crawling down the tube with Garak following behind.

At the intersection, Sisko carefully looked around the corner, saw no trace of Quark, and pushed on.

After two more turns, it was clear where Quark was headed—his bar.

"This is it!" Sisko said to Garak. "Somehow, Quark got the Orb, and he's taking it up to hide in his bar, exactly where we'll find it six years from now!"

"Except," Garak pointed out, "didn't you say someone else will steal it?"

"Not if we steal it first!" Sisko said decisively.

He was positive there was a chance his last desperate plan could work. *If* he could get the Orb from Quark. *If* he could take it into the future. And *if* he could then hide it again in Quark's bar just before he himself went to search for it after returning from Jeraddo. If he could make that chain of events work out, everything else would, too.

Sisko, with Garak still following, proceeded as quickly as he could through the tubes for one more deck, until he saw an open hatchway. He leaned forward to peer through it, just in time to see Quark hurrying along a corridor, Orb in hand.

Sisko jumped down after his quarry. Garak dropped in pursuit an instant later.

And then, two levels below the Promenade and what Sisko *knew* was Quark's final intended destination, everything changed.

Sisko charged around a corner to find Quark rolled up against a bulkhead, blood trickling from his mouth, completely unconscious.

And the Red Orb of Jalbador was gone.

"No," Sisko gasped, leaning forward, hands on knees, breathless from the long pursuit. "How could it have been stolen already?"

"Unless it was stolen to begin with," Garak said, wheezing slightly as he arrived at Sisko's side a moment later.

"But how?"

"This might not be the time to explore that question, Captain. We have barely enough time to reach the transporter, let alone—"

"GET THE FERENGI!"

At the far end of the corridor, a group of Cardassian soldiers had appeared and now began running forward, eager to complete the lynching that had almost occurred on the Promenade.

"We can't leave him!" Sisko said.

"Captain! We *know* he survived this day!"

"No one could survive *this!*" Sisko cried as he swept up Quark's limp body and began to run back the way he had come.

"You're going the wrong way!" Garak called after him.

But Sisko didn't stop.

He had finally accepted that there was only one thing left that he could do.

What Kira had told him to do from the start.

Trust in the Prophets.

CHAPTER 26

WITH ONLY eight minutes remaining, Sisko finally stopped in front of the door to Terrell's lab. His chest heaved. His lungs burned with each breath. Quark's body was a dead weight in his arms.

But the door to Terrell's abandoned lab still glowed faintly with the power of the Orb.

The power of the Temple.

Garak stumbled to a stop beside him. "You . . . can't be . . . serious," he gasped.

"They entice corporeal beings by offering them what they want most," Sisko said. He shifted Quark's body once again. "I know what I want most. What about you, Garak?"

Garak's weary smile brightened with his understanding. "By all means, then. May I?" He held his hand over the doorplate.

Sisko nodded. Without the Orb, they would have to enter the lab just as Jake and Nog had, not by passing *through* the door but by opening it.

"If it *is* an illusion that we find," Sisko said, "you *can* get us out, can't you?"

Garak cocked his head to one side, looking intrigued by the possibility. "Assuming there *is* someplace else to go, I believe I am well versed in the techniques Dukat used."

"Good enough," Sisko said.

The door opened.

Sisko stepped through it with Quark in his arms.

Thinking only of what he wanted most—

"Captain!" Odo shouted.

Sisko spun around to see that he was exactly where he had wanted to be.

Deep Space 9.

In Quark's bar.

Surrounded by all the rescued crew and passengers with whom he had traveled through time.

Almost all.

Odo stepped forward to take Quark's unconscious body from him.

Then Sisko saw Worf on a stretcher, badly injured.

He saw Jadzia seated at a table far off in the back, working intently at a communications terminal.

"What timeframe is this?" Sisko asked.

Then Garak appeared beside him.

Sisko looked but could detect no obvious portal or distortion that might indicate a wormhole or its precursor field. He and Garak had simply both materialized in the center of the bar's main room.

"We're about ten minutes *after* the station was destroyed," Bashir explained quickly. "And in about two minutes, we'll be swept back to just about ten minutes *before*."

"The evacuation is about to get under way back there," Odo said. "We've got a chance."

Sisko didn't know how that could be possible. He

didn't understand how the timeline could continue unchanged. Not without the presence of the stolen Red Orb. But he had an even more important question to ask them all. "Where's Jake?"

Bashir's expression was not reassuring. "He's still on the *Defiant*," the doctor said. "It's Arla . . . she's been infected by Grigari nanites, and she's a follower of Weyoun now. She won't drop the shields to let us beam Jake off."

Bashir led Sisko to Jadzia, who looked up at him with surprise. "Jake!" she said excitedly. "Your father's here!"

"Dad!"

Sisko felt a heartrending surge of joy tinged with sorrow as he heard his son's voice crackle from the small device on Jadzia's table.

"Jake! It's going to be okay. We'll get you off the ship!"

Sisko saw Jadzia's silent shake of her head, but he couldn't—he *refused* to—believe there was no hope. Not when he could hear his son. And his son could hear him.

"We'll get you off the ship!" Sisko said again. There had to be a way, and he would find it.

Then Weyoun's voice obnoxiously intruded. *"Oh, Benjamin, you shouldn't lie to your son."*

"You can stop this, Weyoun!" Sisko said. "Tell Arla to drop the shields!"

"Why?" Weyoun asked. *"So the pain of life can continue forever?"*

"No!" Sisko exploded. "So the joy of life can continue! You were alive once! You know what—"

"I assure you, I am alive now as well," Weyoun coolly interrupted.

"Are you?" Sisko demanded. "Remember when I hit you, Weyoun? I broke your nose! And now it's perfectly restored, isn't it? Rebuilt by those damned nanites. They're in you, Weyoun. They're making you forget what it even means to be alive. They've programmed you just the way your Founders did! They've turned you into a soulless machine, and *that's* what wants this universe to end!"

"Coming up on ninety seconds!" someone in the bar called out. The earnest young voice sounded like Ensign Simons.

Jadzia lifted the communications device under one arm. Sisko held out his hand for it—it was his only contact with his son. But instead, the Trill held out her other hand to him. "We have to link hands, Benjamin," she said. "It's the only way we can overcome the temporal inertia or whatever it is that kept Weyoun and Dukat and everyone they touched locked in a specific timeframe."

Jadzia took his hand in hers when Sisko made no motion of his own. "We'll come back to this timeframe at least once more," she said softly. "I promise you'll be able to talk to Jake again."

Sisko heard the unspoken words at the end of her sentence. He'd be able to talk to his son one last time.

"All right, everyone," Odo shouted. "It's going to be getting dark on the other side. Lots of confusion. Stay to the back wall and out of sight so we don't interfere with anything!"

In a daze, Sisko saw all the temporal refugees in the bar begin to move to the back wall of the bar's main room. Jadzia used her grip on his hand to move him in the same direction, to join the others.

"Why's Odo saying that?" Sisko asked in sudden alarm. "We have to be *evacuated* on the other side. *Before* the station's destroyed."

"No, sir," O'Brien answered as he hurried over to join Sisko and Jadzia. "Dax and I, we've worked out the equations. If we leave the station too soon, all bets are off. Our one chance to not create an alternate timeline is to reenter our own timeframe at the exact moment the wormhole fully opens."

"Is that even possible?" Sisko asked. He saw the way Jadzia and O'Brien looked at each other. It meant they both had their doubts.

"I'm going to have to blow the station's reactors," O'Brien gruffly admitted. "A full explosive overload."

"What?"

"For what it's worth, Benjamin," Jadzia pointed out, "the force of the explosion might have been what threw the *Defiant* into the future in the first place. I did the calculations, and between the wormhole opening and Terrell's ship firing at us, there wasn't enough energy hitting our ship to put us into a slingshot around the wormhole's mouth."

"But what will blowing the reactors do to this part of the station?" Sisko asked.

"This part of the station's destroyed anyway," O'Brien said. "We all saw it implode. But if the next time we come back to this timeframe *after* the station's destruction—if we can run up to Ops so when we switch back, it'll be completely evacuated—and if I can blow the reactors then, with any luck, all the airtight doors will seal, and the whole Ops module will pop free of the wormhole."

"That's a lot of ifs, Chief," Sisko said.

"It's all we've got, sir. Short of setting off a trilithium planetbuster outside the habitat ring."

"Ten seconds!" Odo shouted. "Everyone link arms!"

Sisko stood, arm in arm with Jadzia and Kira against the back wall with the others, linked arms with them, and was suddenly blinded by a flash of blue light.

But when the flash faded, full visibility did not return as it had so many times before.

Instead, like everyone else, Sisko staggered to one side

in the skewed gravity field. Staring in disbelief at the three floating Orbs of Jalbador, now in perfect alignment. They were suspended in midair, just a meter or so above the deck, spinning and glowing, each just like an Orb of the Prophets, except that the energy they shed was the hellish hue of blood and fire.

"But the third Orb was stolen!" Sisko said.

"I don't know how it got back," Kira told him, almost yelling to be heard over the wail of the pressure alarms, "but the last time we were in this timeframe, we were watching from upstairs, and we saw you find it again. Right behind the mural."

Now, just as Sisko had witnessed six years in the past outside the door to Terrell's secret lab, coiled tendrils of red energy began to unfurl. This time, they curled away from each Orb to link up with tendrils sent forth from the others, until they merged and defined an equilateral triangle of shimmering crimson light.

And in the middle of that formation, a distortion was growing.

The doorway to the Second Temple.

And to DS9's destruction.

To Sisko's profound amazement, *everything* was as it was before. It was as if *all* the actions he and the others had taken in the past had had no effect on the present. Unless, as Garak had said, what had happened in the past was what had *always* happened in the past. What was *supposed* to have happened.

On the other side of the room, Sisko observed the O'Brien of this timeframe try to touch an Orb, only to be thrown back in a flash of red lightning.

He observed the growing wind generated by whatever dimensional forces the Orbs were unleashing that blew at the other Jadzia's hair as she tried to take readings with her tricorder.

He heard that other Jadzia shout, "We've got intensive neutrino flux! A definite wormhole precursor!"

And then Sisko was electrified to hear his *own* voice shout back, *"Here?!"*

There was a flash of phaser fire as someone tried to disrupt an Orb but was disintegrated by his own beam's precise return.

Then Kai Winn and Kira appeared in the entrance to the bar, astonishment stretching their mouths open wide even as the howling wind attempted to drive the women back.

Sisko watched, mesmerized, as these earlier versions of himself and his crew began to withdraw.

And then he remembered . . .

"Chief!" Sisko shouted to the O'Brien of his own timeframe. "You wanted to shut down the reactors! To cut off the power you thought the Orbs were using!"

Sisko saw the sudden fear that struck his engineer. "But if I do that, I won't be able to set them to overload!"

Sisko knew there was no more time to waste.

He ran away from the others, away from the back wall, skirting the glowing triangle of light to race out onto the Promenade, just as the power grid failed and the station was plunged into darkness.

This is it! Sisko thought. This was when O'Brien made his suggestion to shut down the reactors.

And in the halflight, Sisko turned, remembering he himself was just about to give that order, until . . .

The Sisko who had survived his journey into the future ran up to the Sisko who had yet to depart, pushed the Quark of the past to the side, and with all his strength punched *himself* as hard as he could.

Even as his past self fell to the deck, Sisko took command.

"Abandon station!" he cried out, exactly as he remembered hearing himself say so many days, so many years, so many millennia ago. "Chief! Jadzia! Pass the order on to abandon station!"

He checked on himself on the deck, saw himself rubbing his jaw, beginning to get up. He remembered how he felt momentarily confused at the time. As if he had missed out on something important.

He heard O'Brien of the past urgently call out a question. "What about the reactors?"

"Now, Chief!"

The Sisko of the future saw that his order had just the same effect on O'Brien now, as he remembered. A moment later, the station's siren wailed with two long bursts, two short. Over and over.

The order to abandon station.

Sisko watched, fascinated, as his past self got to his feet, looked around in confusion and then tapped at his combadge to issue more orders.

At the time, Sisko remembered, he hadn't known who had given the order to abandon the station, but he had assumed it was in response to something that had happened when he had been hit and half-conscious. So he had not countermanded it.

The Sisko of the future ran back into Quark's bar, felt the floor already beginning to buckle, evaded the debris that was flying everywhere.

He ducked bouncing chairs and rolling tables, went charging for the back wall, reaching out his hand to grab Kira's as—

A red light flashed over him, and he was back in a silent restored version of Quark's bar.

The sudden calm was jarring to Sisko, almost physical.

"We're eight minutes past the destruction of the station!" O'Brien shouted. "Everyone up to Ops!"

Sisko watched in confusion as the others began to run

past him, out of the bar. He didn't understand. "Why is the station restored in here? Why aren't we floating in imploded debris?"

"I wondered the same thing," Odo told him as he hurried past to join the others. "Even Vic is operational in this version of the station. I met him walking around the Promenade."

Sisko decided to think about the implications of that later. It was time to run. Time to try Jadzia's and O'Brien's last-ditch plan to return them all to their timeline.

And then Jake's voice called out to him from Jadzia's communicator.

"Dad! I know what to do! I know what to do!"

Jadzia stopped so Sisko could speak to his son.

"Are the shields down?" Sisko asked him.

"No—Arla's not saying anything. But I can save the station!"

"What? How?"

"By blowing up the Defiant."

Sisko's blood turned to ice. "No!"

"Dad, it'll work. All I have to do is cut the power to the magnetic bottles, release the matter and antimatter, and, according to the computer, the explosion will have enough force to create a subspace compression wave."

"There is no subspace in the wormhole," Sisko said.

"I know!" Jake answered. *"But the explosion will create it, and that's what'll push the station free."*

"You will not blow up the *Defiant!*" Sisko raged. "That is an order!"

"Dad, the channel was open. I heard what you were talking about with O'Brien. The reactors. The planet-buster. I worked it out with the computer. Tell him, Dax."

Sisko looked at his friend in sudden hope, but she had none to give him. "He's right, Benjamin. A subspace bubble generated by the *Defiant* would be enough to push us from the station, with far less risk than overloading the station's reactors."

"Less risk?" Sisko cried. "What about my son?"

"Dad! I'm trapped here! In seven minutes, I won't exist!"

"I'll get you out!" Sisko promised, pleaded.

"Dad, please. Let me help!"

"Don't, Jake . . ."

"Dad, I have to. I know . . . I know you'd do it for me . . ."

Tears burned Sisko's eyes.

He had raised his son too well.

"I love you, Dad . . ."

"Jake . . . I love you . . ."

Sisko swayed on his feet. He couldn't go on. He just couldn't believe that after all he and everyone he loved and cared about had been through, after he had trusted in the Prophets to deliver him and his people and his universe, that *this* would be the price they would demand.

"Benjamin," Jadzia urged as she tugged on his arm. "We have to go."

Sisko let his friend guide him to safety.

But what did it matter that a universe was saved, if the cost was the life of his son?

In the engineering room of the *Defiant*, Jake finally felt at peace.

This was something he could do. Something that would matter.

He touched the command lines that would make the computer think the ship's matter-antimatter fuel had been vented—one of O'Brien's tricks for interfering with a starship's operational readiness.

Then he activated the commands that would permit him to order a powerdown of the magnetic coils—the ones that generated the containment fields in which the matter and antimatter were stored.

Three seconds after he entered that command, the ship would explode. But the timing had to be precisely right.

Jake watched the countdown on the console. Three timeframes gradually coming into phase, only a few seconds off right now.

He was surprised at how good he felt.

He thought of his father.

He was proud to be Ben Sisko's son.

Sisko lost track of timeframes and elapsed time and whether the light that flashed over him was blue or red.

Because nothing mattered anymore.

It was all confusion anyway.

And then he was in Ops with all the others.

A perfect Ops, with gravity level and restored.

"Thirty seconds," Odo said.

Everyone joined hands.

Almost everyone. Three Bajorans had died on the *Boreth*. Two Denevan technicians on the *Defiant*. Vash had escaped to the past. Quark had simply vanished, leaving his past self alone.

And Jake—Jake was somewhere beyond time and space.

In the hands of the Prophets.

"Fifteen seconds," Odo said.

Jadzia squeezed Sisko's hand.

"This will be the final transfer," she told him. "We'll be switching to a timeframe about five seconds before the station was destroyed. We'll actually be on the station as it falls into the red wormhole. And then, just before the wormhole closes, just as the *Defiant* of that time is attacked by Terrell's ship, the subspace bubble will push us out again."

And Jake will die, Sisko thought, remembering the accusations he had hurled at Weyoun. Now he felt like a soulless machine himself, beyond all care, beyond emotion.

"Five seconds," Odo intoned. "Four . . . three . . . two . . ."

The flash was blue, and when it faded, the others cried out in terror as they toppled to the side, the gravity more off-balance than it had ever been before.

Every alarm in Ops was screaming. Distant explosions echoed through the deck. Consoles exploded in sparks and flame.

And then a red glow infused everything in Sisko's field of vision, as if the very air had combusted.

"We've entered the wormhole," O'Brien shouted.

Jake, Sisko thought—one final time.

And then he was in—

—the light space.

"What happened?" the Sisko asks.

He is by the reflecting pool in the meditation garden.

"What happens," Kai Opaka corrects him. She smiles at him as she reaches for his ear.

"No," the Sisko says. "This isn't right. This isn't what was supposed to be."

Captain Picard turns away from the table in the conference room of the Enterprise. *Behind him, Bajor is resplendent in full sunlight, a world reborn. "Supposed?" Picard asks.*

"I trusted in you!" the Sisko laments.

He falls to his knees in the ruins of B'hala. "I trusted in you."

"You always trust in us," Opaka says.

The Sisko looks up at her, and even on the Promenade as it is on the first day he sets foot on it, he feels the tears run down his face.

Not the tears of the Prophets.

His tears.

The tears of a father.

"I hate you," the Sisko says.

His own father stands behind him in the kitchen of the restaurant in New Orleans, holding the Sisko's hand in his as he guides the whisk through the eggs that swirl like galaxies.

"Hate? What is this?" the Sisko's father asks.

The Sisko stands behind Jake in his own kitchen in his apartment in San Francisco, Jennifer looking on as the Sisko holds his son's hand in his as he guides the whisk through the eggs that swirl like galaxies.

"No . . . ," the Sisko says. "This isn't fair . . ."

"Yes," Opaka tells him. "It is."

The Sisko walks the paths of the Academy as a student.

"Just as there is no time—" Boothby says.

The Sisko is under the stars of Earth, outside the tent in Yosemite, cradling Jennifer in his arms the night Jake is conceived.

"—there is no hate," Jennifer says.

The Sisko stands on the deck of the Saratoga *as it burns.*

"But there is death!"

Prylar Rulan bows his head outside the Temple on the Promenade. "Another time."

"Not another time," the Sisko says. "This time! This time Jake died! Not because of time! Not because of anything at all except for you!"

The Sisko expects to be taken to the light space, where he is always taken when his emotions overwhelm the Prophets.

Instead, he is on the pitcher's mound in Ebbets Field.

The Sisko does not understand.

"You brought me here?"

"We always bring you here," Jackie Robinson says.

The Sisko looks around the perfect field, inhales the rich scent of the grass, hears the growing tumult of the crowd.

They are on their feet, cheering. He hears a cowbell

*ringing in the outfield stand, a ragtag band plays Dix-
ieland off-key.*

The Sisko turns again, sees the scoreboard.

"Someone pitched a no-hitter," the Sisko says.

*He looks at the baseball in his hand. The Prophets, for
once, do not correct his incorrect use of tense.*

"I don't understand," the Sisko says.

"You throw the ball," Picard says.

"They hit the ball," Opaka says.

*Twelve-year-old Jake points to the scoreboard again.
"This is what happens."*

Sisko turns back to the board, reads it carefully.

"The home team won?" he says.

The Sisko is in the Wardroom on Deep Space 9.

"The war ends," Locutus says.

The Sisko is in Vic's.

"You threw the ball, pallie. Heckuva game."

The Sisko stands on the bridge of the first Enterprise, a
glimmer of understanding beginning to grow in him.

"The War of the Prophets," he says. "You won."

*Captain Kirk turns in his command chair, holds out his
hands. "We* always *win, Lieutenant."*

The Sisko hangs his head, in the ruins of B'hala, alone.

"But I have lost," he says.

*He grimaces as Opaka's thumb and finger squeeze his
earlobe, feel his* pagh.

"What is this?" she asks.

*In the light space, the Sisko hears the answer to the
question she has asked.*

The voice is Jake's, but the boy cannot be seen.

*"It is, quite simply, your journey, Dad, the one you've
always been destined to take."*

"What is this?" the Sisko asks.

And the Prophets answer as they always do.

CHAPTER 27

SISKO STUMBLED over the deck and opened his eyes to see—

Ops.

Everyone who had been there before was there again, even Worf on his stretcher.

Sisko tapped his foot on the deck. The gravity *felt* right, but . . .

"Chief?" he asked.

O'Brien looked up from an engineering console, shook his head. "We're not in the wormhole, if that's what you mean."

Sisko wasn't sure what he meant. Nor what he was looking for.

He saw Kira watching him.

"You were with Them, weren't you?" she asked, no question as to whom the word 'them' referred.

Sisko nodded. Touched a communications control on the console beside him.

And instantly a squeal of subspace static raced through

379

the speakers surrounding Ops, until a single voice rang out.

"Dad? Are you there?"

"Jake?!"

And then father and son both spoke together, asking the same question at the same time.

"What happened?"

They knew the answer in minutes, provided by Captain Halberstadt of the *U.S.S. Bondar* and Captain S'relt of the *U.S.S. Garneau*. The two *Akira*-class starships had been dispatched to Deep Space 9 when the Bynar computer virus had degraded its defensive capabilities. That deployment had proved invaluable when the time came to evacuate the station as the red wormhole opened.

But what had happened at that time was most easily understood by viewing the visual sensor data the *Garneau* transmitted to the main viewer in Ops.

At first, Sisko had trouble concentrating on the images he watched. *His son had been returned to him!* The *Defiant* was powerless but intact, safe within the protective grip of the *Bondar*'s tractor beams. Jake would be beamed back to DS9 within the hour. Once some routine radion isotope decontamination had been performed on his section of the ship.

The *Garneau*'s sensor log showing the fate of Deep Space 9 was no more than ten minutes old, and it began exactly like the one Sisko had been shown almost twenty-five years in the future.

A glow began on the Promenade as the red wormhole opened in Quark's. The station was deformed by the tidal stresses of the wormhole's immense gravitational well. Escape pods misfired and were drawn to their destruction. Docking pylons collapsed toward the opening mouth of the wormhole as the *Defiant* released her docking clamps and pulled away.

And then, like the familiar Bajoran wormhole seen through a colored filter, the red wormhole opened in just the same way, and Deep Space 9 shrank faster than the sensor log could smoothly record, as if the station had suddenly plunged into a bottomless pit.

This was where the record Sisko had seen in the future had ended.

But here on Ops, the log continued.

The *Defiant* suddenly swung past, gyrating wildly, taking phaser fire from an unseen enemy.

Terrell's ship, Sisko knew.

The *Defiant* spun on its y axis like a sailing ship in a maelstrom. It shrank just as Deep Space 9 had, into the still-seething energies of the red wormhole.

An instant later, Terrell's *Chimera*-class vessel—a Cardassian warship engineered to resemble a Sagittarian civilian liner—blurred into view as its illegal cloaking field failed, and the craft followed the *Defiant* into a hyperdimensional realm.

Yet this time, unlike the fall of Deep Space 9 or of the *Defiant,* as soon as Terrell's ship vanished within the red wormhole, an enormous gout of energy burst from its mouth, and the wormhole collapsed far faster than its blue counterpart ever had.

Sisko watched as the background of stars and the Denorios Belt suddenly shifted, although the timecode at the bottom of the log continued to count without interruption. That told Sisko the transmission from the *Garneau* had switched from one visual sensor to another to show events as they occurred in quick succession.

From this second viewpoint, Sisko saw the Bajoran wormhole open slowly and majestically as always, and when its mouth was open and the passageway revealed, he saw Deep Space 9, intact, tumble out of the blue wormhole like a child's toy rolling out of a funnel.

And just behind the station, the *Defiant* followed, the ship slowly spinning, out of control, but out of danger, too.

Then the image on the Ops viewer changed again, this time to show Captain S'relt on the bridge of the *Garneau.* If Sisko didn't know better, he'd swear the elderly Vulcan was smiling.

"Captain Sisko, were the events clearly depicted?" S'relt asked.

"Clearly depicted," Sisko agreed. "But what exactly were we seeing there at the end? When Terrell's ship entered the red wormhole?"

The captain referred to a padd he held. "According to spectral analysis of radiation and debris ejected from the red wormhole at the moment before its abrupt collapse, we were observing the result of a high-speed collision between two vessels. Molecular samples recovered positively identify one vessel as the *Chimera*-class ship observed entering the wormhole immediately prior to the collision. Additional molecular samples and fragments of unusual hull debris suggest the second ship was of some undocumented Klingon design." The captain looked up again. "My science officer has so far been unable to identify the class."

For Sisko, however, the picture was complete. "The second ship was called the *Boreth,* Captain. An advanced-technology Klingon vessel. We will provide a full report."

"I am certain I will find it fascinating," the Vulcan replied. "*Garneau* out."

The viewscreen looming over Ops became an empty frame.

Sisko's silent contemplation of it was broken by the voice of his chief engineer.

"Am I getting this right?" O'Brien asked. "Terrell's

ship *collided* with *Weyoun's,* and *that's* what pushed us out of the wormhole?"

"More likely, it was the subspace bubble formed by the explosion of the two ships that pushed us out of the wormhole," Jadzia said.

Sisko had no real interest in the details. All that was important to him was that *something* had pushed them out of the wormhole before Jake had been able to follow through on his plan to sacrifice himself by destroying the *Defiant.*

And then a different puzzle came into Sisko's mind. His brow became furrowed as he searched for an explanation he wasn't at all sure he had.

"Captain?" Kira asked in concern. "Is something wrong?"

"I was just trying to remember who shut off the—"

"Benjamin!"

Everyone in Ops instantly stopped talking and turned to see Jadzia at her science station, absolutely dumbfounded.

"Benjamin," she said again, "you are not going to *believe* the lifesigns readings I just found."

Two minutes later, Sisko sympathized with Jadzia's amazement. He, on the other hand, had the experience of punching himself in the jaw. Compared to that, what was waiting for them in Quark's was just another day on Deep Space 9.

This time, the temporal refugees numbered four. Five if Sisko included the still unconscious version of Quark whom he had rescued on the Day of Withdrawal.

Two of the refugees, dazed and considerably confused, were the blue- and brown-suited Cardassians whose autopsies Bashir had performed no more than a week ago.

The other refugee was a less dazed but even more confused Odo, accompanied by a remarkably calm Garak.

Wherever these people had been taken on the Day of

Withdrawal, when Sisko had seen them pulled into Leej Terrell's lab, the collapse of the red wormhole had now deposited them in this place and time.

Sisko couldn't help noting that all four of them were gathered in the center of the main room, in the same location where he and Garak had also appeared after their passage through Terrell's lab.

The same site had been the center point of the triangle formed by the Red Orbs of Jalbador as they had floated together in perfect alignment.

Now the Orbs were scattered widely in the bar, all three glowing but not near enough to each other to cause any dimensional effects. To ensure this secure state, before Sisko even approached the disoriented group of time travelers, he instructed O'Brien to delegate a team to gather the Orbs, one at a time, then take them to three different and widely separated storage sites on the station, in the constant company of armed security officers.

Sisko still couldn't be certain who among the group of travelers had stolen the Orb from Quark's bar six years ago and then replaced it just before Sisko had searched for it, but he did have his suspicions.

He was certain that none of those present was a suspect, though.

In the debriefing that followed, the Odo from the past doubted everything he was told, even when he was told it by his counterpart of this day. Sisko thought it might actually benefit Odo to see his stubborn streak through his own eyes, the way others usually did.

The Garak from the past easily accepted what had happened to him, and from what Sisko could overhear of his conversation with the Garak of this time, it seemed that someone had 'forgotten' to take a certain neural inhibitor. Sisko made a mental note to discuss that with Dr. Bashir.

From the first, there was no question that Odo, Garak,

and Quark would have to be returned to their own time. Since they had already lived through those intervening years, it was obvious that they *had* been returned, though with their memories of what had happened carefully excised.

As he considered the Quark of the past, who had finally regained consciousness with Bashir's help, Sisko realized he would be sorry to see this version of the Ferengi go back. The Quark Sisko knew in his own timeframe appeared to be the one casualty of the journey through time whose fate wasn't known. The last time the barkeep had been seen by anyone was by Odo, after Dukat had been neutralized. And where Dukat had ended up was anyone's guess as well.

But the most problematic decision Sisko had to make was what to do about the two Cardassian soldiers.

For now, they both conveniently believed that they were the victims of an elaborate Bajoran plot, one whose purpose was to make them think the conflict between the two worlds was long over and that they should feel free to reveal military secrets.

These two sat together, apart from the others, stoutly refusing to talk with anyone except to supply their names, ranks, and DNA samples.

To send them back, Sisko knew, would be to condemn them to death. Their bodies already had been found, merged with the hull of the station. Yet if Sisko didn't send them back, how could the investigation of Dal Nortron's murder ever be linked to their deaths? The past would be changed.

Sisko could see no way out of the hard decision he must make soon.

Until Bashir came up with a solution.

"I could clone them, and we could send the clones back," the doctor suggested. "The clones wouldn't have to be perfect. I'd make sure they had no nervous tissue so they wouldn't really even be alive. But after six years in hard vacuum fused to the hull plates, even I wouldn't be able to tell the difference between them and the real soldiers, so the past could remain unchanged."

Sisko gratefully accepted Bashir's audacious plan and told him to begin work right away.

As for Odo, Garak, and Quark, everyone was in agreement that the less time these three spent in their future, the better. So, on Sisko's instruction, Bashir set to preparing the memory inhibitors he would need to wipe out their entire experiences of the Day of Withdrawal.

"At least now I know why I was so impressed by the way their memories were erased," the doctor said with a chuckle.

Within the hour, Sisko was satisfied that all the plans were in place. The Cardassian soldiers would remain on the station for another two weeks while Bashir engineered their pseudo-clones. But Odo, Garak, and Quark would be sent back at once.

And the technique to use was one Sisko already knew would work.

He would carry the third Red Orb of Jalbador to Terrell's lab himself.

"Are you ready?" Sisko asked the three time travelers.

Odo looked from Sisko to his present-day self with dour skepticism. "Can you at least tell me if by now I know where I come from?" he asked.

But the Odo of the present crossed his arms and shook his head. "No one told me," he said.

Garak, on the other hand, appeared to be having immense fun. "I shall enjoy going back, knowing how much I have to look forward to."

"Undoubtedly," Garak of the present agreed. "Except this time, I shall watch you take the memory inhibitor myself."

The Quark of the past, however, was not enjoying himself and had moved well beyond skepticism. "If this is my bar," he said suspiciously, "then where am I?"

"Uh, don't worry, Brother," Rom tried to reassure him. "It all works out."

"Don't be too sure," Quark snapped. "As soon as I get back, I'm changing my will, and *you* are out."

"What . . . ever you say," Rom agreed.

The past Quark threw up his arms, perplexed. "All right, what's the deal? Who's this pushover, and where's my real brother?"

Sisko had called ahead to security to make sure the way to Terrell's lab was clear. "Rom's right," he assured the travelers. "We just have to—"

And then a Ferengi squeal shook the few unbroken glasses behind the bartop as Quark of the present came flying out of his back room as if chased by a demon.

"I'msorryI'msorryIdidn'tmeantolethimgoRUNNN!" Quark screeched.

A heartbeat later, Sisko knew exactly what Quark meant.

Dukat was behind him.

Red sparks flew from every centimeter of exposed gray skin as he floated over the deck, both outstretched hands encased in writhing globes of red energy.

"You are the dead!" he proclaimed in a voice that seemed to come from everywhere at once. *"Give me an AMOJAN!"*

Then, with his white hair flying out in all directions, he raised his hands as the fires intensified, and just before he could release his first blast of energy—

—a phaser beam struck him from behind.

An attack Dukat had not expected.

His personal forcefield briefly flared into life but faded just as quickly.

The phaser beam stayed in operation, and once the red glow left Dukat, the blue haze of phased dissolution began to spread over his body.

Dukat hovered for an instant in front of the open-mouthed victims he had intended to immolate.

But then what life he had left him, and he fell dead to the deck, his dark eyes dulled and empty, a curl of blue smoke rising from the back of his robes.

Only then did Sisko see who had shot him.

Jadzia.

She was shaking.

Sisko went to her. He took away the phaser she had grabbed from one of Odo's officers.

"He would have killed us all," she said.

"I know," Sisko told his friend, understanding her remorse at taking the life of even a monster like Dukat. "But that's the end of it, Old Man. The Pah-wraiths. The Ascendancy. Kosst Amojan . . . it's over."

Jadzia didn't look convinced.

Later, they assembled by the door to Leej Terrell's hidden lab. The two Cardassian soldiers were part of the group, though under guard, because Sisko wanted them to see the truth of how they had come to this time, to prove that there was no deception. The three other time travelers—Odo and Garak and Quark—were accompanied by their counterparts, for reassurance more than any other reason. O'Brien and Jadzia were also present to take readings with various probes. Two weeks from now, when the two Cardassians' lifeless clones were ready, this procedure would have to be duplicated.

Sisko had the Orb.

With a look to Sisko, Bashir now injected the three time travelers with an inhibitor so sophisticated, he said with a smile, that he absolutely guaranteed it would fool even him.

With the Orb so close to whatever equipment Terrell had installed in her lab, the door began to glow.

"It's still there, Benjamin," Jadzia said as she studied her tricorder. "The wormhole precursor field."

"Don't worry," Sisko assured her. "Once these Orbs are off the station, the whole lab's coming out as scrap." He turned to Bashir. "You give the word, Doctor."

Bashir used his medical tricorder on the three he had injected. "Another minute for the reaction to begin."

Sisko sighed, believing for the first time that it was almost over. Jake and Kasidy were already back on the station. Already waiting for him in his quarters.

"I wish I could leave you with something from this future," Sisko told the three travelers. "You will all survive. And Quark, you will prosper."

The past Quark snorted as he looked at his present self. "Not very much, by the looks of it. You call that a suit?"

But present Quark ignored the insult. "Norellian eel hide," he blurted. "In three years, it'll become a fad on half the planets in the Alpha Quadrant. The price goes up by *five thousand* percent in two months!"

"Don't bother, Quark." Sisko laughed. "He'll never remember. You didn't, did you?"

Quark stared at his past self. Mouthed the words *Norellian eel hides*. Gave himself a quick thumbs up.

The past Odo looked over everyone again, as if comparing each face he saw to a mental file of mug shots. "At least I keep my job," he said. "There's some small comfort in that, I suppose."

The past Quark looked up at him with a sly smile. "And I'm still in business in spite of you doing your job." The past Quark suddenly looked at his counterpart. "Hey—is Odo finally on the take?"

Dejected, the Quark of the present shook his head.

"Keep trying," his past self urged. "He's got to come around sooner or . . . or . . ." He stopped in mid-sentence. Yawned.

"I think we're ready," Bashir said drily.

Jadzia opened the door to the lab.

Sisko concentrated on the Orb just as he would with an Orb of the Prophets.

Red light began to glow within the lab.

"It doesn't look any different," Jadzia said.

O'Brien showed her his tricorder. "But look at the chronometric flux. We're at six years. We've got a link just like when we were in the wormhole."

Sisko nodded. Bashir guided a stumbling Quark to the open door.

Inside the lab, the Ferengi began to swerve left and right like Morn after a party, then fell to one side and was gone before he could hit the floor.

Odo guided himself to the door next. The changeling from the past appeared to have difficulty holding his shape, and when present Odo released him, he seemed to pour into the lab, then disappeared just as Quark had.

"Garak," Sisko said.

Garak also escorted himself to the door, then politely shook hands with himself.

Sisko saw a sudden furtive movement between the two.

"Stop!" Sisko ordered.

The past Garak looked back at Sisko, then ran into the room to vanish like smoke.

"Garak!" Sisko said, furious. "You passed him something! What was it?"

Garak's usual pleasant expression became deadly serious. "A small memory rod with Gul Dukat's personal codes. For switching off the station's self-destruct sequence. Did *you* remember to shut it off, Captain Sisko?"

Sisko hesitated, as if waiting for some part of the present to change as a result of Garak's unwise decision.

"But Garak," Bashir said, "what about the inhibitor I gave him? He won't remember how to use the codes. Or even if he should."

But Garak only smiled. "As expert as you are in the

field of memory control, Doctor, rest assured that there are those whose techniques are even more advanced. In fact, I am quite sure that should your inhibitors not function as you had planned, I can be counted on to take one that will do the job required. *After* the self-destruct is terminated, of course."

"And did *you* take the inhibitor?" Sisko asked.

Garak smiled. "Really, Captain, I can't remember."

Sisko shifted the Orb in his arms. "Time to call it—"

"*Look out!*" Odo shouted.

But the warning was too late.

As one, the two Cardassian soldiers jumped away from their guards and barreled past Odo and O'Brien and Jadzia, diving through the open door to the lab to make their escape.

But they didn't vanish as quickly as the first three had.

Their bodies hung in midair for a moment, becoming more transparent, then finally settled through the deck at the far end of the lab where they disappeared from view.

O'Brien moaned. "The field was collapsing."

"Then they wouldn't have been able to punch through on the other side," Jadzia said. "They'd just . . . merge with the . . ."

O'Brien stared into the lab. "And the trajectory they were on . . . with the station's rotation . . ." His shoulders sagged. "Well, at least we know where they ended up, poor devils," O'Brien said. "That makes it full circle."

Bashir nodded. "Then everything's back where it belongs."

The Orb suddenly felt very heavy in Sisko's arms.

"Almost," he said.

Because there was still one last mystery to solve.

CHAPTER 28

THEY MET AT the second-floor safety railing, where they always had met, where they had bedeviled Odo, played too many pranks, shared their dreams and their secrets, planned their futures, and watched the stars.

The awkwardness lasted only a moment, and then they hugged. Not as friends, but as brothers.

That was how Jake felt. And he knew Nog felt the same.

"It's stupid," Nog said as he stepped back to lean against the railing, "but it feels like you were gone for years."

"I was," Jake said.

"But it was only a minute to us."

Jake nodded. "Ten days for us. Not that long." *Only a lifetime,* he thought.

They both leaned forward on the railing, watching the crowds pass below. There were many more Starfleet personnel than usual. Jake had heard the rumors that a major new offensive was being planned, to take the war to Cardassia.

"I saw Commander Worf," Nog said. "Dr. Bashir says he'll be good as new in another day."

"Helps to have two hearts," Jake said.

"Dr. Bashir also says you're a hero. He says you saved Commander Worf's life."

Jake frowned, thinking of the technicians from Deneva. "I had help," he said.

Nog pursed his lips, bobbed his head. Silence returned.

"How is your father?" Nog asked.

Jake thought about the question. "Different. He's going to Bajor tomorrow with Major Kira. He says . . . well, he says he's almost got everything figured out."

Nog suddenly thrust out a package Jake hadn't even noticed he'd been carrying. "I got him this!"

Jake smiled, took the package. "Great." It felt like a book.

"You can open it," Nog said eagerly. "See if he'll like it. It's one of Chief O'Brien's favorites."

Jake slipped the paper wrap from the object inside. It was a book. An old hardcopy of an Academy text from the Starfleet Institute Press.

He read the title. *"On Time Travel: Three Case Studies in Effects and Cause."* He read the author's name. "Admiral James Tiberius Kirk. Oh, my dad likes him."

"I know. Chief O'Brien likes to quote him." He put a hand on Jake's arm. "Do you know what James T. Kirk's first rule of time travel is?"

Jake shook his head.

"Don't!" Nog grinned.

Jake shared the smile. "I think my dad can appreciate that."

The silence returned. Jake wrapped the paper around the book again.

"You met me, didn't you?" Nog asked at last.

Jake had been expecting the question for the past two

days, dreading it, but he was relieved now that it had finally been asked.

"I . . . really can't talk about it," Jake said. "All the civilians had to sign all these security oaths about not revealing future technology and politics, and . . . basically, I could end up spending the next ten years in New Zealand, you know."

"I am not interested in future technology," Nog said. "And that future you saw, it won't come to pass now, correct? Because . . . because the station's still here and . . . the red wormhole's gone . . . and . . . and like that."

Jake was puzzled by how much of the story his friend already knew. "Who've you been talking to?"

Nog squinted at Jake in confusion. He tapped a finger to an ear. "I'm a Ferengi. I hear things."

Jake sighed. He couldn't avoid it forever. "Okay, I met you."

"Well . . . what was I like?"

"Pretty much the way you are now. A big pain in the lobes."

"Jake!" But Nog laughed along with him. Until the silence returned. "Seriously."

Jake knew the promise he had made to Captain Nog of the future. But he also knew the demands of his friendship with Nog in the present.

"You were a great man," Jake said. "You worked at the highest levels with one of the greatest heroes of our time. You were brave. Hardworking. If we hadn't come along, you would have been the guy who saved the universe."

Nog stared at Jake as if he had forgotten how to speak.

"And I really can't say more than that," Jake told him.

"Just one more thing," Nog said, moving closer like a salesman about to close a deal. "Was I happy?"

Jake knew that was always the question. Bashir had told him that Garak's past self had asked the same of his counterpart. Jake wondered that about his own life. The details of what was to come weren't important. But the emotions were.

"No one was happy," Jake said, skirting the truth without really lying. "It was pretty grim. But you were good at your work. People knew it. And . . . and you were the best."

"Was I still in Starfleet?"

Jake almost started to laugh again. He wondered if Captain Nog had made him promise not to tell his past self about his future just to play one last trick on his human friend. After all, who could withstand relentless Ferengi persuasion for a lifetime?

"Nog, just this once. Just this one thing, all right?"

"Of course."

"You, yourself, made me promise not to tell you where you worked or what your job was, because you didn't want your . . . um, you in the future didn't want you in the past to make decisions about your new future based on what the old future . . . this makes no sense."

"But it does," Nog said. "Basically . . ."

"Yeah?" Jake said with a grin. "Basically what?"

"Basically, I didn't want to spoil the surprise for myself."

"Exactly," Jake said.

"But . . . did I happen to give myself any investment advice?" Now Nog laughed.

"Yeah," Jake said. "You told yourself always to be sure to pick up the check when you have lunch with me."

Nog poked Jake in the ribs as he pushed away from the safety railing. "Yeah? Well, today you're buying," he said.

Jake fell into step beside his friend, heading for the stairs that would take them down to the main level.

"Did I mention that you'd put on fifty kilos and your ears had fallen off? Very attractive."

By the time they had reached the stairs, they were both giggling as if they were twelve again, as if nothing had changed or ever would.

Then Nog stopped with his hand on the stair railing. "When the evacuation started, I was in Ops. I . . . I thought I saw you. Like a ghost or something. I thought you were trying to talk to me or something."

Jake put a hand on his friend's shoulder. "Nog, you have to start getting out more often."

But Nog, shook his head, smiling. "No, I don't." He looked all around the Promenade. "I like it right here."

Jake knew what he meant.

For now, at least, the future could wait.

CHAPTER 29

BENJAMIN SISKO breathed deeply of the air of Bajor, picturing the molecules of it entering his bloodstream, becoming part of his body, just as his soul was part of this world.

"It's beautiful," Kira said beside him.

Sisko looked out at the vista of the Cirran Mountains—bold, craggy, snow-capped peaks stretching to the northwest; gentle foothills to the southeast melting gracefully into green meadows tens of kilometers away; transparent clouds high brushstrokes on the scarlet sky as dawn changed to day, red turned to blue.

And the silence of this altitude, Sisko thought. So far removed from the cities and the farms, the roads and air-traffic corridors.

Perfect stillness. Perfect peace.

The peace of the Prophets.

"Beautiful," Sisko agreed, knowing how insignificant that word was, how inadequate. "I can see why they built their monastery here."

Kira nodded. "Not even the Occupation touched it. As if the Cardassians didn't even know it was here."

They probably didn't, Sisko thought. And if any had discovered it, he doubted if Obanak's followers would have let them live long with that secret.

A brisk wind suddenly danced around them, and Sisko and Kira both secured more tightly the heavy coats they wore. Though they hadn't discussed doing so beforehand, when they had met at the airlock for this day's journey, they were both outfitted in civilian clothes. To each of them, it had seemed the right thing to do, coming here to this place of peace on Bajor.

"There," Kira said, and she gestured with one hand toward the old stone path that led from the small parapet they had beamed to, to the entrance of the monastery, where two figures emerged from a small doorway and made their way down the path in a leisurely manner.

As the two figures came nearer, Sisko's gaze traveled beyond them to the monastery behind. The structure was enormous, built of hand-cut stone blocks that seemed to Sisko identical to those that had been used in the construction of B'hala's earliest buildings. Yet the quarries for that fabled city's stones were hundreds of kilometers away.

Sisko tried to comprehend the driving passion that would compel a people to transport the massive stone blocks from such a distance, then carry them up to this mountain peak.

To his surprise, after all he had been through, he found that he could.

The two figures were closer now and Sisko recognized one of them. His identity was unmistakable despite his flowing russet robes. Prylar Obanak's broad shoulders and powerful stride could not be disguised.

The second figure, though, who walked behind the prylar, cloaked in the simpler robes of a monk, was unfamiliar to him.

Sisko sensed rather than saw Kira's glance at him. He adjusted his shoulder bag, felt the Red Orb inside shift slightly to one side. "It's the right thing to do," he said.

She nodded. "I know. I'm just surprised that . . . that you think so, too."

"I'm not a Starfleet officer today."

Kira's smile was thoughtful. "Oh, yes, you are. You were born a Starfleet officer, just as you were born the Emissary."

"Is it possible to be both?"

"If it is, you'll find the way."

Particle or wave. This time or another. His wasn't a quantum condition. Perhaps Kira had always understood that better than he had, Sisko thought. That his choice had never been to be one or the other. It had always been to find the way to be both.

"Captain Sisko," Obanak said as he and his follower came up the path to the parapet on which Sisko and Kira were standing. "Welcome to Cirran."

"Ben," Sisko said. "Not Captain."

"Ben," Obanak said. He looked at Sisko's shoulder bag. "You once tried to give these to Kai Winn."

"Before I knew what they were."

"Do you know now?"

Sisko shook his head. How could he? How could anyone? "If I thought that the entities in the wormhole were merely aliens, and these . . . devices were simply artifacts of an immeasurably advanced technology, I would destroy them."

"And if the entities are gods?" Obanak asked quietly. "And the Orbs known throughout Bajor are their tears? What does that tell you about these Red Orbs and the entities who created them?"

Sisko looked deep into Obanak's eyes but saw only the prylar's conviction.

"Whatever they are," Sisko said at last, "they belong here, because they've been here before."

Obanak's face was unreadable. "Why would you say that?"

Sisko had had a long time to think on the trip from the station, to weave the final strands of the tapestry and complete the missing elements of the picture. "You, your order, are the keepers of these Orbs. You hid one on Jeraddo just before the moon was abandoned, then gave the map to Dal Nortron. And in the chaos of Withdrawal, you stole the Orb from Quark after he had stolen it from Terrell, watched over it for six years, then hid it in Quark's bar when you came back to Deep Space 9 just before all the Orbs were brought together."

Sisko knew it was the only explanation. Where the Orbs were concerned, there were no other times. It all had happened. It all had been real.

"Emissary!" Kira said in surprise. "Do you know what you're saying?"

Obanak held up a hand to assure Kira. "It's all right, Nerys. I'm sure he does."

And Sisko *was* certain, even more so now. "In fact," he added, "I wouldn't be surprised if you had somehow arranged the sale of the third Orb to Vash, knowing it would start the search for the other two."

Sisko heard Kira gasp as Obanak gave him an enigmatic smile before responding. "Oh, we would never *sell* an Orb, Ben." But that was the only part of Sisko's suppositions that he bothered to deny.

"Prylar, I apologize," Kira said hotly. She was about to continue when Obanak stopped her.

"Nerys, really, no offense is taken. But I am curious to know why it is you think what you do, Ben. How you could even consider such . . . manipulation of events to be possible."

Sisko remembered back to his time-bending meeting with Prylar Rulan, in the Temple on DS9, just before he had *first* arrived at the station. To the way Rulan had read his *pagh* and how the prylar hadn't been surprised that the Sisko before him was out of time. *I ask you to accept that there is a reason why the Will of the Prophets must sometimes be seen as difficult to interpret for the many, even while it is understood perfectly by the few.*

"No one thing in particular," Sisko said. He looked up at the magnificent edifice of the monastery, struck by the way it seemed almost to grow from the mountain, attesting to the length of time that had passed since it had been built and the centuries, the millennia, of weathering it had endured to blend its walls and parapets into the natural flow of the existing rock.

"But in that monastery," Sisko said without rancor, without judgment, "I would suggest there exists the complete texts of the mystics of Jalkaree. Every word written by Shabren, Eilin, and Naradim. Not just the fragments known to Bajor at large, but everything—the details that you dare not reveal because if too many people knew the future, that future might change."

Sisko saw Kira look from him to Obanak and back again, her eyes wide with an emotion he was not sure he could identify.

"An interesting theory," Obanak said at last. "They must teach you well at Starfleet Academy." He held out his hand.

Sisko gave him the shoulder bag with the first Red Orb.

"And the others?" Obanak asked.

Sisko reached inside his coat, pressed his combadge. "Sisko to *Rio Grande*. Mr. O'Brien, you may beam down the second Orb."

"*Energizing*," O'Brien replied.

A few moments later, a safe fifty meters farther down the path, a Starfleet packing crate shimmered into existence.

Sisko touched his combadge again. "Sisko to *Defiant*. Dax, you may beam down the third."

"*Energizing*," the Trill said.

The second packing crate took form halfway up the path toward the monastery.

"Thank you, Ben," Obanak said. "They will be quite safe here."

"As I'm sure they always have been," Sisko replied.

Obanak glanced down at the time-smoothed stones of the path for a moment. "If it were true that we had the *complete* prophecies of the mystics, it would also be true that those prophecies extended to a particular time, to a particular set of events, and then . . . ended. As if the mystics could see no farther through the veils of the ages." He looked up at Sisko again. "If it were true."

Sisko nodded. *I know because those who came before me knew,* Prylar Rulan had told him, to explain how it was that he recognized Sisko as the Emissary. *Because those who came before them knew, all the way back to the first writings of the great mystics in the time before Lost B'hala.* "So they set forth their prophecies, and your order made sure they would come to pass," Sisko said.

But Obanak betrayed no inclination either to agree or to disagree. "To respect the mystic texts to such a degree, that would be a worthy undertaking, I believe."

Sisko smiled in defeat, accepting that Obanak would give him little else. "Very worthy."

Obanak bowed his head. "Again, we thank you, Ben. All of Bajor thanks you, even those who cannot know what you have done, or will do."

"Will do?" Kira repeated, eager to finally seize her chance to ask her own question of the prylar. "So there are still prophecies to come?"

Obanak grinned. "The mystics of Jalkaree are not the only ones who have seen the future, Nerys. All you have experienced has been but the first chapter in a book that is still to be written."

"Which book?" Kira asked, frowning.

"The Book of the Emissary."

Kira stared at Obanak, puzzled, confused. "But you don't believe the Sisko is the Emissary."

Obanak looked surprised. "Nerys, I never said the Sisko was not the Emissary."

She waved a hand at Sisko. "But you won't even *call* him Emissary."

"No," Obanak agreed. "Not Ben."

Sisko exhaled, at last understanding. "And not Jake," he said.

Half-smiling, Obanak shook his head, as if to confirm Sisko had finally come to the right conclusion.

"But I don't understand," Kira said.

"It's all right," Sisko told her, and meant it. *Maybe Kas and I will have to talk,* he thought. Then he held out his hand to Obanak. "I look forward to our next meeting, if there is to be one."

"After so many others at such interesting times, you can be sure of it," Obanak said. Then he handed the shoulder bag to the monk at his side. "Rees, if you would. I'll get one of the others."

Obanak started down the path, but Sisko reached out to the prylar's companion, pulled lightly on the hood of the monk's robe.

"Captain," Arla Rees said. She looked at Kira. "Major."

The former Bajoran commander's hair was cut short and ragged in the style of a novice. Her eyes were shadowed, her skin pale.

As if she saw and understood the concern in Sisko's eyes, Arla smiled reassuringly. "I'll be all right, Captain. I'm still taking Dr. Bashir's medications, to be . . . to be sure there's no trace left in me."

"Is this the right place for you?" Sisko asked her quietly.

Arla nodded. "It always has been. I just didn't know it until . . . well, just until."

Kira suddenly stepped forward and threw her arms around Arla and hugged her. Sisko saw the bright tears in Kira's eyes.

Arla lifted a hand to touch one of those tears with her finger. " 'I know why the Prophets weep,' " she said softly, and Sisko recognized the words from an ancient poem.

" 'For joy,' " Kira answered, smiling warmly at her former adversary.

Arla nodded and completed the quotation. " 'In time. In time.' " Then she stepped back from the major, pulled up her hood, turned, and followed after Obanak, who stood waiting for her on the path.

Sisko and Kira watched Arla walk past the prylar, carrying the Red Orb to the doors of the monastery. Then she stepped through those doors and into her new life. Carrying the second Orb a safe distance behind her, Obanak walked the same path up and into the monastery. The crate holding the third Orb remained on the path, awaiting its turn once the other two had been carefully put away.

Sisko took another deep breath of the mountain air of Bajor, each breath linking him closer to this world.

"Time to go home?" Kira asked after a while.

"We already are," he told her, though he knew that until his part of that story still to be told was complete, he could not stay.

He took a final look at the monastery of Cirran, wondered about the mysteries still within it, thought of the Emissary named Sisko still to come, then called to his ship to return to the stars, to the Gateway to the Temple, to Deep Space 9.

EPILOGUE

In the Hands of the Prophets

JAKE SISKO breathed deeply the dry air of B'hala and, as softly as a kiss, blew it out again.

The finest particles of dust danced away from the standing stone, caught in the bright sunlight to swirl like stars in a distant galaxy, swept away by Jake's exhalation and the gentle sweep of his archaeologist's brush.

Jake knelt to examine more closely the last details of the ancient carving he had discovered and now revealed.

Among those details was a single, simple glyph of ancient Bajoran, more familiar to him than his own name.

"There," he said, and the word hung in the still, silent air. He touched his finger to the stone, to trace out the worn but unmistakable lines carved by passionate hands long since turned to dust. Kasidy's shadow fell over him.

"Welcome, Emissary," she said, reading the inscription as easily as could Jake.

Jake turned to her, smiling as he saw the child asleep in her arms. Her child. His father's child.

The child of Bajor, to whom even the kai bowed her head in reverence.

"There's no question now," Jake said.

At the mouth of the cave on the outskirts of what once had been the first and oldest section of the city, Kasidy leaned down to peer more closely at the stone embedded in the rock. "But the way they're depicted, Jake. It's so different from the others."

"Because it's the first time they *were* depicted."

Kasidy's smile lit up her face. The expression came more easily to her face now than it had that first year, before the child was born. Before the new prophecies had been revealed. Before so many things.

"Is it?" she asked as she straightened up. "Or is it someone's idea of a joke?"

Jake understood why she asked the question. He couldn't blame her. Every other representation of the mystics of Jalkaree were almost identical in their presentation of three learned men.

But this carving, buried for millennia, clearly predated all the rest. It had been carved while the mystics had walked this world, before legend and tradition had compromised fact.

"Twenty-five thousand years ago," Jake said, "this wasn't something the Bajorans *could* joke about."

He pointed to the silhouettes beneath the glyphs.

"See? This is Shabren as he's always depicted." The first silhouette showed the traditional stooped figure of an old man; above him, the hourglass shape of a Prophet's tear—the Orb of Prophecy. "But here, beside him, Eilin is clearly a woman." The lines of the second silhouette made that obvious.

"Then how can you be sure it *is* Eilin?"

"Because she's at Shabren's right hand—where Eilin is always depicted. And it really makes more sense when you consider that to the Bajorans who inhabited this area when B'hala was founded, that's the position that would have been taken by an elder's spouse. And see here . . ." Jake lightly drew his brush back and forth across the weathered carving of the second great mystic. "Here's Eilin's bag of knowledge. It all fits, Kas. Shabren stooped with an Orb over his head—the symbol of the knowledge of the Prophets that he gave to Bajor. Eilin with the bag in which she kept her scrolls—the symbol of her knowledge of the world that she gave to Bajor."

"But what about Naradim?" Kasidy asked. "Shouldn't he be carrying his abacus—symbol of the knowledge of mathematics that he gave to Bajor?"

Jake grinned at her formality. "Naradim didn't *need* an abacus. That came much later, as a way the Bajorans could keep up with him."

"But look how much shorter he is. Doesn't that mean he's younger than the other two?" Kasidy asked. "And don't the texts say the three were the same age?"

"They might say that," Jake said. "Or they might be saying that the three *arrived* at the same time. The old glyphs are . . . imprecise. The explanation could just be as simple as we see it here: He's not younger, just shorter. And see here . . ." Jake tapped his brush against the third silhouette.

"His hood is up," Kasidy said. "That's traditional, at least."

"But now we know why," Jake said. "It had to be in that position so the Bajorans wouldn't know he was . . . from someplace else."

Jake laid down his brush, stood up, stretched, scratched at the beard he wore.

The child in Kasidy's arms stirred, half-awake, half-dreaming in this lost city.

Kasidy stroked the child's head and timeless sleep returned.

"This makes things very complicated, don't you think?"

she asked. "I mean, not just time travel but circles of events looping from one alternate time to affect events in another . . ."

"Maybe there aren't any alternates," Jake said. He had spent long nights thinking of all this during his time in B'hala, during his voyage through the wormhole. One of his friends in Starfleet had hinted to him that this interconnection among different histories had been suspected before in events involving the Romulan Empire. "Maybe the way we see time as being quantum, as going either one way *or* the other, isn't the way it really is. Maybe all the different timelines are like the planets were to our ancestors. Individual worlds with their own existence. Their own destinies. And maybe . . . eventually . . . we'll learn to travel between them, instead of just stumbling around like we do now."

Jake had no doubt about what could be used to travel among the timelines, the pathway that linked all times.

"Infinite worlds," Kasidy mused. "And infinite times. An infinity of infinities." She looked down at the child of Bajor. "So what about the timeline you saw? The future where everything ended."

Jake closed his eyes and turned his face upward, toward Bajor-B'hava'el, savoring the heat he had come to associate with B'hala. The moment in his life that Kasidy was asking about, the journey into a future that now could never be, it was more like a dream when he remembered it.

"I think that was a warning," he said. "For us or for the Prophets, I don't know. But it was a warning that had to be, so that . . ." Jake opened his eyes and looked down again, at the three silhouettes on the stone—Shabren, Eilin, and Naradim, to be sure. Picard, Vash, and Nog—who could say for certain? "So that the circles could wheel within circles. So that we could see that one time doesn't exclude another."

"Another time," Kasidy said beside him.

The child in her arms gurgled happily, still caught within a dream.

A sudden wind gusted up then, sending the dust at the mouth of the cave into a helix of shifting sparkles, glittering almost like an Orb, Jake thought.

And then the heat of the day vanished, and from deep in the cave, it was as if a light flickered somewhere far off.

A light that was obscured by a figure before it, one hand held out to them.

Kasidy stepped forward to the edge of the cave, its depths now shimmering, radiant, as if its walls were lined with Orbs.

The sleeping child's eyes opened wide, dark and lustrous, their shining surface reflecting the light from the cave.

And then the light was no more and the dust drifted downward in the still air as the heat of B'hala returned.

Jake reached out to Kasidy, took her hand in his.

They both knew what had just happened, who had been with them.

Who would always be with them.

"Another time," Jake said as he released her hand. Then he crouched down to touch his fingers to the silhouette of Naradim, completing one circle, knowing an infinite number remained. "We should go home."

The Station would be waiting for them at the entrance to the wormhole. The Gateway would be waiting at the entrance to the Temple. And for the first time, Jake truly understood that the one definition did not exclude the other. Circles within circles.

Jake gazed one last time into the darkness of the cave, then turned away into the sunlight to follow Kasidy, wondering who had walked this same path millennia before him and who would walk it after him.

But when he reached the campsite, he abandoned all his thoughts of past and future for a time much more important. The child was waiting, small fingers wrapped around a favorite toy.

"Heads up!" Kasidy warned with a smile.

And in that timeless moment, accompanied by the peals of laughter of a mother and a child, Benjamin Sisko's baseball arched into the air of B'hala, spinning gloriously in the bright sunlight, a blur of scuffed white leather and frayed red stitches, launched on an erratic path that might take it anywhere.

As he had a thousand times before, and would a thousand times again, Jake leaped up to try to catch it . . .

And from the Temple, the Prophets watched as they always did.

But in this one timeless moment, as they had learned from their Emissary, even the Prophets wondered what would happen next.

ACKNOWLEDGMENTS

When it comes to concepts of nonlinear time, we admit to being experts, much to the chagrin of our editor and the entire production and design team who labor to turn our manuscripts into finished books in readers' hands, on schedule and on budget, despite everything we do to ensure they live in interesting times.

So, in the tradition of saving the best for last, in this third book of the trilogy, we must do our best to express our inexpressible gratitude to our magnificent editor, Margaret Clark, and to those in charge of *Millennium*'s production, Erin Galligan and Joann Foster, for allowing us to exploit Parkinson's Law to new—and never-to-be-tried-again—limits.

Thank you for your truly impressive forbearance under pressure of our own making. And one final additional thank you to M. Clark for not having us whacked, even after we turned in the final revision and finally became expendable.

The normal timeline will now resume.

—J&G

A CLASSIC RETURNS

Ten years ago, Judith and Garfield Reeves-Stevens
created an extraordinary and unusual new band of
heroes fighting to save our world *and* the real world,
in the first two volumes of

THE CHRONICLES
OF GALEN SWORD

Now, Galen and his team are coming back in the
special new omnibus collection:

THE RETURN
OF GALEN SWORD

complete with the first two Galen Sword novels

SHIFTER and NIGHTFEEDER

and the all-new third novel in the ongoing series

DARK HUNTER

Look for THE RETURN OF GALEN SWORD
from Babbage Press
in bookstores everywhere,
or log on to REEVES-STEVENS.COM
for more information.

The following is a preview of
GALEN SWORD #3: DARK HUNTER
Be sure to look for previews of
SHIFTER and **NIGHTFEEDER**
in Books I and II of
DEEP SPACE NINE: MILLENNIUM.

THE CHRONICLES OF GALEN SWORD #3:

DARK HUNTER

Galen Sword is an aimless New York twenty-something with no friends, no family, and a multimillion-dollar trust fund. After a night of indulgence, he crashes his sports car, and the doctors in emergency write him off—his injuries are too extensive for him to survive. Then a mysterious man with blue glowing hands heals Galen, and as Galen's body is restored, so are long-buried memories of his early childhood, a childhood he appears to have spent in another world of exotic beings and magical forces. Filled with new purpose, Galen uses his wealth to become an investigator of the unknown and the unexplainable—not to disprove such things but to find his way home.

DARK HUNTER, the third book in the series, brings Galen full circle as he makes the unexpected discoveries that tie his exile from the First World of Adepts to a terrible danger threatening the Second World of humans. If Galen is to uncover the truth about his past—and if our world is to survive the forces assembling against it—Galen must first learn the secret of the mysterious woman he encountered in Greece and then, for the very first time, take his team into the First World and to his family's home . . .

ONE

That's the problem with Hong Kong these days, the hunter thought, *too many humans.*

She had not expected the population of the city to have changed so greatly in the four years since she had last visited. Everywhere she looked, she saw humans. Nothing but humans. Their presence in such numbers depressed her and made her long for the days when the crowded and twisted streets of the city had been filled with the life of both worlds, the First and the Second combined.

But the treaties had changed that intermingling of worlds. The British had turned over the colony at the end of their ninety-nine-year lease. The People's Republic of China had made Hong Kong a special economic zone to encourage international business and banking to remain. And the Clans Seyshen and Akhenaten had sealed the layer at the same time, to sever forever the Second World's Hong Kong from the First World's Western Isles, in exchange for continued and unrestricted access to Macao. As those agreements had been enacted, the adepts had begun to abandon the city, leaving it to humans. Only humans.

The hunter sighed, too long without sleep on her journey,

jarred back and forth by the lurching of the rattling cab she rode in this early morning, and hemmed in by the crowded wooden buildings and signs that appeared to have grown in place rather than being built. She longed for the tall trees and cool mists of Deep Forest. And the Ark.

She ran her fingers idly across the sleek surface of the black leather Haverhill attaché case at her side, feeling the subtle power of the trollstone resonate within. *Soon,* she thought, *soon. When the transfer is complete, I shall go home.* There was peace at home in the desert jungles of Australia. And, she hoped, answers for what she had seen two nights earlier in a refuse-strewn back alley in New York: a shifter halfling, a vampire, and—

The cab shuddered to a sudden stop with the metallic squeal of worn brake pads. A bright red plastic banner proclaiming the Year of the Dragon swung violently from the rearview mirror. The driver rolled down his window halfway and launched a breathless verbal assault against the ancestors of the old woman who had stepped in front of his vehicle. The hunter listened carefully, making sure that no signals or code words concerning his passenger were hidden in the driver's tirade. When she had hired him, well away from the limousines and immaculate cabs of the Mandarin Oriental Hotel, she had placed his Cantonese as coming from the northern regions, across the border. She had sought a driver without friends among the Second World police or appetites that could be satisfied only by suppliers from the First World. A dark hunter could not risk exposure so close to the layer no longer open.

The old woman whom the driver had insulted to the fifth generation trembled with indignant anger that made the faded turquoise garment she wore wrapped around her thin body flutter as if caught in a wind. She slammed her bony hand against the dull yellow hood of the cab, bouncing the metal panel against the loops of wire that held it in place. She screamed back at the driver in a tobacco-thickened voice, cursing the animals from which he and his ancestors had sprung. All around the cab, interested passersby stopped to watch the altercation. Some eyes came to rest on the foreigner in the cab's backseat, their gaze apparently drawn by her red-gold hair and the almost unnatural serenity of her strange eyes and austere features.

The hunter leaned forward and said in Cantonese, "Do not attract attention. Let her pass."

The driver started like a frightened hare, his thin black mustache betraying a nervous twitch. His passenger had just spoken with his own northern accent. But his shock lasted only an instant. He didn't care if he did attract attention. He didn't intend to let the old woman pass. He would lose too much face.

The driver tried to explain. "The witch has cursed us both. She must learn her lesson and—" He shuddered and fell silent as the hunter touched his shoulder.

Despite the driver's protestations, the hunter had seen that the old woman was not a witch adept—she had no aura of substance. And if there were any lessons to be learned here, it would be the driver who would become the student.

"Drive on," the hunter said. She had abandoned the voice of the familiar, and the northern accent no longer encased her words. This time, she used the voice of the hunt.

Through the open window, the flow of the old woman's invective had not ceased or slowed. The hunter could feel the driver's innate resistance ripple through the muscles of his shoulder. She was commanding him to go against a lifetime of social conditioning. The hunter had to speak a second time, rare when dealing with a human who was not in combat.

"Drive on," she repeated. It was a voice that could lure tigers to cages, shifters to silver, and nightfeeders to the dawn.

Like them, the driver had no choice. He jerked the taxi forward, ignoring the old woman's triumphant cackle.

The hunter settled back in the cab, one hand returning to the black case beside her. The driver proceeded more cautiously, as though he knew he would face additional humiliation if another confrontation with a pedestrian should take place. His cab crept through the shifting walls of humans that clogged the complex warren of narrow streets near the demolished ruins of the old Walled City. The driver turned according to the hunter's directions until even he was confused and lost in a section of the ancient metropolis for which maps had never existed.

"Here," the hunter said at last.

The cab stopped instantly. The driver hunched over his steering wheel, peering into the darkly shadowed and twisting street for some clue to his location. Eventually, he became aware of the hunter's hand beside him, offering a thick roll of Hong Kong dollars.

The driver took the money from the hunter, avoiding direct contact with her hand. Even before counting it, he began to complain that it was not enough. But the hunter recognized the well-worn pattern to the words he spoke. She simply stared at him with the eyes of the forest until his voice died away and he looked down at the cash in his hands. The money was more than enough. It was also coated with an unnoticeable dusting of a First World dried resin that would ensure that two hours from now, he would no longer remember from whom he had received it.

The hunter stepped down from the cab, one hand firmly locked on the handle of her attaché case, the other quickly adjusting the sleek jacket and trousers of her custom-cut suit. She scanned the immediate area with the speed and exactness of a machine. There were twenty-two individuals watching her at this moment: eighteen on the street, one from an inset doorway seventeen feet away, and three from windows overhead. The hunter returned her attention to the man who hid in the doorway. His eyes were locked on the single strand of South Sea pearls she wore at the neck of the silk shirt that concealed the dark fabric of her shadowsuit. The man's interest in the pearls was a typical human response, nothing to worry about.

The hunter stepped back from the cab and lowered her left arm with a small sideways twist, as if adjusting the cuff of her shirtsleeve. The handle of the sandcutter fell perfectly into her waiting fingers. She turned her back on the man in the doorway and began walking to the meeting place. Behind her, the cab slowly rolled off along a roadway that gave it only two feet of clearance on either side. When the cab had turned its first corner, the hunter heard the footsteps of the man from the doorway as he began to follow her.

In case the cab driver were to be questioned before the clouding effect of the resin took hold, the hunter had directed him to let her off a half-mile from her actual destination. In this part of the city, that half-mile could encompass a thousand different meeting points and a month of searching. Thus, she did not expect to be followed because of anything the driver might do. But the man who had stared so fixedly at her necklace was another matter.

She came to a passageway formed by the overhanging second floors of two buildings that had come to lean against each other over decades of slowly settling on their foundations. She glanced around again, saw that fourteen individuals were now watching her with limited degrees of interest, then stepped into the shadows of the passageway so that none of her observers could see her.

She listened carefully over the sounds of market haggling and children crying, an old truck's erratic engine, and radios tuned to a dozen stations, to catch the footsteps of the man from the doorway as he quickened his pace. He stepped into the passageway seconds after she did, then paused in surprise, unable to see his prey against the small portal of sunlight at the passageway's end.

The hunter waited in pure stillness less than four feet away. When dealing with humans, her own skills were such that her shadowsuit and other weapons of deception were seldom needed.

"To your left," she said quietly.

The man wheeled to his left. He was no more than twenty, wiry, edgy, and the short-sleeved white shirt he wore over loose dark trousers was stained with circles of sweat. He squinted nervously at the hunter. One hand reached behind his back, and, just as it reappeared with a knife in place, the hunter lifted her sandcutter. Its projecting blade was shaped like that of a hand adze—a flared petal of unpolished iron the size of a child's fist. But unlike an adze, designed to cut, the sandcutter's blade was thick and perforated with a thousand fine holes. The hunter squeezed the weapon's iron handle, feeling the wizard's script engraved there.

The man's knife clattered to the rough cobbled floor of the passageway and he sank to his knees, moaning in shock as he pressed both hands against the suddenly abraded skin of his face.

In a fluid move, the hunter bent down to scoop up the man's knife, then deftly tossed it so it was embedded in a wooden beam ten feet overhead, lost in darkness.

The man looked up at her through bloodied fingers, and the hunter was able to judge the effectiveness of her aim. *Good,* she thought, *his eyes are untouched.* Then she walked calmly from the passageway, and this time no one watched her.

She arrived at the meeting place ten minutes later—a large abandoned building, blackened with age, which had once been a warehouse for a trading company that had dealt in First World artifacts. As such, it was far removed from the harbor and the transport lines that served the rest of the city. The shipments of the goods it had handled would have passed through fardoors or the layer itself, making it a secure locale for the coming transfer.

The main door was unlocked and the hunter stepped in from the street. Inside the building, the musty air was heavy with a hundred years of stale incense ineffectively masking the spoor of generations of humans and adepts alike. The hunter glanced behind her. The glass panes of the entrance door were plastered over with thick grime and the tatters of old posters. Ahead of her, a wide hallway punctuated by closed doors caked with thick green paint was unlit and undisturbed. She listened as she studied the layers of dust on the worn wooden floorboards. She walked forward, sandcutter held out, though she sensed no threat.

At the end of the corridor were two large doors. She pushed on them with her case and they swung so smoothly and silently open that the hunter knew there had been working crystals somewhere in the making of their hinges. The doors closed just as silently behind her.

"Welcome, Diandra."

Eric Hong waited for her, two hundred feet away at the far end of the empty warehouse.

The hunter paused, waiting for her eyes to adjust to the odd lighting in the cavernous space; broad shafts of iridescent sunlight pierced the gloom in patterns determined by the long cracks in the three-story-high roof. The shafts slashed the wooden floor with alternating streaks of brilliance and blackness. The dust-filled air glowed where the sun swam through it.

The hunter was wary. Too much detail was obscured by the harsh glare of the light. Even she could not see what might be waiting in the corners of the huge warehouse, or what might be observing her from the wide balcony that circled the empty walls ten feet above her head.

"We are quite secure," Hong called out to her, his voice booming in the vast volume of empty space; He stepped forward into the band of light that striped the long silver hood of his Bentley. The hunter was perturbed anew. She never understood how Hong could believe he could travel inconspicuously through this part of the city in such a car. His father had always chosen nondescript Korean sedans, old, dented, and unwashed.

"Who is with you?" the hunter asked. Unlike Hong's, her voice did not echo in the empty warehouse. Indeed, with the voice she had used she knew Hong had heard her question as a mere rustle in his ear, like the whisper of a ghost.

Hong raised his hand in a clumsy wave. From either side of the Bentley, two figures moved forward. One was a man, older than Hong, though not his father. He was dressed as Hong was, in a conservative dark suit with pale pinstriping. His hair was white, his face extravagantly lined, and despite his suit's exquisite construction, the hunter could see the irregular shape of a shoulder holster beneath his left arm. Her vision at two hundred feet was the equivalent of any Second World hawk's. She had learned the lessons of the forest well.

The second figure was a woman, much younger, in a blue windbreaker and black jeans. There was no attempt to hide her purpose at the meeting. She carried an M-16 automatic rifle, held ready.

Hong's companions halted in the light. The hunter sensed no others waiting behind them and felt reassured. Three humans and two Second World firearms would not be a problem.

"Is that necessary?" she asked, beginning to walk across the warehouse floor toward the car. The measured tread of her unhurried footsteps filled the air.

Hong waved his hand again, discounting the hunter's question. If his companions were with him, then they were necessary.

The hunter stopped by the gleaming silver grille of the Bentley. The woman with the rifle did not watch her. Instead, her eyes moved ceaselessly around the room.

Hong smiled at the hunter. His teeth were the color of the pearls she wore, in striking contrast to the rich black of his hair, carelessly brushed over his forehead like a child's bangs. "In case you are wondering, I have another car outside the back entrance. Two cousins, both armed."

The hunter nodded. She had expected no less.

"And you?" Hong asked foolishly, as if he expected her to reveal the nature of her own defenses and backups. It was a question his father never would have asked. She was a dark hunter. She needed no backups. And as for defenses . . .

The hunter ignored the question and held up her attaché case. Hong's eyes went to it instantly. Clearly, he was not as cautious as his father had been, even though he was as single-minded. Still, the hunter missed the elder Hong's sense of wonder, displayed whenever he had dealt in the treasures of the First World. She detected the slight tremble in the corner of the younger Hong's mouth and the sheen of sudden sweat on his brow, and she knew then that his negotiations had been a lie. Hong was not to be a middleman in the transaction. He had no other buyer waiting for the trollstone. He had become a user of his own goods.

The hunter felt both sorrow for the elder Hong's line and contempt for the man who waited expectantly before her.

Hong turned to the older man at his side and nodded with visible excitement. The man slipped off his jacket, revealing the stark black straps of his shoulder holster against the white of his shirt. The gun he kept there was a long-barrelled Magnum, chosen more for show than for the subtle use the nature of his employment demanded. The hunter was not impressed.

The white-haired man spread out his jacket on the hood of the Bentley. Then he stepped back to the rear passenger door and removed a second Haverhill case, identical to the hunter's.

Hong gestured to the shimmering silk lining of the jacket on the car. "So we don't scratch the paint," he explained.

The hunter placed her case on the jacket. The white-haired man laid the second case beside hers. The hunter waited. Hong nodded quickly at the man. The older man's hands went to the case's combination lock and spun the wheels. The hunter saw that the nail of his right index finger was painted red. It was not a sign with which she was familiar. She studied his wrists, looking for a telltale mark of his Tong, but saw nothing. She glanced at Hong, wondering why he had decided to bring this man into her family's organization. Hong met her gaze but couldn't hold it. His face betrayed too much impatience. She sensed the rapid lessening of his control. His desire for what was in her case was threatening to overpower him. She doubted if they would have many more dealings with one another.

With a crisp snap of both latches, the white-haired man opened his case, revealing the neatly banded stacks of American hundred-dollar bills. Though she had never encountered any significant irregularity within the Hong organization before, the hunter suddenly felt the need to count the money. She looked sharply at Hong again and read the truth in his eyes—the money was short.

Hong nodded jerkily at the hunter's case. She considered her next action. To count the money in front of him would cause him to lose face. And if, as she suspected, the full one point four million dollars was not here, Hong's loss of honor would be intolerable. He would have no choice but to try to kill her.

Without betraying her emotions or her conclusions, the hunter reached for her own case and swiftly turned the dials of its combination lock. Like Hong's case, the first combination disarmed the detonator for the thin sheets of plastic explosive sewn beneath the fine black leather covering. By the time she had spun through to the second combination, which would release the latches, the hunter had already choreographed the actions she would take to neutralize the threat of the woman with the rifle and the man with the Magnum.

The hunter lifted the lid of the case and stepped back. The case held a block of dense black foam plastic. In the center of it, tightly embedded in a cut-out section, a narrow metal canister rested diagonally, a foot long, four inches in diameter. To the right of the canister, embedded in a much smaller depression, an irregularly shaped yellow waiting crystal pulsed gently with inner light.

"Get rid of the crystal," Hong said nervously.

The hunter plucked the crystal from the foam plastic, automatically feeling its heat to estimate how many uses still remained in it. Two customs officials had decided to look into her case this trip, and the crystal had faded rapidly under the strain of clouding their vision of what was inside.

Hong reached for the canister as the hunter slipped her hand inside her jacket and through the fold of her shirt to drop the crystal into a pouch on her shadowsuit. In case she had to abandon her street clothes in the next few minutes, it would remain with her. She felt the intense concentration of both of Hong's companions as her hand disappeared beneath her jacket. She heard them begin to breathe again when her hand returned into view, empty of weapons.

But their reaction was too extreme for what was, after all, a simple albeit cautious transfer between parties who had dealt together many times in the past. The hunter went on alert.

Hong seemed oblivious to the moment of tension. The hunter was appalled at how little attention he was paying to his surroundings. Instead, he was holding the canister with trembling hands, struggling to twist off its lid.

"It's very fresh," the hunter cautioned, not understanding why Hong would risk exposing the trollstone to air when he had no chance of using it right away. Unless, of course, he was a complete addict and could no longer even pretend to control himself.

"How long ago?" Hong asked breathlessly.

The hunter had no need to check the Second World watch she wore as decoration only. "Forty-six hours." That was when she had been in the alley in New York, challenging a chittering, scuttling cadre of Close trolls in greenblack living armor as they swarmed their doomed prey. But their prey had escaped because the Close trolls themselves were the target of her hunt. Within seconds of launching her attack, she had neutralized all of them and netted and gutted and relieved the cadre's focus leader of its stone of influence. It would have been a routine hunt, almost boring, except for the presence of the Close trolls' intended victims.

Hong wrested the lid from the canister, and it clattered onto the warehouse floor, rolling through the alternating swaths of light and shadow.

As she watched Hong's fumblings with dismay, the hunter recalled how, in the New York City alley, the immature halfling had been the easiest to deal with. He had been no more than a child, and to him, the appearance of a dark hunter was as if a human infant beheld a true monster crawling out from beneath its bed. But the young halfling had not been alone.

Eagerly, Hong tipped the canister so that the thick, clear sludge of the preserving fluid oozed out and stretched to the ground in a slow tendril. He interrupted the solid flow of it with his cupped, shaking hand, waiting for what must also emerge.

The hunter thought of other things. There had been a nightfeeder in the darkness of that New York alley as well. A nightfeeder and a shifter halfling in common purpose! The hunter still could not comprehend how such a thing could be possible. It was as if the tigers and gazelles of the Ark consorted in Deep Forest, instead of living their dance of predator and prey.

But the nightfeeder and the shifter halfling had not been all of it. They also had not been alone. They had been accompanied by another adept, late of Clan Pendragon—Galen Sword. Little Galen.

The thick preservation liquid puddled and congealed on the dusty floor of the warehouse. A wrinkled brown shape resembling a swollen peach pit slipped from the mouth of the canister and fell into Hong's outstretched hand.

The canister fell to the floor but did not crash or roll. It struck the mound of preserving fluid with a soft, wet noise and was still. Hong moaned as he brought his hands together against the shape he held. He shivered as he tore at the thin paper that encased what lay within.

"Eric," the hunter warned, "the air will make it fade. In an hour, it will be worthless."

Hong was beyond hearing her. He shook thin slivers of the wet wrapping paper from his fingers until the trollstone was revealed: a deep, translucent, red-black jellylike organ that oscillated with its own pale light.

Hong sighed greedily. His companions' eyes were riveted on him and the glistening object he held. The hunter doubted that the two had ever seen such a thing before. She doubted that they had ever worked with Hong before. She wondered what could have driven him to abandon the others who had served his father so well and so long. Or perhaps the others had seen what he was becoming, and it was they who had abandoned him.

The hunter no longer felt safe in the warehouse. Hong's organization was in disarray. There would be too many opportunities for enemies to penetrate its defenses.

The hunter moved closer to the car and the case with the American currency. "You must get that to your buyer within minutes," she said, playing the false game that there was a buyer for the stone. But even if Hong were planning to use it himself, she could not envisage how he could do so. He must know that the stone of a Close troll was worth nothing without a matching organ from a Far troll. The Far troll's organs could last indefinitely and be used hundreds of times, so, though they were harder to obtain, their price was lower. But unless Hong had been reckless enough to bring a Far troll's stone in his car, and unless one of his two companions was also his lover, the dripping trollstone he now clenched in his fist was useless.

"There is no other buyer," Hong whispered. His voice was dry and uncertain. The capacity for using words, for thinking coherently, was quickly leaving him.

"Then you are wasting it." The hunter reached for the second case, on the alert for any sudden movement from either of the still transfixed companions.

"No," Hong said faintly. "I have the stone of a Far troll." His hand gripped the hunter's arm. She could feel the cold wetness of the preservation liquid soak into the sleeve of her jacket. "Use it with me, Diandra. Now."

The hunter stared into Hong's eyes, seeing the madness that threatened to overwhelm his remaining sanity, just beneath the surface, on the brink of breaking through. With two quick moves, less than a second of effort, she could shatter his arm. But for Hong's father's sake, if for no one else's, she knew she owed him one last chance for dignity.

"Release my arm, Eric. Our transaction is over." She kept still, prepared to give him a few more seconds.

"If you've not experienced love with a trollstone, you've not lived," Hong gasped. "The things we could share. Our thoughts, our hearts, our . . ." He dared brush a finger along the hunter's cheek, and a moment later, his shriek filled the warehouse as he clutched his broken arm to his chest. The glimmering trollstone pulsed on the filthy floor, half coated with dust where it had fallen.

The hunter remained unmoving, aware of the woman's rifle and the white-haired man's pistol, both pointed at her.

"The transaction is over," the hunter said again.

The man and the woman looked to their employer for direction. His face was ashen with fear and pain and frustration. With his good hand, he reached inside his jacket and withdrew the narrow, greenblack shape of a Far troll's stone, the size of a finger.

"Not until you've swallowed this," Hong croaked. "Not until you've shared the stones with me . . ."

The hunter felt the cool mist of Deep Forest pass through her and grounded herself in the serenity of her home. The three humans before her would be dead within five seconds. She had been given no other choice.

Hong staggered toward her, his eyes clouded with the madness of a human enslaved by the deadly byproducts of the First World ecology. His companions' firearms locked on the hunter. She reassessed her options. Nothing could save them. She prepared to withdraw her windblade and—

A single dot of red light appeared on Hong's forehead. For an instant, the hunter hesitated, wondering if he had a working crystal implant and what that would mean, what powers it might give him. Then three more dots appeared on his chest. She looked down. Other dots had also appeared on her. Hong's companions whirled to face the shadows as red dots danced on them as well.

The hunter realized what had happened even as an enormously amplified voice blared through the warehouse.

Aiming lasers, the hunter thought with disgust. Not First World crystals but second-rate Second World trickery.

"Hong Kong Police!" the voice bellowed. "Put down your weapons. Do not touch the drugs or the money. Raise your hands. You are all under arrest."

The dark hunter stepped back from the car and lifted her

hands away from her sides. She didn't know whether to laugh or to relieve Eric Hong of his head. The wood floorboard shook with the rumble of advancing police officers running through the old corridor. She heard the crash of the main door behind her as more officers rushed into the warehouse.

That's the trouble with Hong Kong these days, she thought coolly as she readied herself to dispense with the unsuspecting officers.

Too many humans.

OUR FIRST SERIAL NOVEL!

Presenting, one chapter
per month...

The very beginning of the
Starfleet Adventure...

**STAR TREK®
STARFLEET: YEAR ONE**

A novel in Twelve Parts®

by
Michael Jan Friedman

Chapter Nine

Aaron Stiles considered the tiny brown-and-blue sphere of Oreias Nine on his viewscreen.

"We are in communications range," Darigghi announced from his place at the captain's side.

Stiles nodded. "I know that."

"Shall I hail the colony administrator?"

"That won't be necessary," the captain told him.

The first officer looked down at him. "Do you not intend to communicate with the colonists?"

"That's correct," Stiles responded evenly. "I don't intend to communicate with them."

Darigghi licked his fleshy lips—a gesture that the captain had come to know all too well. "The people on this world have been living in fear," the Osadjani observed. "Knowledge of our presence in this system will give them a sense of security."

"I'm not here to hold anyone's hand," said Stiles. "I'm here to take care of whatever attacked Oreias Five. When that's done, the colonists will feel plenty secure."

Darigghi didn't seem satisfied with the captain's response. "Then what *will* you do? Proceed directly to Oreias Five?"

"I'll proceed in that *direction*," he told the Osadjani.

Darigghi tilted his head, confusion evident in his deep-set black eyes. "But you will not stop there?"

"I don't see any need."

"No need?" the first officer asked, a strain of incredulity in his voice. "When the colony may hold clues to its attacker's identity?"

Stiles chuckled dryly. "There are captains in this fleet who would give their eyeteeth to examine that colony—and I'm only too glad to give them the chance. Me, I'm going to sniff around this system and see if I can't pick up the enemy's propulsion trails."

Darigghi stared at him for a moment, as if weighing the utility of arguing the point. In the end, he must have decided that opposition was futile, because he made his way to the lift and disappeared inside.

The captain wasn't going to miss him. Turning to his navigator, he said, "Ms. Rosten, set a course for Oreias Eight. And scan for propulsion trails, maximum range."

Rosten got to work. "Aye, sir."

Sitting back in his chair, Stiles eyed his viewscreen again. Every vehicle known to man left some kind of residue in its wake. He was betting that his adversary's vessels were no exception.

With luck, he thought, he would get a notion of where the enemy had come from before the rest of the fleet arrived.

"Here he comes," said Cobaryn, as a gleam appeared in the sky over the pristine curve of a bone-white dome.

The husky, fair-haired individual standing beside him shaded his eyes against the brittle sunlight. His name was Sam Lindblad, and he was the administrator of the Oreias Five agricultural colony.

"I still don't get it," the fair-haired man told him.

"I beg your pardon?" said the captain.

"Why Earth Command didn't respond. This is an Earth colony, after all. And Earth Command knows how to fight."

"Starfleet can fight too," Cobaryn pointed out.

Lindblad grunted disdainfully. "Not from what I've heard." He glanced at the Rigelian. "They say you're just a bunch of scientists."

"And that bothers you?" asked Cobaryn.

"Right now it does," said Lindblad.

"Even though you are a scientist yourself?"

"*Especially* because I'm a scientist myself. I know what I can do and what I can't do—and going toe to toe with some alien invader is one of the things I *can't* do."

By that time, the gleam in the sky had grown into a shuttlepod. As it descended toward the plaza in which they were standing, it raised a cloud of amber dust with its thrusters. Then it settled on the ground, joining the pod in which Cobaryn had come down from the *Samurai.*

"Perhaps we can change your mind," said the Rigelian.

The colonist frowned. "I sure as hell hope so."

A moment later, the pod door slid open and Cobaryn's colleague stepped out. Squinting as his eyes adjusted from the relative darkness of his vehicle, he said something to his crewmen, who were still inside. Then he made his way across the plaza.

"Administrator Lindblad," said the Rigelian, "this is Bryce Shumar, captain of the Peregrine."

Shumar shook hands with the colonist. "Sorry about all this," he said with what was obviously heartfelt sympathy. He turned to Cobaryn. "Have you had a chance to survey the damage yet?"

The Rigelian shook his head. "We just arrived ourselves."

Shumar looked to Lindblad. "Shall we?"

"This way," said the fair-haired man, gesturing for the Starfleet officers to follow him. Then he led them on the straightest possible course through the colony, a complex comprised mainly of large geodesic domes and the occasional pyramidal supply hut.

Cobaryn had sent his team ahead with its portable scanners to conduct their analyses while he waited for his friend to land. As a result, the Rigelian's only exposure to the stricken parts of the colony had been through the observation port of his pod.

Now, as he and Shumar followed Lindblad, Cobaryn began to see firsthand what had drawn the Federation's fledgling Starfleet to this planet. There were burn marks on the walls of some of the domes along with rents in the fabric from which they were constructed.

And the farther they went, the worse it got.

The punctures and scorch marks gave way to splintered supports and major structural damage. In fact, some of the domes seemed unsalvageable, though the teams of men and women attempting to make repairs might have taken issue with that verdict.

As Cobaryn and his companions went by, the colonists stopped and scrutinized them. The captain wondered if they were more fascinated with his alien appearance or the blue uniform he wore…and decided that neither answer would have surprised him.

"Here's the worst of it," said Lindblad, as they came around the shoulder of a half-shredded dome that still smelled of burning, and looked out toward the edge of the human settlement.

It was the worst, all right. There was no question about that in the Rigelian's mind. Perhaps a dozen of the colonists' residences, all of them situated between a pair of rounded hills, had been seared and pounded into the ground. What was left looked like a collection of blackened carcasses baking in the afternoon sun.

Cobaryn's landing party—his science officer and two crewmen—had all hunkered down among the wreckage with their scanners. After all, whatever residue had been left by the directed-energy weapons of the colony's assailants would be in greatest evidence here.

Shumar frowned as he gazed at the carnage. "And no one was hurt?"

"Miraculously, no one at all," said Lindblad. "But we were plenty scared, I can tell you that."

Shumar nodded soberly. "I've been fired on myself. I know what that can feel like."

The Rigelian negotiated a path through the ravaged domes and joined his science officer, a stern-looking woman named Kauff. Her scanner was cradled in her arms and she was playing it over a blackened strut.

"Anything yet?" Cobaryn asked.

Kauff put her scanner down and stretched out her back. The device was too heavy for a human to carry for very long, especially when one was working in such an obstacle course.

"One thing's for sure," said the science officer. "It wasn't the Romulans who did this."

"Why do you say that?" the captain inquired.

Kauff pointed to her scanner's digital readout. "The Romulans use electromagnetic beams, just like we do—and there's no electromagnetic beam in the universe that can cause this kind of molecular disruption."

The captain bent over and studied the readout. The woman was right. The colony's assailants boasted weapons much more advanced than those employed by the Romulans.

"So we know who it is *not*," he concluded. "Now all we need to determine is who it *is*."

"We'll get there," Kauff assured him. "Eventually." Then she bent, hefted her scanner again and moved to another section of wreckage.

Next, Cobaryn went to check on Crewman Miloso-vich. The fellow was analyzing the soil to see if the aliens might have been after some kind of mineral wealth. They wouldn't have been the first group to try to scare a rival off a potentially valuable piece of land.

Stopping behind Milosovich, the Rigelian ventured a guess. "Precious metals?"

The crewman looked back over his shoulder at his commanding officer. "No, sir. At least, nothing to write home about. But there are heavy concentrations of or-ganic materials."

"Oh?" said Cobaryn.

"Yes, sir. A certain polysaccharide in particular. It suggests that this area was once teeming with life."

The captain took a look around at the surrounding landscape, much of which had been turned into dark, carefully ordered farmland by Lindblad's people. Only in the distance was the terrain still dry and barren, a broad expanse of yellow plains dappled with dusky or-ange hillocks. Outside of a few small, spiky scrub plants, Cobaryn couldn't find any obvious signs of in-digenous biological activity.

"Teeming with life," he repeated ironically. "That must have been a long time ago."

"That would be my guess as well, sir," said Miloso-vich. "Though I would have to conduct some lab tests to determine *how* long ago."

Catching a glimpse of blue out of the corner of his eye, Cobaryn turned and saw Shumar's team ap-proaching. Their captain deployed them to an as-yet-unexplored area with a gesture, then followed them.

After all, Shumar was a planetary surveyor by trade. When it came to performing scanner analyses, he was as qualified as anyone.

For that reason, Cobaryn disliked the idea of interrupting the man. Nonetheless, he walked over and knelt beside Shumar as the latter adjusted the data input on one of his scanners.

"So tell me," said Cobaryn, "how is Lieutenant Kelly?"

His friend looked at him, his expression one of surprise tinged with amusement. "You never give up, do you?"

Cobaryn smiled. "In my place, would you?"

Shumar thought about it for a moment, then shook his head. "Maybe not. But then, I haven't thrown in the towel yet insofar as the *Daedalus* is concerned, so I'm probably the *last* person you want to ask."

"Anything new on the Dumont front?" the Rigelian inquired.

"Nothing," his colleague confirmed. "And what happened here isn't going to help our cause one bit. If the Federation believes they've got a new enemy to contend with, they're not going to be devoting a lot of resources to science and exploration."

Cobaryn weighed the comment. "I suppose that's true," he was forced to concede.

"Look at the bright side," said Shumar, managing a humorless smile. "When the fleet becomes Ed Walker's toy, you and I can quit and do what we wanted to do all along."

"Explore the galaxy," the Rigelian responded.

"And forget about people like Walker and Clarisse Dumont." With a grunt, the human went back to work.

Quit Starfleet? Cobaryn thought. Somehow, "the bright side" didn't seem all that bright to him.

For the better part of an hour, he watched his men and Shumar's as they went through one pile of charred debris after another, gathering all kinds of data. During that time, Lindblad came and went a few times. So did some of the other colonists, including a few children, seeking to satisfy their curiosity or gain some sense of reassurance...or perhaps both.

Then, as the sun approached the horizon and they began to lose its light, both teams agreed that they had accumulated all the information they could. Lugging their scanners back through the heart of the wounded colony, they returned to their pods and prepared to analyze the data in greater depth.

But as Cobaryn took his leave of Lindblad, he knew that they hadn't uncovered anything that would lead them to the colony's attackers. For all intents and purposes, they had come up empty.

Hiro Matsura considered his viewscreen, where a bony-faced man with small eyes and thick brown hair looked back at him.

"So you've heard about what happened on Oreias Five," the captain recapped, "but you haven't seen any sign of alien vessels yourselves?"

"No sign at all," confirmed Tom Orlowski, the administrator of the Oreias Seven colony. "But that doesn't mean a thing. If they attacked Oreias Five, they may decide to attack us too."

Matsura could hear the strain in the man's voice. Clearly, the last few days had been difficult ones for him.

"That's why we're here," the captain said. "To figure out who staged the Oreias Five attack and why...and to make certain that sort of thing doesn't happen again."

Orlowski frowned. "You sound so confident."

Matsura smiled. "And you don't."

That caught the administrator by surprise. "With all due respect," he said, "we asked for—"

"Experienced help," the captain noted. "And that's what you're getting. Don't let the uniform and the age fool you, Mr. Orlowski. I was at the Battle of Cheron.

So were two of the other captains assigned to this mission. Whatever it takes, we'll get the job done."

The statement seemed to calm the administrator a bit. "That's good to know," he told Matsura.

"Now," said the captain, "I'm going to send a team down to scan your colony and the area around it. When we're done, we'll compare notes with our teams at Oreias Five and the other colonies."

"And if you don't come up with anything?" Orlowski asked.

"Then we'll pursue other strategies," Matsura assured him. "In fact, at least one of our vessels is doing that already."

The captain looked forward to joining that pursuit—just as soon as his scanner team took a look around.

Hours after his visit to Oreias Nine, Dan Hagedorn could still see the faces of that planet's colonists, their eyes full of fear and uncertainty and the desperate hope that he could help them.

He had grown accustomed to that look during the war, seeing it at civilian settlements from one end of Earth space to the other, but there was something unsettling about seeing it now that the war was over. As hard as Earth had battled the invader, as high a price as she had paid, she should have earned a respite from armed conflicts.

Unfortunately, Hagedorn mused, it was a cruel universe. As he had seen all too often, one seldom got what one deserved.

Just as he thought that, his navigator turned from her control console to look at him. "Sir," said Glendennen, a slender, dark-skinned woman, "we've picked up an unusual ion concentration. And unless our instruments are off, it seems to describe a pretty coherent line."

The captain felt a twinge of anticipation, but he was

careful not to show it. "Sounds like a propulsion trail," he observed.

"It certainly could be," his navigator responded.

Hagedorn tapped his fingers on his armrest, considering the discovery from all angles. After he had rejected the idea of a trap, he said, "Get me Captain Stiles. He'll be interested to hear what we've found."

"Aye, sir," said Glendennen.

Hagedorn leaned back in his center seat. If this had been an Earth Command mission, its next stage would have been a simple one: seek out the enemy and destroy him.

But this was different, wasn't it? It wasn't just a matter of tearing their adversaries' ships apart. Somewhere along the line, they would have to find out why hostilities had begun in the first place.

It raised the level of difficulty considerably. But then, the captain reflected, that was the nature of the job.

Once, when he was a teenager, Aaron Stiles had seen a hawk pounce on a field mouse. Right now, he felt a lot like that hawk.

His viewscreen showed him four alien ships—the ones whose propulsion trails he and Hagedorn had been tracking. The vessels were small, dark, and triangular, with no visible nacelles. For all Stiles knew, they weren't even capable of faster-than-light travel.

He opened a communications link to his colleague's bridge. "I've got visual," he told Hagedorn.

"Same here," said his fellow captain. "And they don't seem to know we're on their tails."

"That's my impression too," Stiles responded. "Remember that maneuver we pulled near Pluto?"

Hagedorn grunted audibly—as close as the man ever came to a laugh. "How could I forget? I'll work on their starboard flank."

"Acknowledged," said Stiles. He glanced at his helm officer, a woman named Urbina who wore her flaxen hair in a tightly woven braid. "Heading two-six-two-mark one, Lieutenant."

"Aye, sir," Urbina responded.

Over his comm link, the captain could hear Hagedorn giving the same sort of orders on the *Horatio*. Though Hagedorn was no longer Stiles's commanding officer, Stiles liked the idea that the man was working alongside him.

He regarded Weeks, who was sitting in front of him at the weapons console. "Deploy power to all batteries, Lieutenant."

"Power to lasers and launchers," Weeks confirmed.

"Range?" asked the captain.

Weeks consulted his instruments for a moment. "One minute and fifty-five seconds, sir."

"Thank you," said Stiles. Finally, he turned to his navigator. "Raise shields, Ms. Rosten."

"Raising shields," came Rosten's reply.

The captain studied the viewscreen. The enemy ships were maintaining their course and speed. Apparently, they hadn't spotted the *Christophers* yet. Or if they had, they weren't giving any indication of it.

It felt good to be in battle again, he thought. It felt good to have an enemy in his sights. Stiles wasn't a scientist or a diplomat, and he didn't think he could ever become one.

He was a soldier, plain and simple.

And right now, he was in a situation that called for a soldier's skills.

"Range in one minute," said Weeks.

The words had barely left the weapons officer's mouth when the enemy squadron began to split up. The captain frowned.

"Stiles to Hagedorn. Looks like they're on to us."

"Looks that way. Let's go after the two nearest ships first, then worry about the other two."

"Agreed," said Stiles.

He pointed out one of the vessels on his screen. "That one's ours, Urbina. Get us in range."

"Aye, sir," the helm officer returned, her slender fingers dancing over her control console.

The *Gibraltar* veered hard to port and locked onto the alien's tail. It wasn't long before she began to gain on her prey, which seemed incapable of full impulse.

"Range?" asked Stiles.

"Twenty seconds," said Weeks.

"Target lasers," the captain ordered.

"Targeting," the weapons officer confirmed.

The Starfleet vessel continued to narrow the gap. Stiles remained as patient as he could, the muscles working in his jaw. Finally, he got the word he had been waiting for.

"Range!" called Weeks.

"Fire!" the captain barked.

Twin bolts of blue energy stabbed through the void. But somehow, the alien ship eluded them. And as it curled back around, it spewed a string of fiery crimson packets at the *Gibraltar*.

The charges loomed on Stiles's viewscreen until all of space seemed to be consumed in ruby-red fire. He took hold of his armrests, expecting the aliens' volley to send a brisk shudder through the *Gibraltar*'s forward shields.

Instead, the impact sent his ship heeling steeply to port and nearly tore him out of his chair. Amazed, he turned to his helm officer and called out, "Evasive maneuvers!"

Urbina sent them twisting away from the enemy, allowing them to escape a second blazing barrage. But before they knew it, another alien vessel had slid onto their viewscreen.

"Target and fire!" the captain snapped, instinctively grasping an opportunity to reduce the odds against them.

But the enemy was quicker, unleashing a stream of scarlet energy bundles that slammed into the *Gibraltar* with skull-rattling force. The Federation vessel reeled, and a plasma conduit burst above the aft stations, releasing a jet of white-hot gas.

"Report!" Stiles demanded.

"Shields down eighty-four percent!" Rosten barked.

The captain swore beneath his breath. The enemy's weapons were more powerful than they had a right to be. One more hit like the last one and their hull would look like a sieve.

"What about the enemy?" he asked.

"No apparent damage," said the navigator, her expression one of disappointment and disgust.

Abruptly, the triangular shape of an alien ship swam into their sights again. But this time, Stiles wasn't so eager to confront it—especially when he sensed he was about to become the target of a crossfire.

"Move us off the bull's-eye!" he told Urbina. Then he leaned toward his comm controls. "Captain Hagedorn!"

As the *Gibraltar* swung sharply to starboard, avoiding another alien barrage, the other man's voice came crackling over a secure channel. "I'm here. What's your status?"

"Not good," said Stiles. "Shields are down to sixteen percent, and we haven't done any damage ourselves."

"We're taking a beating here too," Hagedorn confessed. "We need to break off the engagement."

The idea of conceding defeat was poison to Stiles. During the war, his squadron had only done it twice—and on both occasions, they had been facing vastly superior numbers. This time, the odds were only two to one.

But the aliens hit harder and moved faster than any Romulan ship ever built. The Starfleeters didn't have any choice but to slink away with their tails between their legs…

At least for now.

"Get us out of here!" Stiles told his helm officer, each word like a self-inflicted wound.

Suddenly, the *Gibraltar* hurtled away from the battle, going back in the direction from which she had come. On her starboard flank, Hagedorn's ship followed a parallel course.

Stiles wasn't the least bit certain that the enemy wasn't going to come after them. But as it turned out, the aliens were perfectly content to let their adversaries escape.

For a moment, the triangular ships just cruised back and forth, as if defending an invisible border. Then, after the Federation vessels had put some distance between themselves and the aggressors, the aliens recreated their original formation and resumed their course.

They acted as if there hadn't been a battle at all…as if Stiles and Hagedorn weren't even there.

On Stiles's viewscreen, the enemy ships diminished rapidly with distance, shrinking to the point where they were barely visible. But the captain didn't have to see them to remember what they looked like.

Or to promise himself that they would meet again.

Look for STAR TREK fiction from Pocket Books

Star Trek®: The Original Series

Enterprise: The First Adventure • Vonda N. McIntyre
Final Frontier • Diane Carey
Strangers from the Sky • Margaret Wander Bonanno
Spock's World • Diane Duane
The Lost Years • J.M. Dillard
Probe • Margaret Wander Bonanno
Prime Directive • Judith and Garfield Reeves-Stevens
Best Destiny • Diane Carey
Shadows on the Sun • Michael Jan Friedman
Sarek • A.C. Crispin
Federation • Judith and Garfield Reeves-Stevens
Vulcan's Forge • Josepha Sherman & Susan Shwartz
Mission to Horatius • Mack Reynolds
Vulcan's Heart • Josepha Sherman & Susan Shwartz
Novelizations
Star Trek: The Motion Picture • Gene Roddenberry
Star Trek II: The Wrath of Khan • Vonda N. McIntyre
Star Trek III: The Search for Spock • Vonda N. McIntyre
Star Trek IV: The Voyage Home • Vonda N. McIntyre
Star Trek V: The Final Frontier • J.M. Dillard
Star Trek VI: The Undiscovered Country • J.M. Dillard
Star Trek Generations • J.M. Dillard
Starfleet Academy • Diane Carey
Star Trek books by William Shatner with Judith and Garfield
Reeves-Stevens
The Ashes of Eden
The Return
Avenger
Star Trek: Odyssey (contains *The Ashes of Eden*, *The Return*, and *Avenger*)
Spectre
Dark Victory
Preserver

#1 • *Star Trek: The Motion Picture* • Gene Roddenberry
#2 • *The Entropy Effect* • Vonda N. McIntyre
#3 • *The Klingon Gambit* • Robert E. Vardeman
#4 • *The Covenant of the Crown* • Howard Weinstein
#5 • *The Prometheus Design* • Sondra Marshak & Myrna Culbreath

#6 • *The Abode of Life* • Lee Correy
#7 • *Star Trek II: The Wrath of Khan* • Vonda N. McIntyre
#8 • *Black Fire* • Sonni Cooper
#9 • *Triangle* • Sondra Marshak & Myrna Culbreath
#10 • *Web of the Romulans* • M.S. Murdock
#11 • *Yesterday's Son* • A.C. Crispin
#12 • *Mutiny on the Enterprise* • Robert E. Vardeman
#13 • *The Wounded Sky* • Diane Duane
#14 • *The Trellisane Confrontation* • David Dvorkin
#15 • *Corona* • Greg Bear
#16 • *The Final Reflection* • John M. Ford
#17 • *Star Trek III: The Search for Spock* • Vonda N. McIntyre
#18 • *My Enemy, My Ally* • Diane Duane
#19 • *The Tears of the Singers* • Melinda Snodgrass
#20 • *The Vulcan Academy Murders* • Jean Lorrah
#21 • *Uhura's Song* • Janet Kagan
#22 • *Shadow Land* • Laurence Yep
#23 • *Ishmael* • Barbara Hambly
#24 • *Killing Time* • Della Van Hise
#25 • *Dwellers in the Crucible* • Margaret Wander Bonanno
#26 • *Pawns and Symbols* • Majiliss Larson
#27 • *Mindshadow* • J.M. Dillard
#28 • *Crisis on Centaurus* • Brad Ferguson
#29 • *Dreadnought!* • Diane Carey
#30 • *Demons* • J.M. Dillard
#31 • *Battlestations!* • Diane Carey
#32 • *Chain of Attack* • Gene DeWeese
#33 • *Deep Domain* • Howard Weinstein
#34 • *Dreams of the Raven* • Carmen Carter
#35 • *The Romulan Way* • Diane Duane & Peter Morwood
#36 • *How Much for Just the Planet?* • John M. Ford
#37 • *Bloodthirst* • J.M. Dillard
#38 • *The IDIC Epidemic* • Jean Lorrah
#39 • *Time for Yesterday* • A.C. Crispin
#40 • *Timetrap* • David Dvorkin
#41 • *The Three-Minute Universe* • Barbara Paul
#42 • *Memory Prime* • Judith and Garfield Reeves-Stevens
#43 • *The Final Nexus* • Gene DeWeese
#44 • *Vulcan's Glory* • D.C. Fontana
#45 • *Double, Double* • Michael Jan Friedman
#46 • *The Cry of the Onlies* • Judy Klass
#47 • *The Kobayashi Maru* • Julia Ecklar

#48 • *Rules of Engagement* • Peter Morwood
#49 • *The Pandora Principle* • Carolyn Clowes
#50 • *Doctor's Orders* • Diane Duane
#51 • *Unseen Enemy* • V.E. Mitchell
#52 • *Home Is the Hunter* • Dana Kramer Rolls
#53 • *Ghost-Walker* • Barbara Hambly
#54 • *A Flag Full of Stars* • Brad Ferguson
#55 • *Renegade* • Gene DeWeese
#56 • *Legacy* • Michael Jan Friedman
#57 • *The Rift* • Peter David
#58 • *Face of Fire* • Michael Jan Friedman
#59 • *The Disinherited* • Peter David
#60 • *Ice Trap* • L.A. Graf
#61 • *Sanctuary* • John Vornholt
#62 • *Death Count* • L.A. Graf
#63 • *Shell Game* • Melissa Crandall
#64 • *The Starship Trap* • Mel Gilden
#65 • *Windows on a Lost World* • V.E. Mitchell
#66 • *From the Depths* • Victor Milan
#67 • *The Great Starship Race* • Diane Carey
#68 • *Firestorm* • L.A. Graf
#69 • *The Patrian Transgression* • Simon Hawke
#70 • *Traitor Winds* • L.A. Graf
#71 • *Crossroad* • Barbara Hambly
#72 • *The Better Man* • Howard Weinstein
#73 • *Recovery* • J.M. Dillard
#74 • *The Fearful Summons* • Denny Martin Flynn
#75 • *First Frontier* • Diane Carey & Dr. James I. Kirkland
#76 • *The Captain's Daughter* • Peter David
#77 • *Twilight's End* • Jerry Oltion
#78 • *The Rings of Tautee* • Dean Wesley Smith & Kristine Kathryn Rusch
#79 • *Invasion!* #1: *First Strike* • Diane Carey
#80 • *The Joy Machine* • James Gunn
#81 • *Mudd in Your Eye* • Jerry Oltion
#82 • *Mind Meld* • John Vornholt
#83 • *Heart of the Sun* • Pamela Sargent & George Zebrowski
#84 • *Assignment: Eternity* • Greg Cox
#85-87 • *My Brother's Keeper* • Michael Jan Friedman
   #85 • *Republic*
   #86 • *Constitution*
   #87 • *Enterprise*
#88 • *Across the Universe* • Pamela Sargent & George Zebrowski

Star Trek: The Next Generation®

Metamorphosis • Jean Lorrah
Vendetta • Peter David
Reunion • Michael Jan Friedman
Imzadi • Peter David
The Devil's Heart • Carmen Carter
Dark Mirror • Diane Duane
Q-Squared • Peter David
Crossover • Michael Jan Friedman
Kahless • Michael Jan Friedman
Ship of the Line • Diane Carey
The Best and the Brightest • Susan Wright
Planet X • Michael Jan Friedman
Imzadi II: Triangle • Peter David
I, Q • Peter David & John de Lancie
Novelizations
Encounter at Farpoint • David Gerrold
Unification • Jeri Taylor
Relics • Michael Jan Friedman
Descent • Diane Carey
All Good Things... • Michael Jan Friedman
Star Trek: Klingon • Dean Wesley Smith & Kristine Kathryn Rusch
Star Trek Generations • J.M. Dillard
Star Trek: First Contact • J.M. Dillard
Star Trek: Insurrection • J.M. Dillard

#1 • *Ghost Ship* • Diane Carey
#2 • *The Peacekeepers* • Gene DeWeese
#3 • *The Children of Hamlin* • Carmen Carter
#4 • *Survivors* • Jean Lorrah
#5 • *Strike Zone* • Peter David
#6 • *Power Hungry* • Howard Weinstein
#7 • *Masks* • John Vornholt
#8 • *The Captain's Honor* • David and Daniel Dvorkin
#9 • *A Call to Darkness* • Michael Jan Friedman
#10 • *A Rock and a Hard Place* • Peter David
#11 • *Gulliver's Fugitives* • Keith Sharee
#12 • *Doomsday World* • David, Carter, Friedman & Greenberger
#13 • *The Eyes of the Beholders* • A.C. Crispin
#14 • *Exiles* • Howard Weinstein
#15 • *Fortune's Light* • Michael Jan Friedman

#16 • *Contamination* • John Vornholt

#17 • *Boogeymen* • Mel Gilden

#18 • *Q-in-Law* • Peter David

#19 • *Perchance to Dream* • Howard Weinstein

#20 • *Spartacus* • T.L. Mancour

#21 • *Chains of Command* • W.A. McCoy & E.L. Flood

#22 • *Imbalance* • V.E. Mitchell

#23 • *War Drums* • John Vornholt

#24 • *Nightshade* • Laurell K. Hamilton

#25 • *Grounded* • David Bischoff

#26 • *The Romulan Prize* • Simon Hawke

#27 • *Guises of the Mind* • Rebecca Neason

#28 • *Here There Be Dragons* • John Peel

#29 • *Sins of Commission* • Susan Wright

#30 • *Debtor's Planet* • W.R. Thompson

#31 • *Foreign Foes* • Dave Galanter & Greg Brodeur

#32 • *Requiem* • Michael Jan Friedman & Kevin Ryan

#33 • *Balance of Power* • Dafydd ab Hugh

#34 • *Blaze of Glory* • Simon Hawke

#35 • *The Romulan Stratagem* • Robert Greenberger

#36 • *Into the Nebula* • Gene DeWeese

#37 • *The Last Stand* • Brad Ferguson

#38 • *Dragon's Honor* • Kij Johnson & Greg Cox

#39 • *Rogue Saucer* • John Vornholt

#40 • *Possession* • J.M. Dillard & Kathleen O'Malley

#41 • *Invasion! #2: The Soldiers of Fear* • Dean Wesley Smith & Kristine Kathryn Rusch

#42 • *Infiltrator* • W.R. Thompson

#43 • *A Fury Scorned* • Pamela Sargent & George Zebrowski

#44 • *The Death of Princes* • John Peel

#45 • *Intellivore* • Diane Duane

#46 • *To Storm Heaven* • Esther Friesner

#47-49 • *The Q Continuum* • Greg Cox

    #47 • *Q-Space*

    #48 • *Q-Zone*

    #49 • *Q-Strike*

#50 • *Dyson Sphere* • Charles Pellegrino & George Zebrowski

#51-56 • *Double Helix*

    #51 • *Infection* • John Gregory Betancourt

    #52 • *Vectors* • Dean Wesley Smith & Kristine Kathryn Rusch

    #53 • *Red Sector* • Diane Carey

    #54 • *Quarantine* • John Vornholt

#55 • *Double or Nothing* • Peter David
#56 • *The First Virtue* • Michael Jan Friedman & Christie Golden
#57 • *The Forgotten War* • William Fortschen
#58-59 • *Gemworld* • John Vornholt
  #58 • *Gemworld #1*
  #59 • *Gemworld #2*

Star Trek: Deep Space Nine®

Warped • K.W. Jeter
Legends of the Ferengi • Ira Steven Behr & Robert Hewitt Wolfe
The Lives of Dax • Marco Palmieri, ed.
Millennium • Judith and Garfield Reeves-Stevens
 #1 • *The Fall of Terok Nor*
 #2 • *The War of the Prophets*
 #3 • *Inferno*
Novelizations
  Emissary • J.M. Dillard
  The Search • Diane Carey
  The Way of the Warrior • Diane Carey
  Star Trek: Klingon • Dean Wesley Smith & Kristine Kathryn Rusch
  Trials and Tribble-ations • Diane Carey
  Far Beyond the Stars • Steve Barnes
  What You Leave Behind • Diane Carey

#1 • *Emissary* • J.M. Dillard
#2 • *The Siege* • Peter David
#3 • *Bloodletter* • K.W. Jeter
#4 • *The Big Game* • Sandy Schofield
#5 • *Fallen Heroes* • Dafydd ab Hugh
#6 • *Betrayal* • Lois Tilton
#7 • *Warchild* • Esther Friesner
#8 • *Antimatter* • John Vornholt
#9 • *Proud Helios* • Melissa Scott
#10 • *Valhalla* • Nathan Archer
#11 • *Devil in the Sky* • Greg Cox & John Gregory Betancourt
#12 • *The Laertian Gamble* • Robert Sheckley
#13 • *Station Rage* • Diane Carey
#14 • *The Long Night* • Dean Wesley Smith & Kristine Kathryn Rusch
#15 • *Objective: Bajor* • John Peel
#16 • *Invasion! #3: Time's Enemy* • L.A. Graf
#17 • *The Heart of the Warrior* • John Gregory Betancourt

#18 • *Saratoga* • Michael Jan Friedman
#19 • *The Tempest* • Susan Wright
#20 • *Wrath of the Prophets* • David, Friedman & Greenberger
#21 • *Trial by Error* • Mark Garland
#22 • *Vengeance* • Dafydd ab Hugh
#23 • *The 34th Rule* • Armin Shimerman & David R. George III
#24-26 • *Rebels* • Dafydd ab Hugh
    #24 • *The Conquered*
    #25 • *The Courageous*
    #26 • *The Liberated*

Star Trek: Voyager®

    Mosaic • Jeri Taylor
    Pathways • Jeri Taylor
    Captain Proton! • Dean Wesley Smith
Novelizations
    Caretaker • L.A. Graf
    Flashback • Diane Carey
    Day of Honor • Michael Jan Friedman
    Equinox • Diane Carey

#1 • *Caretaker* • L.A. Graf
#2 • *The Escape* • Dean Wesley Smith & Kristine Kathryn Rusch
#3 • *Ragnarok* • Nathan Archer
#4 • *Violations* • Susan Wright
#5 • *Incident at Arbuk* • John Gregory Betancourt
#6 • *The Murdered Sun* • Christie Golden
#7 • *Ghost of a Chance* • Mark A. Garland & Charles G. McGraw
#8 • *Cybersong* • S.N. Lewitt
#9 • *Invasion! #4: Final Fury* • Dafydd ab Hugh
#10 • *Bless the Beasts* • Karen Haber
#11 • *The Garden* • Melissa Scott
#12 • *Chrysalis* • David Niall Wilson
#13 • *The Black Shore* • Greg Cox
#14 • *Marooned* • Christie Golden
#15 • *Echoes* • Dean Wesley Smith, Kristine Kathryn Rusch & Nina Kiriki Hoffman
#16 • *Seven of Nine* • Christie Golden
#17 • *Death of a Neutron Star* • Eric Kotani
#18 • *Battle Lines* • Dave Galanter & Greg Brodeur

Star Trek®: New Frontier

New Frontier #1-4 Collector's Edition • Peter David
    #1 • *House of Cards* • Peter David
    #2 • *Into the Void* • Peter David
    #3 • *The Two-Front War* • Peter David
    #4 • *End Game* • Peter David
#5 • *Martyr* • Peter David
#6 • *Fire on High* • Peter David
The Captain's Table #5 • *Once Burned* • Peter David
Double Helix #5 • *Double or Nothing* • Peter David
#7 • *The Quiet Place* • Peter David
#8 • *Dark Allies* • Peter David

Star Trek®: Invasion!

#1 • *First Strike* • Diane Carey
#2 • *The Soldiers of Fear* • Dean Wesley Smith & Kristine Kathryn Rusch
#3 • *Time's Enemy* • L.A. Graf
#4 • *Final Fury* • Dafydd ab Hugh
Invasion! Omnibus • various

Star Trek®: Day of Honor

#1 • *Ancient Blood* • Diane Carey
#2 • *Armageddon Sky* • L.A. Graf
#3 • *Her Klingon Soul* • Michael Jan Friedman
#4 • *Treaty's Law* • Dean Wesley Smith & Kristine Kathryn Rusch
The Television Episode • Michael Jan Friedman
Day of Honor Omnibus • various

Star Trek®: The Captain's Table

#1 • *War Dragons* • L.A. Graf
#2 • *Dujonian's Hoard* • Michael Jan Friedman
#3 • *The Mist* • Dean Wesley Smith & Kristine Kathryn Rusch
#4 • *Fire Ship* • Diane Carey
#5 • *Once Burned* • Peter David
#6 • *Where Sea Meets Sky* • Jerry Oltion
The Captain's Table Omnibus • various

Star Trek®: The Dominion War

#1 • *Behind Enemy Lines* • John Vornholt
#2 • *Call to Arms...* • Diane Carey
#3 • *Tunnel Through the Stars* • John Vornholt
#4 • *...Sacrifice of Angels* • Diane Carey

Star Trek®: The Badlands

#1 • Susan Wright
#2 • Susan Wright

Star Trek® Books available in Trade Paperback

Omnibus Editions
    Invasion! Omnibus • various
    Day of Honor Omnibus • various
    The Captain's Table Omnibus • various
    Star Trek: Odyssey • William Shatner with Judith and Garfield
      Reeves-Stevens
Other Books
    Legends of the Ferengi • Ira Steven Behr & Robert Hewitt Wolfe
    Strange New Worlds, vol. I and II • Dean Wesley Smith, ed.
    Adventures in Time and Space • Mary Taylor
    The Lives of Dax • Marco Palmieri, ed.
    Captain Proton! • Dean Wesley Smith
    The Klingon Hamlet • Wil'yam Shex'pir

STAR TREK
THE EXPERIENCE
LAS VEGAS HILTON

Be a part of the most exciting deep space adventure in the galaxy as you beam aboard the U.S.S. Enterprise. Explore the evolution of Star Trek® from television to movies in the "History of the Future Museum," the planet's largest collection of authentic Star Trek memorabilia. Then, visit distant galaxies on the "Voyage Through Space." This 22-minute action packed adventure will capture your senses with the latest in motion simulator technology. After your mission, shop in the Deep Space Nine Promenade and enjoy 24th Century cuisine in Quark's Bar & Restaurant.

- -

Save up to $30

Present this coupon at the STAR TREK: The Experience ticket office at the Las Vegas Hilton and save $6 off each attraction admission (limit 5).

Not valid in conjunction with any other offer or promotional discount. Management reserves all rights. No cash value.
For more information, call 1-888-GOBOLDLY
or visit **www.startrekexp.com.**
Private Parties Available.

CODE:1007a   EXPIRES 12/31/00